I0849810

Praise for Kate Breslin

"Within a few pages of a Kate Breslin novel, I'm not just reading historical fiction, I'm living it. *In Love's Time* is an exceptional story of courage and sacrifice, fidelity and love against all odds, set amid the escalating intrigue and danger of 1918 Europe. Riveting!"

Laura Frantz, award-winning author of *The Rose and the Thistle*

"Readers begging for more of Kate Breslin's gorgeous prose, compelling characters, and faith-filled insight will savor each word of *In Love's Time*. Perfectly plotted with a skillful balance of history, action, and romance, *In Love's Time* kept me turning the pages until the utterly satisfying ending."

Stephanie Landsem, author of *In a Far-Off Land*

"Kate Breslin for the win! *In Love's Time* has it all—romance, history, intrigue, and of course a beautiful happily-ever-after."

Rachel Fordham, author of *Where the Road Bends*

"As usual, Kate Breslin's ability to spin a beautiful tale that pulls at the heartstrings shines in her new novel, *In Love's Time*. I was rooting for Marcus and Clare from the flirty beginning to the achingly sweet ending. Marcus's depth of character and Clare's faithful love for him show the steadiness of true love even when all odds seem stacked against them. With intrigue, heartache, and a tender romance, this novel is a delight!"

Pepper Basham, award-winning author of *Hope Between the Pages*

"Kate Breslin mixes wonderful imagination with historical nuggets to create a dramatic novel of the First World War. This engaging story will keep you wondering how everything can possibly turn out well right up to the end."

Terri Wangard, author of *The Storm Breaks Forth*

"Kate Breslin has gifted us with another heartfelt WWI tale filled with intrigue, romance, espionage, plot twists, and compelling characters. Her thorough research and historical detail are impressive. *In Love's Time* also delves into some of the characters introduced in *Not by Sight*."

Janet S. Grunst, award-winning author of *A Heart Set Free*

IN
LOVE'S
TIME

Books by Kate Breslin

For Such a Time
Not by Sight
High as the Heavens
Far Side of the Sea
As Dawn Breaks
In Love's Time

IN LOVE'S TIME

KATE BRESLIN

BETHANYHOUSE

a division of Baker Publishing Group
Minneapolis, Minnesota

Published by Bethany House Publishers
11400 Hampshire Avenue South
Minneapolis, Minnesota 55438
www.bethanyhouse.com

Bethany House Publishers is a division of
Baker Publishing Group, Grand Rapids, Michigan

Library of Congress Cataloging-in-Publication Data
Names: Breslin, Kate, author.
Title: In love's time / Kate Breslin.
Description: Minneapolis, Minnesota : Bethany House Publishers, a division of
    Baker Publishing Group, [2022]
Identifiers: LCCN 2022037861 | ISBN 9780764237492 (paperback) | ISBN
    9780764240799 (casebound) | ISBN 9781493439010 (ebook)
Classification: LCC PS3602.R4575 I6 2022 | DDC 813/.6—dc23
LC record available at https://lccn.loc.gov/2022037861

Scripture quotations are from THE HOLY BIBLE, NEW INTERNATIONAL VERSION®, NIV® Copyright © 1973, 1978, 1984, 2011 by Biblica, Inc.® Used by permission. All rights reserved worldwide.

This is a work of historical reconstruction; the appearances of certain historical figures are therefore inevitable. All other characters, however, are products of the author's imagination, and any resemblance to actual persons, living or dead, is coincidental.

Cover design by Kathleen Lynch / Black Kat Design
Cover image of woman by Richard Jenkins, London, England
Cover image of soldier by Stephen Mulcahey / Arcangel

Author is represented by Hartline Literary Agency.

Baker Publishing Group publications use paper produced from sustainable forestry practices and post-consumer waste whenever possible.

22 23 24 25 26 27 28   7 6 5 4 3 2 1

For my readers

And for the courageous and talented staff
at Endell Street—doctors, surgeons, nurses, scientists,
orderlies, clerks, cooks, laundresses, and volunteers—
your dedication and hard work proved your success
in establishing Britain's first all-female-run
military hospital during WWI.

There is a time for everything, and a season for every activity under the heavens . . . a time to love. . . .

Ecclesiastes 3:1, 8

1

WHITEHALL, LONDON
MONDAY, AUGUST 5, 1918—2130 HOURS

Would the human destruction never end?

Captain Sir Marcus Weatherford returned the telephone receiver to its cradle. Leaning back in his seat behind the desk, he stared at the tall oak bookshelves lining one wall of his Admiralty office. The leather tomes on government law, rules of the sea, and Britain's war history seemed to mock any peace of mind he might seek.

Tonight, a German Zeppelin struck over Norfolk's coast to the north, and if not for an RAF squadron's ability to shoot her down, the body count of British citizens over the past four years would have increased.

He rubbed the back of his neck. Only a year past his thirtieth birthday and yet he was tired. Four years of the fighting had worn him down. Though he hadn't been on the battlefields of No Man's Land across the sea, he'd performed his silent duty to the Crown, both in Britain and abroad, and sported the scars from more than one bullet to show for it.

How many times had he coached his men—friends and colleagues—with talk of a coming peace? Like the Allied armies, the Germans were also exhausted; and with the Americans now in the fray, victory seemed plausible. Yet in his bones, Marcus refused to believe it. Not until the sounds of the guns stopped and the men began returning home.

In fact, he rarely considered what he might do after the war. Why torment himself with expectations that would amount to nothing, especially if he was killed during the next mission? At times he'd briefly entertained the idea of taking up life where he'd left off so many years ago, before Oxford and the Royal Naval Academy. Montefalco, his family estate, was in Hampshire, where he'd grown up surrounded by Mother and Grandfather and Fannie, though his baby sister was now a grown woman. Would he like settling down one day, being a family man and taking up farming? Overseeing the yearly harvest of Montefalco's grove of chestnut trees instead of his clandestine assignments?

His mouth curved upward. He couldn't imagine being satisfied with a sedate life of planting and harvesting or picking fruit. Not after years of chasing enemy spies across Europe. *Ah, man, but your sweet Clare could certainly persuade you otherwise* . . .

His pulse quickened. Soon he would see her again. He'd been away from London much during the past few weeks completing his latest assignment, and he'd missed their time together. Perhaps they would steal away to the shores at Margate for the weekend, and afterward play a game of chess. His smile broadened. He enjoyed matching wits with her, and it *was* Clare's turn to win back the white king.

He opened his desk drawer and reached inside for his small framed photo of her. His tension eased as he rubbed his thumb slowly across her smiling lips. How had he been so fortunate last year, finding a woman both smart and beautiful who would tolerate him *and* his frequent absences working for the Crown? And her enchanting two-year-old daughter, Daisy, had instantly claimed his heart—

"Marcus? Ah good, you're still here."

He glanced up at the opened door and, after replacing the photo, swiftly rose to his feet.

10

"Take a seat, boy." His boss, "C"—Captain Sir Mansfield George Smith-Cumming, head of Britain's Secret Intelligence Service—entered his office and strode toward one of two wing-back chairs across from the desk.

Marcus marveled anew at the man's smooth gait, despite his wooden leg. The horrible car crash in France four years ago cost him his limb and the life of his only son. Legend held that C dug into his pocket for a knife and finished cutting off his own partially severed leg in order to free himself to crawl to his boy and hold him as he died.

Easing down into the chair, C gazed at Marcus through his monocle. "You're here past your bedtime."

"As are you, sir." C was known to spend most of his waking hours at the Admiralty.

"Well, I'm glad to catch you. Not ready to leave just yet?"

"No rush at all, sir." C was a man he'd always admired. His own father had served with Captain Smith-Cumming in the Royal Navy before Marcus was born, and then years later when Marcus was old enough, Father introduced him to this enigma of a man who now ran MI6 at Whitehall.

Marcus had decided after Oxford to enlist in the Navy as well. Once he'd made midshipman, C offered him a post at the Admiralty and Marcus readily accepted. His subsequent training in naval intelligence, cryptography, and fieldwork with Scotland Yard had held him in good stead while he'd risen through the ranks, first as a lieutenant and then as a captain on assignment with MI6.

"How is Sir Geoffrey? It has been a while since he and I had lunch together."

"Grandfather is doing well, sir. Still designing prosthetics for the wounded."

C nodded and sighed. "Sadly, I imagine we keep him busy—too busy, in fact."

"Sir, did you wish for me to brief you on the closing of the Kahverengi case?"

"Not exactly." C hesitated. "While I commend you on that

most successful conclusion to the munitions debacle, I'm here for another reason. I'd planned to discuss this with you in the morning, but since you're still here . . . I have an assignment that needs your immediate attention."

Marcus's weariness evaporated. "Yes?"

"Day after tomorrow, I need you on a ship bound for the Russian port of Archangel. There's been a sighting west of the Ural Mountains." C eyed him through the monocle. "Empress Alexandra and her son, Alexei."

Marcus blinked and leaned back in his seat. Last year, Tsar Nicholas abdicated his throne in the face of revolution. Then just weeks ago, Russian newspapers shocked the world by reporting that the tsar, head of the Romanov dynasty, had been murdered in Yekaterinburg, and his family was relocated to a place of safety.

MI6 inquiries into the whereabouts of the tsarina and her five children, however, had so far proved fruitless. "Sir, I thought our agents there had determined the entire Romanov family was also killed."

"So they did. Until I received this coded telegram." C handed him a yellow sheet.

Marcus scanned the paper, frowning at the sender's initials.

"Sidney Reilly sent that to me yesterday from Moscow," C said, confirming Marcus's suspicions. "He learned of their location but insists on an in-person meeting to hand over the details. I can only surmise he's concerned the Bolsheviks will get wind of it."

Or another example of Reilly's eccentricities. Marcus returned the note. Years before the war, C had recruited the Russian agent to work for Britain, but Sidney Reilly had a reputation as a wildcard. "Why doesn't Reilly go himself to collect the Romanovs?"

"That's a bit of a pinch, I'm afraid. With Lenin back in Russia and the Bolsheviks in power, Reilly's having to stay one step ahead of the Cheka secret police in Moscow. He claims he can get as far north as the city of Vologda and meet you there in a week's time.

I'll wire him back for details." Again C eyed him sharply. "Once you've located the empress and her son, I will inform His Majesty."

Marcus nodded. No doubt King George would rejoice to learn that both the wife and the heir of his cousin Nicholas still lived. "How will I know for certain it *is* the empress and *tsarevich*?" He'd only seen a few old photographs.

"You will be accompanied by Natalya Bryce, Sir Walter's young widow." C smiled. "At one time Natalya was intimate with the Romanovs, and I've asked her to help us."

Marcus raised a brow at his boss. Natalya *was* Russian—a former ballerina who had married Sir Walter Bryce, their embassy man in Moscow, last year prior to his death.

Yet how did that qualify her to take on this covert assignment with him?

"Natalya grew up near Vologda," C said, reading his thoughts. "And from what I know of her and what Sir Walter relayed to me last year, she can handle herself. More importantly, she's able to make a positive identification of the Romanovs. God willing, once she verifies it's them, you can get everyone safely back to Britain."

He steadied his aging hands on the arms of the chair. "There is another reason I'm sending you. An assassination has been planned against Lenin by some of the Allied agents in Russia. Reilly knows when and where this will take place, and I need *you* to get me that information. This could be a boon for us. Cutting off the head of the Bolsheviks would allow the White Army and the Cossacks loyal to the former tsar to retake the government—"

"And get them back in the war against Germany."

"Precisely." C frowned, tilting his gaze. "These two assignments are of equal importance as they relate to one another, Marcus. To put it bluntly, the king wants his family back, and once the Bolsheviks are defeated, he'll most certainly wish to restore the Romanovs to their rightful throne."

Marcus's pulse raced. Peace could be within their grasp. "Understood, sir."

"I should warn you, too, that this is not only an extremely

delicate situation, but it will be a bit dodgier than your previous missions. Recently, we managed to secure Archangel from the Bolsheviks, but the rest of Russia is crawling with them. And while our embassy people in Moscow are fleeing north to Finland to be smuggled out on ships bound for home, you and Natalya Bryce will be going in the opposite direction."

He paused. "If at any time you decide it's too dangerous for her, use your discretion to come up with an alternate plan." C rose from the chair. "Come and see me tomorrow to receive your necessary travel documents and dispatches for the British authority in Archangel. It's best if Natalya poses as your fiancée on the pretense that you're both visiting her family in the area of Vologda."

He angled his monocle at Marcus. "You'll also need to stop by Barkers on High Street in Kensington and ask for Mr. Price, the jeweler. We use him for this sort of thing, and he knows you'll be coming." He reached across the desk, and Marcus rose to shake his hand. "I'll leave you to it, boy. Enjoy your time in London tomorrow while you can. I hear there's to be a do at Benningham's tomorrow night for some of the staff?"

"A dinner, sir. Director Henshaw from Communications is finally retiring."

"Ah yes, another relic gone." C sighed again. "Henshaw, like your father, once served with me in the Navy a lifetime ago. I'm told these days the director's keen memory falls a bit short of the mark." He turned and ambled toward the door. "It happens to all of us at one point or another," he called back. "But for my part, I'd prefer this war be ended first."

"Indeed, sir." For a moment excitement pulsed through his veins, before frustration seeped in to take its place. His plans to spend time with Clare and Daisy were now dashed.

Retrieving the photograph from his desk drawer, Marcus sighed deeply as he gazed at her lovely image.

What had he once told his young lieutenant friend, Mabry?

Duty and love do not mix.

2

KENSINGTON, LONDON
HOLLAND STREET
TUESDAY, AUGUST 6, 1918—NEXT EVENING

Honestly, Grace, this was a bad idea. What if I embarrass you in front of your guests?"

Clare Danner fidgeted with the powder-blue silk at her shoulders while she eyed her reflection in the mirror. The blue gown, its bodice overlaid in chiffon and seeded with tiny pearls, was unlike anything she'd ever worn.

"Nonsense, Clare. You'll do just fine. And you are here by invitation, don't forget."

Clare's heart thumped with pleasure. Marcus had telephoned her earlier at work asking her to meet him here tonight. "It's been a while since we've seen each other. He just returned from another of his assignments for the War Office."

"And one more reason you should look your very best. The blue color complements your dark hair and lovely gray eyes, by the way. Far better than it does my features."

Lady Grace Benningham finally approached to stand beside her at the cheval glass, a swath of green ribbon hemming in her riotous red curls as her emerald eyes perused Clare in the mirror. "In fact, I shall give you that dress."

"You will not!" Clare turned to her. "Where in heaven's name would I wear such an article? To my hospital job, changing all those soldiers' bloody bandages? Or maybe at breakfast while I attempt to feed my finicky two-year-old. You know Daisy would love to paint her porridge all over this lovely silk. No," she said firmly. "I'll borrow the gown tonight for your dinner party and then you'll take it back, no argument."

"If that's the way you want it." Grace emitted a sigh. "I should know by now that you will always do things 'Clare's way.'" Her eyes twinkled. "Just as you did at the farm."

Clare eyed her with affection, forgetting for a moment the upcoming social gathering downstairs. Instead, she recalled their budding friendship a year ago, when she and Grace had worked together baling hay on one of the vast estates in Kent to aid the war effort. "I'd say you did things your own way, too, Grace Benningham. Falling in love with the lord of the manor—a viscount, no less—and becoming his bride a mere ten months later."

She flashed a mischievous smile. "Viscountess Walenford hasn't quite the same ring as 'Duchess,' but I suppose it will have to do."

"Oh, stop!" Grace laughed, her face turning rosy. "I haven't forgotten you once teased me with that name because my family has wealth. But you know me more than most, Clare Danner. I am as I always was, with or without money or title."

"I do know you," Clare said softly. In Grace she'd found a treasured friend, the kindest, most generous woman she'd ever known. "And you'll never be too fancy for me."

"Let me just fix your hair." Grace stepped behind her and removed the pearl comb to tuck in the errant strands. "Did you ever find the lost mate to this comb? I remember when I made you treat yourself to the lovely pair in that shop in Greenwich last year."

"You called it 'my Christmas present to me,' and no, I haven't found it yet. I'm hoping it will turn up eventually." She glanced at the gold vanity clock and tensed. It was nearly time to go downstairs and mingle with the gentry.

She looked at Grace in the mirror. "So, are you going to keep me in suspense? You told me there was another reason I needed to be here tonight." Her eyes widened. "Do you have an announcement to make?"

"I do not, but someone else I know might." Grace's eyes gleamed.

"Tell me now."

"My, aren't we impatient?" Grace arched a fine brow and smiled. "I was in Barkers department store over on High Street today to purchase a teapot Knowles has had his eye on. He turns sixty next week and I wanted to surprise him."

"Grace." Clare narrowed her eyes. "Enough about your butler."

"All right." She threw up her hands. "I happened to spot a certain gentleman at the jeweler's counter as he purchased a ring."

A rush of heat engulfed Clare. "Who?" she said faintly, not daring to hope.

"Can you not guess?" Grace settled her hands on Clare's shoulders while their gazes met in the glass. "The man who loves you like no other?"

Clare swallowed, her heart pounding. "Marcus . . ."

Grace's eyes glistened. "My dearest friend, who else? And I imagine it's the reason he wants you here with him tonight."

Stunned, Clare could only shake her head. How long she'd waited! A year ago, she'd met Sir Marcus Weatherford, a distinguished naval captain with the Admiralty in London. Admittedly, she'd at first ignored his attentions, but eventually he'd won her heart with his gentle smile beneath the dark mustache and those warm golden-brown eyes. The moments they'd stolen kisses . . .

Every so often she and Marcus talked of a future together, but he had yet to propose. And now he'd bought her a ring!

"I . . . I can hardly believe it." She turned to face her friend. "Are you sure?"

Grace chuckled and nodded, dabbing at her own eyes with a

handkerchief. "I'll grant you, it took him long enough. Still, it's been a worthwhile wait, hasn't it?" She sniffled. "I've prayed so long for your happiness, Clare. You and Marcus are a match made in heaven."

Clare smiled, blinking back her own happy tears. She was about to become engaged to her love—

"Let's finish up so we can go and meet the guests." Grace retrieved a pair of blue satin gloves from her vanity and handed them to Clare. "Hopefully everyone will arrive promptly and Mrs. Riley won't have to delay dinner."

A turnip in a rose garden, Clare. That's what you are.

Clare perched on the edge of the ivory brocade love seat, her satin-gloved hands fisted in her lap as she eyed the Benninghams' lavish surroundings. High walls, colored in shades of lemon and saffron, amplified the last rays of an August evening sun streaming in through the large bay window at the far end of the drawing room.

The stylishly dressed guests were all milling about, most of them middle-aged gents wearing formal "white tie" or military uniforms. They held their lit cigars, pipes, or glasses of amber liquid in hand, and the drone of their conversation sounded to Clare like a swarm of bees bouncing off the high-ceilinged cornices.

Her eyes shifted toward the drawing room's double doors. *Oh, Marcus, please hurry!* The sooner he arrived, the sooner she could relax with him and feel less like flotsam cast adrift on the sea.

The doors suddenly opened, and she held her breath as four more gents and two couples entered the room. No sign of Marcus.

"He'll be here, Clare, trust me." Grace had left her guests to settle in the padded turquoise velvet chair beside her. She grinned as she opened her fan, waving it briskly. "Marcus knows you're here, after all."

Clare forced a smile. She secretly dreaded the coming formal dinner with the Benninghams and their guests. Last summer she'd baled hay for the war effort, and before that she'd grown up working as a domestic belowstairs. How was she to behave seated beside the nobility? Grace and Jack's wedding reception had been somewhat less formal and included the other girls who had worked with them on the farms. But this . . .

Calm down. Drawing a deep breath, she relaxed her grip. Marcus would be here, and he'd bought her a ring. She turned to Grace. "You said this was a retirement celebration?"

"Yes. See that gentleman near the fireplace? Sir Charles Henshaw. He's finally leaving Whitehall. Jack has been working for him over the past year."

Clare eyed the salt-and-pepper-haired man in question, his slight paunch evident beneath the white shirtfront. He didn't look all that old. "Does he wish to leave his job?"

Grace frowned. "I cannot say for certain, but I think it's become difficult . . . to keep up."

Clare's heart softened as her gaze returned to him. If what Grace said were true, that Sir Henshaw's memory wasn't keen any longer, then it was a blessing the Benninghams had decided to send him off with dignity. She scanned the rest of the room. "Are these men all with the War Office?"

"Yes, and the few ladies here are their wives." Grace aimed her fan toward a pair of finely dressed women seated on the rose-print couch nearby. "That is Lady Wippleton on the left and Lady Dooley. Their husbands are standing near the bay window. All are the best of friends. Lady Dooley is an accomplished pianist. I've asked her to play for us after dinner."

A beautiful blonde sat on a floral-patterned chair adjacent to the two wives. Her flowing gray silk matched the lace mantilla pinned to her perfect chignon. Clare noted the other ladies leaned in to listen to whatever she was telling them.

"That is Mrs. Walter Bryce." Grace followed her gaze.

"Where is her husband?"

"Mrs. Bryce is widowed. Her husband died almost a year ago."

She glanced at Clare. "She still chooses to honor him by wearing gray shades, but I don't believe she's hampered by any dictates of mourning, at least those preventing her from attending social functions."

Clare couldn't really blame her. In four years of war, the public had begun to shift its views on bereavement. With so many deceased husbands and their widows needed in the workplace to keep the country going, the stringent etiquette of long mourning periods and avoiding society simply wasn't feasible for most women. "Why is she here with the War Office staff? Does she know Sir Henshaw?"

Grace shrugged. "Mrs. Bryce's name was included on the list of guests I received from Whitehall. Sir Walter was with the British Embassy in Moscow, so likely she knows several here."

Clare observed the animated faces of the two wives. "They seem captivated with her."

"I'm not surprised. Mrs. Bryce is Natalya Savvina, once a rather famous Imperial Russian ballerina who also danced in Paris with the Ballets Russes."

"She's very elegant."

Again the drawing room doors opened. Clare darted a look at the newcomers. Still no Marcus, but instead two older gents and . . .

She gripped the arm of the love seat and stared at the tall, lean man in his twenties who accompanied them. Formally attired, his reddish-blond features were pleasantly handsome.

His familiar blue eyes took in the room from behind a pair of gold spectacles and then widened on her before a footman caught his attention with a tray of drinks.

Clare took shallow breaths as memories of the past flooded her. "Why is he here?" she whispered.

Grace gave her a startled look before turning toward the newcomers. "Which do you mean? Sirs Howard Tarleton, Rodney Blake, or Stephen Lange? All three work in the War Office with Jack and Marcus." Her eyes narrowed on Clare. "What's wrong?"

"Nothing. I . . . I was just curious." She gave another tight smile.

Grace appeared unconvinced. "You will tell me?"

"Later, I promise."

Her relief came when a regal-looking matron broke from another group to stroll in their direction. Lady Bassett, Dowager Countess of Avonshire, took the seat across from Grace. Lifting her diamond-encrusted lorgnette from a gold chain around her neck, she inspected Clare with eyes the color of strong coffee. "Mrs. Danner, is it?"

Clare offered a polite nod. "Yes, your ladyship. I was—"

"You were Lady Walenford's matron of honor. Yes, I recall, it was only back in May. And before that, I saw you at Swan's Tea Room." She leaned forward with the lorgnette. "You are looking very pretty this evening . . . and you have kept our hostess occupied for most of the past half hour."

"The fault is mine, your ladyship, and I do apologize for neglecting my other guests." Grace turned, making bug eyes at Clare, who nearly grinned. "I have mentioned to Mrs. Danner that you are my father's chief patroness at Swan's."

Grace then smiled lovingly at the older woman. "And through your ladyship's generosity and devotion to my mother's memory, you have helped me to rise to the station of polite society for which I now lay claim as a viscountess."

"And one day, Countess of Stonebrooke," Lady Bassett added sharply, though the slight flush in her cheeks revealed her pleasure at Grace's words. Her lorgnette returned to Clare. "And where is your husband, Mrs. Danner? I have yet to meet him."

Again Grace intervened. "Lady Bassett, Mr. Danner became a casualty of the war last year."

Clare averted her eyes. How she despised having to make her friend lie! Yet the truth—that Clare was an unwed mother with a child—would have barred her from getting a decent job and from attending a formal event like this one at the Kensington home of a viscount and viscountess.

Her "widowed status" had been Grace's suggestion once they left behind their hay-baling work to return to London.

"It is frightful how many young men we have lost." Lady Bassett made a tsking sound and then eyed Clare through the diamond lorgnette. "Condolences to you, my dear."

"Er . . . thank you, your ladyship." Clare reached to absently pluck at the seed pearls on the blue chiffon overlay before Grace laid a hand gently against her shoulder.

"Where is our host?" Like quicksilver, Lady Bassett rebounded to glare at the room. "Has Weatherford once again nabbed him into the study with brandy when there are guests about?"

As if the dowager's words had conjured them, the drawing room doors suddenly opened.

Marcus strode into the room first, and Clare's breath caught as she eyed the handsome dark-haired man who had stolen her heart.

He wore his military "mess dress"—the short-tailored navy jacket emphasizing his lean waist and broad shoulders, while the gleaming medals on his breast lapel complemented his gold-laced cuffed sleeves and the matching gold stripes on his dark trousers that indicated his rank as naval captain.

Right behind him followed Grace's husband, Lord Walenford—Jack—clad in his formal white tie for dinner. Though each of them was tall and powerfully built, Marcus's dark good looks were in sharp contrast to Jack's striking blond features, yet both men cut fine figures.

Marcus and Jack soon spotted them across the room and smiled as they approached.

"Have you ever seen such loveliness before you, Marcus?" Jack said once they stood beside them. His teeth flashed white against his tanned face. "And, Clare and Grace, you ladies are also looking splendid tonight."

A chortle escaped Lady Bassett, and she turned to give Jack a playful slap with her lorgnette. "Impudent pup," she said, though her smile clearly held affection. She arched a dark brow at Marcus. "Where have you kept him hidden, Weatherford? You cannot simply run off with the host when he has his duties to attend to."

"My sincerest apologies, your ladyship." As he spoke, Marcus reached to take her gloved hand and place a kiss at her fingertips. He turned slightly and winked at Clare, and her pulse leapt as she smiled.

While Jack kept Lady Bassett entertained, Marcus moved to sit beside Clare.

"Thank you for coming tonight." He leaned to whisper in her ear while the spicy scent of his cologne filled her senses. "You look ravishing."

She turned to him, her skin warm with pleasure.

He glanced around the room and then smiled at her. "You're also far more interesting to talk to than these old goats, Jack included."

A giggle escaped her, and she darted a look at Lady Bassett, relieved to see the matron hadn't noticed. "You had better behave yourself," she said, glancing back at him.

He flashed a devilish smile, the warm golden glint in his eyes making her pulse race. "We could always go to the study." His attention slowly drifted down to settle on her mouth.

She gasped her amused outrage. "Marcus!"

He laughed softly. "I promise you, my intentions are honorable."

Clare swallowed. Did he wish to propose to her in the study?

"There's a chess set ready and waiting, and I'll even give you first advantage to win back your white king."

Her disappointment was quickly followed by relief. She'd rather he ask for her hand somewhere more romantic than Jack's study. "In case you've forgotten, sir, I won the last game." She raised a brow. "You owe me that white king."

He grinned. "We'll go for the rubber match and see if I don't keep it."

She reached for his hand. "I've missed you," she said softly, her humor vanishing. "So has Daisy. I imagine work has been terribly busy for you?"

He nodded, his sculpted features sobering. "I'd hoped you and I could spend some time together . . ."

"Oh yes! I look forward to it. And thank you for inviting me tonight." While she was uncomfortable with the whole formal dining business, being here with him was all that mattered.

"Would you like something to drink?"

"Tea would be nice."

Nodding, he rose and made his way toward one of the footmen.

"Dinner is served!"

The old butler's bald announcement sent a wreath of smiles across the room. Jack escorted Lady Bassett while Grace took the hand of their guest of honor, Sir Henshaw, and afterward others began spilling out of the drawing room toward the dining hall.

Clare still sat on the settee. Would she embarrass herself at the table in front of Marcus and his colleagues?

He was heading back her way, wearing a confident smile, when Mrs. Bryce, the blond beauty, intercepted him with a touch on his sleeve.

"Captain Weatherford, I find myself without an escort. Would you please be so kind?"

Marcus hesitated before casting a glance at Clare, regret in his eyes. "Of course, Mrs. Bryce. If you'll allow me."

Giving her his arm, he looked to Clare once more, mouthing an apology before he and the ballerina joined the others exiting the room.

Anger and humiliation brewed in her as she watched them leave. The nerve of that woman! Hadn't she seen Marcus with her on the settee?

Clare was so furious she didn't notice the tall man approach. She was still glaring at the open doors when a familiar male voice murmured close to her, "May I have the honor, Clare?"

3

Clare's heart lurched as she glanced up to see Stephen Lange straighten to his full height and smile at her. "Shall we?"

She bit back an angry retort. Clare wanted nothing to do with this man who reminded her of a past better left forgotten. Her desperate gaze darted around the drawing room, now empty. What could she do? Be further humiliated by staying here alone and starving to death?

Stephen extended his hand to her.

"Thank you," she said stiffly and reached for him. Accepting his offer seemed the lesser of two evils. Outside of dinner, though, she never wanted to see him again.

They were the last to reach the dining room, and all but two of the twenty-two table settings had been taken. Amid the buzz of conversation and laughter, Stephen escorted her to the place with her name card, and she noted he had been assigned the empty seat beside hers.

"It must be fate." Stephen smiled as they took their places.

Clare's mood lifted to see Marcus seated directly across the table from her. She glanced down several places to find Mrs. Bryce safely out of reach. Good riddance!

Quickly she placed the linen serviette in her lap, having spied the elderly footman assisting other ladies and now looking intently at her. She was no child to be coddled, tucking napkins or spoon-feeding as she did with Daisy.

She tensed over the tableware—an array of spoons, forks, and knives on either side of the setting, along with several empty crystal glasses. When she'd worked as a domestic, her job pertained to polishing banisters and changing sheets, not managing the flat-ware, which was the butler's job.

Clare glanced up to find Marcus watching her from across the table, an amused glint in his eyes. Her spine stiffened. Was he laughing at her?

Again he winked at her, then splayed his hands along the edge of the table. With surreptitious movements, he used an index finger to touch the soup spoon she'd be using first and proceeded to touch the other pieces in the order she would need them.

Shoulders easing, she offered him a grateful smile. He hadn't been making fun of her.

Your old habits die hard, Clare Danner. This is Marcus, after all. She flushed. How could she think he would ridicule her? In the past she'd done her own share of mocking others—her defense against those who might hurt her, either by word or by deed—but then she met Marcus, and they'd talked about trust, something she hadn't been able to do for a long time. She'd been trying to learn ever since.

He and Grace were the two people in her life she *could* count on to always guard her heart.

A bowl of fragrant onion soup arrived, and she tucked in with her proper spoon, careful not to slurp or call attention to herself. Casting another glance across the table at Marcus, her pulse sped with anticipation. When *would* he propose to her . . . surely not here in front of everyone?

"So, how are you, Clare?"

She jerked her head toward Stephen just as the soup bowls were cleared away and the footmen began delivering the second course. "I'm doing well," she said briskly. "And you?"

"Working all hours at the War Office, as you might have guessed." He smiled. "It has been some time since we've met and spoken to each other." He hesitated. "Are you employed as well?"

For an instant she bristled at her memories of the past, when years ago her mum had taken a job as a cook with Stephen's rich and titled relations. Clare herself had worked her way up from being the lowest "slavey" to finally obtaining her post as an upstairs maid before Mum's death.

"I work at the military hospital over on Endell Street," she said, raising her chin. There, too, she'd worked her way up the ranks to eventually become an orderly.

His blue eyes brightened. "You always were smarter than Elliot and me put together."

She startled at the compliment. Mum had been such a fine cook that she'd bartered with the mistress to let eight-year-old Clare tutor alongside Elliot Lange, the viscount's son and heir, and his cousin Stephen. At least until the boys left for Harrow School in London.

"And you must enjoy the work." Regret flashed across his expression. "I became deaf in my right ear, so I could not serve in France. It must be satisfying to be able to care for our brave Tommies coming back from the war."

"It is that," she said softly, her mood thawing toward him just a bit.

"I've seen you in town a few times with Lady Walenford. Have you been here in London the whole time?"

Once more her guard went up. "For several months I traveled with the Women's Forage Corps, baling hay for the cavalry horses overseas."

"Impressive." His look held sincerity. "You've accomplished much since I last saw you."

More than you know. She smiled and turned to Marcus. Hopefully he'd wish to marry her soon, and then she and Daisy would be his family.

Clare was thankful when Stephen tucked into his food again

and their conversation ended. Various courses followed, simple fare due to the rationing, but the Benninghams' cook, Mrs. Riley, outdid herself, and by the time dessert arrived—stewed apricots topped with dollops of whipped cream—it seemed everyone was satisfied.

A clink on the edge of a crystal goblet drew everyone's attention. Jack rose from the other end of the table and made a toast to Sir Henshaw, seated beside him. Clare listened as he commended Henshaw's valued years of service with the Crown and described how much he appreciated working for him. The older man's eyes teared up, and he reached for his napkin to wipe at his face, a show of emotion even she knew wasn't done in such dignified circumstances.

Yet he clearly seemed to know what was happening to him, and it tore at her heart. *Clare, you need to stop this. How will you ever keep doing your job at the hospital if you go soft every time you see someone in pain?*

She glanced at Stephen and was reminded of her days in service with his family. An aging scullery maid, Penny Ann Gruber, had worked with her mum in the kitchens. Clare remembered how Penny became more and more confused over the years, putting the cups back in the wrong place or forgetting to add soap to the dishwater. One night, she had trouble finding her room and took the wrong set of stairs, ending up on the main floor in the midst of the viscount's party. Penny got the sack the next day without so much as a stipend to see her through.

Clare frowned. Yet another reason to despise the family whose money and pedigree had made them callous toward those in need. She prayed Sir Henshaw had people who would love and care for him the way Penny should have been.

Relieved to end the meal, Clare went through with the other ladies to the drawing room and sat beside Grace on a raspberry satin couch as tea was served. The others gathered around, regaling one another with snatches of Paris fashion news or their latest contributions to the war effort.

Mrs. Bryce sat apart, her smile forced as she looked beyond them to the several oil paintings along the wall.

The ballerina seemed no more interested than Clare in the humdrum chatter.

"Lady Dooley, would you honor us with some music?" Grace said, much to Clare's relief.

"I would be delighted, your ladyship." Yet as Lady Dooley rose to go to the piano, she cast a conspiratorial glance at Lady Wippleton and tipped her coiffed head toward Mrs. Bryce.

Lady Wippleton seemed to understand. She smiled at the ballerina. "Mrs. Bryce, would you consider giving us a sampling of one of your lovely performances . . . before the gentlemen arrive?"

Several other ladies tittered at the request while Lady Bassett and another matron both frowned their displeasure. But once Lady Dooley sat down and began to play, Mrs. Bryce cried, "*Chopiniana!*" and with delicate poise rose from her chair, lifting her slender arms high to a smattering of soft applause. She looked toward the piano, then rose on slippered toes and with small, mincing yet graceful steps seemed to float backward toward the center of the room, arms high and flowing.

"Bourrées!" Lady Wippleton murmured, then "Arabesque!" as Mrs. Bryce splayed her arms along either side while tipping her torso forward, raising one leg behind her as far as her flowing gray skirts would allow. She held the graceful pose to more applause.

"Petit allegro!" cried Mrs. Wippleton as the ballerina performed a series of small leaps, her elegant arms moving in unison while she moved back and forth, her pointed feet at times aloft and criss-crossing rapidly like beating wings.

All eyes were upon her, some clearly shocked at the dance, while the rest stared in fascination at the elegant woman in gray. Lady Wippleton applauded once more and turned to inform everyone it was Natalya Savvina of the Imperial Ballet and Ballets Russes in their midst. Several gasps arose, then more applause until the ballerina twirled once, twice, with more small leaps, before her final rushing steps across the room.

Mrs. Bryce didn't see the drawing room doors opening until it was too late. Her upper body jerked to the left to avoid hitting the wood just as Stephen Lange came through the opening and grabbed for her as she began to fall.

He held her at that angle for an instant, her back arched while her hands clutched at his sleeves. Then Marcus came through, and Stephen shoved her onto him. He grabbed for her and held her in much the same fashion while the ladies again began to applaud.

Clare's shock turned to anger. Why didn't Marcus just let her go?

That's uncharitable, Clare. Still, she fumed at the ballerina. Must that woman have all the attention?

Jack walked through right after Marcus and took in the sight. "Are we having a dance lesson in the drawing room, old boy?" he said, and a few of the ladies laughed while Marcus helped to right Mrs. Bryce back onto her feet.

The other gents filed in, yet the rest of the evening was a blur to Clare.

Her mood seesawed between envy at seeing the ballerina in the middle of conversations between Marcus and some of the other gents, and her nervous anticipation at his upcoming proposal. *These are the people he works with, Clare, and you need to be patient.*

Yet despite her efforts to overcome the sense, she still felt like an outsider.

At least she hadn't been obliged to talk with Stephen Lange again before he left the party.

The clock finally chimed the hour of eleven, and Clare breathed a sigh as the rest of the guests stood and prepared to depart.

"What an entertaining evening." Sir Henshaw made the remark to Grace and Jack once most of the others had left.

Clare took the initiative and sidled up beside Marcus. He smiled at her and leaned close. "You were wonderfully patient with me tonight, especially after I asked you to be here," he whispered. "May I make it up to you and escort you home, madam?"

Again he winked at her, and Clare thrilled as she grinned. "You may, sir," she whispered back.

Mrs. Bryce had also remained behind, and chose the moment to move forward into the group. "Captain Weatherford, have you arranged a car for this evening? I would be pleased to offer you mine if you need a ride home."

Clare stiffened, glancing at Marcus.

"Thank you for your kind offer, Mrs. Bryce. I have my own transportation well in hand."

Clare resisted a sudden urge to crow right then and there.

Mrs. Bryce turned to the guest of honor. "Sir Henshaw, I extend the same offer to you."

"Oho!" A smile lit his slightly wrinkled face. "How could I refuse the escort of a beautiful young woman? Thank you, Mrs. Bryce."

It *was* a kind gesture. For a moment, Clare's guilt outweighed her distrust of the woman.

"I thank you, Lord and Lady Walenford," Mrs. Bryce said after Sir Henshaw had made his farewells. "It has been a lovely evening." She turned a smile to Marcus. "Until tomorrow." And taking the older gentleman's arm, they departed to her waiting transport.

Until tomorrow. What had Mrs. Bryce meant?

It was minutes later when Clare sat beside Marcus in the darkened back seat of the Benninghams' Daimler, the chauffeur, Raymond, driving them back to their respective homes.

She eyed Marcus's tall, silent silhouette. Despite his efforts to make amends, their romantic evening *had* turned into disappointment. Clare expected him to spend the evening with her; after all, he'd invited her there and Grace had seen him purchase the ring. Yet either by chance or intent, the blond ballerina had claimed much of his attention tonight.

She gazed out at the shadowy streets as the car headed east. The ornate Georgian and Victorian mansions and stylish brownstones eventually gave way to the dingier neighborhoods of St. Giles that Clare called home. The borough wasn't far from London's East End, with flats squeezed in between warehouses and industrial shops, alongside breweries and brothels, which were there to entertain young soldiers who were home on furlough with the intent to carouse and have a good time.

A drunk, his bottle in hand, staggered his way along the lamplit street.

Marcus tensed beside her. "Darling, I wish you would allow me to help you and Daisy move into a better place. I don't like the idea of you living in this rough neighborhood." He turned to her. "It's dangerous."

"We've talked about this before, Marcus," she whispered. "My reputation is already in question by some, and I don't need people thinking I'm a 'kept woman,' especially by an unmarried man. It's not proper and you know it."

Why was he talking like this? Weren't they going to be married soon? "Besides that, my flat is close to the hospital, so I can take the bus or even walk the distance in a few minutes' time."

"I definitely don't want you walking." His voice hardened. "Promise me, Clare. You must avoid taking risks, especially when I'm away."

And that would be much of the time, Marcus. She clamped her mouth shut. He worried about her, and for that she should be thankful.

Clare switched topics. "It was certainly an eventful evening tonight. Mrs. Bryce seems quite lively, especially with her dancing in the drawing room. I thought for a moment she might fall and break her head." She wet her lips. "Do you know her from the Admiralty?"

"I knew her husband first, Sir Walter Bryce. And yes, I've spoken with her on several occasions when she has come to Whitehall." His warm hand pressed against hers while the regret in his tone held some amusement. "I'm sorry about not being able to escort

32

you into dinner. A bit of a tricky situation, and I couldn't very well refuse."

"No, of course not." Earlier, Clare had thought otherwise, but her churlishness was uncalled for. If he'd refused Mrs. Bryce's request for a dinner escort, the woman would have been affronted. Marcus didn't need animosity from the widow of a former friend.

"I saw you conversing with Lange at dinner. What did he have to say?"

Clare noted the strain in his voice, and her heart swelled. Ever her protector. Marcus knew all about her past suffering with the Lange family. "Nothing more than polite conversation, thank goodness."

His body relaxed beside hers. "Has he approached you here in London before?"

"No, I was quite shocked to see him. I think he was just as surprised to see me."

Marcus grunted. "Let me know if you'd like me to speak to him."

Clare squeezed his hand. "I am looking forward to our lunch tomorrow," she said, again changing the subject. When he *was* in town, they always met for lunch on Wednesdays. "Will you pick me up at the hospital or shall I meet you?"

He bent his head to hers. "I'm afraid we'll have to postpone tomorrow's lunch, sweetheart," he said. "I must travel to Hampshire in the morning on business."

"Will you see your family while you're there?"

When he flashed a quick smile and nodded, Clare swallowed past the ache in her throat. He'd mentioned before that one day he would take her and Daisy out to the country to meet them, yet in a year's time and despite her pressing him once or twice, their visit to Hampshire hadn't happened.

Why?

She knew their names—his younger sister, Frances, his mother, Elaine, and his grandfather, Sir Geoffrey, a scientific man who designed prosthetics for the soldiers who were missing limbs.

Marcus's mother had opened half of their house to the British Army as a rehabilitation center for the returning wounded.

"I'll come to the flat once you finish work at the hospital tomorrow. Six o'clock?"

He put his arm around her then, and once more her spirits lifted. At least he hadn't mentioned seeing Mrs. Bryce. "Yes, and I'll win back my white king *without* your advantage, Captain."

Chuckling, he drew her close, and Clare savored his warm strength. She looked to him in the shadows. "And will you join us for dinner, too?"

"I . . . cannot stay long." He hesitated. "I'm sorry, darling. The truth is, I must leave you again."

She tried shrugging off his arm, but he held her tight. "Clare, you know my work is critical to the war, much like a soldier's. I'm given orders and it's my duty to fulfill them."

Clare stilled against him, his words shaming her. "I'm sorry. I do understand and I appreciate what you do for king and country."

"I know it hasn't been easy for you or for Daisy, but I will make it up to you both."

She smiled a sad smile, relieved that he couldn't see her face in the shadows. "Any idea when you'll return?"

"We'll talk more about that tomorrow evening." As he spoke, the car pulled up alongside her flat. Clare saw that, behind the curtains, her live-in babysitter, Ruthie Simmons, had lit the lamp for her.

"Stay put, Raymond," Marcus instructed the chauffeur before exiting to come around and open her door. Helping her to alight, they walked onto the front porch.

Clare gazed up at him in the lamp's reflection, her emotions a tangle of confusion and anticipation. His smile was tender beneath the dark mustache as he reached for her, tipping her face up to his. "You are so beautiful, sweetheart, and tonight especially so."

His deep voice melted through her taut nerves like butter, and as he dipped his head to her, she lowered her lashes, eager to surrender to the warm feel of his mouth against hers—

"Thank goodness yer home!"

Ruthie had suddenly thrown the door open. Swiftly, Clare and Marcus pulled apart while Daisy's loud crying echoed from inside.

"I'm sorry, Mrs. Danner, but she woke up fussin' and hasn't stopped. I fed her and then changed her nappy, but she's still a-cryin'."

Ruthie, looking frazzled, finally seemed to realize Marcus was there. She eyed him with a smile. "Yer looking right fine tonight, Cap'n Weatherford." She then flashed another desperate glance at Clare before retreating into the flat and closing the door.

He smiled. "I suppose that's my cue to say good night so you can go and comfort our sweet Daisy."

"Not so sweet by the sounds of it." It seemed the marriage proposal she'd hoped for tonight must now be delayed. Her eyes rose to his. "I'll be home tomorrow by six-fifteen sharp."

"And I *will* be here." This time he leaned in to kiss her cheek, and his arms held her close, his scent of spice enveloping her. "Take care of yourself tomorrow, my *Chiara*," he murmured into her hair. "No walking to work."

"I'll take the bus." She smiled against him. *My* Chiara. It sounded so romantic.

He released her and brushed a fingertip along the place where he'd kissed her.

Her heart leapt along with her hopes as she followed him with her eyes toward the Daimler.

They would still have another chance to be together before he left.

4

"Clare!"

Clare looked up from signing in at the hospital ten minutes past the hour of six o'clock the following morning to see her co-workers Beatrice Parker and Sally Forbes wave to her from the far end of the hall. Each orderly wore a white smock and kerchief similar to her own, and both had worked on the same shift with Clare several times before.

"You're late, Mrs. Danner." Sally held up her watch, hazel eyes gleaming with mischief. "Did you miss the bus?"

Clare offered a tight-lipped smile. She didn't need the reminder. It was bad enough she'd broken her promise to Marcus and walked to work this morning. Besides that, Sally Forbes was too nosy by half. "And what if I did?"

Sally's eyes suddenly dimmed, and Clare sighed. *Trust, Clare. She means you no harm.* "My daughter woke up fussing this morning, if you must know, and she was the same last night. I checked her for fever, but she seems all right. Maybe just bad dreams."

"Poor tot." Beatrice spoke up, her freckled features full of sympathy.

Clare nodded. If anyone had a right to nightmares, it was her sweet baby. Her chest still hurt, remembering how her infant child was taken away from her at birth. A whole year later and with Marcus's help, they'd discovered Daisy abandoned in a filthy workhouse orphanage in Kent.

"So you couldn't take a cab?" Sally asked.

Clare grabbed up the clipboard with her day's patient roster and duties. She couldn't afford a cab, not with her flat rent for August having depleted over half her wages. And aside from Ruthie's room and board, there was her small stipend to be paid and their food to be purchased. She turned to Sally. "My legs needed a good stretch."

"Walking the streets of St. Giles at dawn?"

"I was fine, though next time I'll do as you suggest and hail a cab."

"I hope so. I wouldn't wish to read about you in the *Times*." Sally tipped her head. "So, Beatrice and I were both called in to work the shift with you today. It seems with the new wounded coming in from France over the past week, the hospital's had three more orderlies come down with influenza—Smith, Casey, and Adams."

Clare tensed. She'd been working the day shift with those three women over the past few weeks. "Where are they? Are they going to be all right?"

"They're being tended to on the second floor," Beatrice answered. "Matron says she has them well in hand."

It was a worry Clare always carried at the back of her mind. What if she took some foreign sickness home and gave it to her daughter or Ruthie? "That means we must all take extra care today. With three down and only two replacements, it's going to be a busy twelve hours."

"That's an understatement. I'll see you both at tea, then." Sally waved again as she turned to leave, and all three went off in their different directions to begin their rounds checking on patients and tending them according to the night-shift nurses' recommendations.

Clare loved her job. Last summer after Marcus helped to reunite her with her daughter, she'd realized that her life of working the farms was no longer suitable. For Daisy's sake, she needed both steady employment and stability.

She and Daisy had then left Kent for London. Yet Clare's job experience was limited—her farming work with the Women's Forage Corps didn't qualify her for a proper city job, despite her years of being tutored alongside Elliot and Stephen Lange. And unless she went back into domestic service—a notion she abhorred—she needed to learn a new skill.

When Clare was injured last year in an enemy air attack over Kent, Grace's cousin Dr. Strom had cared for her. Watching his healing skills helped to foster her interest in the medical profession. In Ireland, too, when Dad was alive, she'd worked with him on the tenant farm, which had included helping him with the animal husbandry.

Still, being unmarried with a natural daughter, she'd shied away from applying at any of the London hospitals. Questions would be asked, and she'd get tossed out on her ear without even a consideration. Yet as the weeks passed and her farm earnings ran out, she worried about how she would care for Daisy.

And that was when Grace stepped in to take charge.

Clare smiled. Her friend was much involved in the suffrage movement and knew where "Mrs. Danner" might succeed in getting a post.

Louisa Garrett Anderson and Flora Murray ran the Endell Street Military Hospital, both women suffragettes as well as accomplished doctors. In fact, except for a handful of soldiers unable to return overseas, their entire hospital staff of cooks, clerical workers, orderlies, nurses, doctors, surgeons, and specialists were women—even the volunteers who maintained the patients' outdoor therapeutic garden.

Clare had been nervous at the interview; yet as the questions were asked, she decided to be truthful about her past and was rewarded for her honesty when the interviewer seemed impressed and supportive of her new vocation. She'd agreed to start in the laundry, and after months of hard work she began assisting the nurses and finally became an orderly herself.

The next several hours passed quickly as Clare took temperatures, fed patients, reapplied bandages, changed linens, and stitched wounds. By elevenses teatime, she was in dire need of refreshment. Along with her lunch she'd packed a tin of biscuits, which she brought with her to meet the others in the small canteen serving hospital staff.

She, Beatrice, and Sally were among several other workers who had stopped to take their break, and the three enjoyed a light snack of the biscuits with their steaming cups of black tea.

"I haven't worked this hard in months," Beatrice complained.

"I had to change the bedding twice for three different patients!" Sally exclaimed, before she closed her eyes and breathed in the steaming fragrant tea. "Just wake me up in a couple of hours."

Already weary from her near-sleepless night, Clare sipped at the strong brew, grateful that though the country rationed food, the British Army took care to provide ample tea for its recovering soldiers—and by way of an unspoken boon, for those who cared for them as well.

When Matron entered the canteen, the chairs in the room screeched as everyone turned to look at her.

Clare opened her eyes to see the woman approaching their table.

"Ladies, I need your assistance. We've received word that three ambulances filled with wounded are on their way from Waterloo Station. Once the soldiers are off-loaded and examined to determine their state of urgency, they will require your immediate attention with bathing and bandaging the minor wounds."

She glanced up at the wall clock. "Which means I must ask you to postpone your lunch by at least two hours today." Gazing at each of them, her soft dark eyes came to settle on Clare.

"Mrs. Danner, I shall rely on you to see that all is organized.

Beds made, bandages ready, and notify the chief cook so she can prepare meals for them. I'll give you an accurate count once they arrive."

Stunned, Clare rose from her seat. She'd imagined Matron about to chastise her for her ten-minute tardiness this morning, yet she was being given this important responsibility? "Why . . . of course, Matron. All will be in readiness." She glanced at Sally and Beatrice, then at another pair of orderlies, who met her gaze. "We shall see to it now—"

"You've still another few minutes." Matron waved Clare back into her seat. "Enjoy your tea while you can. It will be some time before you have the chance to eat again."

With that, she abruptly turned and departed.

"My oh my, Clare! It seems Matron's given you Smith's job while she's laid up in bed."

"Yes." Still a bit dazed, she looked at Sally. "And I'll need both you and Beatrice to help make sure I don't blunder."

5

RUSSELL PARK, LONDON
WEDNESDAY, AUGUST 7, 1918—SAME DAY

Marcus paced back and forth along Russell Square's graveled garden path, his gaze occasionally turning toward the tall bronze statue of Francis Russell, Fifth Duke of Bedford, after which the square was named.

He checked his watch: 1455. Natalya Bryce had requested to meet him here in front of the statue at 1500 this afternoon. Her former husband, Sir Walter, had held a flat somewhere here in the Bloomsbury district.

Once he'd briefed her about the train arrangements, they would embark later this evening to arrive in Folkestone near dusk and board their ship to sail at night for Rotterdam. From there, he and his "fiancée" would sail by naval cruiser the four days it took to reach the port in Archangel.

Marcus pushed out a sigh. He would have preferred Whitehall for this meeting, but he'd just returned an hour ago from Hampshire and her message was waiting for him at his office.

He'd delivered documents in a sealed packet to his grandfather while he was home—a newly revised will in case he didn't make it back from Russia, along with a private envelope for Clare. Grandfather had taken the packet from him and placed it inside the safe, the concern in his wizened old face revealing his understanding.

His grandson was embarking on a very dangerous assignment.

Neither had spoken of it, however. Marcus couldn't offer any details, and the old man knew it.

He cleared his throat to ease the tightness. His grandfather had clung to him as they embraced before he departed, as though he might never see him again.

Marcus looked past the bronze statue toward the square, where people—mostly women—milled in and out of the Georgian-style Russell Hotel, likely having tea at Doll's. He also spied a few soldiers strolling about and sightseeing, no doubt home on furlough. Several offices had taken over the terraced estates, while behind him the British Museum had closed its doors to the public during the war.

He noticed a gathering of older men—cabbies—standing near their taxis and conversing while they waited for fares. For a moment, he envisioned simply being one of them, talking about how the day was going and passing along any amusing anecdotes. And at the end of the shift, heading home to a hot meal with the family. Repeating that process the following day.

Again his thoughts turned to Clare, and his pulse increased. She'd been breathtaking last night at the retirement party, like royalty, floating in a sea of blue that enhanced her midnight hair and eyes like the color of a storm.

He grinned. Those eyes were more than a match for her fiery temper, certainly. But it was that same passion he craved, and he was proud of her. She'd accomplished so much in the past year all on her own.

Marcus wasn't happy, however, when she continued to refuse his help in moving her and Daisy out of that slum. He understood the concern about her reputation, but still he worried. In fact, a few weeks ago he'd called in a favor with his friend at Scotland Yard, and they'd made an arrangement: The bobby who patrolled the area was keeping an eye out for Clare in the mornings as she left the flat, making certain she caught the bus to Endell Street.

He checked his watch again . . . 1510. Already fifteen minutes had elapsed.

Marcus turned to scan the gardens, the untended lawns and overgrown shrubbery a sign of how the war had reduced the workforce here at home. Natalya was late.

Regardless of the reasons C had offered him, why risk taking a woman completely unskilled in the business of espionage into a country swarming with Bolsheviks?

He fished from his uniform pocket the ring he'd collected for Natalya at the jeweler's yesterday, completing their ruse as an engaged couple off to visit her family in Russia before they married.

Guilt pricked him as he flipped open the velvet box and stared at the gaudy jewel. *How is it, Weatherford, that you're standing here in the park about to give an engagement ring to the wrong woman?*

His mother had also given him a ring, months ago, his grandmother's garnet. The red gem surrounded in tiny yellow chrysoberyl stones was not nearly as pretentious as this chunk of glass, though far more valuable.

Mother's hint hadn't been subtle: Marcus needed to start looking for a wife.

He'd taken the offering and for the hundredth time considered asking Clare to marry him. He'd even had the ring resized. And then he'd hidden it away for another time.

His tracking down enemy spies and saboteurs here and across Europe, and the threats against him, could put at risk a wife and family. Only after the war, when peace finally brought an end to the fighting, would he no longer be an enemy's target.

Duty and love do not mix.

Again, his own maxim. Yet guilt, and a deep longing, battled his self-control, making him ache with uncertainty.

Were the sage words always true? *Was* his making Clare wait really safer for her and Daisy? It didn't seem fair . . .

Marcus snapped the box closed, returning the costume ring

to his pocket. For now, for this assignment, he must rely on duty first, though it didn't relieve his pain at having to leave his sweet Chiara once more.

"Now, isn't this a lovely spot?" Sally remarked as she, Clare, and Beatrice passed through a black wrought-iron gate into the garden square.

"It's heavenly." Clare took a deep cleansing breath. "The air doesn't smell of carbolic disinfectant or the stench of blood."

Once they'd been allowed their lunch hour, Sally suggested the park, and Clare was grateful to get away from the demands of the hospital. Her fatigue from working over the past several hours only added to her already exhausted state from Daisy, and yet being here among the trees and the sweet smell of grass seemed to rejuvenate her. "I've never been to Russell Square gardens before, and it's only a ten-minute walk from Endell Street."

"I've been a few times." Sally led them along a footpath edged by overgrown grass. "Once in a while I stop to take tea at Doll's inside the hotel." She pointed toward the massive structure across from the park. "Then I usually come here and stroll through the grounds."

"Oh, look! There's the perfect place under that tree where we can sit," Beatrice cried. "Though the grass might be long enough to tickle our noses."

Grinning, she headed them toward an area off the path beneath the shade of a yew tree and surrounded by grass that hadn't been mowed in what looked like weeks.

Still, it faced the south gate, and the square Sally had mentioned was visible.

"Yes, I think I shall like this spot," Sally said as she dropped down beside Beatrice, both sitting cross-legged in their skirts amid the grass. "We can see out, but no one can see in, and I so enjoy watching people."

No doubt about that. Clare smiled as she sat down beside them. Sally Forbes was curious about everyone and everything, so it was easy to imagine the stories she'd concocted with her impressions of passersby. "And I suppose after nine steady hours of watching over patients, you haven't had enough to satisfy your curiosity for one day?"

"You'd think so." Sally sighed and opened her small jug of tea. "So much for a two-hour lunch delay. It's been three already, and I don't mind telling you, I'm starved."

Clare nodded. The past several hours had been grueling, and they'd gone without food beyond Matron's estimate. Three hours on the shift remained and they were all tired and hungry.

"Our lunches could have been postponed altogether if Clare hadn't organized our workload of patients so brilliantly today." Beatrice turned to Clare as she unwrapped her sandwich. "I'm sure you impressed Matron with your efforts."

"Our efforts," Clare corrected as she opened her own jug of tea. The soft, cool grass beneath her skirt was a welcome change from the overheated patient wards at the hospital. "I couldn't have accomplished nearly as much today without the two of you. Truly, I am thankful to you both."

"You're welcome." Sally grinned before taking a sip of her tea. "And I suspect there will be a promotion in this for you, Clare. Our new chief orderly, hmm?"

"I'm sure once Smith recovers, all will go back to the way it was before," Clare assured her. Still, she could hope. If her abilities had made an impression today, she might get that promotion and it would mean an increase in pay. Maybe she, Daisy, and Ruthie could then move into a better neighborhood.

Of course, if Marcus proposed tonight, it would change things for all of them . . .

"I've never been here before, either," Beatrice said. "What's that statue over there?"

"The fifth duke of Bedford," Sally said. "Bedford Square and

Russell Square were both named after him. His lands once extended over much of this area."

Clare followed their gazes. Staring at the back of the imposing statue, she glimpsed beneath the bronze figure a familiar profile, the man's tall height and broad shoulders unmistakable in his naval uniform. *Marcus?*

As Sally continued to explain the duke's history and holdings, Clare only half listened, her attention still focused on Marcus.

He checked his watch. Was he waiting for someone?

"I enjoy history, so I suppose it's another reason I like coming here to stroll the gardens and admire the Georgian and Renaissance architecture across the square. Do you like history, Clare?" A pause. "Clare? Are you listening, or are you too busy watching that handsome officer?"

Clare turned to Sally, only vaguely noting her amusement. "Er . . . yes, history," she said, and her cheeks warmed as Sally and Beatrice burst into laughter.

"Seems I'm not the only one who's curious today." Sally winked at Beatrice.

Clare darted a quick glance back at Marcus. Why was he here in the park?

"Well, I'm not really interested in history about dukes and kings or learning about old architecture," Beatrice was saying. "I'd much rather go to the cinema and see Charlie Chaplin. He always makes me laugh."

Clare smiled noncommittally while she watched Marcus reach into his pocket and remove a small box. He flipped the top open and stared at the contents before tucking it back in his pocket.

The ring! Her heart thumped against her chest. He was going to propose tonight!

She started to rise to go to him and then stopped. He'd said last night he must travel to Hampshire today on business. Did that mean he'd gone to speak with his family first about his impending betrothal to her? Clare's breath hitched. Had they returned to London with him? Perhaps he wanted to introduce them to her tonight . . .

"Ah, I see you're right on time, Captain."

Marcus glanced up at Natalya's approach and frowned. She seemed oblivious to the fact that she was late.

"Mrs. Bryce." He nodded briskly. "I trust you're completely recovered from last night?" Her display in Jack's drawing room could have resulted in an injury and delayed their assignment.

"I am fully recovered, thanks to you and that other gentleman," she said softly. "I admit that it was an oversight on my part, dancing so close to the door."

Oversight? How foolhardy did she intend to be during their time in Archangel? "I trust that once we leave London, you will restrain yourself from any more dancing?"

She chuckled. "Indeed." Her dark eyes narrowed as if reading his thoughts. "And I promise I shall not become a burden to you on this trip."

We'll see about that. "Why this place?" he asked. "I thought we'd agreed to meet at Whitehall."

"I had to arrange for a final fitting with my dressmaker here in Bedford Place, and thought to meet you directly afterward." She smiled. "I can hardly travel in mourning clothes when we are supposed to be an engaged couple."

She did a slight turn. "What do you think?"

Gone were the more subdued widow's weeds, and in their place was an impractical, flamboyant dress as red as the currants growing on his family's estate. A wide-brimmed hat also hid part of her face.

"I suggest you focus more on bringing warm, sensible clothing."

At her crestfallen look, he added more gently, "Not only are we in for a rough sea journey over the next few days, but the less attention we draw to ourselves, the better."

She brightened again and nodded, then glanced across the street. "Since we are here, I thought we might take tea over at the hotel?"

"Sorry, but I've still some business to finish up at the office." After that, he'd have just enough time to return to his flat and clean up a bit before heading over to see Clare and Daisy and say his good-byes.

Natalya seemed to pout, but Marcus wasn't impressed. Would she be an asset to him on this mission . . . or a liability? He didn't need the added disruption of this woman's eccentricities, especially when he had to stay focused. For both of their sakes.

He withdrew an envelope from inside his tunic and handed it to her. "Your train tickets and ship's boarding pass. In the event we fail to meet at the station. Once we're aboard the ship in Folkestone, I'll brief you on our Rotterdam connection to take us on to Archangel."

She reached for the envelope and tucked it inside her purse.

Mrs. Bryce?

Clare blinked, taking in the scene. No longer in mourning gray, the ballerina strode toward Marcus, looking fashionable in a dress of deep scarlet.

She stopped to speak with him, and Clare's mind flashed with the woman's words to Marcus last night. *"Until tomorrow."*

An ache pressed against her chest as she watched Marcus offer Mrs. Bryce an envelope. What was he giving her?

"I also want you to pack light. A small valise, nothing more." Again he eyed Natalya's frivolous costume, and leaning in, he lowered his voice. "If all goes according to plan, we'll meet with our man in Vologda. Once we've located Russia's mother and son, we can extract them and be back here in less than two weeks."

"It is my wish as well, Captain," she whispered, huddling closer. "I do pray they are indeed the tsarina and tsarevich. To know they are alive and have not been lost to the Bolsheviks' brutality . . ."

"My, my, what do we have going on over there by our good Duke of Bedford?" Sally said in a low voice. "Clare, it looks like your handsome man in uniform has found himself a lady."

Clare ignored her as she kept her eyes fixed on Marcus. The pain in her chest now rose to her throat as she watched that . . . that Russian tart! . . . lean into her love and practically cling to him in front of the statue. The woman was like a dark red spider, drawing him into her web. *Marcus, you must get away from her!*

"He's certainly a handsome bloke." Beatrice had joined them in observing the couple. "As tall as one of your courtly knights, Sally. And the lady with him seems very elegant. Do you think she's his wife?"

"Who can tell?" Sally murmured. "But let me see. Golden-blond hair, tall and slender and dressed like a queen. And, Beatrice, you said he's a knight. What if she's his paramour and they're having a secret tryst?"

Sally nudged Clare. "What do you think, Clare? Could he be Sir Lancelot with his Lady Guinevere?"

But Clare couldn't tear her eyes away from Marcus's tall, broad-shouldered frame, now bent slightly as he spoke to the beautiful ballerina beside him. Her upswept hair was perfectly coiffed beneath an expansive hat, and as she turned her head, Clare saw her pink mouth suddenly part in a broad smile.

"Just so," Marcus said as he straightened. "We'll take the seven o'clock from Victoria Station. I'll meet you at the ticket office. Any more questions before I leave?"

"Just one." Removing the glove on her left hand, she smiled

and fluttered her fingers at him. "I was told by our mutual friend that you would have something for me?"

The ring. He fished the velvet box from his pocket, then opened the lid and held the ring out for her inspection.

She leaned forward to study it. "It is rather a large diamond."

"It will certainly draw the attention of any who see you wearing it," Marcus agreed. "Perhaps that's the idea our mutual friend had in mind. Reinforcing our cover."

"Shall you put it on my finger?" She glanced toward the gardens. "In case we're being watched?"

Marcus resisted another urge to check his watch. He had paperwork on his desk to complete, and he wasn't going to miss seeing Clare before leaving town.

He curbed his impatience and scanned the area. At this end of the park, only a few people—a nanny with a small child and two elderly gentlemen deep in conversation—walked the garden paths.

Earlier, Marcus had heard female laughter emerging from the copse of trees just ahead and spotted at least two women seated in the tall grass, though he couldn't make them out.

In any case, they seemed harmless. "I don't believe we're being watched," he said, turning back to her. "Take the ring and make certain it fits."

He needed no last-minute delays before they left tonight.

She reached for the jewel and slid the diamond onto her finger. Holding her hand up toward the sky, the showy glass glinted in the sun. "It does not seem so garish now that I have it on." Her dark eyes sparkled as she stepped forward, raising her other hand to his cheek. "I accept—"

A sudden keening cry brought them both up short.

Marcus turned and narrowed his gaze toward the copse of trees. Was someone hurt?

"Did you hear that?" Natalya whispered.

He didn't answer her but instead strode in the direction of the sound and the women seated in the grass.

One of them, still crying, rose to stand in the tall grass. Her familiar form, the soft curves and hair the color of blackest night, made his gut clench. *Dear God, no . . .*

Even from this distance, the shine in her eyes—tears—made him want to roar at the sky. "Clare!"

Clare heard the howling cry and quickly looked around her. She saw Sally and Beatrice staring at her.

It was her own wailing.

Body shaking, she clambered to her feet, the sandwich and jug of tea falling from her lap into the grass. The keening sound in her throat wouldn't allow air inside, and she couldn't breathe. As it grew louder, she clamped a hand over her mouth.

"Clare!" Marcus paused, his face a mask of horror. Then he started moving toward her again. "Wait!"

But she'd seen enough. She couldn't stand to be here another moment longer.

Spinning on her heel, and without a backward glance at her co-workers, she stormed in the direction of the west gate leading out of the park.

She had to get away, somewhere she could think . . .

Pain flooded her chest. He'd given another woman the ring. *Her* ring, and then he'd smiled when that outrageous flirt reached for him! How could he do it? After their embrace last night, his gentle caresses? *My sweet Chiara . . .*

"Darling, wait!"

Mired in her own devastation, she didn't realize when his longer stride caught up with her. A hand touched her shoulder. "Clare, please listen."

Her fury kicked in then, nearly blinding her as she stopped and whirled to face him, quickly stepping outside of his grasp. "What could you possibly say to me?" she rasped, her heart ripping apart. "I watched you propose to her! Grace told me you bought the ring and I-I thought it was supposed to be for me." Despite her anger, her voice broke. "Why would you ever hurt me like this, Marcus?"

He looked stricken for a moment, his eyes desperately searching hers. "Clare, it's not what you imagine—"

"I *imagined* nothing!" she snapped, her pain tying her into knots. "I saw what I saw, and after last night's dinner, that woman said she'd see you today. Do you think me a complete idiot?"

He frowned, looking as if he were trying to recall the ballerina's words. Then he breathed an oath. "Her remark meant nothing, sweetheart, and I want to explain, but I cannot . . ." He wet his lips. "You must trust me. Remember, we've talked about trusting—"

"Trust?" Clare cut him off as she pointed to the ballerina in red still standing at the bronze statue. "Does that mean I should blindly pretend *she* doesn't exist? Or pretend she wasn't trying to . . . to *charm you* last night while I sat like a wallflower watching it all?"

Heat flooded her face. "If that's your idea of trust, then I never will. I learned my lesson once before, Marcus Weatherford, and I won't suffer being made another laughingstock."

His only response was to pull off his cap and rake a hand through his hair. "Please . . . I'll come over tonight and we'll talk."

"A moment ago, you said you couldn't explain." She raised her trembling chin. "And after you gave her the ring, she . . . caressed your face." Again her disappointment spiraled into a wave of despair, sparking her anger, and she reeled away from him when he tried reaching for her once more.

His heart wrenched as she avoided his touch a second time. Marcus couldn't reveal to her his secret assignment. Nor would he explain that the woman she feared had stolen his heart was leaving with him for Europe tonight.

Blast! For a wild moment he considered refusing the assignment. Surely his boss could find someone else to accompany Natalya . . .

Duty first, man. Tormented, he drew a deep breath. "Clare, there are things I cannot share with you, only—"

"There's so much we haven't been able to share in a long time, Marcus." She looked him in the eyes, hers still red from tears. "And you shouldn't come to the flat tonight." She averted her gaze. "Daisy . . . hasn't been well."

Swallowing hard, he nodded and took a step back, his chest aching.

She seemed to waver for a moment, and he held his breath. But then her chin thrust forward, her stormy eyes dark and as murky as the deepest sea. "I have to leave now. Good-bye, Marcus." She whirled from him, making her exit toward the street.

Marcus stood there, his fists clenching and unclenching as he watched his heart go with her. His only hope was that he could make it up to her when he returned.

If he returned.

6

ARCHANGEL, RUSSIA
SUNDAY, AUGUST 11, 1918—FOUR DAYS LATER

*Y*ou're a blighter and you don't deserve her.

Marcus stood at the ship's rail and gazed out to sea. The cold, blustery winds of Russia's summer blasted his face yet failed to assuage his burning throat. In the four days since leaving London, Clare's reaction in the park before they'd parted still preyed on his heart, her look of pain like a jagged scar marring her beautiful face.

That face still haunted him. *"Grace told me you bought the ring . . ."* He gritted his teeth at the memory of her words. *Blunderer!* No doubt Grace had seen him at Barker's, getting the phony ring for his ruse with Natalya.

It was another reminder of his chosen path years ago, a series of secrets he could never reveal. Including this mission, involving the highest of stakes—the king's own family and an assassination plot that would hopefully pull Russia back into the war and put a Romanov tsar on the throne.

Despite Clare's wish that he stay away, Marcus had stopped by her flat that night after her shift, where he'd waited until a man from the Royal Army Medical Corps delivered a note to Ruthie, telling her Clare would be delayed a couple of hours.

He'd even stopped his cab en route to the train station to wait outside Jack's town house while he went inside, only to learn Clare had been there with Grace and then left.

Afterward he'd had no choice but to leave for Folkestone and the ship.

He could patch things with her on his return, couldn't he?

"Good-bye, Marcus . . ."

Drawing in a shuddering breath, he filled his lungs with another cold gust of air. She'd said they hadn't been able to share much in a long time. Criminy, is that how she really felt? Marcus still had things he wanted to tell her, but . . . what if he didn't make it back?

He'd never get the chance to make her understand just how much he loved her—

"We will . . . wait to begin our search tomorrow, Captain, *da?*"

Marcus turned toward the gravelly female voice beside him. Natalya had finally come up from belowdecks and leaned against the rail. Clad in sensible wool traveling clothes, her bruised eyes stared at him dully from beneath the brim of a snug-fitting wool cap.

She turned her attention to the water but quickly closed her eyes as the cruiser skimmed along the surface of the Northern Dvina River, preparing to dock at the port of Archangel.

"You're still unwell?"

"*Nyet,* I am better." She gripped the steel rail and positioned her feet against the swaying deck. "Just a bit . . . queasy. It will pass."

At least she hadn't been able to cause more trouble. Marcus allowed himself the briefest satisfaction. It was her flirtatious antics that had caused the row between him and Clare.

Yet as he eyed her deathly pallor, his pity again won out. She'd been paralyzed with seasickness the entire four-day trip from Rotterdam, and her meals—at least what she was able to keep down—had been left daily outside the door to her quarters where she'd taken refuge.

"Natalya, I can go on ahead while you remain in Archangel."

"I assure you . . . the train will not affect me in this way."

"Maybe not, but you're still taking a personal risk, especially in this condition."

Her glassy eyes stared up at him from beneath dark lashes. "I am British now, thanks to my dearest Walter, rest his soul. But Mother Russia is still my home. If I can help her by being here, then I am ready to take that risk."

He nodded. For all her mischief, he should be grateful she was here. How else could they prove that the king's relations were genuine and not impostors?

Marcus still had his doubts, however. The city of Archangel was now controlled by the Allies, but there were enemy Bolsheviks and Red Army soldiers infiltrating the south where he and Natalya were headed.

They would be lucky to get out of this alive.

Clare's image rose in his mind, along with his regret at what he should have said.

"I know one thing, Captain. I will . . . be more than grateful to leave this ship."

He leaned toward her. "While we are here, Natalya, you must remember to call me Marcus."

A slight flush tinged her sallow cheeks. "Of course . . . Marcus."

He turned back to the waterfront and the wooden promenade stretching for miles along the riverbank. Above the boardwalk, glimpses of the city could be seen as a continuous line of structures—ornate, multistoried wooden buildings beside orange brick edifices and a scattering of churches with colorful lintels and cupolas.

A tall white cathedral garbed with dark bell-shaped towers and golden onion domes stood to the north. Beyond that, the mild green slopes of tundra and forests undulated in the distance.

Marcus had worn plainclothes for the mission, and like Natalya, he carried only a small valise. Anything else would be supplied by British HQ in Archangel, including an escort from Russia's White Army, still loyal to the tsar and his empire.

Their meeting with Sidney Reilly was to take place tomorrow evening in Vologda, a city three hundred miles to the south. Once they learned the whereabouts of the two Romanovs, he and Natalya could begin their journey.

The cruiser finally docked alongside the quay, and it was minutes before they were met by the naval ensign in charge of driving them to British headquarters.

Marcus glanced at Natalya, who held a handkerchief to her lips. "Ensign, any idea where we're to be billeted?"

"Aye, sir. The Metropole Dvina Hotel is just a few blocks from HQ."

"Please take us there first. My fiancée needs to rest."

"Of course, sir."

Arriving at the hotel, Marcus escorted her inside while the ensign took their bags and checked them into their respective rooms.

Once he'd delivered her to her door, Natalya eyed him woefully. "I am not a very good spy, am I, Marcus? More like a wilting flower."

At his smile, she blinked at him. "You will not leave me here, will you?"

"We'll see, Natalya. Now get some rest. I'll be back in time for dinner." When her pallid features took on a grayish hue, he stifled a smirk. "You'll be all right?"

Her answer was to open the door and slip inside her room. Before she closed it, she whispered, "I will get better at this, I promise."

Marcus could only hope. Again he questioned whether to take her with him beyond Archangel. Without proper skills and in her current state, she was a liability he couldn't afford.

Returning to the car, he slid into the back seat and ordered the ensign to proceed. Soon they were heading toward British headquarters. Marcus stared absently at the passing shops, churches, and houses while considering the more critical part of his mission here: learning from Reilly the exact day and place a group of Allied agents planned to assassinate Lenin, and why C's "wildcard" agent had insisted on an in-person meeting.

Amber skies heralded the onset of dusk by the time Marcus had delivered his London dispatches and finished meeting with the commander in charge, British General Fredrick Poole.

He brooded silently in the car's back seat while the ensign returned him to the hotel.

The general spent most of their time together lecturing him on the danger he and "his fiancée" would encounter once they traveled beyond the city into a country bristling with violence. Afterward, he'd supplied Marcus with the appropriate Russian clothing and a pair of special "Bolshevik" passports the general hoped would be enough to keep them safe. The following morning, they were to arrive at the train station just after dawn to meet up with their security escort: three pro-tsarist White Army soldiers disguised as laborers.

Vologda was still purported to be reasonably safe, as several Allied ambassadors were currently holed up there. Yet it was the distance between here and there that Marcus worried about. Any Bolshevik or Red Army official who decided to stop the train and check passports might start asking questions. And if they didn't like their answers . . .

He and Natalya might end up being interrogated by the Cheka police and thrown into a Russian prison—or shot.

Back at the hotel, he knocked on her door. C had given him discretionary power where Natalya's safety was concerned. And Russian or not, the woman seemed oblivious to the danger they were about to face. Perhaps she could offer him some intimate detail about the empress and tsarevich known only to them? Marcus could then discern the truth on his own while Natalya remained here where it was safe.

When she didn't respond to his summons, he called out to her several times. Only silence met his ears, and his pulse began racing. Was she that seriously ill?

He deftly picked the cheap lock and, upon entering her room, found Natalya lying on the bed coverlet, fully dressed and still wearing her boots. As he inched closer, his shoulders eased at the sound of her steady breathing. She was sleeping.

He left the clothes on her dresser but held on to her new passport. It was too dangerous for her to accompany him to Vologda. He would question her about the Romanovs in the morning before going on alone to meet with Reilly.

Marcus quietly let himself out and retreated downstairs to order up a scant meal of salted herring, pickled cabbage, and rye toast before returning to his room. Once there, he sat on his bed, exhausted. Four days of rough seas had left him weary, and if the general was correct, tomorrow's train ride south promised him added tension as well.

Releasing a sigh, he readied himself for bed while waiting for the food. He turned back the coverlet and spied a scrawled note.

Meet me. Dormition Church. 2200 hours. Belfry.

—S. R.

Hair rose along his nape. Sidney Reilly.

He checked his watch. Forty-five minutes from now. Quickly he re-dressed and left his room, learning from the concierge downstairs that Dormition Church was the tall white structure with the dark bell-shaped towers and golden onion domes he'd seen along the promenade when they sailed into port. Because of the late hour, he requested the hotel's *droshky*, and minutes later the cab was taking him back toward the waterfront.

Darkness had descended as he arrived at the church. Marcus sent the driver away and went inside. He had twenty minutes yet before meeting Reilly.

Standing in the narthex of the church, he peered into the dimly lit nave, where a few elderly kerchiefed women bowed in prayer at the front. He surveyed the lavish classicist architecture of the church, admiring its ornately carved wood and gold candelabras. A gilded chandelier with icons hung at its center, now dark with unlit candles, while painted murals in the iconic Byzantium style covered walls, archways, and the domed ceiling high above.

Dozens of framed holy icons hung near the front of the church, and one he recognized as the Miracle Worker, the Assumption of the Mother Mary.

It wasn't often over the past several years he'd been inside a place of worship—only when he was in town and it meant a chance to be with Clare.

And before that?

Marcus shifted on his feet. In his mind he no longer stood with Clare singing hymns in church. Instead, he sat beside his tall father, breathing in Hampshire's crisp winter morning air. Father always drove them in the family's shiny black carriage to the Anglican church in nearby Mattingley for Sunday services.

Behind them in the carriage sat his mother and baby sister, Fannie, both bundled up against the chill. After services they'd return home to sit down to a Sunday feast, while Father questioned Marcus on what he'd learned from the good reverend's sermon.

It was only when his father failed to return from the war and Fannie got sick that Marcus lost his taste for attending services, and somewhere between naval college and the Admiralty he abandoned the practice altogether. He still believed in God, but church was for others, not him. Besides, with his duty to Britain and the war, he had no time for anything else.

Including love . . .

His mind's eye returned to Clare and the way she'd looked at him with such devastation in her expression. *"I watched you propose to her . . . and I thought it was supposed to be me."* A new wave of self-loathing filled him, and again he thought of his grandmother's ring. He'd justified his reasons for tucking it away, convincing himself it was for the best that he wait until there was no more danger because of his work. But was that the real reason?

Maybe you just lack courage. He coughed to cover his bitter laugh. He'd chased the enemy for years now. He'd been shot at, nearly blown up, his life threatened too many times to count. But he knew the truth—he *was* afraid, afraid to trust, especially where Clare was concerned.

You're a piece of work, man. How many times had they spoken of trust, in particular about *her* trusting *him*? Yet it was he and the future he couldn't believe in that required real faith. Clare's faith was strong enough, and he admired her for it, especially after all she'd suffered. But his own?

Regret pierced him. There was so much he hadn't been able to share with her, making his silence a lie all by itself. And each mission merely added another black mark on his soul, including this blasted assignment. Criminy, he'd given a ring to a near stranger, while *she'd* been forced to watch!

He swallowed past the knot in his throat. *And she told you good-bye—*

The sudden clanging of church bells overhead broke through his musings. His meeting with Reilly.

Duty calls, man. Get your head on straight. Quickly he strode toward the winding stairs leading up to the belfry.

Natalya roused fully awake, her queasiness finally gone. Never had she been so ill in her life. Even the ship from Petrograd to London last year had not encountered such tumultuous seas as those she and Marcus just experienced.

With a yawn she rubbed her eyes and then switched on the nightstand lamp. Hunger had awakened in her, and rising she realized she had slept in her boots. Humiliating! A change of clothes and freshening up must come before satisfying her traitorous stomach.

Her valise sat on the floor near the dresser. She vaguely remembered dropping it there just before she passed out. As she retrieved the bag, she spied atop the dresser a stack of folded garments and ran her fingers over the rough homespun fabric. Peasant clothing. Had Marcus been in her room?

Natalya's skin warmed. She disliked being vulnerable, and it seemed Marcus had already determined she was too weak to travel beyond Archangel. She must purchase some *imbir* to make tea before their return journey home. Ginger soothed the stomach and would minimize any seasickness.

Finished with her ablutions, she changed into her only clean dress and slipped on fresh stockings. Then she opened her door and peeked into the narrow hall. At the next door, no doubt Marcus's room, a covered tray of food rested on the floor.

After darting another glance down the hall, she approached the tray and removed the lid to find his meal untouched. Natalya considered taking it into her room, yet he would need all his strength for the assignment. She knocked lightly on the door. No answer. She rapped once more, louder. Still no response. Her pulse sped as she tried the doorknob. Locked.

Had he simply gone out somewhere . . . or had he decided to leave her behind?

Raising the dish cover, she snatched a piece of the rye toast before going downstairs.

"Comrade, have you seen my fiancé?" she asked the swarthy concierge in Russian, and when he told her of the church and that Marcus had hired the hotel's droshky, she found the man outside. "Take me to Dormition Church as well," she instructed.

Was Marcus at the church praying for their safety in the coming assignment tomorrow? She knew the captain only from their occasional meetings at Whitehall and what little Walter had mentioned before his death. That, and Sir Mansfield Smith-Cumming's remarks when she had agreed to help with this assignment.

Captain Weatherford was certainly no cowardly man, nor did he seem to be one who would spend time praying before the icons in church. Yet he seemed troubled over that crying woman in the park. Was that the reason he'd come here?

Inside the shadowy confines of the church, candlelight revealed only a few babushkas holding candles and bowing in prayer. No sign of Marcus.

Natalya scanned the vast space—within the murky alcoves it was impossible to see clearly—then heard low voices above, and her gaze flew to the bell tower.

She strained to listen. Definitely male voices.

Against the far wall, a set of winding stairs led upward. Natalya approached and very quietly began her ascent, her smile broadening. She had told Marcus earlier that she made a very poor spy.

It was time to prove herself.

7

So you believe the tsarina and her son are in Perm?"

Marcus eyed the silhouette of the man beside him. Both sat hidden against the wall space between the bell tower's many arched open-air windows. He'd met Reilly only once before but recognized him from his dark looks and piercing eyes.

"I have an address with specific instructions." Reilly handed him a scrap of paper.

A single candle was their only light. Marcus scanned the series of numbers and letters: 2E, 5R, 7L, 3R. He glanced up. "What is this supposed to mean?"

"My own code." Reilly's eyes narrowed in the faint light. "Two E is the second major city beyond Vologda heading east by train. You'll arrive first at Vyatka and then at Perm. Once at Perm, you'll travel straight ahead on the main street. Five R is the fifth street and turn right. Seven L is the seventh *kommunalka* on the left."

"How many families live in the communal flat?"

"Too many, thanks to the Bolsheviks."

Reilly indicated the scrap of paper. "Three R is for the third door on the right inside the kommunalka. Once you knock, ask for your *matushka*. An old woman in black will greet you, and you must ask her for a *chotki*." He paused. "The knotted prayer rope used by Russian Orthodox Christians is similar to Roman Catholic rosary beads. You'll then be allowed inside so you can get acquainted with mother and son."

The Romanovs. Marcus studied the bells above his head, every nerve attuned. He wasn't certain if the cloak-and-dagger instructions were Reilly's remedy for boredom or if Russia had so many spies it became necessary to write notes using a Playfair cipher. "Do we still leave in the morning? General Poole has assigned us a three-man White Army escort."

"Yes, in Vologda, take the next train east. The railway is slow because of our rebel Czech friends, but you'll get there eventually."

Marcus exhaled. Any hope for a quick return to Britain seemed futile at this point. Not only must he travel three hundred miles to the south, but it was an additional six hundred to reach Perm. It could take a week, and that was if he didn't run into trouble with the Bolsheviks.

He turned to Reilly. "What about the other reason you sent for me?"

Natalya's pulse raced as she listened from her huddled place on the steps just below the top landing into the belfry. From her perch, she could see a large wooden wheel mounted horizontally against the belfry's rounded ceiling. Several large brass bells were attached, one for each of the arched windows.

Candlelight flickered against their metal surfaces, and Natalya raised her head slightly to peer into the semidarkness. The top of Marcus's head was barely visible, or that of the shorter man seated near him. Yet as the latter held up the candle, she glimpsed his dark complexion and knew she'd met him before. In Moscow when she was there with Walter. *Sidney Reilly, the famous ghost.*

She leaned an ear to them as their voices quieted and managed to grasp words like "Vologda," "Vyatka," and "Perm." Half amused, her eyes widened at Reilly's instruction to meet a *babushka* in black and ask for a chotki. Such dramatic intrigue . . . and as exciting as her past role in *Raymonda* at the Bolshoi!

It seemed Reilly had given them the location of the poor tsarina and her son, and she and Marcus would need to travel to Vologda after all. Relief mingled with her excitement. Their assignment was about to begin, and Natalya intended to contribute her share to the cause.

"What about the other reason you sent for me?"

Marcus's voice. Natalya craned her neck another inch to hear Reilly's soft words.

"Yes, about Lenin," he replied. "But first, I've discovered disturbing news that involves—"

The sudden clanging of bells obliterated the rest of Reilly's sentence. One bell rang just above her head, back and forth with a clamor so loud Natalya gritted her teeth and pressed her hands against her ears.

It was several seconds before the noise stopped, though her ears continued ringing. Another moment passed and she felt the thud of heavy boots against the wooden landing near her head. Someone was approaching the steps!

She could not be caught or Marcus would become angry and decide to leave her here!

Ever light on her feet, she flew down the winding steps and fled the church. Relief outweighed her frustration at seeing the droshky driver had waited for her.

"Take me back to the hotel," she said, and as he obeyed, Natalya gazed out at the lamplit streets, her curiosity on fire. What about Lenin? And what kind of disturbing news had Reilly discovered?

Would Marcus tell her?

Hailing a droshky half an hour later, Marcus headed back toward the hotel, his mood grim.

He'd left Reilly at the church after obtaining the details of the planned Lenin assassination, though now his thoughts circled around the agent's more troubling news and his reason for the in-person rendezvous.

A suspected double agent was working in the British Consul in Moscow, and worse, the agent had an accomplice—a planted mole in London's War Office!

Reilly claimed to have found sufficient proof that both existed, though he hadn't yet confirmed either of their identities. With Russia currently in chaos, the wily agent remained constantly on the run from the Bolsheviks' Cheka police.

Marcus's first impulse was to send a wire to his boss from General Poole's office at British HQ, but then he dismissed the idea. What if his report played into the hands of this London mole?

He withdrew from his pocket the scrap of paper with its numbers and letters, directions he would take to reach the tsarina and her son. Marcus also withdrew the other item he'd received in the meeting, a playing card—the queen of spades.

He fingered the card Reilly had given him, along with the news about the traitors. When Marcus had asked what the queen of spades meant, the agent said only that C would understand.

He ground his teeth. Blast the man for his cloak-and-dagger schemes!

Marcus rubbed the back of his neck, his muscles tense. He'd leave for Vologda in the morning, then travel immediately on to Perm. It could take him a week or more to complete the assignment, but the sooner he returned to London to hand over the card and report the turncoats, the better.

He only hoped that he'd survive to do so.

Dawn rose early in Archangel the following morning as Natalya awoke to a soft knock on her hotel room door. "Marcus?" she called out sleepily.

"Your breakfast is here. I'll be downstairs."

Immediately she washed and dressed in the Russian clothes he had left for her and then opened the door to find a tray and covered dish on the floor. Grateful, she quickly consumed the gruel and toast, and with her valise in hand, she exited her room.

Downstairs, Marcus looked very Russian in his simple home-spun clothing as he waited for her in the reception area. As she approached, Natalya's curiosity kindled anew over the previous evening's rendezvous at the church. Her attempts to eavesdrop had been rudely interrupted by those noisy bells! She tilted her head to eye him appraisingly. Would he share with her last night's conversation with Reilly, the famous ghost?

"Natalya, I've decided that it's best if you stay here."

Natalya halted at his words, noting the way he rubbed the back of his neck, his brow creased.

"What do you mean, Marcus? I need to go with you. I am the only one who can . . ." She cast a quick glance at the hotel concierge, who seemed highly curious about their conversation.

"You must know something," he cut in softly, as he, too, had noticed the swarthy man behind the desk. "Anything specific that I can use to identify them."

"*Nyet*, nothing." Even if she did, she would never tell him. He was not leaving her behind. "Why are you doing this?"

She clutched the valise, cutting off the circulation into her hand. They had a plan, and she must see it through for Mother Russia!

He dropped his arm to his side and stepped closer, blocking her view of the concierge. "There's fighting everywhere along the way, Natalya. I cannot let anything happen to you."

"Oh, you chivalrous man." She eased her grip on the valise handle. "I am Russian, remember? If anyone is in danger, it is you." She searched his eyes. "Please, let me come with you. Let me help my country."

Natalya sensed victory when he pushed out a sigh. "You'll do as I say at all times, without questioning my judgment?"

"Da." She glanced at her homespun blouse and skirt. "And I am dressed for the part."

He handed her a Russian passport. "Take what you need from your bag. The hotel has agreed to hold our belongings until we return. If something happens, we don't want to have to explain our Western-style clothing."

"Excellent point." She turned her back to him and opened her valise, digging through her underthings to find her pistol. Once she'd tucked the small Colt into her skirt pocket, she fished for the purseful of rubles before closing the case.

As she spun back around, Natalya noticed he was staring at her skirt. Obviously he could make out the gun. "Walter bought it for me," she said briskly. "Living in Moscow was—"

"A bit dangerous?"

She nodded. "He made me promise to carry it with me at all times."

Marcus raised a brow. "Do you know how to use it?"

She lifted her brow right back. "Would you like a demonstration?"

"I'll take your word for it." His gaze shifted to her hand. "Leave the ring behind, too. Peasants don't wear diamonds. You can put it on once we get back."

Natalya frowned as she reopened the valise. Pretending to put the ring inside, she instead grabbed a plain white handkerchief, stuffing both into her pocket. She would trust no Russian with her jewels.

"All right, I am ready," she said, smiling.

Marcus frowned as he watched Natalya stroll toward the desk and hand over her valise to the concierge. He still worried about the risks to her coming with him. But what other choice did he have to accomplish this mission?

"I trust that you have fulfilled my request, Comrade?" She was speaking to the man in Russian.

"Da, just as you instructed, miss."

She reached for his hand. "*Blagadaryu vas.*"

"*Pozhaluysta!*" He grinned and bowed. "You are most welcome."

"What was that all about?" Marcus asked once they were outside and climbing into the cab. "What request?"

Natalya settled in the seat and gave him an appraising look. "If you have never before traveled on a Russian train, Marcus, then you might not appreciate my surprise."

She looked pleased with herself. "I had the concierge arrange for us to enjoy cushioned seats rather than hardwood benches, especially since we will be traveling for some time."

Marcus worked his jaw. Once again, her naïveté in light of their circumstances caused him to have second thoughts.

"How do you suppose it will look, Natalya, if you and I and our escort, all dressed as peasants, take seats together in first class? Don't you think we'll draw some attention?"

She blinked at him, her satisfied expression evaporating. "You are right, of course." Leaning close so the driver wouldn't overhear, she whispered, "And not very spy-worthy either." Dropping back against the seat, she heaved a sigh. Then a determined glint resurfaced in her eyes. "I promise I shall do better next time."

He nodded slowly. "Just take care to keep that gift from Sir Walter out of sight. We don't need any trouble." He gave her a hard look. "*Ponimat?*"

She bowed her head. "Da, I understand."

At least she seemed contrite. He gentled his tone. "I appreciate your intentions, Natalya, even if we cannot take advantage of a soft ride this time."

Her smile easily returned. "Perhaps one day we will get that chance."

Marcus made no comment but instead turned to the window just as the driver pulled into Archangel's Isakogorka Station, not far from General Poole's offices.

Once they alighted from the cab, Marcus spied the naval ensign who had delivered them to the hotel yesterday. He was accompanied by three solidly built men dressed as peasant tradesmen, obviously the White Army escort they'd been promised. "Ensign."

"Sir. Ma'am. Your train leaves in ten minutes if you'd like to board. Your escort will remain close by."

"I feel safer already." Natalya smiled at the men before they all boarded the coach, taking their places along either side of the hardwood bench seats Natalya had warned about. Marcus didn't bother to tell her he'd experienced worse last year, traveling for hours on a cattle train during an assignment in Mesopotamia.

They took seats near the open window, and he was grateful for the fresh air. The sultry compartment already reeked with the humanity of dozens of passengers: tradesmen, laborers, women, and children all squeezed in alongside one another on the bench seats.

Leaving Isakogorka Station behind, the train crossed to the western shore of the Northern Dvina River before heading south. Along the way, they passed myriad outlying villages and station stops, where workers embarked or disembarked to their respective jobs.

As the train chugged toward the city of Vologda, Marcus noted the vast changes in countryside as scattered farmsteads and stretches of flat green meadow gave way to forested areas, and he sensed when the train began ascending into the hills. After two hours, the marshy edges of Ozero Lakhta came into view, and farther south the green turned more reddish-brown as miles of tundra changed color in the summer sun.

"She is beautiful, my Russia, is she not?" Natalya asked. She leaned past him to look beyond the window to the red-gold grasses and distant trees. "I grew up in Rostov, a small town between Vologda and Moscow. My heart has never left this country."

"Do you miss it?"

"Sometimes." She leaned back against her seat. "I miss dancing. And I miss Walter."

Marcus eyed her somberly. "My sincerest condolences, Natalya."

"My husband and I were not married long, but we enjoyed

our time together. I have learned one cannot wait for the perfect moment to fulfill a dream. One must act despite all and embrace what the heart holds dear."

One must act. Marcus grunted and turned back to the window, his thoughts again on Clare. Natalya's words had resurrected his uncertainty and also his regret—that he hadn't offered a future to the woman he truly loved. Was it too late for them? *Please, God, let me make it back home.*

"Are we to meet our contact once we arrive at Vologda Station?"

Natalya's question drew him back to the present. He shook his head. "We met last night."

"Oh! And you didn't think to wake me?"

He smiled wryly. "I did try, Natalya, though I doubt cannon fire would have roused you in your state. After days of suffering seasickness, you needed your rest." In a low voice he added, "I have the location of our mother and son. We'll change trains once we arrive and head east."

"East?"

"I'm afraid we are in for a long ride to Perm."

"But . . . that is almost six hundred miles from Vologda!" she hissed.

He winced. "Yes, and I'm certain we'll need those cushioned seats before this is over."

"Did he . . . say anything else to you?"

Marcus glanced at her. The balance of what he'd been told was none of her concern. "Nothing that affects our assignment together."

She turned away from him, looking again at the passing scenery outside the window. "I do hope we can shop and refresh ourselves in Vologda before departing once more." Her shoulders hunched. "I cannot bear to stay in these same scratchy clothes for days on end."

"We'll get food and a change of clothes, perhaps find a couple of rooms to stay the night, but not much else. We've already entered Bolshevik territory, and they will be randomly checking passports along the way."

"I think with your dark features and your command of Russian, you will have no problem with the Red Army soldiers."

He stared at her, incredulous. They were in the middle of a civil war that was spreading throughout the country like wildfire. He hadn't mentioned it earlier, but he'd seen the unmistakable smoke from artillery fire in the distance. They were in a battle zone, and everyone would be suspect, including Natalya.

"I know the Bolshevik mentality, Marcus," she said in English, reading his thoughts. She glanced at their escort seated across from them. "After all, I am Russian."

"I hope you're right." His smile was grim. "Still, we travel light."

He'd no more spoken the words than the train began to slow. Marcus craned his neck out the window but could see no station ahead. His body tensed. Why were they stopping?

"Natalya." He turned to her. "Do you have your passport ready? I think we're about to be boarded by Bolsheviks."

"Oh no! I . . . I must go to the washroom," she whispered quickly. "I will be right back."

"No!" He grabbed for her as she rose from the bench. "You need to stay in your seat."

Her pale skin flushed rosy. "Please, Marcus, I . . . I cannot wait."

"I'll come with you, then."

"Nyet! I shall return before they reach our coach, I promise. Do not worry."

She left the bench and hurried through the door of their coach into the next while the knot in his stomach twisted tighter. One minute passed, then another, and Marcus turned to their escorts, who were staring out the windows. "See anything?" he asked in Russian.

"Nyet." The escort closest to the window shook his head. "It could be just an animal or a cart on the track. I'll go check." He left, and seconds passed before another escort stood and followed him.

The last escort remained seated across from Marcus. "I will stay here," he said in a gruff voice. "Our orders are to protect you both."

Marcus's mouth tightened. What was taking Natalya so long?

He removed his felt cap, brushing his fingers over the playing card he'd tucked up inside the cap's lining. Reilly's coded directions to Perm threatened to sear a hole through his coat pocket.

Another minute passed before he replaced the cap on his head and rose from the bench. "I must find my fiancée."

As he started to leave, the escort was fast on his heels.

Into the next compartment they went. The train remained at a stop. Marcus continued through until he saw the signs for the washrooms. Nearing the place where Natalya should have been, a pair of ironclad fists gripped him from behind.

"If you try anything, Captain, she will die." The escort's deep voice spoke from behind him. "Keep moving."

Beyond the washrooms, Natalya was being held in much the same rough manner by the other two escorts. "What the blazes is going on here?" he snarled as he was shoved against her.

Natalya's dark eyes were huge. "I . . . I think we have been betrayed, Marcus." Her lower lip trembled. "These men, they are not here to protect us."

The two Russian thugs began dragging her from the train. Marcus found himself being shoved along behind them, and he had to grasp the side rail to keep from falling on his face against the rocky ground.

"Move!" the obvious leader barked, glancing back at Marcus. Down the slope he and Natalya stumbled until they'd reached the edge of the forest. Marcus breathed in the smell of gunpowder, the air thick with smoke. Where were the Allied troops?

"Do not get any ideas, Captain." The man holding him read his thoughts. "There is no help for miles. Your soldiers have not yet come this far."

Into the trees they went, stopping minutes later in a clearing surrounded by thick evergreens.

"What do you want from us?" Marcus demanded as he was checked for weapons. They took his Webley revolver. "We have nothing to give you. And we are not here to fight you."

"Ha!" the leader laughed as he examined Marcus's gun. He

opened the cylinder and turned it. "Fully loaded, I see." He glared at him. "But you are not here to fight us?" Snapping the cylinder closed, he aimed the pistol at Marcus's head. "You lie."

"What are you doing?" Natalya screamed, struggling against the hands gripping her. "Do not shoot him!"

The leader eyed her, a smile forming through his long, scruffy beard. "Shall I shoot you, then?" He aimed the gun at her.

"No, wait!" Marcus struggled against his captor's hold, his thoughts racing. If he could just stall them. "We have valuable information. If you shoot her or me, we cannot share it with you."

The leader's dark eyes narrowed on him. "What kind of information?"

"Critical to your cause."

"Marcus, please, do not tell him anything!"

Marcus locked eyes with Natalya. "I will not let them shoot you."

She was visibly shaking. "A-all right."

He turned to the man holding his gun. "I received the information—it's written in code—on a slip of paper back at the train. The time and place for a very important event. Take us there and I will get it for you."

"I think you tell more lies." Cocking back the hammer, the Russian with the gun on Natalya stepped closer to her. "If so, she dies—"

"No!" Marcus roared. Breaking free of the hands on him, he threw himself in front of Natalya to shield her.

"Imperialist!"

Vaguely, Marcus heard the shot before fire ripped through his skull. The world slowed as he dimly observed the leader holding the gun on him now, Natalya's screams rending the air. A sudden heaviness overtook him, each muscle in his body giving way beneath the cold weight of darkness. Like falling snow, settling over him amid flashes of memory—the last winter in Hampshire, his sister, Fannie, his mother and father—and then a stab of excruciating pain with his last thought . . .

Clare.

8

London
Monday, August 19, 1918—One Week Later

You should join us for dinner, Clare."

Sally shrugged into her coat while Beatrice signed out of the hospital after the long shift.

"Yes, you should!" Beatrice turned, beaming at Clare. "I'm making a Saturday pie, even though it's Monday. I had leftovers and I've been saving up my flour rations. The three of us will have tea and for dessert the honey scones I made last night, and we will celebrate your new promotion."

Clare smiled as she secured the hatpin back into her bonnet. Neither woman was very good at masking her concern. And while both meant well, their ongoing sympathy after her disaster with Marcus two weeks ago made her uncomfortable.

Even more humiliating, she'd had to explain to them that "Sir Lancelot" was the man she'd been courting and "Lady Guinevere" her rival.

So much for keeping her private life private, especially with Sally Forbes. "Thank you, Beatrice. That's a sweet offer, but maybe another time? Today was a challenge from start to finish, and right now I just want to go home and sleep."

Her two co-workers shared a glance. "You've been working what amounts to a double shift ever since Smith became ill," Sally said, pinning on her own hat. "Now that she's living with her family in Bristol, you've even more responsibility on your shoulders. You need a bit of fun, Clare, or else you'll work yourself into the ground."

"Sally's right," Beatrice piped up, and the vehemence in her voice surprised Clare. "You deserve so much better than that . . . that—"

"Please, I'm all right. And I do appreciate your support." Clare raised a smile at Beatrice while she shrugged into her jacket. "How about bringing me a piece of that Saturday pie tomorrow?"

Beatrice nodded. "I'll bring the scones, too, and we'll have our own little tea party during the morning break."

Clare waved before she exited the hospital and headed toward the waiting bus for home. Boarding the conveyance, her gaze instinctively sought out the Bloomsbury district to the north and the treetops in Russell Square.

The ache she'd been carrying for the past fortnight continued to throb with each heartbeat, and for the hundredth time she tormented herself with the memory of what she'd witnessed there. *"Clare, it's not what you imagine . . ."*

His words continued to haunt her. Had he been telling the truth? How could she know for sure?

After a year, she still knew so little about Marcus. When they were together, he was silent about his work, and when she'd asked him, he offered her the humdrum, like too much paperwork or being travel-weary. And about the war he said only that he hoped the fighting would end soon.

Rarely did Marcus share any of his particulars, though they did enjoy their games of chess or an evening of reading, and he liked whatever foods she happened to serve for dinner on those occasions he visited. If they did chance on an outing together, he was amenable to whatever she wanted, not what he enjoyed. He'd always been wonderful with Daisy, but her daughter was a two-year-old and easy to please. Clare, on the other hand, needed more from him. But he hadn't been willing to give it. At least not to her.

She blinked back tears as the bus turned onto the dingy neighborhood streets she recognized as her own, and where later tonight she would bury her head in her pillow and sob out her frustration and heartache.

Had he returned to London? She'd been to visit Grace a few times since his departure, and while her friend insisted on prying information out of her husband, Jack's only response had been to say Marcus was still away.

Clare had asked Grace about Mrs. Bryce, too, but her friend had not seen the woman in town. Was she with Marcus? Or maybe she was attending parties and dancing in other drawing rooms while showing off the enormous gem he'd given her!

Her anger rekindled. When she'd met Marcus a year ago, he'd told her he wanted to prove his love to her. But seeing him with Mrs. Bryce . . .

Had his words to Clare been impulsive, offered after he'd taken a passing fancy to her?

You forget the way he held you last year, after believing you dead . . .

That precious memory, his arms wrapped around her when he'd found her alive in the rubble after the enemy air raid over Margate last year. He'd held her so tightly she thought she might suffocate, his whispered words frantic against her hair. *"Sweetheart, dear God, I thought I'd lost you."*

Marcus had seemed a different man then. But as the months passed, while their love grew, the more time they'd had to be apart. He'd become distant, more . . . secretive. And how she had swallowed her shame those times he went to visit his family without her and Daisy.

Still, she'd struggled to hold on to the hope that one day she and Marcus would be together always.

Had his feelings for her simply worn off over time?

Staring at her lap, she gripped her purse until her fingertips turned white. *Let him go, Clare. You've a fine job at the hospital and a beautiful baby daughter who loves you without question. You don't need a man to get you through life.*

But I still love him . . .

No! Raising her eyes, she thrust out her chin. With her recent promotion came more earnings, and she could make plans of her own. Like finding a better neighborhood to live in and increasing Ruthie's stipend. The girl had been so helpful with Daisy while Clare dealt with the double workload.

Perhaps once things settled with the new arrivals at the hospital this week, she could take a short holiday with Ruthie and Daisy. Sally was right. She needed to start living again. Clare was still young and now there was no need to wait any longer.

Seeing her stop just ahead, she stood and prepared to leave the bus. Only after she'd exited did she notice the shiny black motorcar parked alongside her flat.

Approaching the vehicle, a sense of unease settled in her chest. Who was it? The car wasn't Jack Benningham's Daimler.

A Rolls-Royce.

The chauffeur exited the car, and Clare's steps slowed to a halt. Coldness permeated her at the sight of his green-and-gold livery. Viscount Randleton . . .

"Madam, are ye Mrs. Clare Danner?"

He touched the brim of his cap as he spoke while Clare tried to recall his craggy features and slight limp from her years of working at the estate. He must have started driving for the viscount and his family after she'd left. "I . . . yes," she said. "Why are you here?"

Instead of answering, he hobbled forward and offered her a cream envelope embossed with the Randleton crest. "My employer wishes a reply." He stepped back to give her privacy.

"Mrs. Danner? Everythin' all right?"

Ruthie had appeared at the open door to the flat, carrying Daisy on her hip.

"I'm fine, Ruthie. Please go back inside."

Clare's fingers trembled as she broke open the parchment's seal.

Mrs. Danner,

I have important business to discuss that concerns you and your daughter. Would you do me the favor of meeting me tomorrow afternoon? Please name your most convenient time and place. Thank you in advance.

Regards,
Sir Montague Lange,
Viscount Randleton

Mouth dry, Clare reread the note. What could he wish to discuss with her?

Stephen Lange. The viscount's nephew had been at Grace and Jack's party two weeks ago, and he'd spoken with her at dinner. Did this meeting have something to do with him?

After nearly three years, she couldn't imagine why the Lange family would be haunting her life again. She handed the letter back to the chauffeur. "Please tell him I'm unavailable."

The chauffeur tipped his head. "Well, ma'am, ye didn't 'ear it from me, but I 'appen to know there's some quid in it for ye." His eyes surveyed the dingy street, as if to point out she could use any help she could get. "I 'eard it directly from 'is valet, I did. 'Is lordship's wantin' to give ye money."

Money? Clare narrowed her eyes. "Do you know why?"

He seemed to hesitate. "Well, 'is lordship and milady just found out their son was killed in the war. In the second battle at the Marne."

Clare grabbed for the side of the car. Elliot Lange was dead? For years she'd harbored resentment toward him for his callous treatment of her, yet never did she wish Daisy's father dead. "I'm . . . sorry," she whispered. "But I still don't understand what this has to do with me."

The chauffeur shrugged. "Suit yerself, ma'am. But if it were me, I'd meet with 'is lordship and find out. I mean, what 'ave ye got to lose?"

What did she have to lose?

Clare settled into her seat at Swan's Tea Room on Coventry Street in London's West End the following evening. Despite the ornately carved Queen Anne–style tables and chairs and fluted glass sconces set against richly papered walls, she was comfortable here. Grace's father owned the prestigious establishment, and on occasion she and her friend took tea here together when Grace was in town.

Already Clare had scanned the shop to see if Swan's patroness Lady Bassett was in attendance, but the crowd had thinned and only a few older businessmen remained.

Since Randleton had allowed her to choose the time as well as the place, she decided to suit her own schedule and meet him after her work shift. It was gratifying, especially after years of working for his family and having to accommodate herself to their timetables.

She glanced toward the door at the sound of the overhead bell, and her pulse quickened to see a portly, well-dressed gent enter the shop. He removed his hat, and never could she forget the man who had watched while his wife dragged Clare from the house and placed her into that awful home.

Both Elliot and his cousin Stephen had inherited the viscount's reddish-blond coloring. Randleton's full head of hair now held faint traces of silver, while his beard and mustache were painstakingly trimmed. His thickened figure hadn't changed much that she could tell, garbed in a dark blue suit with his gold-and-white-patterned waistcoat.

He nodded in her direction and approached. "May I join you, Mrs. Danner?"

It struck her then that he and his chauffeur had both addressed her by her fictitious married title. Had Stephen Lange mentioned meeting her at the Benninghams' weeks ago?

At least Randleton seemed to want to treat her with respect. "Of course, please sit."

Once he'd taken his chair, she noticed the black armband on his sleeve. He followed her gaze. "You may have read in the *Times* that Elliot . . . recently died in battle."

Clare compressed her lips. She hadn't much time for reading newspapers. "Yes, I do know about his death," she said. "You have my sincere condolences."

And she meant it. Despite their cruelty, she knew what it felt like to lose a child.

"Thank you, Mrs. Danner." His sad eyes belied his smile. "You understand . . ."

"Yes." She swallowed and turned toward the evening sun illuminating the large front window, her mind reliving the horror of having her infant child wrenched from her while nursing at her breast. The harsh tone and accusing eyes of the staffer at the Magdalene asylum. *"Got what ye deserve for all yer sinfulness, harlot."*

It had taken Clare weeks to recover, physically and emotionally, so that she could return to work laundering sheets, sweeping floors, cleaning chamber pots, and any other task given to those relegated to that hellish place. It wasn't until months later—when Elliot, likely defying his father, had paid off the house matron—that Clare was set free.

She hadn't seen her baby's father ever again.

"May I serve you some tea?"

The waiter had arrived. Clare nodded her assent to the viscount, who ordered for them a pot of orange pekoe and a plate of currant scones. As the server departed, she looked directly at Randleton. "Why did you want to meet with me?"

"Ah, yes." He cleared his throat. "I wish to give your daughter, my granddaughter . . ." Removing a white handkerchief from his breast pocket, he pressed it to his mouth before looking up. "I want to give Daisy every advantage she should have had . . . before."

Clare's anger surged. "You mean if I'd been suitable enough to marry your son? Or if you'd not tossed me out, sending me to that prison of a home like some street—"

"Please, Mrs. Danner. What happened then . . . it was wrong, I admit. But now I wish to make amends to you and to Daisy." He leaned forward, his voice low. "With Elliot gone, my wife and I wish to provide for his child. Though I cannot give Daisy the title, she will not want for anything. We will provide her with the best education and eventually arrange a most fortuitous marriage—"

"Wait! Stop." Clare scanned the tearoom to see if anyone else was listening, her thoughts still spinning.

He wanted to help her and Daisy? It seemed too good to be true. Yet with Elliot's death, she could understand Randleton's longing to give to her daughter. His son's daughter.

She recalled the chauffeur's remark about money. "Do you plan to set up some kind of trust for her?"

"That and more. She will thrive with us at Randleton—"

"Hold on! You wish for us to come and live with you at your estate?" She fought back a shudder. Could she ever again walk the halls of that accursed place?

"Not exactly." His bearded cheeks flushed. "We would take Daisy."

Clare blinked. "You mean take Daisy . . . from me?"

"You would be handsomely rewarded." He reached for her across the table. "I would make certain you received a sum each month—"

Wood scraped across the tiled floor, disrupting several of the patrons as Clare launched from her seat, hands curled at her sides. "If you think I'd give up my daughter to you and your wife after what happened, you're barmy!" she shouted, not caring who heard her.

"Please, Mrs. Danner, sit down!" He glanced around the tearoom.

"I will *not* sit down. In fact, I'm leaving." She tossed her napkin onto the table.

"Fine." Randleton stood as well. "If you choose to do this the hard way, these are my terms." He removed from his breast pocket an envelope and withdrew a wrinkled letter. Snapping it open, he held it out to her, and Clare eyed the dirty, bloodstained stationery.

"A letter from my son before his death," he rasped. "A last will, recognizing Daisy as his own and making her his heir to the monies and estate his late grandmother left to him." He thrust the letter at her. "As you can see, it's been witnessed. And there are copies on file with the army chaplain's office."

Clare's mouth went slack as she stared at the paper. In between blood splotches and mud stains she glimpsed her daughter's name and the words "wealth and lands," and then her eyes found the signatures at the bottom—Elliot's, along with signatures of an army chaplain and another officer.

She looked at Randleton, panic squeezing her lungs. "You have no right—"

"I have every right as her grandfather." Randleton replaced the letter inside the envelope and shoved it back in his pocket. His blue eyes bored into her like ice. "You have a fortnight to decide if you wish to deal with me amicably. If so, I shall make it worth your while, and you will never again have financial issues. Or—" he paused, a snarl on his lips—"I will take this to the courts. Believe me, as I am a member of the House of Lords, and with this document from my son, who recently perished fighting for his country, you, *Miss* Danner, a single mother who has been subjecting my granddaughter to the squalor of St. Giles, won't stand a chance."

At his low-spoken threat, her mind went wild with panic. "You . . . you . . . can't do this!"

"I can, and I will. The choice is yours." He tossed three one-pound notes onto the table and retrieved his hat. "You have two weeks. I want an answer, or I'll take action and contact my solicitor."

He brushed past her out of the shop.

Clare watched blindly, her heart thundering in her chest as terror pierced her soul.

Oh, Lord, please help me! I cannot lose my baby again.

9

didn't know where else to turn, Grace. I won't let those horrible people have her!"

As Clare Danner started to cry anew, Jack Benningham shifted in the velvet upholstered chair while his wife sat on the couch, attempting to console her friend.

Marcus had told him of the filthy conditions at the workhouse orphanage where he'd found Clare's daughter last year, not far from Jack's estate in Kent. The babe wore no more than a soiled nappy and appeared grossly underweight for a one-year-old.

Hard to believe Randleton's audacity to demand Daisy back from her mother now after being responsible for the baby's abuse.

"Jack, is there anything we can do?"

His wife looked up at him, her lovely features creased in alarm.

"I can certainly try speaking with Randleton . . ." But how much good would it do? Montague Lange was a powerful lord in Parliament, and he possessed a handwritten will from his recently deceased son—a war hero—naming Daisy as his child and heir.

Clare, unfortunately, was a single mother living in a disreputable part of town, her finances a mere shadow of what the viscount could provide for his granddaughter.

Even at the risk of scandal in publicizing that Daisy was his dead son's natural daughter, Randleton was willing—no, eager—to push it through the courts.

Jack frowned as he considered an uglier side to this—that with Elliot dead, and his small daughter now rightful heir to any of Elliot's private wealth or lands, Randleton meant to control and perhaps profit from his granddaughter's newfound assets.

"See, Clare? Jack will speak with Randleton, and all will be well. That man cannot simply go taking a child from its own mother, regardless of his son's inheritance."

Though he did exactly that two years ago. Still, seeing the hope in his beautiful bride's emerald eyes, how could he refuse her? Jack squared his shoulders. "I will do all I can, Clare, but you must still prepare for a battle. Randleton is accustomed to getting what he wants."

Grace shook her head slightly at him while Clare looked up, eyes reddened with tears. "He's given me only a fortnight to decide, and I can't pay to hire a solicitor to go to court," she whispered. "Oh, how I wish Marcus was in town."

At her anguished look, Jack's chest tightened. He imagined for a moment a child being taken from him and Grace. It didn't bear thinking about.

"Jack, do you know when Marcus is returning home?"

He turned his attention back to his wife. How could he tell her the truth?

"I hope soon." Clare sat up on the couch and wiped away her tears. "Marcus and I had a . . . a terrible row before he left, but he did find Daisy for me once before, and despite everything that's happened between us, I know he would help her now."

Jack found himself looking into the expectant faces of the two women. He couldn't in good conscience lie about one fact. "Marcus is back," he said hesitantly. "At a private hospital near Cricklewood. Though I'm afraid he's off-limits right now."

"Hospital? What's wrong with him?" Clare leapt from the couch and approached. "Is it the influenza?"

When he fell silent, her face twisted in torment. "I need to see him, Jack. Please! My baby girl is my life, and I'll do whatever I must to save her from going back to that despicable family."

"Darling, if she could just speak to Marcus," Grace said. "Clare is chief orderly now at Endell Street, and she takes care of the sick and wounded every day. She knows what precautions to take."

His wife's green pools had the power to sway him, and Jack felt much like a flailing fish about to get reeled into the boat. "Sweetheart . . ."

"I beg you." Clare fell to her knees beside his chair, her expression pleading. "Let me see him, talk to him. At least let me try, can't you?"

He stood and helped Clare to her feet. "Yes, you can try." *And God willing, you will succeed.* "Can you meet me at Cottage Hospital on Gaylord Road at one o'clock tomorrow?"

"Yes, thank you!" She grasped both of his hands, then turned to his wife. "Thank you both so much!"

To him, she said, "I'll leave from the hospital and meet you there. Oh, I know in my heart that once Marcus gets better he'll testify to what he saw when he rescued Daisy last year! Surely that could change everything, couldn't it?"

Nodding, Jack raised a smile as he offered up a silent prayer. "We can hope."

Where was Jack?

Clare checked her watch as she stood outside Cottage Hospital the following afternoon at five minutes before the hour. She'd taken a cab, unwilling to risk being late to meet him due to the erratic bus schedules. And spending the extra shillings would be worth it if it meant she could see Marcus and plead her case to him.

How sick was he? Jack hadn't elaborated. Was Marcus receiving the proper care? Chewing at her lower lip, she stared at the front entrance of the small hospital. The facility did resemble a cottage, nestled against a backdrop of plane trees and surrounded on three sides by a green hedgerow of laurel. Beside the hospital stood an old church building.

The place seemed peaceful enough, and private hospitals were usually well-staffed. Her hopes lifted. Marcus could feel well enough to speak with her.

What should she say to him?

Clare's insides churned as she began to pace. Waiting for Jack, she mentally rehearsed how she might approach Marcus with her dilemma, especially after their awful last parting.

You're a man of honor, Marcus . . . No, that wouldn't work, not after she'd accused him in the park of being just the opposite of honorable. *I know we've had our differences, Marcus* . . . Yes, that was a much better way to start, no need to bring up what happened between them. *Marcus, surely you love Daisy, and you would do anything for her* . . .

She stopped pacing as the tight coil at her middle eased. Marcus would ask her to explain the problem with her daughter, and once she told him, he would contact Randleton and threaten to go to court against him and his wife and reveal their past cruelty toward her baby. And because Marcus was a naval captain at the Admiralty with a very important job aiding in the war, the court would surely listen to him.

Clare looked toward the street. Still no sign of Jack. She glanced back at the front of the hospital. Perhaps he was waiting for her inside?

The possibility fueled her determination as she entered the facility. While she didn't see him in the small waiting area, Clare did spot the admitting nurse in white uniform and cap at the front desk. "Excuse me. Have you seen Jack . . . Lord Walenford?"

Seated in a swivel chair, the thin woman peered up at her through a pair of wire-rimmed glasses. "No one has arrived since this morning, miss."

"I see." Clare's hopes fell. "I was to meet him here and together look in on Captain Weatherford."

The nurse sniffed. "That may well be, but at this time of day we do not allow visitors."

Clare set her jaw. It seemed the stubborn woman wasn't about to give way. She glanced back toward the entrance. What if Jack failed to arrive, and she lost her chance to see Marcus?

She forced a smile at the nurse. "I'm Mrs. Danner, chief orderly at Endell Street Military Hospital near Bloomsbury." Opening her purse, Clare withdrew her hospital card and handed it to the woman. "I was asked by his lordship to personally look in on the captain. It seems Lord Walenford has been delayed." Clare made a show of checking her watch. "However, I need to get back to my hospital soon. We have another trainload of our wounded lads arriving within the hour, and I must arrange for their reception and care."

"You do?" The taut face behind the glasses softened. "I received a telegram that my brother, Norman, was recently wounded in France. He's being sent back to London to be treated." She rose and leaned across the desk, glancing down the shadowy corridor. "Captain Weatherford is in room four, just down the hall on the right."

Clare hid her elation. "Thank you kindly, Sister . . . ?"

"Adgate. Miss Emily Adgate." She added, "My brother is Norman Adgate."

"Well, if I chance to meet your brother at our hospital, I will tell him that we met." Clare flashed a genuine smile this time. "And you can be assured he'll receive the best care with us."

"Thank you, Mrs. Danner." The nurse looked pleased. "And should Lord Walenford arrive, I'll notify him that you are with the patient."

Clare nodded and turned toward the hall, her mouth suddenly dry. Would Marcus agree to speak with her, or would he instead order her from the room? "Good-bye, Marcus . . ."

Recalling her parting words to him, she paused in front of his door, the ache in her heart she'd been trying to overcome now throbbing full force. *Dear Lord, what went so terribly wrong between us that he chose to love someone else?*

For the umpteenth time, she sensed no answer to her plea. *For my baby's sake, then.* With a sigh, she raised a fist and knocked on the door of room four. "Marcus, may I come in?"

The door opened seconds later, and Clare was stunned to see Mrs. Bryce. She was dressed in the same scarlet costume she'd worn that day in the park.

The large emerald-cut diamond glinted from her hand. "May I help you, miss?"

She smiled politely at Clare, though Clare sensed recognition in the dark eyes. Obviously, the ballerina chose not to acknowledge her from the party or the park.

"Hello. I'm Mrs. Danner." She lifted her chin at the woman who had stolen Marcus's affections. "I'm from Endell Street Military Hospital. Lord Walenford asked me to check in on the patient."

"Oh! Of course, please do come in."

Mrs. Bryce stepped back, and Clare entered the dim room, the drapes having been partially drawn against the bright daylight. She scanned the sparse furnishings—a steel table laden with supplies and a high-backed chair beside the bed—before her eyes found the bed's occupant . . .

Seeing Marcus with a white head bandage, she fought back a gasp and rushed to him. His eyes were closed, yet he seemed to be breathing steadily. At his flushed color, she pressed a hand to his skin. He had no fever that she could tell.

She glanced back at the bandage. Certainly not influenza. Sitting in the chair beside the bed, she took up his hand. Gently she traced her fingertips along his palm before pressing them to his wrist to time his pulse.

That, too, seemed steady and normal.

Once she'd resettled his hand against the bedsheet, she turned to Mrs. Bryce. "I wasn't made aware of his condition. Why is his head bandaged?"

"He . . . he was in a terrible accident." Mrs. Bryce removed an embroidered white handkerchief from her sleeve and began dabbing at her eyes. She cleared her throat. "Marcus received injuries to the head."

That much was obvious. "How?"

But Mrs. Bryce could only shake her head.

Clare shifted her attention back to Marcus, startled to see his dark eyes staring at her. "Hello there," she said softly.

"Hello," he murmured, still groggy from sleep. "When . . . did you get here?"

"A few moments ago." His voice sounded different to her. "Jack told me you were here. How are you feeling?"

"Headache." He closed his eyes again. "Very tired. Long journey."

From where? she wanted to ask him. Instead, she wet her lips and leaned forward. "Can I get you anything?"

"Thirsty," he muttered.

"Of course." She rose and went to the steel table and moments later returned with a glass of water. Gently she raised him up to drink.

"How's that?" she asked once he'd slaked his thirst.

"Better."

She lowered his head back onto the pillow, and he closed his eyes. Seconds ticked by. Finally, Clare drew a deep breath. "Marcus, I need your help."

His eyes opened to her once more, searching her face. He didn't seem angry. That was a good sign, wasn't it?

She plunged ahead. "I know you still love Daisy and would do anything to help her, wouldn't you?" Clare spoke quietly the words she'd rehearsed outside the hospital. "They're trying to take her from me again. Randleton and his . . . his awful wife!"

Her voice did rise then, but she didn't care that Mrs. Bryce might be listening. "Elliot's dead, and now they want to take my baby to raise without me! Randleton even offered me money to give her away, and if I refuse, he's going to steal her back through the courts. We can't let them have her, Marcus! You need to tell Randleton you'll testify to what you saw in Kent last year when you found our sweet Daisy. Please, you must make him stop this!"

Clare's chest burned as a sob escaped, and she ducked her head, struggling for calm. Once she'd regained her composure, she sniffled and raised damp eyes to his. He'd said nothing so far, but his tortured look didn't need words.

New hope filled her. "You will help us!" She'd been right to come to him. He would save her precious child for her! Reaching for his hand again, she clasped his fingers. "Oh, Marcus, I knew you wouldn't refuse—"

"Who is Randleton?" he cut in hoarsely, staring at her. "And . . . who are you?"

10

lare gazed dully out at the palace green while the cab took her to Grace's town house in Kensington.

Marcus had no memory of her or of anything else, according to Mrs. Bryce.

Heat flushed her cheeks as she was reminded of the pity in the ballerina's dark eyes at Clare's shock. *"I am very sorry Marcus cannot help you with this trouble."*

Mrs. Bryce had overheard their entire conversation.

Conversation! A bitter laugh nearly choked her. *She'd* done all the talking while Marcus just stared at her as though she were a complete stranger to him.

You are now, Clare.

She'd wanted to ask Mrs. Bryce why Marcus was able to remember *her*, but the ballerina saved her the trouble when she offered that it was *she* who had brought him to the private hospital once they reached London, and he wouldn't let her leave his side.

So, they had been traveling together. And Marcus wanted Mrs. Bryce to be with him. *Not you, Clare, and not Daisy.*

A stab of fresh pain mingled with her anger as the cab pulled up in front of the Benningham town house. Whether he was Grace's husband or not, Jack was going to get a piece of her mind!

Clare had just paid the driver and alighted from the taxi when Jack's Daimler drew up behind them along the curb. She glared at him through the Daimler's windscreen, hoping he could see her while the chauffeur exited and came around to let him out.

Color tinged his face as he spied her and waved her toward the front door.

"You must despise me now," he said once they were inside. "But please understand, I'm sworn to secrecy about Marcus's condition, and the only way to tell you was not to tell you." His eyes held apology. "I counted on your determination and cunning to outweigh any scruples you might have about following the rules, and I was right."

She reared back from him. "You left me waiting there on purpose?"

He nodded. "Unchivalrous, I grant you, but it worked and now you know the sad truth."

"Yes, I do," she gritted out. "And thank you for letting me get the shock of my life."

Jack heaved a sigh before he ushered her toward the drawing room, where Grace was likely having tea.

Her friend looked up at them from the ivory love seat, and seeing Clare's anger, Grace rose to her feet. "What's wrong? What's happened to Marcus?"

"He doesn't remember me." Clare flashed a heated look at Jack. "Or Daisy."

"What do you mean? Come, both of you, and sit. I'll pour tea."

Grace collected two more cups from the side table, and once they were all seated with biscuits and steaming cups of Darjeeling, she leaned toward Clare. "Now, tell me everything."

"I waited for your husband at the hospital, but *apparently* he was running late." Clare cast another sidelong glare at Jack and then relayed to them the events that led to her humiliation after pouring her heart out to Marcus. "To make matters worse, *she* was there and heard everything, and now I don't know what to do."

Grace leaned back with her cup. "She?"

"Mrs. Bryce."

Grace gasped. "She was in Marcus's hospital room?"

Clare nodded miserably. "And she was wearing *the ring*."

"Oh, my dear friend!" Grace quickly set down her cup. "How painful for you, and with all that's happening right now."

"What ring?"

Both women looked at Jack, who seemed confused by their exchange.

Grace chose to enlighten him. "Darling, I've not explained to you about Mrs. Bryce, but before Marcus left town, Clare discovered the two had been having an affair for some time."

Biscuit crumbs sprayed from Jack's mouth as he coughed. "What?" he managed hoarsely.

Grace crossed her arms. "He was unfaithful to my friend, and I will have a difficult time forgiving him for that."

Jack set down his biscuit and leaned back, hands on the arms of the chair. He glanced at each of them, though he failed to make eye contact. "You don't know that for certain . . ."

"Husband." Grace relaxed her arms and sighed. "Clare saw them both with her own eyes in Russell Square gardens the day Marcus left town. He gave Mrs. Bryce a large diamond, along with an envelope containing the funds to purchase her trousseau."

Jack's mouth flattened as he shook his head.

"You've nothing to say?" Grace demanded.

"Only that he was a fool," Jack muttered. He turned to Clare. "I'm heartily sorry you were a witness to that. I'm sure it must have been a terrible shock."

Clare nodded, only half listening while fresh pain seared her at the memory of being betrayed in the park, and her recent humiliation at the private hospital. *I've now lost you entirely, Marcus, in both body and mind.*

She swallowed past the ache in her throat. "It was . . . devastating," she whispered. Then she straightened and drew a deep breath, raising her chin. "But I must think of my daughter now, and our future . . ."

What future? Without Marcus's testimony, she'd certainly lose her case against Randleton and his wife. Leaving her entirely alone, without her sweet baby *and* without the man she'd once loved. Her eyes suddenly burned. *Still loved . . .*

She turned to Jack. "How did he get these injuries?"

"Apparently Marcus took a nasty fall and cracked open the back of his head," he said. "The doctor believes it's the cause of his amnesia."

"Darling, does Marcus remember anything at all?" Grace asked.

"He knows his name, and he seems to recall that he has a family." Jack shook his head. "But not much else at the moment."

"He remembers Mrs. Bryce," Clare said bitterly. "They were obviously traveling together." She tipped her head at Jack. "Do you know her well, too?"

He shrugged. "I knew her husband and I've spoken with her on occasion when she has come to Whitehall. She's also acquainted with Marcus's boss and likely that's how he met her."

Clare nodded. Marcus told her much the same the night before he left.

She set her teacup on the table, despair having replaced her anger. In truth, Marcus's condition *did* worry her, but she had bigger problems at the moment. "I'm at a loss what to do now," she said to Jack. "Unless you're able to sway Elliot Lange's father into changing his mind, he'll take my baby from me all over again."

"I promised you that I'll do what I can," he said, his earnest expression giving her some measure of comfort.

Clare glanced at the mantel clock and rose. "I must return to work. Thank you for the tea."

Jack also stood. "I'll have Raymond drive you back to Endell Street. We'll come up with something, Clare, so don't give up hope."

"Take care of yourself, dear friend." Grace approached and hugged her. "Jack and I will be here in town for some time yet, and one of us will let you know what he can arrange with Randleton. Trust in God," she added, "and all will turn out well."

Moments later, riding back to work in the Daimler, Clare prayed that Grace was right.

Marcus awoke hours later to stare into the darkness. Sweat rolled off him in waves while terror coiled like a knot in his chest, making it difficult to breathe.

He strained to listen for a comforting sound that he wasn't alone, but only his own rapid breathing reached his ears. He raised a hand, groping for the chair beside his bed where Natalya should be sitting, just as she'd been before . . .

Empty. Panic threatened to overwhelm him, and his head began to throb. He groaned and started to rise when he heard the door open.

"*Myshka*, you should be sleeping! Did you have another bad dream?"

Natalya. His body relaxed, the tightness in his chest easing. In the dark, he could make out her form as she took her place in the chair beside his bed.

"The same nightmare," he rasped. In his dream, he was falling, unable to grasp at anything to stop him from being swallowed up in the maw of blackness that haunted his sleep nearly every night.

She turned on the small bedside lamp and he reached for her. "Where were you?"

"I spoke with the evening nurse about putting a cot in here. That way I can be with you all the time, da?"

"Yes." He hated being alone. His mind was a door leading into that crater of darkness, shutting him off from the light. He vaguely recalled seeing a crater once—at least he'd thought it was a crater. He didn't know for certain. Could it have been in his dreams?

"Oh, *milyi*. You are soaked to the skin. Let me get a dry cloth from the table."

Milyi. Darling. He watched her rise from the chair to cross the room. "You'll not leave me again, will you?"

Natalya sighed as she returned and began gently wiping the dampness from his face and neck. "I have not left you, Marcus, and I will never abandon you. You made me promise when you were in the other hospital." She paused. "Do you remember that hospital?"

"Before the ship," he said, comforted by her ministrations.

"Da, before we took the ship home." She smiled, then eased back in the chair.

He stared at the diamond on her finger winking in the lamp-light. Images returned; his awakening to darkness, pain searing his skull. His eyes unable to see. He'd cried out, reaching for his face, when suddenly soft hands had gripped his, pulling them away from what was a partial head bandage. She'd grazed his skin with the large stone.

"Did I give you that ring?"

"You did, Marcus. We are engaged, remember?"

Marcus didn't remember, but he hadn't wanted her to leave him, so he'd agreed. Her touch was soothing, and for some reason the fragrance of her perfume had brought him comfort.

Traces of another scent unlike Natalya's still lingered in the room. "Who was the woman?" he whispered. Eyes the color of liquid silver and the hair beneath her bonnet as black as the abyss tormenting him each night. Her perfume . . .

"Mrs. Danner is from a hospital here in London. One of the men you work with sent her over to look in on you." A pause. "She seemed to know you, Marcus. And you know her and her small daughter. Do you remember them?"

He tried to recall the woman's plea, but his thoughts scattered like bits of tattered paper into the wind. *Focus!* He furrowed his brow, heart thumping, and suddenly words started forming, coming together.

". . . Marcus, I know you . . . love Daisy . . ." Her touch had been warm and gentle like Natalya's, her husky voice soft—until she became upset. *"They want to take my baby . . . you must tell them what you saw . . . please, make him stop this!"*

And then a man's name she kept repeating. *Randleton*.

Marcus had wanted to help, to remember for her, but all that was in his memory was blackness.

His breath hitched in the silence.

"She has upset you, milyi," Natalya said gently. "I am sorry, she will not trouble you again. Now go back to sleep and get your rest. I will be right here. And tomorrow we can try again to help you remember."

Relieved at her soft assurances, Marcus began to drowse off, yet the dark-haired woman again sifted into his thoughts, tears filling her stormy eyes as she'd begged for her daughter's safety. *Daisy*.

As sleep began to overtake him, he imagined a prayer forming in the shadows of his mind.

Let me help her to save the child.

11

WHITEHALL, LONDON
THURSDAY, AUGUST 22, 1918—NEXT DAY

N ow you know what we are up against, Benningham. A race for time, I'm afraid."

Seated in the paneled office at Whitehall the following day, Jack nodded at the man behind the desk. Captain Sir Mansfield George Smith-Cumming, head of MI6, had just given him a full briefing on Marcus's most recent assignment. "I'm amazed he survived a gunshot wound to the head." He breathed a silent prayer of thanks that his friend hadn't been killed.

"Right. According to Natalya Bryce, Marcus fell afterward and cracked his head open on a rock protruding from the forest floor."

Jack winced and held up the peasant's cap C had handed him, noting a dark bloodstain over most of the felt fabric. "How did she manage to get the two of them away from the Bolsheviks?" He couldn't fathom why they hadn't killed her in the process.

"She shot her way out."

"What?" Jack blinked.

C smiled. "Natalya may look like a delicate flower, Benningham, but she's a crack shot. Her late husband, Walter, and I were close friends before his death last year. After they were married, he learned Natalya's father had taught her to use a hunting rifle when she was young. As soon as the Bolsheviks started making noise and threatened revolution, Walter bought her a pistol and showed her how to use it. It wasn't long before her skill with a gun surpassed his. The Bolsheviks who attacked her and Marcus weren't prepared for a pretty peasant woman to start firing at them."

"So . . . she shot them dead?"

He nodded. "Afterward, she ran for help at a farmstead not far from the woods and then got Marcus to a nearby village, where a doctor patched him enough for her to bring him back on the train to Archangel."

Jack whistled. "That woman is full of surprises. I'd be grateful to have her along for any assignment."

"Agreed. Now tell me, what is our boy's status?"

"Unchanged, I'm afraid," Jack said. "I went to see Marcus shortly after his return. The attending physician at Cottage Hospital believes he suffers from retrograde amnesia. He can remember details of his distant past, his name and his family, but he has no recollection of events prior to being hospitalized in Archangel." He paused. "And we don't yet know how far back that lapse goes. It's like a block of time in his mind has gone missing."

"A block that we desperately need to recover."

"Indeed," Jack said. "I understand you asked Natalya to refrain from telling Marcus any details regarding their trip to Russia?"

"I'm concerned about security, Benningham, especially if he cannot remember enough to keep silent. If word got out he'd been in Russia . . ."

"Parliament would start asking questions." Jack leaned back in his seat. Yesterday had been a perfect example with his wife relaying to him the rift between Clare and Marcus.

Having known about the engagement cover story between his friend and Natalya, Jack was shocked to learn Clare had witnessed them in the park exchanging information and the phony ring before their departure.

"This is a bad business," C said. "Since Marcus's return, we've assigned two other agents, including our man Tunney at the British Consulate in Moscow, to search for news on Sidney Reilly. Apparently he's gone into hiding."

Jack grimaced. "And every day without Marcus or Reilly to provide us with information reduces our chances to locate the tsarina and her son. Do we know for a fact my friend spoke with Reilly before the accident?"

"Yes. Natalya reported that Reilly met with Marcus the night they arrived in Archangel and gave him the directions to find the Romanovs somewhere in Perm."

C reached for a folder on his desk and withdrew a note from it, which he handed to Jack.

Jack scanned the series of written numbers and letters. "What does this mean?"

"We believe it to be a code of Reilly's invention. Natalya found the note in Marcus's jacket pocket after she got him to a doctor. It could represent the map directions to Perm."

"Or perhaps the assassination details?"

"Possibly, though Natalya was not privy to that part of his assignment. The two men did meet, however, so Reilly certainly would have told him."

"What will you do now?"

"We've got a man in Archangel we can work with. Like Reilly, Chaplin is Russian and supports the Allied cause. He'll find our agent if he's there and retrieve the information Marcus received about the tsarina and young tsarevich."

"And the plot to kill Lenin?"

"I'll need to have Tunney in our Moscow Consul see if he can obtain the details from another source." C frowned. "Until then, we can only hope Marcus will remember in time to make a difference in this war." He looked up. "Get that cap back to him—it might jog his memory."

"Of course." Jack tucked the soiled felt cap into his briefcase. "Would you actually send Marcus back to Russia?"

"A slim possibility, but yes." C picked up a playing card from the desktop; it was stained with blood. He eyed Jack. "It's one reason why I want Natalya to continue her cover with Marcus, at least for the time being." C studied the card. "There could be other business afoot."

Jack blinked. *What business?*

But the head of MI6 did not elaborate. "Much will depend on how swiftly Marcus regains his memory," C added instead. "And according to my sources, our boy could get that mind of his back at any time . . . or he may never fully recover."

Jack curled his lip. He refused to accept the possibility Marcus might never remember him or Grace or Clare, the woman he'd loved, and her little girl, Daisy.

Memories of the past flooded him: the trust and latitude Marcus had granted him last year during an investigation that ultimately led to his own happiness with Grace; and before that, his friend had helped him to come back from the dead, after an explosion left Jack scarred and blinded in more ways than one.

If Marcus could just latch onto a solid memory, and then hold on until he could grasp another . . .

He straightened to consider his friend's boss. Marcus did remember that he had a family. And clearly C wanted his friend out of the public eye.

"Sir, if you have no objections, I've an idea on how we might speed up the memory process." Jack wasn't about to give up now, and he hoped C would accept his plan.

And if it worked, Jack would have his best friend back.

"I'm taking Marcus to Hampshire."

Clare paused in pouring herself another cup of tea to stare at Jack as he and Grace sat across from her at the linen-covered table in Swan's.

When her friend requested she join them for dinner that evening,

Clare had been surprised when both Jack and Grace arrived in the Daimler to collect her. She was relieved when Grace announced that instead of returning to the house in Kensington and their stuffy formal dining room, her father was hosting a private after-hours dinner at the tearoom for the three of them.

"You believe his family can help," Clare said, continuing to pour tea into her cup. Her nerves were ragged. With each sunrise, she mentally counted off the days—already three had passed!—until her next meeting with Randleton. And time wasn't about to slow down to give her a chance to think of a solution to her problem.

"Indeed, they can." Jack reached for a yeast roll that Becky Simmons, Ruthie's older sister and Swan's chief baker, had prepared for their meal. "The Weatherfords will be able to help Marcus in piecing together the part of his past he does remember and hopefully create a bridge to the present that he's forgotten."

"And if this plan doesn't work?" Clare asked, watching him spread a dab of the precious butter on his roll.

He glanced at her. "Right now it's the only chance we've got."

"It makes sense to me," Grace said, forking a piece of roasted chicken onto her plate. "If he's well enough to travel, then the beauty and peace of Hampshire alone will be so much better for him. Not only his mental recovery, but his physical wounds as well."

Clare weighed their words while she reached for a flaky meat pasty. Since half of Marcus's Hampshire home was now a rehabilitation center for the wounded, it would be a good place for him to rest and heal.

He would also be free of the ballerina, at least for a time. The possibility lightened her mood. "Will it just be you and Marcus, then?" She reached for another celery stick slathered in crowdie cheese.

"Not quite." Jack hesitated. "Mrs. Bryce will be accompanying him."

"I see." Clare crunched hard on her piece of celery, trying to ease the hurt in her heart.

"That's why you're coming with us."

"Me?" She tried talking around her food before she swallowed and said, "I can't possibly leave London. What about my daughter? My job at the hospital?"

"Bring Daisy and Ruthie along with you, and I'll hire you for your medical services while you're there." He smiled. "I'll even convince your hospital matron that you're desperately needed to work for the Crown." His face sobered. "It is critical to the war effort that Marcus make a complete recovery."

"I think it's a marvelous plan!" Grace beamed at Clare. "You've already admitted that you're concerned about the cases of influenza the wounded are bringing back from France, and this would be a chance to breathe in some fresh country air. The Weatherfords should have plenty of good farm food on hand, much like our summer fare last year at Jack's estate."

"But you know I've never been to Hampshire or even met his family," Clare argued. "What do I say if they ask questions, especially now that Marcus is engaged to someone else?"

"Don't go borrowing trouble," Grace chided. "You'll be there as his nurse, and I doubt the Weatherfords would be so crass as to ask you about your relationship with him." She paused and raised a brow. "Or are you afraid to go?"

Clare's pulse sped. Grace made several good points. Yet how could she risk losing her new promotion at the hospital? It could mean a better place to live for her and Daisy, more opportunities in life for herself and her daughter . . .

But if you don't do something, there's every chance Randleton will be giving Daisy those opportunities instead of you!

"Go to Hampshire," Grace said gently, reading her thoughts. "And if you're willing to care for any medical needs Marcus might encounter, it will give you two a chance to spend some time together."

Clare scoffed. "For what purpose? His fiancée will be with him constantly, and I'll just be in the way."

"Consider this," Jack said. "You've known Marcus longer than

Mrs. Bryce has, which means you've a better chance at helping him to regain what he's lost. And when that happens . . ."

"Marcus can then help you, Clare," Grace added with earnestness. "He will testify and ensure that you keep Daisy."

Hope flared as she eyed them both. Could she jog Marcus's memory so that her life wouldn't come crashing down around her once more?

Memories of the torment she'd suffered just two years ago rushed back—the emptiness and grief the moment Daisy was taken from her, and then the agonizing months spent searching, waiting, worrying, and wondering how her baby was doing. The gnawing heartache never lessened, believing her daughter was forever out of her reach.

What would Randleton and his wife do to Daisy this time if her little girl failed to please them or she caused them embarrassment? Withhold her inheritance from Elliot while they shipped her off to some boarding school to become lost among so many other children?

How could Clare ever trust the Langes to love and care for her sweet baby the way only she could?

Grace was right. Clare was afraid. And she was angry. Enough that the hospital promotion, her co-workers, even these two dear friends of hers—all meant little without Daisy. Her baby was her world, and Clare owed it to her daughter to ensure that her mum would always be there for her.

She set down her stick of celery and looked at Jack. "When do we leave?"

"Must we leave, Natalya?"

Marcus struggled against panic while his fiancée walked toward the window. After another terrifying night of dreams, the nurse had arrived early this morning to give him a sedative, causing him to drift in and out of sleep most of the day. "I don't want to sail again. I'm tired of the sea."

"No, myshka, not a ship this time." She drew back the drapes, allowing the early evening sun to stream in through the window of his hospital room. He tried to relax, lifting his face to bask in the light.

"We shall take a train."

She returned to stand beside his wheelchair. The doctor had also checked him over this afternoon, declaring him fit enough to get out of bed and into the conveyance. Though Marcus felt determined to walk on his own, his body's equilibrium disagreed. "To where?" he asked.

"The countryside. Do you remember Hampshire? You are going home to rest and to be with your family."

Family . . . Father? His heart thumped as an image flashed in his mind. *A dark-haired boy, ready for Harrow at thirteen . . . a little girl, crying as he carried her . . .*

A twinge of pain pierced him at the memory. His father was dead.

He looked up at Natalya. "Are you coming with me?" His fear that she might not stay with him returned, and he reached for her.

"Of course." She took his hand. "You do not remember my promise to you?"

His thoughts tangled with the shadowy images in his brain, words colliding with each other until finally the mist cleared. His breathing eased. He did remember her words. She would not leave him. "I . . . sorry, I forgot."

"Do not apologize. I think you will start to remember more and more each day." She smiled, her eyes like onyx. "You can ask me whatever you like, and I shall tell you to the best of my ability. I want to help you to remember."

He managed a weak smile. "When do we leave?"

"In a day or so." She looked toward the window and the yellow-orange light. "Lord Walenford will let us know when he can collect us and take us to the station."

Lord Walenford. Jack. He'd come to the room once before, but Marcus wasn't able to recognize the face smiling at him. Slightly scarred at the temples, yet not enough to mar his good looks. Blond hair, blue eyes, and according to Natalya, a viscount.

Jack had told him they were best friends, and Marcus sensed they must have enjoyed good times together. Jack had a likable way about him.

But as Marcus struggled to recall the man, nothing emerged but the blackness. "How long will we be gone?" he asked Natalya, weary of trying to remember.

"As long as you like, myshka." She turned to him once more. "As long as it takes you to recover."

Would he recover? Marcus reached up with his free hand to touch the bandage. The wound on the side of his head was still tender, while the back of his head continued to throb. Surface wounds could heal quickly enough, but what about his mind? Would he ever pierce the murky fog of his memory, to recognize the scarred, smiling face of the man who had been his friend? Or the woman with midnight hair and eyes like the restless sea they'd encountered sailing back to London?

Would he be able to help her child?

He still held Natalya's hand and squeezed her fingers gently. Because she'd acted quickly to get him to a hospital weeks ago, he was here now. And he could still grasp at a thread of hope.

You're alive and that's a start.

"All right, we'll go," he said, gazing up at her. "Together."

12

Hampshire was like a glimpse into heaven.

Clare held her sleeping baby and gazed out the window as their train headed west on the hour-long ride to the Weatherfords' home. The glass, concrete, and stone of the city had given way to endless stretches of green—patchworks of verdant fields now ripe with sweet corn, rainbow chard, and bright-yellow summer squash, and orchards laden with early apples and purple plums. Crisscrossing each field, white flowering blackberry vines threaded their way through colorful hedgerows of elderberry, golden aspens, copper beech, and silver birch.

In the breaks between the trees, she would often see the sparkle of water—a slow-moving river or the tranquil reflection of a lake, its marshy fringes barely discernible. The scenery, together with the deep rumble of the train's engines, worked to soothe her frayed nerves while beside her Ruthie dozed in the royal-blue cushioned seat.

Much had happened in the past two days—starting with Matron's shock when Clare announced she must leave for the country to take a temporary post as private caregiver. Even with Jack's official letter from Whitehall, her supervisor grumbled that more wounded were arriving at Endell Street and Clare was needed.

In the end, though, Matron had given her blessing, and Clare went off to say good-bye to Sally and Beatrice. Once they got over their surprise, Sally, in typical Sally fashion, wanted all the particulars.

Clare had offered her Grace's argument—the chance to get Daisy away from the city and into the fresh country air. She refused to tell them the identity of her patient in Hampshire, as they'd surely assume she was chasing after Marcus.

It's his memory I need right now. And becoming his nurse gave her the chance to try to save her own happiness with her daughter.

She turned to him, seated directly across from her in the first-class compartment. Mrs. Bryce, now garbed in a green costume, sat beside him.

Ignoring the ballerina, Clare focused on her new patient. A fresh stab of pain mingled with her longing as she studied his face. He looked so vulnerable, with his bandaged head resting against the seatback and his dark eyes closed, his generous mouth gone slack beneath his mustache.

Thoughts of the Benninghams' party just weeks ago flashed in her mind. Then, Clare had wished that their guest of honor, Sir Henshaw, had someone to take care of him and his faulty memory. Now here she was, doing the same for Marcus.

She frowned. He was still too pale. At Cottage Hospital, his pallor had been much the same when she and Daisy accompanied Jack inside to collect the pair. Marcus, in a wheelchair, had seemed disturbed to see her.

So had Mrs. Bryce.

Clare pressed her lips against Daisy's soft curls, allowing herself a scrap of satisfaction. Jack's invitation to her days ago to join them in Hampshire had obviously been on impulse, without a warning to Marcus or the ballerina.

They had all left Cottage Hospital in silence, with Raymond

driving Clare, Daisy, and Ruthie to the station in the Daimler while Jack hailed a cab for himself, Marcus, and Mrs. Bryce.

They'd needed two cars just to carry all the ballerina's trunks. Clare turned to the window and drew a deep breath. Soon they'd arrive at Hampshire Station, and from there travel to Marcus's home, and her first time meeting his family.

What would the Weatherfords think, especially now that Mrs. Bryce was engaged to Marcus? Would they feel sorry for Clare?

A rush of heat singed her face. *Oh, Lord, please don't let them pity me!*

"Hosey, Mama."

Daisy's sudden announcement pulled Clare from her thoughts, while her sleepy daughter pushed against her to sit upright. Her pudgy finger pointed toward the window. "Hosey."

"I see the horse, love," Clare murmured, noting a plow horse tilling soil on a distant farm. She bent to kiss her daughter's plump cheek. Pity or not, keeping her little girl with her was all that mattered.

Satisfied, Daisy leaned back against her mum, and Clare closed her eyes, breathing in the scent of her baby—a mix of talcum powder, traces of milk, and that oh-so-sweet smell imprinted on her soul from the moment her child was born. Cuddling her daughter, she returned her attention to Marcus.

His eyes were now open and watching them.

"Da." As if sensing his attention, Daisy raised her head, this time turning to Marcus. Her dimpled hand extended in his direction.

At the hospital, Daisy had reached for him in much the same way. And just as before, he hunched his shoulders and turned away.

Clare ached at his reaction. It wasn't so long ago when he came to visit that Marcus would swing Daisy in the air like a Ferris wheel, laughing out loud when she squealed with delight. *And then he'd lean over and kiss you afterward, still smiling.*

Clare tightened her hold on her child, even as she noticed Marcus's hands clenching into fists against his thighs, his features taut while he stared out the window as the train rumbled on.

He was afraid. Her heart softened at seeing his stony expression. It struck her anew that she, Daisy, Ruthie, and even Jack, who had stepped away from the compartment—were unknown to Marcus.

Only the stylish blonde seated beside him was someone he was familiar with and trusted.

As if on cue, Mrs. Bryce's gloved hand reached to cover one of Marcus's fists, and pain and jealousy surged through Clare at seeing the way he began to relax. The ballerina knew his signs as well as she did and sought to ease his distress with a simple touch.

The compartment door opened and Jack entered. "This will be our stop," he said as the train began to slow. Clare turned to the window in time to see a town sign that read *Hook*.

He approached Marcus. "Your grandfather has arranged for a car to meet us here at the station."

Marcus jerked a nod, his broad shoulders bunched as he flexed his hands.

Clare watched him, her chest aching. *Lord, please give him the strength to heal and grant him the courage and desire he'll need to see it through.*

Staring down at her baby, asleep once more against her breast, she rested her cheek gently atop her soft crown.

Most of all, Lord, please let him remember us.

"Welcome to Hampshire!"

A pretty, dark-haired woman smiled at them from the front passenger seat as Clare and the others clambered into the large bus to continue their journey to the Weatherfords' home.

The driver helped Mrs. Bryce to climb in first, followed by Ruthie with a sleeping Daisy. The bus, while filled with seats, resembled more the hospital ambulances that delivered the wounded to Endell Street from London's train stations. Clare went in next, then Marcus, helped from his wheelchair by Jack and the driver as he carefully ascended the steps. Clare took his hands and helped to ease him into the seat beside the ballerina.

"I apologize for the accommodation," said the young woman in front once they'd all settled in. Her looks seemed familiar as she first cast a nervous smile at Marcus, whose head was bowed, then looked directly at Clare. "When Lord Walenford told us about the number in your party, it was too many for the Rolls. I thought Vickers fetching you up in the facility's bus might be more expedient."

"Your ingenuity does you credit, Miss Weatherford." Jack had chosen a hard bench seat on the other side of Clare. He grinned. "It's been years since I've taken a ride on a bus, and I'm certain the experience will do me good."

Miss Weatherford . . . Frances, Marcus's sister! Clare studied the woman she'd heard about but never met. Looking near to her own age, Frances Weatherford had fine dark brows arched above deeply set eyes, the same honey-brown color as her brother's. The high cheekbones, small pointed nose, and full mouth emphasized her delicately attractive features.

But what about on the inside where it counts? Marcus had only told her that his sister enjoyed gardening and she'd been away at school last year.

Frances appeared refined and proper, and Clare hoped she would be like Grace, who never put on airs or made those around her feel uncomfortable.

"Thank you for understanding, your lordship." Frances smiled at Jack before her gaze shifted back to her brother. A troubled look creased her brow.

Marcus stared straight ahead, his chiseled face without expression. Did he not recognize his own sister? Clare looked back and forth at the two of them, her pulse ebbing along with her hope. If he couldn't even do that, it meant Jack's plan would surely fail.

And if you give up now, Clare, you'll have failed before you started. She turned toward the sleeping angel in Ruthie's arms and then straightened her shoulders, infused with new determination. She was Daisy's mum after all, and her daughter needed her to try.

Clare lifted her eyes to find Frances looking at her and reflecting similar despair. She offered a smile. "I'm sure once we arrive at your home, Miss Weatherford"—she cast a sidelong glance at Marcus—"we'll get everyone situated and start getting acquainted."

"Why, yes, you are right," Frances said, appearing relieved as the bus pulled away from the station.

"Miss Weatherford, I've been remiss in my manners," Jack said. He turned to Clare. "You must know of Mrs. Danner, who will be caring for your brother while he's home. And beside her is little Daisy, and the child's nanny, Miss Ruthie Simmons."

Frances angled her head at Clare, dark brows veed together. "Mrs. Danner," she said, nodding.

"And next to your brother is his friend, Mrs. Bryce—"

"Marcus's fiancée," Mrs. Bryce interjected. "So wonderful to finally meet his charming sister."

Clare forgotten, Frances's mouth gaped like a mackerel while she blinked at the ballerina. "You are . . . engaged to my brother?" She turned to Jack and then glanced back at Marcus before her face reddened. "Pardon me, Mrs. Bryce. We were . . . unaware Marcus was to be married."

"Please, you must call me Natalya. And I shall call you . . ."

"Uh . . . Frances." Frances continued staring at her.

"Such a lovely name." Mrs. Bryce—Natalya—smiled. "And do not be distressed, my dear. Our engagement was only recent, and Marcus had no chance to tell you before . . ."

She paused in her syrupy speech to look at him, and the smile he offered her was like another blade ripping open Clare's heart.

Clare bit the inside of her lip to conquer her emotion, dismissing the niggling at the back of her mind over Frances Weatherford's initial response. How would she possibly survive a fortnight watching Marcus ogle that tart?

Natalya returned her attention to Frances. "I can certainly see the resemblance between the two of you. You are both quite handsome."

Eyes still wide, Frances gulped and nodded. "Thank you."

"Now, tell me, how far away is your home?"

"Montefalco is five miles from the station." Frances seemed to collect herself and indicated a northerly direction beyond the windscreen. "We'll arrive in a few minutes."

"Montefalco?" Natalya raised an elegant brow. "Is that a town?"

Frances grinned, her teeth white and straight like her brother's. "Montefalco is our family estate. In medieval times it was once a monastery, and the name was bestowed in the fifteenth century to honor an Augustinian abbess, Chiara da Montefalco."

Clare blinked, a lump rising in her throat. *"Take care of yourself, my Chiara."* The endearment Marcus had spoken to her the night of the Benninghams' party.

"Hmm, Chiara . . ." Natalya pressed a finger to her mouth. "My Italian is a bit out of use, but—"

"Clare."

All eyes swiveled toward Marcus, gazing at his sister. "Clare of Montefalco," he said.

"That's right, Brother. Saint Chiara." Her dark eyes shone, and even Clare took hope at his response. Perhaps being here would help him after all.

"It seems a blessing that Mrs. Danner is with us." Smiling, Jack angled his head at Clare. "Were you aware that you share the namesake of this Montefalco saint?"

Frances also eyed her curiously. Clare shook her head, heat crawling up her neck. One more tidbit of his life Marcus hadn't shared with her.

Struggling against the hurt, she averted her eyes . . . and collided with Marcus's piercing look. His brow furrowed beneath the white bandage, the muscle at his jaw flexing. Was he upset at her being here . . . or was he trying to remember?

Her pulse quickened at this last. Yet a moment later he ejected a breath and turned away. The blade in her heart gave a hard twist as Natalya reached for him.

"We're here."

Clare turned at Frances's announcement just as the bus rolled onto an orange brick drive and passed beneath a two-story gatehouse bordered by a hedgerow of laurel. Along either side of the cobbled drive stood a long row of majestic plane trees leading up to the house . . .

Clare's mouth opened as she stared. *Not a house.*

Montefalco was a castle. Standing three stories high, the vastness of dark-gray stone supported numerous wide chimneys and a cluster of sculpted spires high above the arched entrance. Along the front, tall bay windows stretched outward in relief, ending in a red-capped tower at the east wing.

Clare couldn't tear her eyes away from the Gothic grandeur and structure that dominated the landscape. And this was where Marcus grew up?

Beyond the plane trees to her right, the grounds were immense. She marveled at the well-trimmed lawns spanning out to a backdrop of forests—oak and birch and more plane trees. Clare also spied the glint of water—a creek running back through the woods.

On the opposite side of the drive, a grove of broad-leafed trees—an orchard?—stood in the distance, and behind the grove more woodlands that seemed to go on forever.

As the bus drew up to the wide rounded portico at the castle entrance, she turned to Marcus, who stared straight ahead at his home. How was it that this man with his wealth and lands and knighthood had ever given her a second glance?

Their first meeting had been in a barn on Jack's estate in Kent last year, she in overalls, her hair and clothing littered with straw, her blistered hands wiping at her sweaty brow. Marcus for his part had made such a grand entrance, all spit and polish, and he'd singled her out among her co-workers.

A nostalgic smile edged her lips. He'd been the perfect gentleman, though his efforts to impress her that day had come to naught. Clare had tasted the cruelty of the aristocracy with Elliot Lange and his family, and she wanted nothing to do with Sir Marcus Weatherford, Esquire. *But you did surrender your heart,*

Clare, and when he rescued Daisy, you thought the sun and moon rose on him.

A small sound escaped her. She'd thought he felt just as she did.

Reaching to take Daisy from Ruthie's arms, Clare held her baby close. "I will stay here for you, my little Daisy Do," she whispered into the soft curls before kissing her. *Eat my pride if I must and do whatever is necessary to keep you with me.*

Pressing her cheek against Daisy's silken hair, she found Marcus watching them once more, his eyes traveling over her face and then her baby's. *What are you thinking, Marcus? You must help us! Daisy and I have less than two weeks.*

"There's Mother and Grandfather!"

Clare looked up to see Frances waving through the windscreen at a tall elderly gentleman and striking dark-haired woman as both awaited their arrival on the portico. Behind them at the set of double doors stood two men in livery—a tall, older butler and a stocky middle-aged footman manning a wheelchair more extravagant than the one the hospital had provided.

"Goodness!" cried Marcus's mother once they'd tumbled out of the bus and made their way onto the porch. Mrs. Weatherford was statelier in looks than her daughter, yet her light-brown eyes mirrored those of her children as she rushed forward to greet them. Stylishly dressed in a silvery silk skirt and matching belted blouse, her fair complexion revealed the faint lines of age, while gray strands threaded through her pompadour of soft brown hair.

The footman had been quick to retrieve Marcus in the new wheelchair, and as he brought him onto the porch, Mrs. Weatherford turned her full attention to her son. "My darling boy." Her voice broke as she leaned to place a hand against his cheek. "How do you feel?"

Marcus stared up at her for a long moment, then looked away and shrugged.

Clare noted his hands gripped the arms of the wheelchair. He must feel disorientated. She'd seen similar behavior in the soldiers arriving back from France. Even after they were given a clean bed, a hot meal, and warm blankets, they clung to their fear and confusion.

Marcus turned to seek out Natalya, who came forward and extended a gloved hand to his mother. Clare's chest tightened as once again the ballerina introduced herself as his fiancée.

"Oh my!" Mrs. Weatherford pressed a hand to her cheek, tears welling in her eyes. "You and Marcus are to be wed?"

She looked again at her son, this time with a mix of sorrow and happiness. "How very wonderful."

"Let me continue the introductions," Jack said briskly. "Mrs. Danner, of course, and her daughter, Daisy. And the child's nanny, Miss Ruthie Simmons." He smiled. "I thought to surprise you and bring along Clare as Marcus's private nurse. She oversees the orderly staff at the hospital in London where she works, so our patient will be in good hands."

Clare's stomach did somersaults as she nodded at Mrs. Weatherford. The statuesque woman smiled with a look of polite curiosity, much like her daughter on the bus. "Welcome, Mrs. Danner. And thank you for coming all this way to look after my son."

"Ma'am." Clare smiled tightly. "I assure you that he will receive the best of care."

"See that he does, Mrs. Danner." Sir Geoffrey Weatherford came forward. He was nearly as tall as Marcus, his lanky frame encased in a well-tailored brown suit that contrasted sharply with his snowy-white head and mustache. Thick brows of the same color lifted above the pair of wire-rimmed glasses on his prominent nose, while his amber eyes pierced her.

"Grandfather, please." Frances moved to Clare's side and frowned at her grandfather. "Do not frighten Mrs. Danner on her first day here."

But Clare had already drawn her shoulders back to face Sir Geoffrey squarely, though his frown and not-so-subtle dictate rattled her confidence. "You have my word, sir." Did he doubt her capabilities? She hesitated. Or had Marcus told him about her past?

Clare went still as realization struck. *Mrs. Danner.* None of them knew who she was. Certainly not Frances or Mrs. Weatherford. And having clearly interpreted Sir Geoffrey's dubious expression, he'd not known of her existence, either.

Marcus never told them.

Humiliation flooded her, and she raised her chin. She'd worried about being pitied by his family, but this . . . this felt so much worse. Had Marcus been too embarrassed to tell them about her? It would explain why he'd never brought her here.

Eyes burning, she continued to lock gazes with his grandfather. But then a glint entered the amber pools, and he flashed a smile—or was he baring his teeth at her?

Daisy broke the spell with her mewling sounds. Relieved, Clare turned to her sleepy-eyed daughter, who reached for her while Ruthie held onto the small squirming body. "Mama . . . home now!" she whimpered.

"Oh, you poor child!" Mrs. Weatherford's eyes held concern. "Mrs. Danner, I'm certain your daughter must be tired and hungry. Why don't we all go inside and get everyone settled? I'll have Cook prepare something for Daisy."

"Thank you, Mrs. Weatherford." Clare offered a grateful smile as some of the tension eased from her. Marcus's mother seemed kind enough, and Daisy needed to be fed and settled in somewhere.

"Shall we?" Frances indicated the large entrance into the manse. Jack took over pushing the wheelchair while the rest of them trooped inside.

Clare startled at the elegant main hall, which was as impressive as the castle's exterior. A line of uniformed staff stood waiting for them in the foyer, and the butler entered in last to take his place beside a matronly woman Clare guessed to be the head housekeeper.

"Welcome to our home," Mrs. Weatherford said. The staff bowed or curtsied in unison. She nodded toward the butler and matronly woman. "You will find Yates and Mrs. Trask are available day or night should you require anything during your stay with us. And Hanson is outside with our driver Vickers, taking care of your luggage, and will see it reaches your rooms."

Two maids stepped forward as Frances and Natalya began shedding their coats and gloves. Frances peeled out of her stylish linen coat to reveal a dirt-smudged yellow apron beneath, tied at her waist. She looked up then, and at Clare's surprise she glanced down again, her cheeks flaming as she quickly removed the apron and wadded the cloth in her hands.

Fortunately, her mother was too busy delegating servants to notice.

When Mrs. Weatherford faced them again, she said, "I'm afraid we've surrendered our west wing drawing room to the army and nursing staff. However, the Magnolia room is cozy enough, and we shall have our tea there in an hour." She looked to Natalya. "Mrs. Bryce, as you've brought no maid, Ellen will attend you during your stay and show you to your room."

"Thank you, Mrs. Weatherford." Natalya seemed delighted as the capped maid who had taken her coat and purse curtsied again and indicated she should follow her upstairs.

Clare eyed Marcus watching Natalya's ascent, his fingernails digging into the wooden arms of the chair. She could almost sense the shudders coursing through him.

Apparently so could Sir Geoffrey. "Let's get you settled, Grandson," he said gruffly and led the way as Jack pushed Marcus's wheelchair down a long hall to the right.

The staff had begun to disband when Mrs. Weatherford turned to her daughter—or rather the dirty apron in her hands if her sour expression were any indication.

"Frances, please escort Mrs. Danner to her special quarters. I'll have Janet take Miss Simmons and Daisy up to the nursery." She glanced at Clare. "If that meets with your approval, Mrs. Danner?"

"Yes . . . thank you." Clare nodded to Ruthie to take Daisy and follow the other capped maid upstairs.

Mrs. Weatherford departed next, likely to make the food and tea arrangements, leaving Clare alone with Marcus's sister.

"If you'll come with me, Mrs. Danner?" Frances smiled. "I confess your quarters are a bit unconventional, but given the circumstances, I hope you'll find them suitable enough."

Unconventional quarters? Clare's thoughts raced as she nodded, only half aware of Frances's uneven gait as they traveled down the same long hall the men had taken.

Where did this family intend for her to sleep?

13

"Will this suit you, Mrs. Danner?"

Clare's eyes widened as Frances led her into a spacious room, as large as her entire flat in St. Giles. The walls above the white wainscoting were in shades of bluest sky, rising high toward the vaulted ceiling and its crystal chandelier, while the opened floral draperies revealed two large-paned windows facing south.

A gold velvet couch sat beneath the windows and beside it a cherrywood table. Across the room stood a four-poster bed covered in gold satin, with pillows complementing the couch.

Clare smiled. "I think this will do nicely."

"Thank goodness!" Frances released a sigh. "You're certain you do not mind the clutter? Mother's always adding more artwork and her other collectibles." She indicated a table near the bed that held a small Greek statue and a large lavender vase of dried flowers. "There's also her sewing cabinet. It won't be in your way?"

Clare glanced across the room to the cabinet wedged in between the fireplace and a narrow bookcase. Above the furniture, several large oil paintings hung along the wall. An armoire stood tucked into the farthest corner—which like the bed had been recruited for her personal use from another part of the house—and a washstand and mirror.

"I find nothing wrong with this room, Miss Weatherford. I'll do well staying here."

She admired the large windows once more before turning to Marcus's sister, who stood a few inches shorter than herself. "The bed looks comfortable enough, and I love having so much light. It makes any room cheery."

"You've convinced me." Frances smiled. "When Lord Walenford telephoned yesterday with the news my brother was coming home with a live-in nurse, we had to sort things rather quickly. Mother insisted on giving you her sitting room." She gestured to the elegantly appointed space. "This way you'll be close enough to Marcus to care for him should he need anything."

"His quarters are nearby?" She and Frances had taken the same route down the hall.

"Yes, Mother decided he should remain on the main floor for now, so Grandfather has donated his study. Marcus is being settled there as we speak." She nodded toward the bookcase. "Behind the books is a passageway that connects the two rooms."

"Really?" Clare walked toward the books. "Where is it?"

Frances joined her and reached for the center shelf, removing a copy of *Jane Eyre*. Behind the novel was a small brass lever anchored to the back of the shelf. "Just press it down like this."

She demonstrated, and as the *click* of a latch sounded, the bookcase began swinging freely on its hinges.

"How clever." Clare watched her pull back the bookcase, revealing a hidden door.

Frances took a key from the ledge of wainscoting beside her. "We usually leave this door unlocked. However, you're welcome to secure it whenever you like."

She offered the key to Clare. "If for some reason you must get to Marcus quickly, simply open this door and travel the hallway to the study door at the other end. It's just a few yards."

Fascinated, Clare opened the door to peer into the gloomy interior. "Is there a lock on the study door?"

"Yes, but Grandfather plans to leave it unlocked so you'll have no trouble getting in."

Clare closed the door and turned. "Did your family install this secret passageway?"

"Actually, it was one of our ancestors." Frances grinned as she replaced the bookcase. "Hundreds of years ago, when King Henry the Eighth closed the monasteries in England, he gifted this estate to one of his favored nobles, Lord Paget, whose family renovated the abbey from the ground floor all the way up to the top of the spires you saw as we arrived. This secret passage is one of two that we know about, and both are here in the east wing." Her brown eyes sparkled. "I know where that door is, of course."

"You like a bit of intrigue, Miss Weatherford?"

"Oh, yes! I've read Arthur Conan Doyle's Sherlock Holmes series, and nearly all the Violet Strange mysteries by Anna Katharine Green. I enjoy observing people when I get the chance. It's interesting to see what they do."

"You sound like my co-worker at the hospital," Clare said. "Sally Forbes loves watching people. She makes up very clever stories about them."

"I should like to meet her. Is she a writer?"

"I don't know, but she could be. She has the imagination for it." Again Clare glanced toward the bookcase concealing the hidden door. "Where is the other secret passage?"

"So, you enjoy a bit of intrigue yourself?"

Clare chuckled. "I admit, you've captured my interest." She hadn't known any secret passageways at the Randleton estate when she'd worked there.

"The other passageway lies back in the grand hall where we entered the house," Frances said. "It opens onto a set of stairs leading down into the cellarium, used by the monks to make and store their honey wine." Her expression softened. "Years ago, when I was very young, Marcus would carry me down those steps.

The cellarium has a warren of cubbyholes, and we thought them used for storing bottles and kegs. We each found our own hiding place to put our 'treasure box,' and we didn't tell the other where it was hidden."

Her mouth curved upward. "Thinking back on it, I'm certain my brother did all that silliness for my sake." Her eyes shone gold. "As we are ten years apart, I came to realize later that Marcus had been much too old for those sorts of games."

Clare smiled at Frances's wistful recollection while inside she battled a new warmth settling over her bruised heart. Marcus had betrayed her with Natalya, and he'd kept her and Daisy hidden from this lovely woman and her family. Yet she could well imagine how he must have enthralled his younger sister with such a grand scheme as hide-and-seek. He'd been so good at playing games with Daisy.

"It must have been love that prompted him," she said, her voice thick.

"I think you're right." Frances's expression darkened. "Will my brother get better, Mrs. Danner? Will he remember . . . everyone?"

Frances was just a year younger than herself, yet she seemed almost childlike in her fear. Clare's instinct to comfort her warred with her own anguish. What could she tell her?

"I have hope for his full recovery," she said, placing a hand on her shoulder. "And I promise you, I *will* do all I possibly can to help him."

Frances nodded, her eyes glistening. Clare gave her shoulder a gentle squeeze. "Shall we pray together for your brother?"

"Yes, of course. It says in Matthew's Gospel, 'If two of you on earth agree about anything you ask for—'"

Clare finished, "'. . . it will be done for you by my Father in heaven.'" Smiling, they bent their heads together, and she offered up a heartfelt prayer for Marcus's healing. She added silently, *Please, Lord, for Daisy and me, let it happen soon.*

Afterward she glanced at the clock. "I should look in on my

daughter and Ruthie. Where will I find the nursery? I think this place must be half the size of London."

"It can be overwhelming," Frances agreed. "I'll take you upstairs myself. The maids gave the room a thorough cleaning just this morning and it looks grand."

Clare's throat tightened and she nodded. The Weatherfords' generosity toward her and her daughter humbled her. If only she'd been given the chance to meet them before. "You're very kind, Miss Weatherford."

Frances's cheeks turned pink as she gave Clare a shy look. "Would it be improper, Mrs. Danner, if I ask you to call me Fannie? Since we've become acquainted *and* we've prayed together, I think 'Miss Weatherford' sounds awfully stuffy, don't you?"

Fannie. Not the formal Frances she'd offered to Natalya. Clare's heart kindled with the same stirrings of moments ago, her anxiety fading. Meeting with Fannie's mother and grandfather and then being ushered into this lavish castle as if royalty had made her feel like an impostor, that same turnip among the roses who attended Grace's party weeks ago.

She eyed Fannie with new affection. "I'll do it on one condition," she said soberly, hiding a smile.

Fannie's forehead wrinkled. "Yes?"

"You must call *me* Clare." She grinned. "'Mrs. Danner' seems stuffy to me, too."

Fannie's eyes widened before she burst into laughter. "I think we shall get on well together, Clare." Merriment lit her expression and she reached out to her. "Come, let's go find your daughter."

Taking the hand offered to her, Clare glimpsed the dirt beneath Fannie's fingernails. A smile touched her lips. *Salt of the earth.* "Lead the way," she said softly.

"Well, old boy, what do you think? I daresay the bed will fit you, and you've enough reading material for the next six months."

Marcus sat on the coverlet, his quaking finally subsided. Too many faces in the hall staring at him, and Natalya . . .

She'd left him.

"Marcus?"

He stared into the face of the blond man with the scars. *Jack.* The man who said he was his friend and had helped him with the wheelchair during their trip from London.

Marcus leaned forward as Jack assisted him out of his coat and collar. Afterward he loosened the buttons on his shirt, then knelt on the floor and eased off his shoes.

"Do you remember this place?" Jack asked him.

Marcus peered across the expanse of thick Aubusson rug to the opposite side of the room, where floor-to-ceiling bookcases stuffed with newspapers and leather-bound books spanned over half the paneled wall. Adjacent to the books, an oak desk had been shoved into a corner beside a large potted plant, making space for a washstand and the highboy dresser he was to use during his stay.

"Comfortable now, Son?"

He turned at the voice he remembered as Grandfather's. The sherry-colored eyes were deeply set into a face now lined with age. Marcus had recognized his grandfather when they arrived, though he seemed to have more wrinkles than before.

Once Jack had removed his shoes, Marcus flexed his stockinged feet, then shed his shirt, tossing it toward the end of the bed. The suit had been unbearably hot on the train, so he was glad for the opened window as the breeze wafting into the room cooled his skin.

"Study is fine," he said in a gravelly tone. He cleared his throat. "Thank you."

"You're welcome." When his grandfather and Jack exchanged a look, Marcus tensed. He stared down at his undershirt. Had he done something improper?

His pulse slowed when Grandfather smiled broadly. "I'm glad you remember what room you're in, Marcus. A good sign. Perhaps the rest of this place and everyone in it will look familiar in time."

Marcus thinned his lips. *Perhaps.* He'd entered the house only minutes ago to face too many strangers. Except for Yates, their tall, skinny bow-legged butler. And Hanson and Vickers outside, who had aided in getting him out of the bus and into his wheelchair. Though both men seemed older than he remembered.

Even the house looked different. The furniture in the grand hall had changed, the colors not what they'd been before. *Green, not gold.* He remembered helping Hanson to haul in Mother's new credenza, which was now absent. *"Yer a strapping lad, ye are, sir, an' I'm grateful for yer help . . ."*

He'd been a boy. How long ago was that?

Mother's hair had streaks of gray in it now, and her face revealed new creases—sorrows, worries, and maybe laughter he might never recall. *Not since Father's death.* That wound seemed forever branded on his mind and he was grateful for it; the ache in his chest kept the memory fresh and one he could cling to.

Fannie had changed the most. In his mind, Marcus recalled the baby sister he'd once held in his arms and how she'd managed through years of struggle. His weekends home from Harrow and seeing the young girl who liked playing in the dirt. But after that . . .

Blackness.

He swallowed, his heart thumping rapidly.

"Would you like to rest awhile before tea, Son? Cook's preparing a light meal. I'm certain you and Jack and the ladies are hungry after your journey."

Marcus had no appetite. Still, he gazed at his grandfather and then at Jack. "Are you hungry, Jack?"

"I can always eat, Marcus." Jack leaned in, the blue eyes spearing him. "Do you remember our university days when we'd wager two gold sovereigns on Fridays at the Blue Boar pub near Oxford? Whichever of us ate more platefuls of bangers and mash won the money."

He smiled and straightened. "And that was usually me."

"Bangers?" Marcus blinked, confused.

"Sausages, old boy. They're called bangers now because of the war. With meat rationed, the sausage casings have more water than beef so they tend to explode in the frypan." He tipped his head. "Do you recall our wagers?"

War? Marcus knitted his brows as he struggled through the murky haze of his memory. *Sausages. Potatoes.* An image—*Mother's patterned china on the white linen table, his belly rumbling as he cut into the sausage, the meat and soft mashed potatoes swimming in dark gravy beneath his knife . . .*

He looked at Jack, his head beginning to throb. "Sorry, no."

"That's all right." Jack stepped back. "Give it time."

"We'll leave you to rest now, Son. You have an hour until tea, when Jack will return to take you to the Magnolia room." Grandfather crossed to the window and partially closed the heavy drapes, leaving the room in cool shadow. Returning, he laid a gnarled hand on Marcus's shoulder. "All will be well. Just be patient with yourself."

As he and Jack made to leave, Marcus dug his fingers into the bed coverlet. He didn't want to be alone with the dark void of his thoughts. "Where is Natalya? Why isn't she here?"

"She's likely upstairs in her room." Grandfather turned, eyeing him steadily. "She will be coming down for tea, so you will see her soon enough."

Marcus wet his lips, scanning the cavernous room. "She could stay here with me. You could move the table and put a bed over there for her."

He released the coverlet to point toward the corner opposite the oak desk. A chessboard and set of carved soapstone pieces rested atop a small table surrounded by two padded chairs.

"Marcus, it would be most improper." His grandfather frowned. "Your nurse, Mrs. Danner, is in the room next door. She will check on you and help you with whatever you need."

Mrs. Danner. The woman with midnight hair. *"Please, Marcus, they want to take her! Help me . . ."* Daisy. The blond little girl on the train with eyes like polished slate, darker than her mother's.

All at once, the urgency he felt at the hospital returned, his need to remember, to save the child. Marcus ground his teeth. He could remember nothing. "I do not *know* Mrs. Danner." He glared at his grandfather. "I want Natalya here. Now."

"Marcus, you'll be all right." Jack retraced his steps to the bed. "I told you that Clare works at a hospital in London and she's here to help you. She *will* take care of you, I promise." He offered a smile. "Natalya will be at tea, and if you like, afterward you two can spend the rest of the afternoon together. How would that be?"

"Not safe," Marcus growled.

"Son, she *is* safe, never fear," his grandfather said.

But I'm not safe. "I . . . I need Natalya." His voice cracked.

"That's enough, Marcus." Grandfather stood with hands on hips beneath the suit coat. "You *will* see her in an hour. Is that clear?"

Marcus's pulse jumped, and he again fisted the coverlet. *"Never argue with Grandfather, Fannie. His word is law . . ."* He tried to steady his breathing, staring at the man who helped to raise him. "Yes, Grandfather."

"Now rest up." His grandfather's expression gentled. "You're exhausted."

He exited the room while Jack held back, his face troubled. "You'll manage, old boy?"

"I'll be fine." He forced the words past the bile in his throat.

"Capital." Jack's smile was back. "Then I'll see you in a tick."

Marcus's gut wrenched as the thick oak door to the study closed on Jack. Every muscle tense, he lay down on the bed, the back of his head throbbing. He turned onto his right side to try to ease the pain and stared out at the dim room. The light from a small lamp on the desk helped to illuminate the space.

He focused his attention on the bookshelves and not his fear, vaguely recalling the leather tomes. Could he read them all now and learn again what he'd forgotten?

His eyes drifted toward the chess set on the table. He *knew* how to play the game. *"Your turn, Father, but I'm taking your queen in the next move . . ."*

Father. The exquisite ache of memory pierced him. He'd been just a boy when Father taught him the game of chess, and he quickly learned the strategy of winning. As he excelled in recognizing the swiftest moves to achieve a decisive checkmate, he began to best his father, and then his grandfather.

He swallowed, his mouth parched. How long ago had he played chess with Grandfather? Months? Years? *How far back have you forgotten?*

Forcing his gaze from the board and hand-carved pieces, he noted the patterns in the rug, which also looked familiar. He spotted his valise beside the bed and reached for the bag, sitting up again so he could inspect the contents.

The pungent smell of brine filled his nostrils as he opened the case on his lap. Natalya had carried his valise onto the ship and then brought it with him to Cottage Hospital. He rummaged through it: undershirts, socks, a clean waistcoat, toiletries, and an unfamiliar felt cap. He removed the cap. The brim was stiff, the felt material rough and darkened with stains. It reeked of sweat and a foul metallic stench . . .

A chill rippled beneath his skin. It had the odor of fear, or perhaps the felt had become wet. He closely examined the dark stains. *Blood.*

Gingerly, he reached to trace the bandage along his left temple and scalp, then carefully probed the lump at the back of his head.

He must have worn the cap when he'd had the accident. But why wear such a thing?

Natalya had asked him over and over if he recalled where he was or what had happened to him, but he couldn't tell her. She'd finally explained they were overseas, but not *where*. Marcus vaguely recalled men's voices when he'd been carried onto the ship. British. And . . . Russian? The hat was made of a rough felt . . . like a peasant's clothing.

He scanned the room with its rich furnishings, the expensive rug, and imagined Natalya, dressed in her fine green silk on the train. *Where and why had he worn this cap?*

Closing his eyes, he again saw flashes of the ship, the rough sea, and Natalya . . . unwell. Her face pale and dark circles beneath her eyes. Yet she'd stayed by his side in the cabin.

Before that he could see the hospital and smell carbolic mingling with the candied scent of her perfume. Her soft hand in his while he clung to her, his lifeline, and her promise to stay with him always. And before that . . .

Blackness.

He opened his eyes and fisted the cap. "You must . . . remember," he whispered, then tossed the valise onto the floor where it landed with a thud. A new wave of exhaustion had settled over him, and he lay down again, this time on his side. He tucked the cap under the mattress. He didn't want them taking it away from him, not until he could figure things out.

Closing his eyes, he willed the darkness to stay away and let him sleep. Yet the silence preyed on him, but for the ticking clock on the wall. He was alone in this room, in a house he only partially remembered. Natalya was gone, and he wasn't safe . . .

His racing heart competed with his throbbing head as he covered his eyes with a pillow to shut out the terror. *God, if you are there, please help me!*

14

The faint, low noise reached her ears.

Holding a lock of her hair, Clare paused in front of the washstand mirror as she readied herself for tea. She listened a moment but heard only the soft screech of a branch outside brushing against the window.

"Your imagination at work," she muttered, pinning the loose dark strands back into place. She'd been relieved to find her two-year-old upstairs crowing with delight as she rode back and forth on an old wooden rocking "hosey" in the nursery, showing off for the wide-eyed, ever-watchful Ruthie.

Smiling, Clare inserted the last pin. The innocence of childhood. She prayed her daughter would savor these moments. Before long, Daisy would become a grown woman facing the challenges of adulthood—like meeting with Marcus's family for tea in the Magnolia room.

She hesitated before dabbing on a bit of her eau de toilette, surrounding herself in the scent of honeysuckle. Sir Geoffrey's fierce look on the porch earlier still unsettled her. Why such censure? He obviously didn't know her. Did he disapprove of her child?

At least she and Fannie had formed what promised to be a bond of friendship. Could she be assured of doing the same with

Fannie's mother and grandfather? What should she say to them if they asked about Daisy or found out she knew Marcus? What if they asked about the fictitious Mr. Danner!

She grimaced at her reflection as she straightened her necklace, centering the daisy pendant at her opened collar, then reached for the single pearl hair comb.

Clare still hated the lie. After all, it was lies that had landed her in trouble in the first place, when Elliot Lange once filled her head with sweet nonsense. Featherheaded as she was, she'd believed him and conjured dreams of a life that would never come true . . .

"Ahhh!"

Dropping the comb in the washbasin, she turned to the bookcase. *Marcus?*

Quickly she strode across the room, and after removing *Jane Eyre* from the shelf, she turned the hidden lever inside. The latch clicked, and soon she was swinging the bookcase back to reveal the door to the hidden passageway. As she opened it, sunlight from her room streamed into the darkened hall, revealing the door at the other end.

"Ahhh . . . no!"

Clare rushed through the small space and tried the knob to the study door.

Locked.

She muttered under her breath, digging into her skirt pocket for the key. Soon she had the door open. Thankfully no furniture blocked her way as she stormed into the study.

Marcus lay on his back in bed, the rumpled coverlet twisted beneath him. He thrashed about, tossing his bandaged head back and forth against the pillow.

Clare approached carefully, keeping her distance. He was obviously in the throes of a violent nightmare. Sweat soaked his undershirt as well as the gauze above his brow, and when he moaned again, the agonized sound pricked at her heart. His face was the color of chalk, and beneath the dark mustache he bared his white teeth.

Many times she'd witnessed the nightmares that accompanied her patients suffering from "shell shock." The nervous phenomenon affected many of the wounded returning from France. Having learned the hard way, getting a good cuff to her ear, she never repeated the mistake of touching a man during the sleeping hallucinations the illness brought on.

A strategy she sometimes used at the hospital was needed here. Casting a glance toward the half-closed drapes, she went to the windows and threw back the heavy fabric, allowing light to flood the study. "Marcus, wake up!"

He lay still for several seconds, his lungs pumping air while his muscled arms and shoulders tensed. He twitched once or twice as though trying to flee something awful in his dream.

Clare slowly approached the bed. "Marcus, I need you to open your eyes."

Despite her soft appeal, the tendons in his neck and limbs continued to bulge. She looked at his hands fisted against the bed. She'd seen them clenched on the train and anchored in a deathly grip to the wheelchair when he'd faced his family.

The balled-up fists meant fear. Wherever his mind had taken him, he was terrified.

She risked leaning close to his ear and whispered soothing words. "You're safe, Marcus. I'm here now, and you're safe with me."

It was a moment before the knots in his neck eased, though his breathing remained fast. He turned slightly, his thick dark lashes flickering until he was looking up at her.

"You are safe," she repeated gently and reached to lay the back of her hand against his cheek, marking his temperature.

He flinched at her touch, before his eyes focused on her. "Who . . . are you?"

"Clare," she said softly, and raw anguish flooded her when he continued to stare, uncomprehending. "Mrs. Danner . . . your nurse. We were on the train together." *Oh, Marcus, why can't you remember me?*

He raised a hand, shielding his eyes against the light. "Where am I?"

"You're home with your family in Hampshire."

He dropped the hand, his heavy-lidded eyes searching her face. "Eyes like . . . storm," he muttered, before his nostrils lifted slightly. "Honeysuckle."

Clare's heart thumped. "Yes."

"Where's Natalya?"

"She's probably getting ready for tea." She reached to touch him again, forcing her mind to the task of nursing. She inspected the gauze. "We'll need to change this bandage before you go anywhere. I'll be right back."

Clare felt his eyes on her as she slipped through the secret door, which from this vantage point was camouflaged rather well using a sizable map of Great Britain. Along with a recessed doorknob, the opening could easily be mistaken for part of the wall.

She returned with her medical bag in hand and went to his bedside. "Can you sit up?"

He started to rise, and she helped lift him into a sitting position on the bed. "This won't take long."

"You have experience?"

Clare paused at the question. Of course, she must start again with him. "I do. At the hospital where I worked, changing bandages was part of my job."

She placed her bag of hospital supplies on the bed and then carefully started cutting away the soiled gauze.

"You said 'was' part of your job. You're not working there anymore?"

She paused with the scissors. He certainly seemed lucid enough now. "I honestly don't know if I'll have a job when I get back."

His dark eyes studied her. "Why?"

She moistened her lips. How much to tell him? If he didn't recall her earlier pleas at Cottage Hospital, she didn't want to scare him off now on their first day in Hampshire. "Jack asked me to come along. To take care of you."

He tilted his head. "Is Jack your—?"

"No!" she rushed out. "He's a friend. His wife, Grace, and I are best friends."

He grunted. "Where is Mr. Danner?"

"No more questions for now. Let me work." Conscious of his attention on her, she finished cutting away the bandage. Carefully she pried the gauze back from the wound and stifled a gasp at the sight.

A thin furrow of flesh along the left side of his scalp had been sheared away, and a neat row of stitches covered the length of the wound. A sickly feeling invaded her. She'd seen this before—the familiar tear and powder burns. A pistol by the looks of it, for a rifle would have taken off half his face. *Dear Lord, he'd been shot . . .*

She worked to steady her hands as she gently turned his head to inspect the back. A portion of his dark hair had been shaved away to reveal an egg-shaped knot, the wound still oozing blood. Here, too, the flesh had been stitched neatly near the center.

He must have fallen against a sharp object—a rock or maybe a steel edge, or perhaps he was struck with the butt of the pistol? Likely his thrashing around had opened the wound.

"Not too terrible." She forced a smile. *Jack Benningham, you and I are going to have a talk!*

Fishing from the bag a bottle of antiseptic she'd brought from the hospital, Clare began dabbing with a cloth at the stitched areas. His low hiss sounded in her ears. "I know it stings, Marcus. But it will kill any infection so you can heal more quickly."

Once she'd finished wrapping his head with fresh gauze, she went to the washstand and returned with a wet cloth. "Shall I give you a quick wash?"

Frowning, he snatched the cloth from her hands and ran the wet rag over his eyes, nose, and mouth before offering it back to her.

Clare bit back a sigh. It would have to do for now. She then made the mistake of surveying his soiled undershirt, and her willful attention continued beyond the fabric to the bronzed arms and broad shoulders. And his chest . . .

Grabbing the rag, she returned it to the washstand. *You're acting like a novice, Clare. You've seen hundreds of bare chests at the hospital.* Only none of them were Marcus's.

In fact, she'd rarely seen him out of uniform, let alone like this, with power and strength carved into every inch of his exposed flesh. Clare recalled their visit to Margate by the Sea last year, shortly before she and Daisy had come to London. There, he'd worn a bathing costume on the beach that revealed the same corded muscles in his shoulders and chest while the two of them reveled in the sun and salt spray, mere weeks after the air raid nearly took her life.

Marcus had seemed much more relaxed then. Later that afternoon, they'd returned to Jack's estate in Roxwood while he was away and played their first game of chess in his drawing room. Soon afterward, Marcus had found her little girl . . .

"I need a clean undershirt."

Had he read her thoughts? She set the rag against the basin and turned, almost relieved to see his features still sullen.

A dark shadow of whiskers covered his face, and his mustache also needed a trim. "Before you change, let me get the razor, and we'll give you a shave."

"No."

His look turned stubborn, and Clare crossed her arms, having dealt with this kind of mutiny at the hospital. "You'd rather not go and have tea with your family?" She gritted out, "Or Mrs. Bryce?"

Marcus's strong chin jutted out like stone. He was more stubborn than Daisy! She tried a different tack. "What will your mother think, Marcus, if you show up at tea looking like . . . like . . ." She searched her mind for the right word.

"Yes?" His brow arched beneath the edge of the gauze, his mulish expression gone. "Like what, Mrs. Danner?"

Was he taunting her? "Like a wild boar!" she blurted, and heat flooded her face as she realized she'd spoken aloud. *An orderly is supposed to maintain control of her patient.*

A gleam came into his honey-brown eyes. "I'd imagine . . . I've been called worse."

Amusement? Relief battled her pride, bringing with it the familiar longing at her core. "I'll have you know I've shaved a lot of faces at Endell Street Military Hospital and never received a complaint."

"Did they not live to do so?"

A jest! She blinked, her emotions becoming tangled. "Of course they lived!"

Her traitorous heart leapt when a slow smile touched his lips. He pointed to a leather valise on the floor by the bed. "Razor is in there. And the undershirts."

Clare retrieved from the bag a clean shirt for him, along with a small shaving duffel. Removing the razor first, she checked the blade's edge with the pad of her thumb. It seemed sharp enough.

She took up his shaving cup, lathering brush, and soap next, and after whipping up the desired foam at the washstand, she returned to hand him the cup. "This will be your job."

Brush in hand, she proceeded to lather his face while his eyes stayed fastened to her every move. "How long did you work at the hospital?"

She dropped the brush back into the cup and withdrew the razor from her pocket. "Better let me do the talking now." Clare eyed him with a straight face as she opened the blade. "I'm running short on bandages."

When his eyes widened, she smiled sweetly, and it was a moment before the amused glint returned to his eyes. "Fair enough."

"I took the job at the hospital almost a year ago." She began scraping the blade deftly across the right side of his face. "I started out washing bedsheets, blankets, and soiled smocks before I was finally allowed to assist the nurses and orderlies on shift. Then I became an orderly myself." She straightened, pausing with the razor in hand. "And before I arrived here, I was promoted to chief orderly."

"You're not a nurse?"

She bent forward to start shaving the other cheek. "I said no talking." When she caught the light in his eyes, she tried to ignore her fluttering pulse. "I'm not a qualified nurse, but an orderly is just what you need as you're recovering from your injuries. Someone to change your bandage and your bedding, and if necessary, to help you into your wheelchair." She glanced at him, unable to resist. "And even bathe you."

"The deuce you will!"

He reared back from her, and Clare struggled to contain her amusement. His look of shock was comical. "You actually bathe men at this hospital?"

"Of course." She shrugged. "How else are they to get clean?"

When he held his guarded look, she released the grin she'd been holding. "There is a method we use with bathing that provides modesty for both the orderly and the patient. And oftentimes the poor man is unconscious or so injured or ill that he takes little notice of what's going on."

"I am fit enough for the task," he growled. "And if I'm not, I'll call for Hanson."

He remembered the stocky footman. Her spirits buoyed. "Very well. Now, please, can we finish this? I refuse to hurry with skimming a blade across your throat, and your family is expecting you to be on time for tea."

He straightened, sitting very still while she finished scraping the foam from the underside of his jaw. As she stopped to wipe the blade, she caught him staring at the pendant resting at her open collar. "Daisy. Your little girl's name."

A crease had formed above the bridge of his nose, his wide mouth bowed beneath his mustache. Clare watched him, hardly daring to breathe. Was he remembering how she'd come to him at Cottage Hospital? "My daughter, yes. Daisy is two years old."

He looked up from the flower pendant. "Her eyes are darker than yours."

She nodded.

"And her father?" His curious gaze met hers above the striking face still half covered in white foam. "Mr. Danner?"

Clare absently wiped at the already clean blade. Should she tell him the truth . . . that there was no Mr. Danner? The tightness in her chest rose to her throat. Once, she'd thought Marcus loved her, and she'd let that belief claim a whole year of her life.

But his recent tryst with Natalya . . .

Surely that was like a death. "I'm a widow," she whispered.

"I'm sorry."

Her gaze lifted. "Shall we continue?"

He sat motionless as she finished working the blade's edge along his skin, the silence between them strained. Clare had no idea what he thought about her or if he even had thoughts about her.

But he *had* asked about Daisy.

It was a hopeful sign.

"How did you meet my brother?" Fannie asked the question as she sat down beside Clare in one of a matching pair of pink damask chairs and faced those gathered for tea in the Weatherfords' elegant Magnolia room.

Clare noted her new friend now wore a soft green silk skirt and blouse that complemented her dark features—and her fingernails were clean of dirt.

"Was it love at first sight?" Fannie leaned forward. "You must tell me—"

"Frances Marie!"

"Oh, Mother." Fannie rolled her eyes at Mrs. Weatherford, who sat beside Sir Geoffrey on an emerald-and-beige-striped couch near the hearth. "If she's to be my sister, then I hope my asking questions will not bother her."

Clare's stomach knotted as she reached for a steaming cup of tea from the table. All eyes had turned to Natalya, who took her place on the forest-green settee across from the Weatherfords. Marcus sat in his wheelchair beside her.

Natalya seemed amused. "Frances, you are quite right and I applaud you for being curious." Now in a sapphire silk dress and matching jaunty feathered cap, the ballerina leaned back in the settee and held her teacup aloft. "I insist you all dispense with Mrs. Bryce and call me Natalya."

Fannie straightened and smiled triumphantly at her mother before turning a mischievous wink on Clare, who would have smiled back if the knot in her stomach hadn't given a painful twist. Soon she'd be forced to listen while Natalya relayed the sordid details of the treachery Clare had suffered at their hands.

Natalya set her cup in its saucer and reached for Marcus's hand. "In answer to your question, Frances, I first met your brother many months ago in London, after I had fled Russia and the revolution." She turned to smile at him. "Marcus was a good friend to my dear late husband, Walter, and showed me kindness after my arrival here. He introduced me to some of Walter's friends at Whitehall, and that is how I met Lord Walenford. After that . . ."

Natalya raised a brow at Jack, who stood at the hearth beneath an enormous oil painting of white magnolia blossoms. He shifted, looking ill at ease. "Yes . . . we all knew and respected Sir Walter and wanted to ensure his widow was well received and taken care of."

Clare gripped her teacup. Surely Marcus had done more than his part in that regard.

Though she ached at having to listen to Natalya's words, Clare needed to know the truth—all of it.

She drew a deep breath and turned to the ballerina. "When did you and Marcus actually start courting?" She pretended mild interest despite her thundering heart. "I would imagine with the war on, finding time to be together must have been difficult."

"Oh, we managed well enough."

Eyes the color of sable gazed at her knowingly, and Clare looked away, her skin hot.

KATE BRESLIN

A horrible thought pierced her. What if the times she had thought Marcus away with his work . . . he'd been with Natalya? The possibility made her ill.

"Frances, your brother and I did not court for a lengthy period of time. However, we knew we were meant for each other." Natalya had turned to his sister. "So, you were not far from the truth. It may not have been 'love at first sight,' but it was shortly after that Marcus gave me this ring."

Lifting her hand from his, she removed her dainty lace glove to reveal the sizable diamond on her finger. The gem winked in the light from the overhead chandelier, and while Fannie gasped her pleasure, Mrs. Weatherford's eyes rounded in surprise.

Clare eyed the jewel miserably.

"It *is* an impressive stone, yes?" Natalya said, reading their reactions.

"Indeed, like nothing I have ever seen." Mrs. Weatherford glanced at her son, then turned to exchange a look with Fannie's grandfather, whose sudden scowl produced more wrinkles in his face.

"I think it's splendid!" Fannie declared. "Where and how did he propose?" She looked to her brother, and sadness came over her features. "I wish he could tell us in his own words."

Her attention swiveled back to Natalya. "But you will tell us everything, won't you?"

Natalya grinned. "I shall do my best to leave nothing out."

Clare rose abruptly, rattling her teacup as she placed it on the table. "If you'll excuse me, Mrs. Weatherford, I must return to the nursery to check on my daughter."

She kept her eyes on Fannie's mother, not daring to look anywhere else.

"Of course, Mrs. Danner. Daisy is settling in well, I hope."

"Yes, she loves the rocking horse." Clare squeezed out the words, the scab on her heart ripping wide open. She would rather chew glass than have to sit here and relive every degrading moment of that awful day in the park.

143

"Oh, my dear! You haven't eaten." Mrs. Weatherford waved toward the table, where tiered trays of patterned china offered an array of tiny cucumber sandwiches, blackberry scones, and sugar-glazed biscuits.

"I'm . . . really not that hungry." Clare sidled farther away from her chair.

Mrs. Weatherford eyed her kindly. "Well then, I hope you shall join us tonight for dinner. Here at Montefalco, we serve at seven." She paused and glanced at Natalya and Jack. "Unless you are all weary after a long day of preparations and traveling here with my son. In that case, I shall have a maid bring trays to your rooms, if you prefer."

Clare seized on the opportunity. "That would be lovely, Mrs. Weatherford, thank you. I'm a bit done in."

"Of course." Mrs. Weatherford smiled. "I'll arrange it."

Nodding at Fannie, who smiled and winked at her, Clare left the room.

Once she'd made her escape, she hurried into the grand hall and ran up the stairs toward the nursery, fresh anger searing her heart. Why had she let Jack talk her into this scheme . . . so that she could watch another woman claim the man she loved? A man whose absences Clare had endured for days and weeks over the past twelve months as she waited for his return. Like poor Jane with Rochester . . .

Marcus had even missed Daisy's birthday in July, when he explained he must leave for an assignment elsewhere. *Had* he been away because of the war, or had he arranged for some secret tryst with that . . . that seductress, Natalya?

Oh, how she'd wanted to wipe the smile off that woman's face!

The pair had even taken a recent trip together when Marcus was shot and lost his memory. Where had they gone? Had she traveled with him before?

It hurt to breathe, air cutting into her lungs like the razor's edge she'd used to shave Marcus earlier. Clare paused to grip the banister and catch her breath. She should leave this place tonight! She and Daisy . . .

And do what? Surrender to Randleton's demand?

Tears welled against her lashes. She couldn't leave, not when she'd made a promise to her child to do *anything* to keep them together.

Clare drew in several deep breaths until the ache in her chest subsided. Standing at the rail, she gazed toward the next landing before continuing upstairs. *To Daisy.*

Her only salvation in this unrelenting nightmare.

15

A decent morning for a stroll, wouldn't you say?"
Marcus didn't respond as Jack pushed him along the
walkway at the back of the house. The flagstones were new,
as well as the yellow and orange zinnias edging the path. Before it
had been only a border of green shrubbery along a graveled track.

The trees he remembered—the familiar line of oak, pine, poplar, and birch bordering the estate, where he'd once played as a
boy. His shoulders eased at the memory. Scott's *Ivanhoe* had fascinated him at a young age, and Marcus decided to become the
hero bandit Robin Hood, fighting for freedom and for the good
of the innocent in his own Sherwood Forest.

A smile edged his mouth. He'd recruited some of the local village boys to be his merry band of men. They had no Maid Marian
of course, but then they were too engrossed in mock battles with
wooden swords or bows and arrows to think about girls. *But the
years changed the way you thought about them.*

His attention returned to the path ahead, and he stared at the mortared slate near his feet, gray stones blurring past as the wheel-chair moved quickly with Jack's pace.

Her eyes were a similar shade of gray. Marcus knitted his brows. She'd been upset at tea yesterday and he didn't know why, her fair skin like fire as she rose from her chair, her stormy eyes wet with unshed tears.

Had she been worried about her daughter? Is that why she'd left?

After tea, Jack and Natalya had taken him back to his room, where he'd slept fitfully through the night, missing dinner. And this morning, when Hanson brought him a tray, Marcus still had no appetite.

He'd sensed someone in his room last night. Had Mrs. Danner come to check on him?

Marcus realized he wasn't frightened when she was there. His thoughts drifted back to her visit yesterday when he'd suffered another bad dream. Her touch had been soft, her voice soothing his agitation.

Mrs. Danner had even made him smile. His lips curved upward. A wild boar, indeed! She seemed wholly unaffected by him, even teasing him—and oddly, it made him feel more like himself, whoever that was. Not the same anxiousness as when the other nurses in hospital had fretted and hovered over him. Nor did she press him with questions about things he couldn't remember, not like Natalya did.

His grip tightened on the arms of the wheelchair. Natalya's eagerness to help him remember was doubtless because she cared, but trying to force his foggy brain to grasp images and words that scattered like the cattail wisps off the poplar trees only made him wearier and more afraid that he was losing his mind.

Mrs. Danner had merely asked him how he felt.

His nostrils lifted as the breeze brought him a waft of fragrant honeysuckle from the pink and golden-white flowers dominating the east hedgerow. Her scent. Different from the candied perfume Natalya wore . . .

Guilt made him shift against the confining wheelchair. At tea yesterday, he'd been grateful to Natalya when she revealed to him and his family how he came by his injuries—a bad fall in the woods just outside Paris. Though his instincts told him the place they'd been when they boarded the ship to London hadn't felt like Paris.

Natalya also shared how she and Marcus had met and about his giving her the diamond. Marcus recalled none of it but merely sat next to her, holding her hand and watching her. Having no other direction for his thoughts.

He was surprised to learn he'd proposed to her at Russell Square in London, a place Grandfather once took him when Marcus was let out from Harrow for a summer season. Natalya told his family how romantic he'd been with his proposal, going down on one knee and offering her the large ring. Fannie had clapped her hands in delight.

Marcus tried again to imagine it now, but his only memory was gripping Natalya's hand at the hospital like a drowning man to a floating piece of wood. Asking about the ring and then making her promise that she would never leave. Surely the emotions of a man in love?

If only he could remember . . .

"Anything looking familiar to you, old boy?"

He turned his head slightly. "Yes." He owed Jack an answer for carting him around like a wheelbarrow full of sod. "The grounds, and that fountain." He pointed to the water feature at the center of the garden, surrounded by more of the new slate walkway and bordered by copper-colored shrubbery. A trio of white marble angels spewed water from their mouths into the low round pool beneath them.

"And?"

"The climbing roses." Just twenty yards ahead he'd spied his mother's red, pink, and white blooms flourishing along one corner of the wall beside the west wing.

Marcus sat up in his seat as he noted half a dozen wrought-iron tables and chairs that had not been there before. Who were those men seated in their nightclothes, having tea and reading the newspaper in his home?

"What's going on there?"

"Those are a few of the patients," Jack said. "Your family opened up that half of the estate to the army for the rehabilitation of wounded soldiers returning from the front. Shall we venture over?"

"No." Marcus's heart began thumping.

The wheelchair halted, and Jack suddenly came into view beside his chair. "What's wrong? I thought you might like to see the place."

Marcus wet his lips, a frisson of fear chasing down his spine. He didn't want to be with the wounded. He looked at Jack. "Where is Natalya? Is she at the church?"

"Everyone's already back from the village. Natalya wanted to write some letters before lunch."

Yes, Jack had told him that. He tried to quell the panic fraying at the edges of his mind. He didn't want to go to the hospital again. And he didn't know Jack.

Would this man take him back to the house if he asked? "I need to see her," he whispered. "Make sure she's all right." *I need to be all right.*

Jack's dark eyes scrutinized him before he sighed. "Very well."

Marcus eased out a breath as Jack rose. Then he felt his hand on his shoulder. "Are you going to marry her one day, Marcus?"

"Yes." He turned to stare back at the lawns and his Sherwood Forest.

"What do you remember of her?"

Not nearly enough. "She took me to the hospital . . . after I was injured." He looked up, swallowing hard. "Stayed with me."

"And yesterday she told us how you courted her." Jack tipped his head. "What I want to know is, do you love her?"

Marcus furrowed his brow. Did he love Natalya? The question had continually circled his thoughts as he tried to remember back before the accident when she'd said he proposed to her in the park.

Each time his mind slammed against the dark wall.

He did know that he was very fond of her, and she made him feel comfortable. Safe.

He'd also given her the ring. "I will marry her once I am better," he said. *If I am better.*

Jack's blue eyes clouded. "All right, old boy." He returned to manning the wheelchair. "Let's get you back to your fiancée."

How far did Natalya intend to go with this cover of hers?

Returning his friend to the house, Jack mused once more over the detailed reiteration she'd given at yesterday's tea. Telling the Weatherfords much of what he already knew: the proposal in the park, the ring, and his friend whisking her off to Europe.

She'd also fabricated a new cover story—that they'd traveled to Paris and not Russia to visit her family, with Marcus taking a serious fall during a hike just west of the city. Finally, her returning with him to London to remain by his side at the hospital.

He understood that piece of subterfuge was for the benefit of his family and keeping the security C insisted upon. Yet Natalya went so far as to fawn over his friend, giving him affectionate looks and warm smiles and squeezing his hand. Marcus watched her constantly, turning anxious when she wasn't with him and then latching onto her when she was there, as though he feared she might leave him again.

Marcus had also just declared to him they would marry once he recovered. Had he transferred his affections to Natalya Bryce?

It seemed incredulous, but with his friend's inability to remember, and no doubt some amount of shell shock after the incident, Jack could well imagine Marcus forming a new attachment to her. But why did Natalya insist on taking advantage of his friend's vulnerability?

They returned to the house and found her in the hall, placing outgoing letters into the tray on the foyer table. She glanced up in surprise at their approach. "Myshka, why are you back so soon? You have not been away more than twenty minutes."

"He wasn't comfortable outside." Jack refrained from voicing his friend's fear of the rehabilitation center. He narrowed his gaze. "Marcus also wanted to see *you*."

"Ah, how dear you are to me, milyi." She smiled and approached the wheelchair, leaning to kiss his friend on the cheek. "I have written to my friends back in London, giving them our good news now that your family knows of our engagement."

Writing letters announcing their phony engagement? Jack frowned. Why was that even necessary?

Natalya touched Marcus's hand. "It is already warm outside, and I imagine you are uncomfortable wearing that blazer. Would you like to return to your room?"

His friend nodded, and Natalya raised a brow at Jack.

"Of course." He pushed the wheelchair back toward the study, and once inside, helped Marcus to sit on the bed and remove his jacket and vest.

Natalya pulled a chair over from the small table and sat down.

Jack took his time hanging the garments over the wooden clothes valet near the bed. He worried at his friend's increasing involvement with Natalya. Why would she continue to allow Marcus to become so completely dependent on her?

His jaw tightened. Yesterday at tea she seemed to enjoy being the center of attention as she regaled them all with her stories while Clare had clearly been distressed.

"To make matters worse, she was there and heard everything . . ." Clare's words to him and Grace after she'd made her pleas to Marcus at the hospital. Natalya must know the two were once intimate. Did she now stoop to some game of female rivalry at the cost of Marcus's health? Maybe even his life?

Jack intended to find out.

"A word, please?"

Natalya found Lord Walenford waiting for her in Montefalco's grand hall shortly after she left Marcus asleep in his room.

"Of course, my lord." She smiled. Jack Benningham was an attractive man, despite the scars. He also had that commanding presence, born of the aristocracy. "What do you wish to speak to me about?"

"Shall we walk outside so you can view the gardens?"

Though curious about what he had to say, Natalya readily nodded and walked with him toward the rear exit. Since arriving at Montefalco yesterday afternoon, she'd spent time getting her clothes and other sundries settled into her new room, then sitting at the bedside of her poor myshka. There had been no time to fully appreciate the green manicured lawns or the profusion of flowering trees and colorful gardens the castle estate had to offer.

Just outside, she spied a curved bench beside a marble fountain with angels rising out of a clear pool. It seemed the best vantage point to view the lovely flower garden. "Shall we sit here?"

"Of course."

Settling herself on the bench, she was surprised when he remained standing. Her mood dimmed. Not a good sign. "I am listening, my lord."

"I'll get right to the point." He eyed her sharply. "What is this farce you're playing at with my friend?"

"Excuse me, Lord Walenford?" Natalya blinked. Surely he had spoken with their mutual friend in the War Office and knew their circumstances. Why was he so displeased?

His features grew taut as he scanned the gardens. Then he turned to her, leaning in. "Look, we both know Marcus has no recollection of his proposal to you in Russell Square weeks ago, or much of anything else. I'm also aware that you've been instructed to keep your cover. But you're taking things a bit too far, don't you think? First, that yarn you spun out for everyone at tea yesterday, and now mailing out letters about your engagement. Seriously, Natalya?"

She wanted to laugh. Obviously, he had never been onstage.

"Merely props to give the illusion, my lord. In truth, those letters contain instructions to my housekeeper in London and a bank draft to my dressmaker. Trust me, it was all for show."

He didn't seem amused. "And how far do you plan on leading my friend into this romantic illusion you've created? Why didn't you simply tell him when he regained consciousness that you were an acquaintance, or any number of other things, rather than make him believe the two of you are to be married?" He straightened, his mouth bowed. "Clearly, he's become besotted with you, and he has no idea why."

Natalya stiffened, memories of those horrible few days rushing back to her. Anger stirred anew remembering how Marcus lay so very still and helpless, bleeding onto the forest floor.

She offered a tight smile. "If you are expecting an apology for what I have done, my lord, I must disappoint you. I have no regrets."

"What do you mean?"

She folded her hands in her lap, glancing at the large diamond on her finger. "I have merely elaborated on my story with Marcus for his sake alone." She tipped her face to him. "Can you even imagine how he must feel? Unable to recall anyone from his past, save perhaps his family? Not his friend Lord Walenford or your lovely wife or Sir Mansfield Smith-Cumming . . ." Natalya turned toward the fountain, recalling the woman who visited Marcus in London, her pleas for her child coming to naught. "Even Mrs. Danner and her daughter are unfamiliar to him."

"You are aware of Clare and Marcus's relationship?"

The scene from Russell Square flashed in her mind. Marcus's brooding afterward. "Yes, I know all about them, just as I understand what is at stake for her and her daughter right now."

"Yet you don't seem to be helping their situation with this . . . playacting."

At his somber look, Natalya stifled her annoyance. How could he possibly understand what she owed to Marcus? "You should have seen him, my lord. How frightened your friend was when he finally awoke at the hospital in Archangel."

She lowered her voice. "I was there keeping watch over him. Earlier, I had tried searching out our contact to see if he could help, but Reilly had vanished."

"C told me you knew of the rendezvous in Archangel between Marcus and Reilly," he said softly. "What happened after that?"

"I tried going back to our hotel. We had left our luggage behind, and I wanted to get him some things. Marcus would not let me leave his bedside. Your friend is quite strong." Though she smiled, Natalya would never forget the terror she'd seen in Marcus's eyes. "I stayed with him, and when he noticed the ring on my finger, he asked me if we were engaged. It was prudent at the time to say yes, as we were both still carrying false passports."

She sighed. "Honestly, he was already too distraught to be left alone, and I did not have the heart to tell him no."

"Indeed." He grimaced. "You and Marcus could have incurred even more danger if the truth of your assignment had leaked beyond the Bolsheviks you encountered."

Lord Walenford knew? Natalya stared at him before she finally nodded. "Our mutual friend told you, of course."

"He did." His eyes appraised her. "It seems your aim is quite accurate."

Natalya dipped her head. Thank goodness Marcus had not argued with her about bringing along her pistol. She had taken great pleasure in shooting all three of those *nevezhdy!*

She looked up at him. "My lord, to Marcus this is all very real, and as you said, our mutual friend wishes us to keep our cover, at least until the mystery in Perm is resolved." She clasped the ring on her finger. "I will continue to do my part as I see fit. And if you or anyone else say otherwise to him about this, I will deny it."

Seconds passed before his expression softened, much to her relief. "Your loyalty to my friend and our country does you credit," he said.

Natalya smiled. "It is my country, too." Solemnly, she added, "I have not said anything before, but as we left Archangel to go south, Marcus tried to convince me to stay behind. He even asked

if I knew anything about . . . mother and son that might prove
their identity. So that I would not have to go with him. It was to
be a long and dangerous journey."

She leaned forward as memories rushed her: Marcus, throwing
himself in front of her, followed by the blast of the pistol and her
screams, the blood . . .

"He wanted to protect me, my lord. Marcus was willing to
sacrifice his life to save mine. And yet I was to save him instead."
She eyed him fiercely. "Now he needs to know that he can trust
me to stay with him, at least until he regains his memory." She
whispered, "If he regains his memory."

Heat tinged Jack's face. It seemed he'd misread Natalya's actions entirely. "Forgive me," he said. "I thought—"

"You thought what anyone who knows Marcus so intimately
would think." Her gaze warmed. "You are a good friend to him,
Lord Walenford."

"Jack, please." He offered a smile. "I appreciate all that you're
doing for him, Natalya. Let's hope he improves quickly so you
both can finish what you set out to do."

"I have been praying for that very thing."

Jack didn't add MI6's critical need to discover the plan for Lenin's assassination. He checked his pocket watch. "I must leave you.
I need to pen some letters myself and then speak with Sir Geoffrey
before lunch." He started to move away, then turned back to her. "I
realize that until Marcus is himself again, or Reilly can be reached
to resolve things, you must continue to pretend, not only with my
friend but with his family and all here at Montefalco. That cannot
be easy for you. I thank you, for Marcus's sake and for my own."

"My deception is not so difficult. I am a performer, after all."
She grinned and then eyed him through lowered lashes. "And Marcus could be an easy man to love if things were different . . ."

"But he already has someone, Natalya." Jack gave her a pointed look. "So please tread more carefully and do not become overly enthusiastic in your current role."

She rose from her seat. "Thank you for the advice, but I think I can safely say that Mrs. Danner and I will not compete for him once the truth is known."

"Good. Then I'll see you later."

"I look forward to it . . . Jack."

She gave him a mock curtsy, and he chuckled before heading back into the house.

Natalya's intentions seemed altruistic enough. Jack, too, was impressed with her assessment of Marcus and his need to anchor himself.

Certainly, in his friend's current state of mind, Marcus must be feeling cast adrift into murky and unknown waters. Jack's gratitude was short-lived, however, as he battled his conscience. Clare's pain was no charade, and he must keep Natalya's secret while his wife's dearest friend suffered in her perceived loss.

And if his own plan here at Hampshire failed?

He strode through the elegantly appointed hall and jogged upstairs toward his room.

It would mean his friend would never know the truth and Clare might well lose her daughter to Randleton. That the tsarina and her son, the heir to the Romanov throne, might never be found, while the Allies' best chance to get Russia back into the war against Germany would be lost.

Jack reached the second landing, where he looked out at the pair of enormous chandeliers illuminating the room below, like beacons of light shining down from heaven. Reminding him of a time when he'd met Grace and began believing in miracles. "*We live by faith, Jack, not by sight.*"

He continued down the hall toward his room. He would keep that faith, praying for a miracle to heal his friend.

Because any other outcome was simply not an option.

16

MONTEFALCO ESTATE, HAMPSHIRE
SUNDAY, AUGUST 25, 1918—SAME DAY

dinna want to be here, Deering. Take me back to my room."

At the grumbling male voice inside the conservatory, Fannie Weatherford poked her head up over the top of the *Citrus x citrofortunella mitis* she was replanting, her hands grimy with soil and fertilizer mixture. Having to relocate the dwarf Calamondin orange tree, plus two crates of *Hosta ventricosa* that still needed to be settled into the earth, she'd likely miss lunch with her family and their guests. Would Marcus finally show up for the meal?

She tried not to worry over her brother, but he was so pale and a bit alarming seated in that wheelchair with a white bandage wrapped around the top of his head. She did take comfort from knowing she and her new friend Clare Danner, his nurse, had prayed for his swift recovery yesterday after their arrival. And she'd prayed for him again this morning at church.

Fannie was a true believer in miracles.

"Come now, Lieutenant. Ye've not yet been to the conservatory. I figured this place would spark yer interest, given yer background.

Ye'll be right at home here with all these green leaves and vines and such."

Fannie turned, recognizing the voice of Deering. Built like an oak and nearly as tall, she'd spotted him in the conservatory twice before over the past few months, his pressed white tunic and trousers marking him as one of the hospital staff from the west wing.

"You had no right reading my private records, Deering. You're a neb, poking into other people's lives. 'Tis a sorry trait."

"Sticks and stones, Lieutenant," Deering responded good-naturedly. "I'm yer orderly, and my job while yer recovering is to learn all I can about yer interests and see if we can't speed up yer healing."

"Unless you can wave your magician's wand and give me another leg, that's not likely to happen. Now take me back."

Fannie finally rose to her feet to view the man who had spoken. She'd glimpsed that reddish-brown hair before, a week ago when she visited the west wing and assisted Mr. Bauer, their gardener, with fertilizing Mother's rosebushes. The lieutenant had sat off by himself in his wheelchair, his back to her while he'd gazed out at the dahlia garden in full bloom on the north side of the patio.

Her pulse gave a leap now as she took in his full features—the thick tussle of russet hair complementing his brooding green eyes. His sculpted mouth thinned above the strong jaw as he stared toward the cluster of beautiful *Strelitzia reginae* she'd recently transplanted.

His face was dark with freckles, too—like the beautiful bark of a cedar. A rush of heat stole into her cheeks. She hadn't realized before, but he was altogether quite handsome.

He wore a dark robe and pajamas, much like she'd seen him in before, though this time she noted that just one slippered foot rested against the foot pegs.

"Good afternoon," she called softly, moving around the dwarf orange.

The green eyes immediately locked onto her, surprise replacing their glittering anger of moments ago. She drew in a breath at their beauty and smiled. "I'm Miss Weatherford, the curator for the conservatory. Have you come to see the fragrant *Stephanotis floribunda*? They have all bloomed at once, giving us more flowers than we've had in three years."

The lieutenant turned away from her. "I've seen enough jasmine." Impatience laced his words. "Deering, I wish to leave."

"Excuse our boorish manners, Miss Weatherford." Deering frowned at his patient before looking up to smile at her. "I'm Corporal Owen Deering, an orderly here at the rehab hospital, and this young lad in my care is Lieutenant Peter Ainsley."

Lieutenant Ainsley at least had the grace to bob his head in acknowledgment.

"It's nice to meet you both." Instinctively her dirty fingers went into her apron pockets. "I believe I've seen you here before, Mr. Deering, so you probably know that there is a smooth path that winds through the entire conservatory. You are welcome to explore the various plant life on your own if you wish." She eyed the lieutenant hesitantly. "You may also visit anytime, day or night. We always leave the side door near the patio unlocked." Indicating the door in which they'd entered from the west wing patio, she added, "My wish is to maintain this conservatory for the relaxation and enjoyment of all who enter."

"You're very kind, Miss Weatherford."

The lieutenant had returned her look, and Fannie's breath caught once more as she met the dark fern-green eyes, the very color of her favorite *Asplenium scolopendrium*.

Deering cleared his throat. "We'd like to visit and perhaps find some task that would take the lieutenant's mind off things."

"Deering . . ."

The lieutenant's tone held a warning.

What sort of task? Fannie glanced toward the two crates of leafy hostas still to be worked into the soil. Too low to the ground. Then she spied the elongated concrete planter near her dwarf date palm. The soil was good, having lain fallow since last year, and because it was raised, he could easily reach to plant while seated in the wheelchair. "Would you help me with the *Plumbago auriculata*, Lieutenant? I have a few starts that need planting. I'll go and get them now—"

"Do I look like I'm capable of planting shrubs, Miss Weatherford?" Again, his striking features were charged with anger. "Or am I expected to crawl around in the dirt like some . . . some *Microtus agrestis*, digging holes all day?"

Like a field vole? Fannie took a step back. "Of course not, Lieutenant."

"I think we're done here." Deering's mouth curled, crimson tinging his normally jovial face. "Miss Weatherford, my apologies for intruding upon yer work." He scowled at the lieutenant. "It would seem today is not convenient, after all."

He touched a lock of his hair before maneuvering the wheelchair with his patient back toward the exit door. Fannie watched them, the pounding of her heart over the lieutenant's outburst battling her constricted throat. The man clearly imagined that because of a missing limb, his life no longer held meaning.

She'd seen it before, in the patients Grandfather had treated over the course of the war. And though he'd tried his best to patch them up on the outside, using prosthetic arms, legs, and even faces, only God could reach inside a person's soul, showing them their true worth through His love and grace.

Still, to receive His gift, one had to learn to accept oneself. Fannie understood only too well how angry and full of despair Lieutenant Ainsley must be. Hadn't she once stood on the same precipice?

Yet God had given her a guardian angel—someone who believed in her and helped to show her that she did matter, warts and all. Peter Ainsley seemed to be badly in need of that belief.

Perhaps she could help him . . .

"So this is where you hide out, Sir Geoffrey."

Having consulted the butler for directions, Jack entered the large laboratory Marcus's grandfather kept in the west wing. Here, he was closest to the patients recovering in the rehabilitation hospital on the estate.

"Ah, Jack, good to see you found your way without getting lost." Seated on a wooden stool, Sir Geoffrey glanced up from his worktable, screwdriver in hand.

"Thanks to your man Yates." Jack surveyed the spacious room, now littered with arms and legs, hands and feet, even a few partial faces. He'd accompanied Marcus home for a visit a few times over the years, but never had he ventured into this private domain. "I see you're doing a brisk business with prosthetics."

Sir Geoffrey grimaced while he fastened a screw into what resembled a wooden knee joint. "I wish it were otherwise. But the army insists on sending us back these young fellows with missing parts, so I must continue to try to make them whole again as much as I can."

Jack sobered. "Sir, you do Britain a great honor with your work. You're giving a second chance to those who have risked their lives for our country."

Sir Geoffrey grunted. "Pretty speech, Jack." He glanced up and grinned. "Truth is, I enjoy my work. I've always been fascinated with the dexterity and movement of the human body, and it's a challenge for me, finding ways to imitate what God has easily managed on His own in nature."

"Pretty speech or not, your fascination is a blessing to those chaps in the hospital next door." He took up another of the wooden stools beside the worktable. "You and I haven't yet had a chance to talk since we arrived yesterday. How is Mrs. Weatherford holding up?"

"As well as can be expected." Sir Geoffrey tightened another screw into the knee trapped in a pair of metal grips. "Elaine is still a bit stunned over this business, especially seeing her son in his current state. She went to check on him sometime after dinner last evening, but he was asleep. She's grateful that at least he's sitting upright and able to speak and observe his environment." Sir Geoffrey glanced up again. "How are your eyes doing, by the way?"

"I have nearly perfect vision, thank God." He raised a brow. "Why? Did you have a spare set?"

Jack had expected him to laugh, but instead the old man surprised him when he reached for a small black case containing a pair of blue eyes made of glass. "Would you be needing these?" he quipped, his sherry eyes gleaming.

Jack snorted and pushed the case back at him. "Save them for someone else. I happen to be very attached to mine."

Sir Geoffrey chuckled, and Jack grinned before his humor faded, recalling his reason for the visit. "Sir, as I told you on the telephone before we arrived, it's my hope that by being here, Marcus can bridge his past memories of you and the family back to the present and regain what he's lost. He seems to remember you."

Sir Geoffrey nodded, his seamed face now troubled. "He knows me, yes, and he seems to recognize his mother and sister, but I also sense it distresses him. However, he only arrived yesterday. Given more time, I hope his being here will help him to heal completely."

"Time is the real question." Jack made a face. "I'm afraid I must return to London tomorrow, but I plan to come back later in the week to see how my friend is faring. I'd also like to bring my wife's cousin along. Strom is a physician, and he evaluated Marcus in London. I thought to have him come out, check on my friend, and give you and the family an accurate assessment of Marcus's present condition."

"A good plan," Sir Geoffrey said, then released the knee joint from the metal grips. He reached for a steel appendage—an elbow?—before he paused. "What is this fiction with Mrs. Bryce?"

Jack eyed him sharply. The old man obviously understood the situation. "I . . . cannot say, but trust me, she's here to look out for Marcus's best interests."

Sir Geoffrey sighed. "Some secret war business of my grandson's, no doubt. That's what his boss always tells me whenever we meet in town and Marcus is off to God-knows-where." He looked up. "Sometimes I think that boy must have a death wish."

Thinking of his friend's gunshot wound, Jack silently agreed.

"It does in fact involve secret war business, but Marcus is unaware, and any revelation to this 'fiction' would upset him gravely at this early stage. As you've noticed, he clings to Natalya like lint to a dinner jacket."

"What have you told him so far?"

"Only what she has explained to you and the family earlier."

"Probably all that he can cope with right now," Sir Geoffrey agreed. "And you brought Mrs. Danner as well, along with her daughter and nanny. She must be a good nurse."

"Clare will give Marcus the best care, you have my word."

"It doesn't hurt that she's pretty, too." Sir Geoffrey wore the hint of a smile beneath his mustache. "Think she'll be able to rattle my grandson's cage and make him remember?"

"I'm counting on it, sir. There is . . . much at stake."

"I never doubted it, Jack." He set down the artificial elbow he'd been working on. "Though if my grandson cannot recall the past . . ."

"Let's hope that's not the case."

Sir Geoffrey rested his own bony elbows on the worktable, his eyes piercing. "Be that as it may, do you believe it possible for two people to fall in love a second time?"

Jack held his gaze while an image of Grace rose in his mind. Over the past year, they'd shared laughter together and their dreams, their mutual faith and values. Even shouldering each other through sorrow. Would he fall in love with her all over again? "I do believe it," he said with conviction.

"Good." Sir Geoffrey straightened and picked up his screwdriver. "Then I believe things will work out well enough for Marcus, regardless of the outcome."

But perhaps not for Clare if Marcus can't help her. Jack frowned. She had less than a fortnight.

Was it enough time?

17

MONTEFALCO ESTATE, HAMPSHIRE
SUNDAY EVENING, AUGUST 25, 1918—SAME DAY

t seemed her prayers had been answered.

> *Mrs. Danner,*
>
> *Marcus has not eaten since our arrival yesterday, and as his nurse you must ensure he finishes his evening meal. I look forward to receiving a good report.*
>
> *—N. Bryce*

Clare eyed Natalya's note, feeling almost giddy. The maid Nelly, its messenger, now hovered near her bedroom door awaiting a response.

"I already put the tray in 'is room, Mrs. Danner."

Clare grinned at the young maid. "That's fine, Nelly. Thank you."

Once the girl had left, Clare slowly folded the missive. She couldn't believe her good fortune. Two nights in a row she'd managed to dodge what would surely be a disastrous event—formal dining with the Weatherfords.

Her spirits buoyed, she quickly opened the bookcase and entered the passageway.

"Marcus?" Clare knocked lightly, and when he didn't answer, she entered the room and glanced toward the bed. Her patient was sitting in his wheelchair, watching her.

Crossing the rug toward the small table at the far end, she noted the chessboard nudged aside to make room for a tray laden with chicken stew, a cheese tart, teapot and cups, and for dessert, bread pudding drizzled with blackberry compote.

"Are you hungry?" she asked while removing the food from the tray. More silence. She turned to him. "Well, Marcus? Yes or no?"

"No."

Clare drew her brows together. She'd dealt with plenty of Daisy's fussy eating habits and there was always a way. "Would you at least *try* to eat something?"

Ignoring her question, his dark gaze traveled her length. "You look . . . nice."

Disarmed by his compliment, she eyed the blue silk and chiffon folds of her costume—the elegant dress that Grace had insisted she keep. "Thank you," she said softly. "I'd planned to wear this to dinner tonight, so it's good to know I would have passed muster."

"Indeed," he said, his voice low. "I will not keep you from your meal."

"Trust me, it's all right. In fact, if you eat something from the tray, I can stay here and avoid all those awkward dos and don'ts in fine-dining etiquette."

His eyes took on a warm glint. "In that case, I will eat."

"Thank you." She smiled. "Now, shall I fetch you over here, or would you rather come to the table on your own?"

In answer, he gripped the chair's side wheels and began pushing himself forward a few inches, the muscles in his upper arms bulging beneath his shirt as he came up against the thick carpet.

"We'll have the rug removed tomorrow so you can get around

easier." She went to him and helped to push the wheelchair over the thick fibers until he was seated at the table. Quickly she arranged the food and laid out his tableware. "Would you like some help?"

"I think I can manage. A fork and a spoon are not entirely foreign to me."

More of that dry humor? *Oh, how I've missed this!* She slid into the chair beside him, her elbow on the table while she rested her chin in her hand. "Prove it."

He gave her a sharp look before he picked up the napkin. As his unsteady hands worked to unfold the cloth, she fought an urge to assist him. *You're not his mum, Clare. Let him try on his own.*

Once he'd settled the napkin onto his lap, he reached for his spoon and stirred the hot stew. She bit down on her lip as the bowl tipped slightly, his hand resting heavily against its edge. Finally, he raised a serving of the stew and brought it toward his lips . . . before the spoon listed at an angle and a glop of chicken chunks and vegetables landed in his lap.

He breathed a mild oath as he dropped the spoon back into the bowl, then tossed his soiled napkin onto the tray. Next, he took up his fork and plunged the tines into his cheese tart.

"That poor tart did nothing to offend you, I hope?" She lifted a brow at him.

He shot her a wry glance and then managed to spear a chunk of the cheese and bring it to his mouth. Bless him, he only missed by a fraction of an inch before achieving his goal. When he offered her a smug smile, she couldn't help but laugh as she fished the handkerchief from her sleeve and began wiping the cheese from his mustache.

"You're getting better," she said, grinning.

He watched her face, his eyes focused and intent. Once she'd finished cleaning him up, he asked, "Were you here in my room last night?"

"Multiple times, and once with your mother," she replied. "I wanted to make sure you didn't tear your stitches again. And I

came in to check on you a few hours ago, but you were asleep."
She narrowed her eyes. "Or were you not asleep?"

"I . . . thought I was dreaming that you were here."

If only you did dream of me, Marcus. She pursed her lips, then
said, "It wasn't a dream. Any more nightmares?"

"No." She glimpsed a hint of a smile before he added, "Would
you like to share my dinner with me?"

Her pulse sped at his unexpected invitation. Did she dare? Eating with him would make their nurse-patient relationship more
personal, leaving her sore heart even more exposed.

Yet she found herself willing to take that gamble and enjoy his
company. *He has no idea what happened between us in the park
that day.* "All right," she said, reaching for the spoon in the bowl.
She refilled it with the stew. "You go first."

And just like Daisy, Clare zeroed in on his mouth, her awareness of him mounting as she gazed at his lips, remembering how
warm and tender his kisses had been. The lingering smell of coffee
on his breath, which mingled with the spiced scent of his skin . . .

His eyes remained fixed on her as he accepted her offering, and
once he'd closed his mouth around the spoon, she quickly removed
it and again dipped into the bowl.

This time she indulged her own appetite, and when she turned
to him, mouth full, her eyes widened as she swallowed the stew.
"That was delicious, don't you think?"

His eyes gleamed. "Mrs. Connelly can make tree bark taste like
beef Wellington."

He remembered their cook! Hope flared as she hid her shock.
She refilled the spoon with stew and navigated his open mouth.
"So how was it?"

His brows slanted while he chewed. Swallowing, he asked, "How
was what?"

"The tree bark." Her breath hitched in her chest at his sudden, slow smile. *You're playing a dangerous game here, Clare.* She
ignored the little voice. "You remember Mrs. Connelly, do you?"

He seemed startled by the realization before nodding slowly. "She always made me strawberry trifle for my birthday."

"Oh, trifle is a wonderful dessert! What else do you remember about her meals?"

"Pea soup." He ran his tongue across his lips. "She added rosemary, ham, and potatoes, and it was the finest I'd ever tasted." His forehead creased as he seemed to recall more. "Mrs. Connelly also refused to give us dessert if we didn't finish what was on our plates. Fannie went without the sweets more often than not. I learned early on not to be particular about eating my vegetables."

He seemed relaxed as he looked beyond her shoulder. Was he remembering more of the past? She scooped a spoonful of the cheese tart next and brought it to his lips. "I practice that same rule with Daisy," she said. "Speaking of which, you're falling behind, Marcus. I'd hate having to deprive you of your bread pudding."

His grin sent a thrill through her before he accepted the mouthful of cheese tart.

"My mum was a cook at a fine house," she said. "She could create wonders in the kitchen, just like your Mrs. Connelly."

He chewed, his eyes on her.

"She made the best shepherd's pie." Nostalgia swept through her like the soft breezes from the window. "Dad and I would sit at the table in our small kitchen, our mouths watering over the smells coming from the oven. It's a miracle I stayed so slim with Mum cooking all the time."

His expression warmed as he swallowed. "How old were you?"

She gave a shrug. "Seven, I think. Dad was a tenant farmer in Wicklow, and I'd help him in the barn and the fields, which is why I grew so reedy, despite the delicious food."

"Are your parents still alive?"

Her mood dimmed at his question. *Oh, Marcus, I've already shared this with you,* she wanted to tell him. She shook her head. "Dad passed away shortly after we arrived here in Britain. And I was nearly eighteen when Mum died."

"I'm . . . sorry." Compassion deepened the lines in his face, making her ache anew for what they'd once had with each other. "Any brothers or sisters?"

"No. I have Daisy, though. She's my family." But for how long? Clare drew a shaky breath and sought to turn the conversation. "You said Fannie often went without her dessert? She must have been very young."

"Just three or four years old." He now seemed to be studying the tines on his fork.

"Did you never help her out by eating a few of those carrots or peas so she could enjoy some sweets?"

"I might have." He flashed a devilish smile and then reached to stab again at the cheese tart with his fork. This time he managed to reach his mouth without mishap.

He winked at her, and she swallowed against the lump in her throat. She always loved it when he did that.

He reached for the teapot next.

"Please, let me. The tea is quite hot." Taking the pot, she poured him only half a cup of Darjeeling before adding a dash of cream and two lumps of sugar.

Eyeing the half cup, he frowned at her, and she gave him an equally stern look.

A sigh gusted from him as he picked up the cup and saucer, rattling both in his grip as he succeeded with great care in touching the rim of the teacup to his lips. He sipped at the hot brew.

"Do you remember your grandfather?" she asked as she helped him to return the cup and saucer to the table.

He blinked at her. "Yes. But he was much younger the last time I was here."

Her pulse quickened. "When was that?"

"I was attending Harrow School in London, and he took care of Mother and Fannie while I was away."

Clare sat back in her seat. Harrow was the same prestigious school Elliot and his cousin Stephen Lange had once attended. Marcus must have been between thirteen and eighteen years of age when he last recalled seeing his grandfather.

"Where was your father, Marcus?"

"Boer War. He never came back." Picking up the fork again, he glanced at her with eyes full of challenge before turning to attack the bread pudding.

Was his father dead? She studied him while he ate. Marcus had never offered any information other than to say his father had been gone for some time. "Your mother looks quite well, and she's happy to see you."

His broad shoulders lifted. "She kept to her room much of the time after . . ." He paused and looked her in the eye. "Fannie and I spent a lot of time by ourselves. When Grandfather returned from the continent to live with us, it was better. He ate dinner with us and talked to us."

Clare's chest tightened. She imagined two young children rattling around in this colossal mansion with all its rooms and secret passages. They'd been alone, mourning their father while their mother receded into the throes of her own grief. It couldn't have been a very happy childhood for either of them. "I haven't yet spoken with your grandfather, but I hope he approves of my being here."

He smiled. "Trust me, he'll like you."

He scooped up another serving of the bread pudding and this time held it to her lips. When her eyes widened, he said, "You are not keeping up, either."

She gazed at him a moment before parting her lips, much the way he'd done for her earlier. Slipping the pudding into her mouth, he grinned. "I don't mind breaking Mrs. Connelly's rules just a bit for you."

Her heart quickened its pace. "Thank you," she murmured around the mouthful of dessert.

"You have fire," he said, holding the fork while he seemed to consider her. "Grandfather likes that in people. I do too."

He reached again for his teacup and saucer, doing a better job at raising the cup to his mouth and taking a sip. "What do you like?"

You. I like everything about you. "I enjoy cleverness and a sense of humor." She gazed at him through lowered lashes. "A person who cares about others and who adores children and is ready to walk through fire for someone they love." *Someone like me and Daisy.*

"Was your . . . was Mr. Danner like that?"

She didn't answer him right away, her mind too full of the memory of Marcus, tall and strong and cradling her tiny baby girl in his arms after he'd rescued her from the horrible workhouse orphanage. Finally she smiled, her eyes burning. "Oh yes, he was like that, and so much more."

He stared into his cup. "You must miss him terribly."

Marcus, you have no idea. "I do miss him." She glanced toward the chessboard and soapstone pieces on the table. "We often played chess together whenever we had the chance, and he and I were very closely matched."

"You play the game?"

"I do. And you?" *Do you remember how to play chess, Marcus?*

"Father taught me when I was just a boy, maybe nine years old." His tone held a note of pride. "I was quick to learn his strategy, and before long I was taking his king most of the time."

"Perhaps you and I shall play a game sometime." She gave him a mischievous smile. "So long as you're not a poor loser."

He laughed, and a shimmer of pleasure rippled through her at the deep rumbling in his chest. Clare remembered the night of the Benninghams' party when he'd laughed with her and teased her in that rare show of lightheartedness. Usually he was more reserved or distracted by work. And sometimes sad, as if he carried the full weight of the war on his shoulders.

"You should do that more often." She spoke the thought aloud.

"What, laugh?"

She nodded, and surprise lit his face. "How do you know I don't?"

A heartbeat's hesitation. "Call it intuition," she said. "And laughter is an order from your nurse."

He grinned. "Do all your patients at the hospital cower when you talk to them like that?"

"Who said I talk to them like that?"

His gaze narrowed on her, and this time Clare grinned. "Only the patients who argue with me."

"I'll remember that," he said.

She checked her watch. The dreaded formal dinner must be over by now, yet she was reluctant to leave him. "I should go and check on Daisy and make sure she ate her meal. Will you be all right here?"

"Yes." He glanced toward the bed. "I would just like to rest awhile."

"Want to try walking the distance, or shall we wheel you back through this carpet wilderness?"

Pushing back from the table, he gripped the arms of the wheelchair and started to rise.

"Wait for me." She rose to stand beside him and held out her arm, letting him lean on her as he hoisted himself out of the chair until he stood.

"The easy part is over," he said, his breathing labored.

No doubt that being bedridden for two weeks and not eating properly had weakened him. "Put your arm across my shoulders," she said.

Clare then tucked her arm around his waist and looked up at him, keenly aware their faces were mere inches apart. Warmth flushed her skin. "Ready?"

He looked at her for a long moment before finally nodding. Together they took slow steps toward the bed, she shouldering his weight when he lost his balance. A full minute later, she'd eased him onto the coverlet.

He looked up at her, eyes gleaming in triumph.

"Yes, you did well." She smiled, then froze as he reached for her hand and raised it to his lips.

"Thank you, Clare," he said, all humor having faded. "I enjoyed our dinner together."

"I did too."

As he lay down, she covered him with a light blanket. "I'll be in later tonight to check on you."

His answer was to close his eyes, a smile playing on his lips.

She took a moment to study every sculpted line in his handsome face while compassion, confusion, and resentment tangled with the hurt she still felt. Yet love remained as she remembered his tender looks and each knowing smile he'd ever given her.

She glanced at her hand, the one he'd kissed. *He called you Clare.*

Moving back through the passageway to her room, she ignored her rapid pulse, forcing herself instead to remember why she was here—replaying in her mind their conversations, his laughter, and most importantly, his memories, sparse as they were.

Her hope rekindled at this last. In less than an hour's time, she and Marcus had made surprising progress together.

But would it continue?

"There you are! We missed you at dinner."

Clare had started upstairs when Fannie approached from the direction of the dining room.

"I was making sure your brother had something to eat."

"Oh, good! Mother was worried." Fannie eyed her blue silk dress. "You look lovely."

"Thank you." Clare's heart warmed. Marcus had said as much. She noted Fannie's beige silk dress with flowing chiffon sleeves. "And you clean up rather nicely yourself."

Fannie laughed. "Would you listen to us, like two peacocks flattering each other? Come with me now. Mother and Natalya are in the Magnolia room, and the men will be coming in soon. I know they all want to visit with you. I certainly want to visit with you!"

Smiling, Clare hesitated. "I'd planned to check in on Daisy . . ."

"She and Ruthie are both quite happy," Fannie assured her. "Janet's looking after them, and they just finished dinner in the nursery." Her eyes widened. "My goodness, you must be starved! Shall I have Hanson bring a tray to the Magnolia room?"

"Heavens, no, I'm fine." Her pulse sped. "Actually . . . I had dinner with your brother. He offered to share his meal, and we had a nice chat."

"You did?" Fannie leaned forward. "Pray, what did you two talk about?"

"You." Clare smiled, secretly pleased at the way Marcus had opened up to her so easily. "He remembers you, Fannie, and your mother and grandfather. Even Mrs. Connelly, the cook."

Fannie's eyes grew misty. "If only I could have eavesdropped on the two of you in the study. To hear him speak, I'd gladly have turned into a ladybug and hid beneath Grandfather's leafy philodendron."

Clare tipped her head. "Why don't you go and visit with him?"

She hunched her shoulders. "I . . . I didn't know what I should say to him. He's my brother, yet he's so changed. And he's hardly said a word since you arrived with him yesterday." Her eyes pleaded with Clare. "What did he say about me exactly?"

"That you missed out on a lot of dessert when you were little."

"He did?" A grin broke through Fannie's tears. "Mrs. Connelly was rather strict with us about cleaning our plates, though Marcus often came to my aid and ate my cabbage." She made a face. "I still detest that vegetable, though I love growing it. What else did he say?"

"He said your grandfather looks older . . ." Clare hesitated to share the rest of the conversation, then changed her mind. She wanted Fannie's assessment. "He mentioned Sir Geoffrey likes people with fire."

"That is true. Grandfather respects people who stand up for themselves and their principles, who aren't afraid to pursue their dreams. He's done that himself with his work in prosthetics. And he's seen so much of the world, traveling throughout Europe." Her eyes gleamed. "Most of all, my grandfather loves to tease, so don't let him get to you. He's as gentle as a kitten and wily as a fox, and loves putting on a good show, especially if he knows it's working."

Clare forced a smile. "He certainly convinced me."

"Come." Fannie held out a hand. "I feel guilty that you're telling me all of this wonderful news about my brother when Mother and Grandfather would beg to hear you speak!"

Fannie stood just a few steps below Clare, her delicate features animated. Clare sensed her new friend's excitement, and she also understood that Marcus's family needed hope . . .

And, Clare, you can give that to them.

She descended the steps and took Fannie's hand. Clare could handle an hour of Natalya's sugary speech, even Sir Geoffrey's odd manner of teasing.

It was time to stop being a wallflower.

18

eoffrey mentioned you are leaving us, Lord Walenford?"

Mrs. Weatherford sat on the emerald-striped sofa, looking regal in her rose taffeta and pearls while she eyed Jack across from her.

Leaving? Clare turned from Fannie's mother to stare at Jack, who had taken up his drink as he sat beside Natalya on the settee.

"Yes, tomorrow morning," he said. "I've a meeting in town in the afternoon that will not wait." He offered an apologetic smile. "I appreciate your hospitality, and I hope to return midweek to check on my friend."

"My lord, our home is yours." Mrs. Weatherford beamed, while behind her Yates stood at the side table, pouring small glasses of sherry from a decanter. "And be assured, Natalya and Mrs. Danner will want for nothing while they are here."

She turned to Sir Geoffrey beside her. "In fact, we are all so grateful . . ."

Mrs. Weatherford gazed at Natalya and then to Clare, her face mottled with emotion. "Mrs. Danner, your daughter and her nanny are welcome, too."

"Thank you, ma'am." Clare hid her anxiety beneath a smile.

Jack had said he would remain several days . . . and now he was going to abandon her?

She considered her delightfully warm cocoon of the past hour with Marcus. Sharing his food and his laughter, listening to his quiet revelations of the past, secrets she suspected he'd never told anyone.

Yet in that time she'd allowed herself to forget about his reluctance in bringing her here to Montefalco to meet his family. She was an outsider in this place, with only Fannie's friendship to make her feel at ease.

Jack must have sensed her attention, as he flashed her a hesitant smile.

Her nostrils flared. He'd likely known from the start he was leaving and decided not to tell her. "My lord, if I might have a word with you about the patient before you go?"

Clare ignored their curious audience, though not before she'd glimpsed Sir Geoffrey's dagger-like stare. She shifted in her seat. How could Fannie mistake her grandfather's manner for teasing? He looked grim enough to do battle.

"Of course, Mrs. Danner." Jack set his drink on the table. "We'll find a moment before everyone retires for the evening."

Clare nodded. Once she'd given him a piece of her mind, she intended to find out about Marcus's gunshot wound.

Yates offered her a glass of the sherry when Fannie blurted, "Clare told me that Marcus remembers us!"

Suddenly all eyes were on her.

"Mrs. Danner?" Mrs. Weatherford edged forward on the sofa, her anxiety and grief evident. "Please, you must tell us everything!"

Clare took a sip of the sherry, remembering Marcus's painful confession about the loneliness he and his sister had suffered after losing their father.

Yet their mother had suffered greatly, too. "He remembers strawberry trifle on his birthdays."

Joy transformed Mrs. Weatherford's face, and Clare relaxed

her grip on the glass as she relayed to them all that she'd told Fannie earlier.

"Yes, the children would beg me to demand Mrs. Connelly give them dessert." Mrs. Weatherford chuckled, and even Jack smiled.

Sir Geoffrey's hard look had thawed as well, so Clare took a chance. "Sir, your grandson told me that he's always enjoyed your talks together. He was especially grateful for your care of his mother and sister while he was away at Harrow."

The old man blinked, and Clare caught the sudden sheen in his eyes. "He also remembers learning how to play chess. To hear him talk, he became rather good at winning against all his opponents."

"Indeed, he did." Sir Geoffrey's eyes warmed and he ventured a smile.

Clare was thrilled by the reaction.

"Remarkable," Jack said, clearly amazed. "I'm pleased to know my instincts were correct."

Clare eyed him sharply. Instincts?

"It gives me hope that my friend has come this far on his second day home. With time, perhaps he will also remember me"—he glanced at her—"and Mrs. Danner."

Clare cast a covert look back toward Mrs. Weatherford and Fannie, hoping against hope for some glimmer of recognition. She'd love nothing better than to be wrong about her earlier assumptions.

But Marcus's mother and sister merely eyed her pleasantly, while Sir Geoffrey's smile disappeared. Staring into her glass of sherry, Clare fought against the old shame, letting her righteous anger burn like the amber liquid she'd just swallowed.

"Mrs. Danner, I agree with Lord Walenford," Mrs. Weatherford said. "Already you have done wonders with my son. Please tell us, is there anything more we can do for Marcus?"

As she gazed into the mother's eyes, so much like her son's, Clare's indignation cooled. These people were strangers, yet they also wanted Marcus back desperately. Their reasons might be different from hers, but they were hurting just the same. "I believe all of you should simply relax with him. He remembers this house, and he has memories of the staff and each of you, but they're old memories—as far back as his school days at Harrow." She turned to Jack. "I do not think it's a good idea to pressure him with too many questions, but if he offers a memory, then ask him about it. See how far his mind can take it forward." She lifted a shoulder. "That's really all I did with him, and he opened up freely."

"Good advice, Mrs. Danner," Sir Geoffrey said. "If we continue treating my grandson like a hospital patient, he may never feel at ease long enough to unlock those memories. And we don't want to overwhelm him."

Elation filled her. Marcus's grandfather had actually given her his approval!

"Which makes it even more astounding that *you*, Mrs. Danner, as his nurse have managed to accomplish so much in such a short time." Natalya finally spoke from her place beside Jack on the settee. "Perhaps the reason he responds so freely and feels none of the pressures to remember is because he feels no emotional ties with you?"

Though the remark stung, Clare held onto her composure. She wasn't about to give Natalya the satisfaction of seeing her arrow hit the target. Raising her chin, she offered her brightest smile. "And that's why it makes me the best choice in seeing to his care, Mrs. Bryce."

A muffled male cough issued from the direction of the sofa. Clare glanced at Sir Geoffrey, whose eyes gleamed while his mouth twitched beneath the mustache.

He was amused by that? Startled, Clare swung her attention back to Natalya. "Please be assured I plan to help my patient heal as quickly as possible and by whatever means are at hand. The sooner the better, wouldn't you agree?"

"Oh, indeed I do, Mrs. Danner." Natalya's polished features now wore a feline look. "The sooner Marcus gets his memory back"—her gaze darted to Fannie and Mrs. Weatherford—"the sooner we shall be married."

This time it was Jack who coughed, and his severe look at Natalya would have puzzled Clare if she wasn't already incensed by the woman's remarks. "Of course you are anxious to marry," she said sweetly. "I can imagine that for a woman in *your* position, time is of the essence."

Natalya glowered, while Clare eased back in her seat. *I'm not such a drudge that I can't fence pretty insults with you, Ballerina.*

As the strained silence stretched, Fannie launched from her seat. "Clare, when you have time tomorrow, I'd like to take you on a tour of the estate." She turned hesitantly toward Natalya. "Perhaps you would like to join us, too?"

"Oh, yes!" Like quicksilver, Natalya's features glowed with excitement. "I would especially like to visit the rehabilitation hospital." She smiled, ignoring Clare. "I also have some ideas about Marcus's care, and I feel it would do him good to be among others who are coping with injuries. Perhaps he will feel less isolated, and it might relax him and help with his memory." She turned to Clare, brow arched. "Would you not agree, Mrs. Danner?"

Teeth on edge, Clare stared at the woman while Mum's words came back to her. *"Cast away your pride, lass."* And it was true—Natalya's idea did have merit. Except for the patients in isolation at Endell Street, most of the wounded thrived and healed more readily when placed among their fellow soldiers.

"I do agree," she said, each word tasting like grit on her tongue. "But we will inspect this facility first before deciding to introduce my patient."

"Excellent!" Natalya clapped her hands. "Frances, you shall be our guide tomorrow." She looked back to Clare. "After Marcus is resting comfortably, of course."

Natalya looked so genuinely pleased, Clare found her own hostility toward her wavering. Such whimsical moods! Memories of the Benninghams' party flashed in her mind, Natalya dancing about the drawing room before landing straight into the arms of Stephen Lange—and then Marcus—as she avoided crashing into the opening door.

The woman *was* a performer, impulsive and a bit full of herself, yet she seemed to care a great deal about Marcus. And regardless of her own pain, Natalya's concern for his welfare oddly gave Clare a measure of comfort.

Was it possible the two of them could keep his recovery in mind and, instead of bickering, form some kind of truce during their stay here?

Natalya glanced at her, dark eyes dancing in triumph.

Clare curled her lip. *Maybe when pigs can fly.*

"What would you like to discuss, Clare?" Jack gave her a sidelong glance as they stood on the front portico steps. Already the evening sun cast shadows along the tops of the plane trees lining Montefalco's long drive.

"Why didn't you tell me that you only intended to stay the weekend?" She crossed her arms and turned to him. "Leaving me here alone with the Weatherfords and *that woman.*"

He emitted a sigh. Hadn't he expected this? Especially after Natalya's well-aimed barbs at Clare earlier. Poor Mrs. Weatherford and Fannie looked bewildered as their attention bounced back and forth between the two sparring women, like watching a tennis match at Wimbledon.

At least Sir Geoffrey seemed to enjoy the volleys, especially when Clare shot one back. Jack fought a smile. Clare Danner could certainly give as good as she got. He'd almost forgotten her temper. "Clare, despite Natalya's—"

"Obnoxiousness?"

He coughed to cover a laugh. "Yes, despite *that*, you're not alone. This is Marcus's family, after all."

"Why should that matter? They have no idea who I am." She angled her head. "Or haven't you noticed?"

Jack blinked. Sir Geoffrey certainly knew who she was. *"Do you think it possible two people can fall in love a second time?"*

The old man's words to him in the laboratory earlier. And Fannie Weatherford had called her Clare in the drawing room a while ago.

As for Mrs. Weatherford, well, he'd just assumed she heeded to good manners addressing Clare formally. Especially after Natalya shocked them all with her engagement to Marcus.

"Are you certain?" he asked. "You haven't been at meals, and we only arrived yesterday afternoon. There hasn't been much time—"

"Of course I'm sure!" Even in the fading sunlight, her face revealed anguish. "Otherwise, Fannie would have said something to me by now, don't you think?"

True enough. Jack breathed an oath. What had Marcus been thinking? And why would he wish to keep his mother and sister in the dark? "I'm sorry," he said. "There must be some reason . . ."

"Maybe he was . . . ashamed." Her chin trembled.

"Of you? Oh, Clare, you're mistaken. Marcus holds you in the highest regard."

"Does he? Is that why he asked Natalya to marry him?"

Crikey, what a tangle! He couldn't very well tell her the truth and blow Natalya's cover story. *Devil take it, Marcus! You'll have some explaining to do—that is, if you can ever remember.* "Clare, please . . ."

"Save your words, Jack." She flashed a tight smile. "The reason Marcus never brought me here is the same reason he never asked me along on any of his trips abroad, like he did Natalya. *She's* the one who brought him back to London after he was injured."

Jack couldn't argue the point, yet he refused to leave her believing she was unworthy of the Weatherfords and their son. "Trust me, despite this . . . relationship he has with Natalya, Marcus has a deep affection for you."

"Did you say 'trust me'?" Clare snorted. "I'm beginning to think that's a catchphrase men like to use when they'd rather steer away from the truth."

Jack eyed her sharply while scouring his mind for reasons to justify Marcus's actions. Sir Geoffrey knew about her but obviously hadn't mentioned Clare or Daisy to his kin. The old man was also well acquainted with the head of MI6, Marcus's boss. Had Marcus sworn his grandfather to secrecy as a protective measure? With numerous clandestine assignments over the course of the war, Marcus *had* received his share of enemy threats. "Clare, I believe Marcus had good reason to keep you and Daisy a secret," he said. "He wanted to keep you both safe."

"Safe from what?"

Jack hesitated. "His work for Britain, as oftentimes it comes with a certain amount of risk."

"Yes, I've witnessed it." She leaned in, hands on her hips. "As for my other reason for this meeting—" she paused, her eyes narrowed on him—"who shot Marcus in the head, and why?"

19

Even in the waning hours of sun, Clare was satisfied to see shock and guilt skitter across Jack's face.

Though her pride had been bruised, she tried to focus on her duties regarding her patient. "Why wasn't I told of the exact nature of his wounds? You said back in London that Marcus had taken a nasty fall and cracked his skull. Did it slip your mind to mention that he'd been shot first?"

Jack shifted. "Clare, it was confidential—"

"Oh, so you thought I wouldn't figure it out. I do work in a military hospital, you know."

"Yes, of course." He looked away. "It's complicated."

"Why is that? You hired me to take care of him, Jack. That means I need to know everything about his wounds so I can treat Marcus properly."

"You are perfectly right." He breathed a sigh and turned piercing eyes to her. "I'm speaking to you now in the strictest confidence, you understand? Tell no one. Not his family, not even Marcus."

Her pulse leapt. "Yes, I promise. Please, I need to know what happened."

"He received the gunshot wound while he and Natalya were in Europe."

So the ballerina had been with him. Clare swallowed hard. "Was it thieves?" she whispered. "Or street thugs?"

"Thugs in a manner of speaking." He looked away. "They were held at gunpoint. One of the men aimed his gun and—"

"And Marcus took the bullet." She pressed her lips together. "He was protecting her, wasn't he?"

When Jack nodded, Clare's admiration for Marcus merely increased the ache in her heart. She loved that he'd always made her feel protected and his tender care of Daisy. No wonder he and Natalya now seemed inseparable. "But how—?"

"I'm sorry, Clare, but that's all I can tell you." Regret lined his face. "I understand how difficult this is for you being here, especially with the pressures you're facing from Randleton. But you're strong, and I have every faith in your success with Marcus."

She looked up at him, recalling his earlier remark about his instincts being right.

"Consider how he's already responded to you," he continued, reading her thoughts. "When I took him into the garden today, he said maybe a dozen words to me, and those I practically had to pry from him. But you . . ." He shook his head. "Marcus opened up to you like a lockbox full of gold." He eyed her intently. "Clare, *you* are his key. In more ways than you know."

She searched his face, his words confusing her yet igniting a tiny flame in her soul. What was he saying? Or rather, what was he trying not to say?

"You must never give up hope," he added with a smile. "Being here is also your opportunity to become better acquainted with Marcus's family. They're really very good people."

"Yes, Jack, but it's not *me* they need to be acquainted with." His words had doused her small spark of light, recalling her to the present. "Natalya is to be his wife, not me."

"But *you* still need to be here. Your daughter and Britain are both counting on you. And the Weatherfords can help you with Marcus."

Though annoyed, she agonized over the fact that he was right.

It was true that Fannie and Mrs. Weatherford *had* been kind to her. And while Clare was still unsure about Sir Geoffrey, he did support her views about Marcus's care.

Anyway, did she have a choice? "I *will* make an effort to know them better, Jack."

"Good." His expression softened. "Now, I leave early tomorrow, but I hope to return by midweek. I'll even bring Grace along. How would that be?"

"Yes, thank you." Clare's eyes began to burn. How she missed her friend!

"Consider it done."

They returned inside, and after saying good-bye to Jack as he went upstairs, Clare made a beeline for her room. She combed back over their conversation, the tiny flame inside once again alight as she recalled Jack's words. *"Marcus opened up to you like a lockbox full of gold . . ."*

As she turned her mind back to the meal she and Marcus had shared earlier, a flush of heat stole over her. Yes, he had opened up to her, revealing intimacies from his boyhood she felt sure had remained locked in him his whole life.

How she longed to cling to Jack's assurances about Marcus's high regard for her! Yet reasoning, and the ache in her heart, reminded her he was engaged to someone else and that he'd kept her and Daisy away from his family all this time.

Was it, as Jack suggested, to protect them?

The gunshot wound. Clare shivered. Jack's demand for secrecy, his reluctance to offer her more about the incident, still bothered her. Had Marcus been involved in dangerous work? And if so, why had Natalya been with him?

Tension had settled into her neck and shoulders by the time Clare entered her room. She eased down onto the bed's gold coverlet and reached for one of the satin pillows. A maid had switched on the bedside lamp, leaving the room in soft, comfortable shadows.

As she lay there, she again imagined the wound from the bullet that had grazed his head. Was it street thugs who shot him, leaving him for dead . . . or something more sinister?

She rolled onto her back and sighed. Maybe Jack had another reason he wanted it kept quiet. *"Tell no one. Not his family, not even Marcus."*

Surely if the news got out, the Weatherfords would be beside themselves. And Marcus obviously had no idea how he got wounded, and knowing would only distress him further.

Besides, she couldn't imagine him intentionally putting any woman at such great risk, especially one to whom he'd promised the rest of his life . . .

A hard knot settled in her chest. It must be Jack's reason for silence. And he'd only been guessing at why Marcus had kept her and Daisy away from Hampshire, staunchly denying any shame on his friend's part. But bless him, that was simply because she was his wife's closest friend. Clare and Grace had toiled together in his hayfields last year, getting dirty and sweaty, their clothing full of straw.

But this wasn't the farm. Montefalco was a castle, complete with its own prince now sleeping next door. And Clare wasn't his princess, but merely his live-in nurse.

Her gaze went to the mantel clock. Speaking of which . . .

She rose from the bed, despite her stiffness. Marcus needed a fresh bandage, and she wanted to look in on Daisy and Ruthie before going to bed.

Quickly she exchanged her blue silk and pearls for her regular clothes and grabbed up her medical bag. Removing *Jane Eyre* from the bookcase, she opened the secret door and slipped through the passageway into the study. "Marcus?"

"Ah, so that is your little secret, Mrs. Danner. A late-night rendezvous?"

Smiling, Natalya arched a brow as she sat beside Marcus's bed. The large diamond winked in the soft light.

"Clare?" Marcus raised his head slightly to look at her.

"Hello, Marcus." Her pulse leapt at the sound of his husky voice.

She turned toward Natalya. "It's not a secret, and I'm available to Marcus at all hours," she said smoothly, gratified when the ballerina's smug look disappeared. "Sir Geoffrey and Mrs. Weatherford made the arrangement, so that in the event of an emergency—"

"You can come to his rescue."

"That's right."

Natalya smiled once more. "I meant what I said earlier, Mrs. Danner. I appreciate the care you are giving my fiancé. The sooner he heals, the better. For all of us, yes?"

She tipped her head knowingly, and Clare stiffened at the subtle reminder of her own trouble with Randleton. "I'm here to change his bandage now. If you'd care to wait . . ."

"I think not. It is rather late." She rose from her bedside perch, breaking the connection with Marcus. "You are in good hands, are you not, milyi? I shall see you in the morning at breakfast, all right? I insist. You need to regain your strength."

His throat bobbed as he swallowed. "All right, Natalya."

He looked away then, and Clare's heart stirred at his obvious anxiety over having to eat in the dining room with the others. She knew how he felt.

"Excellent!" Natalya sashayed toward the door that led into the main hall before she paused and looked back. "I cannot imagine it is much farther to your room going this way. But as you say, in an emergency Marcus would be quite helpless at this point. Your promptness in reaching him could only be beneficial." This time her smile was tight as she nodded slightly. "Good night."

After she'd left, Clare released a breath. Natalya's moods shifted like the winds of a coming storm. Was it just her nature or were all performers like that?

She dismissed the ballerina from her thoughts and turned to Marcus. "Ready to sit up and have your head examined?"

Her heart thumped as his golden-brown eyes lit with humor. *"Clare, you are his key . . ."* Memories rushed her, moments not so long ago when he'd looked at her in just this way, filling her with such joy.

Surely he couldn't have feigned those feelings? Or when he'd kissed her . . .

Drawing a deep breath to collect herself, she moved to stand beside his bed. "Well? Are you ready?"

"You're in charge, Nurse."

"I'll remember you said that the next time you decide to argue with me." She leaned close and helped raise him to a sitting position. "Did you have enough to eat earlier?"

"Yes, I enjoyed the food . . . and the company."

Clare nodded, images still fresh in her mind of the way his mouth curved beneath his mustache when he'd smiled at her teasing. Her pulse racing, as it did now, when he offered to share his food with her, and a deeper awareness as she'd let him feed her from his own hand.

Even now the intimacy made her skin tingle. "I enjoyed it, too," she said softly. "Thank you for being so generous."

"It was my pleasure."

She blushed at his knowing look, then turned to reach into her bag for her scissors.

Marcus's pulse quickened as he watched the rising color in her cheeks. Was she sharing with him his recent dream?

Earlier, before Natalya arrived, he'd been dozing, his sleep filled with flashes of Clare at their dinner. Her gray eyes were soft, like clouds after a gentle rain, as she'd accepted the dessert he offered her, and the way she'd looked at him as she fed him in turn . . .

Her teasing had made him laugh inside, banishing the blackness that normally haunted his dreams. She helped him remember his favorite foods and his life with Fannie after Father died. Months of loneliness and fear that even now made him ache.

In his dream, he'd told her even more about his past—how he'd sometimes carried his little sister down through the secret passageway into the monk's cellarium below the house. Hiding treasures in their secret boxes.

The dream then changed suddenly, and she was kneeling beside his bed and sobbing in the darkness, begging him to save her child. Marcus had tried to reach for her, but someone had chained his wrists, keeping him shackled to the bed frame. He was unable to free himself, to help her . . .

"It won't take long to change your bandage, I promise."

His breathing eased at the sound of her voice. She was here with him now, and she wasn't crying.

He glanced at his wrists. No chains.

His eyes followed her movements as she cut away at the gauze with a pair of scissors. He breathed in her scent, the honeysuckle fragrance, and felt a deep sense of longing. For what, he didn't know—only that it felt imperative he find out.

He closed his eyes while his mind searched, going beyond the hazy tendrils and into the dark jungle of his thoughts. Beyond flashes of words and images without meaning or understanding, until he stood once more at the great black wall forbidding him entrance.

He gritted his teeth. *Must remember!*

"I'm pleased to see you haven't torn your stitches."

He flinched, returning to the present as she dabbed the burning antiseptic to the side of his head. "This is quite a wound you've managed to get."

He heard the concern in her voice. "Natalya said we were in a forest when I tripped and fell, and my head landed on a rock."

"I see. And you've another bump on the back of your head. That must have been a terrible landing."

"Yes," he said, though he wasn't certain how he'd injured both the side and back of his head in the same fall. And all that blood. He remembered the felt cap he'd hidden beneath his mattress. "I suppose after I fell, I could have rolled and hit some other obstacle?"

"Possibly." She leaned closer and applied the antiseptic to the back of his head, her softness touching his face. Though he winced once more, he took pleasure in her warm contact.

"The knot back here isn't too bad, but you need to lie on your side. I'll bring pillows to prop behind you so you don't roll over."

He was deprived of any further sensation when she moved away to retrieve a package of clean gauze and began bandaging his head. She glanced at him, and he noted her frown, eyes as turbulent as a coming gale.

"Is Daisy all right?" he asked.

He marveled at the rosy patches coloring her creamy skin. "She's doing well . . . for now. I'm on my way to see her in the nursery once I get you patched up again."

"She likes the horse."

"Ah, you remember from our tea yesterday. Yes, she loves that rocking horse."

"And on the train. The horse in the field?"

She paused, her eyes searching his face. "That's right. And a good sign that you're retaining your thoughts." She finished tying off the bandage and replaced her supplies in the bag.

"Would you sit with me for a few minutes?"

She nodded, taking Natalya's chair and placing the doctor's bag at her feet.

He held out his hand to her and waited. She seemed to hesitate before taking it.

Gently he turned it over to study her palm, running his thumb along the slightly roughened skin. Not the smoothness of Natalya's hand, but of one who had seen much hard work, no doubt caring for him and for others.

He turned it back and studied the thin gold band on her finger. Not a diamond like the ring he'd given Natalya . . .

Another ring—an image—flashed in his mind, and instinctively he understood it was tied to this woman. He struggled to recapture the past, knowing with some innate sense that the memory would fill the hollowness in him.

His mind betrayed him. He looked up at her. "Do you ever . . . think of him?"

Startled, she tried to pull her hand away, and he saw the stark vulnerability in her face.

He breathed an oath and held on to her fingers. "Clare, wait! Don't be angry. That question . . . it just came into my head. Forgive me, please."

She stopped fighting him, and when he let her go, she clasped her hands together in her lap, hiding the plain ring. Her gray eyes glistened with unshed tears and remorse seized him, making his throat ache.

"Yes." She spoke in the barest of whispers. "I think of him all the time."

Her wet eyes searched his, and the longing in them nearly undid him. He couldn't fathom why it should, only that it touched him deeply, like nothing else.

"I try to forget . . . I know he's lost to me, but my heart, it won't . . ."

"Let go?" he finished for her, his own voice hoarse. Her words echoed his sense of confusion and loss. His need to fill the emptiness. "You still ache for him?"

She nodded, grief written in her expression, and he almost reached for her but then held back, the invisible chains again on his wrists. On his mind.

He released a ragged breath. "There is so much I *must* remember . . ."

Her warmth touched him then as the slender hand once more rested against his. "Hush," she said, her quiet voice calming him. "You *will* heal, but you must be patient."

He looked at her. *But I need to know about you, about us . . .*

He suddenly remembered more of his dream. "When you came to see me . . . you said that I still loved Daisy and would do anything to help her."

Her face turned to chalk before surging with color. "You remember that?"

He nodded. "We knew each other, didn't we?"

"Yes."

Her soft answer drifted to him. He swallowed. "Where?"

"In Kent. We met in Roxwood, Jack's estate."

He nodded. Jack, his blond friend. "When?"

"A long time ago." She swiftly rose to her feet. "I . . . I must go and check on Daisy now."

"Clare, I want to remember."

She looked at him. "I know you do, Marcus."

"In here." He pressed a fist to his heart. "Something I know, but I can't . . ." Frustrated, he exhaled. "It's important."

"Is it Natalya?"

Their eyes met, hers filled with pain in their questioning. His heart thudded against his rib cage, his mouth tasting like sand. He should tell her yes, shouldn't he?

Marcus recalled how he'd shuddered awake less than an hour ago, the memory of that hospital room, the darkness, and Clare crying. Yet he'd said nothing of his dream to Natalya when she arrived to find him out of breath and restless. Nor when he'd dozed again, his thoughts drifting back to those happier moments when he and Clare shared his dinner.

Even now he couldn't help gazing into the gray eyes, remembering her scent of honeysuckle and her softness, warm against his skin. The bone-deep knowledge that they were somehow connected . . .

You're a rotter, man. He looked away as guilt seized him. Natalya was his anchor, the woman he'd reached for the moment he first roused into consciousness and panicked in that strange place, his memory blind beneath the thick bandage.

She wore his ring, and he'd proposed marriage to *her.* Surely that meant he'd loved her.

"Yes," he said, looking back at Clare, shame battling the inexplicable tie he felt to her. "Natalya. She . . . saved me and stayed with me at the hospital."

He watched as she moistened her lips, the color of ripe cherries. "You were in Paris?"

"Yes . . . no, I don't think so." He'd visited France when he was young, but the place where he'd been wasn't the same. "It was dark and cold there, but I don't know where I was."

"That must be why it's so important you remember."

Her brow creased, lips trembling before she pressed them closed. He'd upset her again. "Clare . . ."

"I have to go." Pushing away from the chair, she fled toward the passageway. "I'll send Hanson to help you ready for bed," she called back. "And I'll come see you after breakfast tomorrow to check on you."

She turned at the secret door, however, her eyes wounded despite her smile. "Good night."

And then she was gone from him, closing the door behind her.

He leaned forward, gripping his knees, staring at the forgotten doctor's bag beside her chair. He had distressed her, though he wasn't certain how or why. And there was much she hadn't told him.

How did he know her . . . before? She hadn't told him when Mr. Danner died. Had they met sometime after that?

"In Kent, at Jack's estate." At least she'd told him that much. And Jack would know.

Marcus lay back on the coverlet, remembering her face and the soft wet eyes staring back at him.

Tomorrow, Jack would tell him why Clare Danner made him ache.

***

Once Clare made her escape through the passageway, her tears fell. Marcus couldn't remember his feelings for her *or* for Natalya, and it saddened her knowing he longed to feel whole again. That *she* had kept from him what was in her heart and what she'd most wanted to say.

Sensing his eyes on her, hearing his deep sigh as he'd pressed his face against her while she'd tended his wounds, was like no torment she'd ever experienced. How much she'd wanted to hold him and tell him how they'd met, and the time they shared together that summer when he once loved her, or thought he did, and how after rescuing her baby daughter in Kent, the three of them remained in Roxwood. "Our sweet Daisy" he'd called her little girl.

Clare had never been so happy in her life. Hoping for a future with him.

She couldn't tell him any of those things; they were dreams of the past. And what purpose would it serve? He'd been fully aware just weeks ago when he'd chosen Natalya and not her. Perhaps what he suffered now was some unconscious guilt over what he'd done.

Entering her room, her cheeks hot with tears, Clare poured fresh water into the washstand basin and cooled her face and neck before gazing at her reflection in the oval mirror.

"Shall you tell him how he chose to love the ballerina over you?" she whispered.

"Clare, you must trust me, it's not what you imagine . . ." Marcus had said those words to her that day in Russell Square, and she desperately wanted to believe, to trust, but . . . could she? He had no recollection of what he'd done to her.

She spun from the mirror and left her room, intent on visiting the nursery and holding her baby girl in her arms. Distressing Marcus with his betrayal at this point would only slow his healing, and regardless of their past together, Clare desperately needed him to remember.

20

Y ou were not at breakfast."

The statement blasted Clare the following morning as she opened the secret door into the study. Marcus sat in his wheelchair looking fine in a three-piece linen suit, the dark green color like the forests she'd seen from the train on their way to Hampshire.

"Where were you?" he said, frowning.

Was he upset? From the moment she'd awakened, her thoughts had circled around their emotional exchange last night, her mood alternating between heartache and hope.

"Daisy . . . had a restless night, and I needed to tend to her." She didn't mention that while her daughter *had* awakened in a bad mood, Ruthie could have handled things. It would have been truer to say, with Jack gone, she hadn't been ready to face a meal alone with the Weatherfords, at least not yet.

His voice gentled. "Is Daisy ill?"

"She's perfectly fine." Clare searched his troubled expression. "How did you sleep?" She'd heard no noises coming from the study bedroom last night and hoped he'd slept through the wee hours peacefully.

He shrugged. "The same nightmare, though not as bad as before."

"That's good." She crossed the polished wood floor to him. "And I'm glad to see Hanson removed that dreadful rug. Now you can do spin-arounds and race across the room with abandon."

The lines in his face eased, his mouth twitching with humor. "The idea has merit," he said. "Actually, Hanson directed Teddy and Lewis to the task. I think he enjoys having two younger footmen to push around, aside from myself."

She grinned, relieved his dark mood seemed to be mending. "Were Teddy and Lewis among those in the foyer to greet us when we first arrived?"

"Yes, Hanson mentioned them last night. Lewis is the son of our groom, Mr. Jamison." His expression faltered. "Like my father in the Boer War, Jamison was killed in this one. Hanson told me that since Grandfather surrendered all our riding horses to the army, Lewis needed a job. So Yates hired him to train as a footman."

Surprised, she asked, "Did you remember all of this yourself? The war and the horses?"

He studied his hands. "Hanson did mention the high points of our war with Germany. He also explained the shortage of horses for the cavalry in France."

"Oh." Her excitement dwindled. She'd hoped his mind was beginning to heal.

And his father *had* been killed in the war.

Marcus looked up, and she ached to see his sad expression. Without the missing pieces of memory that took him beyond the trauma, it must still be fresh in his mind. "Anyone else at the estate you remember?"

"Mr. Bauer, the gardener. He was working the grounds yesterday with a couple of lads I've never seen before." His jaw muscle flexed. "I didn't recognize anyone else."

Clare decided to find out from Yates when the first of the newer staff had hired on. It might help to determine where Marcus's memory had left off. "Let me take a look at your wounds."

She inspected the gauze she'd applied last night, pleased to see the absence of blood at the back. "I can remove these stitches on the side tomorrow, but I'm going to wait on the back. You've been tearing them with your tossing and turning." She glanced at him. "Did you sleep on your side?"

"As much as I can—the pillows help. And I awoke without a headache today."

She nodded her approval. "So, tell me, did you behave yourself at breakfast? No dropping jam toast into someone's lap or flinging a forkful of egg into the porridge?"

The sound of his chuckle filled her with pleasure. "I managed to hit the bull's-eye every time," he said proudly, pointing to his mouth.

"Thank goodness for that." She adjusted the tension on the bandage. "Now you can feed yourself and save me the trouble."

When she glanced at him, she found him watching her, his eyes warm. "I'm sorry to hear it," he said softly. "Perhaps I'll have to start slopping my tea and chewing with my mouth open so they'll relegate me back to my room to eat."

She laughed, then heaved a sigh. "Honestly, I'd much rather dine with you here than out there with your family."

"Why is that?"

Warmth tracked along her cheeks. "I'm not an expert on the exact duty of each piece of silverware at my table setting."

Dawning lit his eyes. "Then I shall fling my potatoes and gravy across the table tonight, so that everyone will be so busy dodging the mess they won't notice which spoon you're eating your pudding with."

She giggled at the image of such a scene, and soon they were both laughing until tears threatened to come. "I appreciate your chivalry," she said once they'd finally stopped, "but there's no need for drastic measures. I promised Jack I'd get to know everyone in your family while I'm here, so you'll see me at dinner tonight."

His features clouded again. "I was told he left this morning before breakfast. I wished to speak with him."

"About what?"

He ignored her question. "Do you know when he'll be back?"

Not soon enough. "He told us he'd try for midweek. He's bringing his wife, Grace, back with him."

Curiosity erased his troubled look. "Grace is your best friend. That must please you, Clare."

"Yes, indeed." She smiled to realize he remembered her friend from their earlier conversations. "Grace and I have known each other for over a year."

"And . . . Grace knows me?"

"She does," Clare said. "And she thinks very highly of you."

"What is she like?"

"Well, she's kind and compassionate . . . and she never puts on airs despite being a viscountess. Grace has a very generous heart."

"Like you."

She met his warm gaze. "Oh, she's much more generous than me. But you'll get to meet her for yourself soon enough."

She glanced at the clock. "I should go. I'm meeting your sister in the conservatory. By the way, have you spent any time with her since you've been back?"

He shrugged. "Just table conversation this morning, along with the others."

"I know Fannie would love a special visit from her big brother. As a matter of fact, she, Natalya, and I are going to visit the rehabilitation hospital at the other end of the estate." She angled her head. "Would you like to join us?"

"No." His mouth twisted. "I don't want to go there."

She crouched beside him. "Why not, Marcus?"

"Too many wounded, and I am not sick . . . not like that."

"Like what?"

"My head."

"Of course not!" A spurt of anger rose in her. Had someone at the other hospital told him that nonsense? "Marcus, your wounds are healing nicely, and you've had a terrible blow jar your ability to remember, but it's not the same as being mentally unfit." She tipped her head. "Tell you what, if I find out it's a nice place to spend a few hours with other men who have wounds similar to yours—and nothing more—would you agree to go and see for yourself?"

He stared at her. "Will you go with me?"

"Yes. And we'll stay only as long as you like, I promise."

He raised his eyes, looking past her. "Then I'll think about it."

It was the Garden of Eden, surely.

Clare had never seen anything like it. Not even Randleton and his wife had such an exotic-looking paradise at their country estate in the north.

She passed through a set of glass doors at the back of the house, entering a world foreign to her with its impressive array of plants— many of which were uncommon to Britain—crowding one another throughout the vaulted space.

Being so immense, the conservatory reminded her of the tropical jungles she'd seen only in books while she was being tutored along with Elliot and Stephen. She recognized the enormous green leaves of a banana tree, nearly touching the pointed fanlike fronds of some kind of palm planted just a few feet away.

Across from the trees, purple blooms and winding vines of fragrant wisteria climbed unchecked up the white lattice of wood mounted on one wall. At the center of the conservatory, the thick trunk of a Japanese maple rose from an enormous planter and stretched upward toward the glass ceiling. And the tall shoots of bamboo growing throughout the space had reached high enough to create natural partitions, making the place look like a lush wilderness.

Waiting for Fannie, Clare idly strolled along the stone path running through the conservatory's greenery. Her gaze met with a rainbow of colors, every size and shape of flower imaginable, each bloom bursting and surrounded by dark green leaves. Halfway down the path she found her new friend, turning the soil in a large planter using a spade. Fannie held an elongated root bulb before looking up.

"Oh, goodness!" She dropped the bulb onto the soil. "Clare, I hadn't realized the time."

"What is it you're planting?" Clare asked.

"This is *zantedeschia aethiopica*—a calla lily," she explained, indicating the root bulb. "A bit late for planting, but once this variety sprouts next year, it will produce beautiful green leaves and rose-colored flowers."

Fannie wore the same dirty yellow apron she'd hidden beneath her coat the other day when they'd arrived, her gloved hands now working dirt and fertilizer over the bulb.

Clare gestured around her at nature's sanctuary. "Did you do all this?"

"Oh, heavens, no!" Fannie laughed as she reached for the watering can beside her, drenching the dirt around her fresh planting. "This was my grandmother's creation. After she died, Grandfather continued to add to the conservatory plants, sending them home from all the different places he traveled. Our gardener, Mr. Bauer, has maintained the conservatory through the years, with my help, until I went off to university. Once I returned, I followed in my grandmother's footsteps, making this oasis even more beautiful." She stopped and glanced around. "I've only been back a year now, but I hope I've made a contribution, even if a small one."

"It's amazing," Clare said.

"Follow me while I clean up. Natalya should arrive soon and then we can all go over together."

Clare let Fannie lead the way into a screened area that included a sink. Stacks of empty wooden crates and terra-cotta pots lined the wall alongside shelves of books on gardening. Various tools stored in buckets stood nearby.

"How is your daughter feeling?" Fannie picked up a small brush, dipping her hands into a tub of water.

"Much better," Clare hedged. "I apologize for not being at breakfast this morning."

"Please don't worry." Fannie began scrubbing her fingernails. "Marcus was there, and it was wonderful to see him eating with us, though he didn't say much, only that he liked the food when Mother asked him." She grinned. "Natalya took up most of the conversation, telling us about her ballet career in Petrograd and Paris. So, other than eating, little was required of my brother."

"You like Natalya, don't you?"

"She seems quite nice . . . most of the time." Fannie gave her a knowing look, no doubt recalling the sparring match between Clare and Natalya last night. "She's very stylish, too. Not like me in my dirty apron."

Her head bowed. "I'm sorry for that, by the way. When we came to collect you at the train Saturday, I'd forgotten to take it off before leaving the house."

"No apology necessary." Clare smiled. "When I'm at work in London, I wear a white smock and kerchief all day, and both get very soiled."

Fannie made a face. "I can imagine." She slipped the wet brush into her other hand and continued scrubbing her nails. "How long have you worked at the hospital?"

"Almost a year."

"And you must like it, especially overseeing other orderlies. That *is* something!"

"I do like it very much. The hospital has an all-women staff, even the doctors, and they gave me the chance to better myself."

"All women, even doctors?" Fannie's dark eyes rounded.

"It's the only one of its kind in London," Clare said proudly. "The two surgeons who founded Endell Street Military Hospital are very forward-thinking women in my view." She eyed Fannie. "How about you? You went to university, right?"

"Only because my family has the money and Grandfather had the clout to get me into the school I requested, to pursue my vocation. I received my degree in horticultural science, naturally." She gave Clare a cheeky grin.

Clare laughed. "I suppose you're in your element here, then?"

"I am." She sighed. "Except for one or two young women in the village, living out here in Hampshire is rather solitary for me. I spend most of my time in the conservatory taking care of my plants."

"Not much of an opportunity for observing people. Don't you get lonely?"

"I have my mystery novels." Fannie's face turned pink. "And I talk to my plants."

Clare smiled. "I'm sure it must help them grow."

"I hope so. In any case, I'm comfortable here. My plants do not ask questions and they are true to me."

Clare eyed her curiously. "What questions?"

Fannie dropped the brush into the tub and grabbed a cake of soap from the sideboard. "About my legs, for one. And they don't call me 'gimping girl' or 'hobbledehoy' and laugh over it."

"What happened?" Clare asked softly. She'd noticed Fannie's awkward gait and wasn't about to insult her by pretending she didn't.

"Polio."

Clare raised her brows. "When?"

"I was three years old, but by the time I turned five, I was walking on my own again."

"You accomplished all of that in a couple of years?" Clare could only marvel at her. "Fannie, you've got more courage and strength than you give yourself credit for. You must have worked very hard to overcome a condition that so many others have not. God gave you that strength. It was His gift, and that makes *you* very special."

Her dark eyes blinked, the soap frozen in her hands. "You think so?"

"Absolutely." Clare nodded. "And I work in a hospital, remember? I've seen all kinds of suffering. Few can rise above their condition and challenge their shortcomings, turning them into something better."

"I like that, Clare. It makes me feel I've accomplished rather than failed at something so simple as walking, even though I still have a limp."

"That's your badge of courage and you should be proud. In fact, I've witnessed more than one soldier showing off to his chums some wound he received in battle."

Fannie grinned. "I'm a warrior, then?"

"Exactly." Clare's mood sobered. "We've all faced one obstacle or another in our lives, but if we believe in ourselves *and* we trust God, we can benefit from those difficulties. It may sound trite, I know, but those hard things can be preparing us for greater challenges."

"You mean like taking an examination in class. If we learn from our mistakes, we'll do better the next time."

"Yes, that's it. Like building up strength." She bent her right arm at the elbow, flexing her muscle for Fannie. "I discovered that laboring in the fields for the war effort provided me with the physical strength I would need later to handle my patients at the hospital."

"You . . . labored in the fields?" Fannie's eyes rounded.

"The Women's Forage Corps—now the Women's Land Army. We baled hay for the cavalry horses overseas."

"I think it's wonderful what women are doing for the war effort," Fannie said. "I should like to do something myself, but . . ." She glanced at her feet.

"You could try growing moss for bandages," Clare suggested. "We've had shortages here in Britain, and I know they need bandage material at the front."

"Of course! *Sphagnum* has the right antibacterial properties and absorbency." Her eyes glowed. "I will start cultivating the moss right away."

"See? You understand my point." Clare beamed. "All your hard work in earning that degree in horticulture will now aid the wounded."

"Yes, it makes sense," Fannie agreed. She finished rinsing and then drying her hands on a towel. "I should be honest, though, and confess that my recovery was all my brother's doing. If not for Marcus, I never would have walked again."

"Truly?" Clare's buoyant mood shifted. Did Marcus remember the polio? He hadn't mentioned it to her.

"My brother worked with me every day for nearly two years, helping me to exercise my legs. He stood beside me while I walked the floors of the house on crutches and then outside on the grounds once the weather was nice. He applied hot wet cloths to my legs when the pain was so unbearable that I cried for hours." Love filled her gaze. "He had to take over my care, as I was told later that our mother was absent much of the time."

Her smile was tinged with sadness. "I told you when you arrived how he would take me through the passageway into the cellarium where we'd hid our treasure boxes, so he knew my hiding place, and he's never violated that trust."

"So your brother was, what, thirteen years old when you had polio?"

"Yes, the same year Father died." Fannie's eyes misted. "He gave up two years at school in order to make me well again. Yet he's so brilliant, he entered Harrow at fifteen and worked twice as hard to catch up. He'd excelled at his studies by the time he finished three years later and went on to Oxford."

Tears lodged in Clare's throat at the boy's incredible love and sacrifice for his sister. Yesterday during their meal, Marcus had shared his memories of Fannie and himself at those ages and about their father's death. Why hadn't he mentioned her polio at the time and that he'd missed school while helping her?

Because he's never been one to boast. "Fannie, you're very lucky to have such a brother."

"I know it." Fannie's face had turned splotchy with emotion. "And that's why I'm so afraid he'll never remember what a truly fine man and a wonderful brother he is to me."

Clare reached for her, misery looming as she considered her

own present troubles. But then she thought back to her trauma in the Magdalene asylum and Daisy's birth when she'd been a new mother, naïve and weakened by her circumstances. Like Fannie, she'd grown stronger from experiencing such trials. And they could both withstand and overcome this hurdle before them with Marcus.

"We can do it, Fannie," she said before releasing her. "We'll work with Marcus every day, the same way he once worked with you, until he becomes whole again." New conviction filled her. "And we'll continue to pray for him."

Fannie dabbed at her eyes and then hugged Clare. "I'm so glad you're here. I think God must have brought you to Montefalco to help us with my brother."

Clare's smile faltered. *More like Jack Benningham brought me here.* In truth, if she hadn't needed Marcus's help, Clare wouldn't be here. The last thing she wanted was to endure daily the ballerina's fawning over the man who still held her heart.

Yet Fannie's words gave her pause. *Was* this God's intention for her? Was she, as Jack had said, the one to bring Marcus back to them all?

"Helloooo! Where are you, Frances?"

Both women turned at the sound of Natalya's greeting. Fannie stepped back and removed her apron. "I suppose it's time we toured the rehabilitation hospital to see if it will suit Marcus."

Clare breathed a sigh, remembering the deal she'd offered Fannie's obstinate brother. "And if it does, let's hope we can convince him to visit the place."

21

We've all faced one obstacle or another in our lives, but those hard things prepare us for greater challenges.* Clare mocked her own sage advice to Fannie as she sat in the Weatherfords' dining room later that evening, her palms damp as she eyed the extravagant table filled with a host of crystal glassware, patterned china, fine linen napkins, and a sea of silverware.

Three different forks sat to the left of her china plate. Should she use the smallest or the midsized fork for the salad? The large fork must surely be for the main course.

What *was* the main course?

"How was your tour of the facilities today, ladies? Was my daughter able to show you the grounds and the rest of the estate as well?"

Mrs. Weatherford's question drew Clare's attention as Natalya answered, "We had a lovely tour of the hospital, Mrs. Weatherford. Not only is it perfectly suitable for Marcus, but we also spoke with the physician and two of the nurses, and they seem quite competent to take care of his needs."

Clare straightened in her seat. She and Natalya had *not* discussed Marcus moving there. She turned to her patient and saw he, too, stared at Natalya, his hands fisted against the tablecloth.

"Marcus," she said gently, "I think it's a good idea that you should *visit* the rehabilitation hospital rather than stay there as a patient. You're making good progress here, and as Natalya pointed out to me yesterday"—she offered the ballerina one of her own syrupy smiles—"the occasional company of the other soldiers might help you." She tipped her head. "What do *you* think?"

The color had returned to his face. Eyes gleaming at her, he relaxed his hands on the linen cloth. "I think it's a good idea for me to stay here," he said.

Mrs. Weatherford's soft gasp was followed by a look of elation, while Fannie reached under the table beside Clare to squeeze her hand.

Clare squeezed back.

"Myshka, I assure you, it was only a suggestion." Natalya turned a smile on Marcus. "I thought consistency might do you more good than switching back and forth, and it is an excellent facility."

"It is a wonderful facility," Clare agreed, yet she was determined to hold her ground. Her eyes went back to her patient. "For now, however, you should get reacquainted with your home and your family. When you're ready, you can decide about seeing the hospital for yourself."

Marcus smiled at her, while Natalya shrugged. "As long as he remembers everything as quickly as possible." She offered him a coy look. "So we can plan our wedding."

"Ah, the soup has arrived." Mrs. Weatherford greeted the first course as though she was relieved to avoid any further sparring between Clare and Natalya, either about nuptials or whether to incarcerate her son in the west wing.

Annoyed by Natalya's reminder of the upcoming wedding, Clare was nonetheless reassured that Marcus would remain home to recover and would do much better spending his nights here instead of the hospital. The thought of his suffering a nightmare in that strange place made her heart twist. Who would check on him or soothe him if he awakened again thrashing in the night?

"Madam?"

She looked up as Hanson stood beside her ready to serve her the creamed pea soup. Once he'd finished and moved on, Clare eyed the small spoon next to her crystal water glass, then the spoon beside the knives. Which should she use? At the Benninghams' party weeks ago, she'd been so rattled by Stephen Lange's presence beside her at dinner, she hadn't paid much attention once Marcus had offered her hints from across the table on the order of each utensil.

Perhaps it's time he flung his gravy and potatoes . . .

She almost giggled as she recalled his earlier promise: to create such a mess tonight that no one would notice which spoon she used.

Clare looked up at him, hoping he'd share her humor, but Hanson was serving him. She glanced at Fannie instead and mirrored her actions in taking up the spoon beside the knives. Careful to sip and not slurp, she tasted the fine fare and agreed with Marcus that Mrs. Connelly's soup was delicious.

"Mrs. Danner, what captured your interest today on the tour?"

Startled that Sir Geoffrey had asked the question, Clare quickly set down her spoon. "The conservatory is a wondrous place, Sir Geoffrey. Your granddaughter told me that her grandmother started the project?"

"Yes, my Charlotte was an avid gardener, much like our Frances here." He looked to Fannie, love shining in his eyes. "She has inherited her grandmother's gift for making every kind of flower, fruit, vegetable, and tree thrive. Which I'm sure you witnessed today."

Clare nodded. "I understand you sent home exotic plants from your travels?"

"That's true. After my wife passed, I decided to journey through much of Europe and parts of Asia, where I collected the different species."

"They're all so beautiful," Clare said. "Many of the plants I've only seen before in books."

"I also was impressed with the conservatory," Natalya said. "Fortunately, I've traveled extensively and recognized many of the foreign species. And you, Frances, have continued your family tradition marvelously."

Fannie blushed, looking pleased by all the attention, while Clare smiled, hiding her irritation at Natalya's words. Though it stung knowing she wasn't as worldly as the ballerina or Sir Geoffrey, Clare *was* happy for her friend. Fannie had surely earned the praise, and after the cruel taunts she'd endured in the past, she deserved to be recognized for her gifts.

Clare's soup was only half finished when the bowls were taken up by Teddy, the second footman, and Hanson followed with the next course—a silver platter of roasted potatoes, carrots, onions, and tiny bits of bacon.

Was this the salad . . . or the meat course? Clare tensed a moment, before more humor touched her lips. Marcus would likely suggest she be fair about it and use each fork to take a bite of the food.

Again she looked at him, and saw he'd read her thoughts. Grabbing up all three forks from beside his plate, he held them in a fist against the table, as though he planned to eat with all three at once. While she bit her lip to keep from laughing, he set them down again and touched the middle fork as he gave her a wink.

The vegetables were considered salad, then. She was still smiling as her gaze shifted to Natalya, who had been watching their exchange.

The ballerina was shaking her head, her look of amused pity branding fire on Clare's skin.

Leaving the salad fork, Clare reached for her goblet of water and took several sips to collect herself while she tried bolstering her courage. *The Weatherfords invited you to sit at their table. Don't let her get to you . . .*

Yet Clare's lightened mood evaporated as the old shame came crashing down around her. She set down her glass, her eyes burning as she again took in the crystal and china, the elaborate floral table arrangements. Why was she fooling herself? She shouldn't be here, dressed in gauzy silk and seed pearls and dining at this beautifully elegant table, in a mansion that was more palace than country home!

Her appetite had deserted her, and she wanted nothing more than to escape. These people, having so much, hadn't any idea about who she was, or what she'd been before, or how her life had changed due to circumstances.

Be strong. Your baby needs you.

Clare gritted her teeth. She had to stay and see this through.

Picking up her fork, she began to eat, hardly tasting the food yet determined to chew every morsel. Ignoring the others at the table, she only looked up to follow Fannie's cue as each new course was served.

Forty-five minutes later, as the dessert cups were being collected, Clare realized she'd succeeded in getting through the entire meal.

It was time for the ladies to go through, and she leaned toward Fannie, ready to make her excuses to visit the nursery.

Her friend turned to her, brown eyes gleaming. "You were wonderful with my brother tonight," she whispered. "I'm so glad you spoke up for him, and you spoke *to him.*"

Fannie glanced toward Natalya, who was already exiting the dining room with Mrs. Weatherford. "Some people don't realize that a person's dignity is inherent to them, a gift from God. And no one has the right to trample on it or dismiss it. Or talk over it."

Clare's heart swelled at Fannie's words. No, she wasn't rich, and she didn't know much about etiquette or fashion. Her days at the hospital were long and exhausting, and she lived in the shabbier part of London. Yet Clare had her dignity, just like everyone else, and she'd lost sight of that fact, until Fannie reminded her.

She would continue to do her job, working toward Marcus's healing. And no more browbeating herself—Fannie had accepted her easily enough, and it was time Clare did the same. She'd also promised Jack that she would become better acquainted with the Weatherfords, but they would have to make an effort with her, too.

"Shall we?" she said to Fannie. And rising from their seats, Clare linked an arm with hers as they headed in the direction of the other two women.

She'd come too far to let the ballerina win.

22

S he was angry with him.

Marcus sat in his wheelchair the following morning as the woman in question silently pushed him along the gray slate path leading toward the west end of the estate.

Last night at dinner he'd appreciated the way she'd championed his freedom, speaking up about the hospital arrangements in the west wing and asking him what *he'd* like to do.

But then it seemed in the next minute, her smile had disappeared and she was staring at him red-faced, before ignoring him entirely for the rest of the meal. What had he done?

By the time she'd come to check on him for the evening, her mood had completely transformed. Gone was the teasing and laughter, and in its place, a cool reserve any nurse might use with a patient.

And this morning, she'd arrived to remove his stitches wearing a white hospital smock for the first time. She'd even checked his temperature with a thermometer instead of using the back of her hand, as though she wished to avoid touching him entirely.

"I think you will like being here, myshka."

Jarred from his brooding, Marcus turned to Natalya, who had paused on the path ahead, her hand raised toward the west wing of the estate. "Is it not beautiful?"

He took in the large patio area, now scattered with several tables and chairs, and at its farthest corner, the knotted old plane tree that had offered shade in that spot since before he was born. Behind the patio, a colorful dahlia garden bloomed in profusion.

Despite the serene setting, Marcus tightened his hold on the arms of the wheelchair. How could he enjoy the place? His only recent memories were those of him lying in a shadowy hospital room, disorientated, and being directed about. And the stench . . .

A shiver coursed through him as his mind returned to those first moments of consciousness: the smell of blood, disinfectant, and gunpowder attacking his senses as he'd awakened in the cold gloom of that place. He couldn't understand why the odors affected him now, only that he feared being around them. The smell of the sick and the dying . . .

The sudden jostle of the wheelchair nearly unseated him as the wheels hit a section of uneven stone.

"Marcus, are you all right?"

Clare's breathy words sounded behind him as she halted the chair.

"Fine," he bit out, his insides coiled with tension.

"Just hold on, we're almost there."

Again her husky voice reached him, and as they resumed their progress, she leaned in to push him over another bumpy patch in the path. He could smell the honeysuckle, her labored breathing warming the back of his neck.

And you're nothing but a lump in this infernal chair. He reached down and began pushing forward on the chair's wheels in an effort to help her. He lasted only a few seconds before he was out of breath, the muscles in his arms trembling.

Blast! He was as helpless as a babe. "Let me . . . out."

The wheelchair halted.

213

"Myshka, what is wrong?"

Natalya had turned on the path, concern in her expression. "Are you in pain?"

Clare moved to the front of his chair, blocking his view as she leaned over him, still somewhat winded. "Are you ill, Marcus?"

"I want to walk," he ground out. "No need to push me."

She looked toward Natalya, then back at him. "We tried that once in your room, remember? Your sense of balance was quite off then."

"That was two days ago. I want to try again." Staring up at her, he couldn't help noticing her shining hair and fine brows black as jet. The heart-shaped mouth that had laughed with him, scolded him, and those full cherry-red lips seeming soft . . .

He swallowed. "You're tired, and I'm useless in trying to manage the wheels, and much too heavy for you to be carting about."

Beneath the black lashes, her gray eyes had darkened to thunderclouds. She straightened and rested her hands at her small waist. "You don't remember, Marcus, but I baled hay for many months last year. Since then I've been handling patients your size on a daily basis at the hospital. I'm perfectly capable of pushing you in this wheelchair from here to Bristol if necessary."

Suddenly she was behind him again, and they were moving.

"Listen to your nurse, milyi." Natalya returned to his side. "Soon you will be well enough to walk on your own again. Just give it time."

Marcus didn't like Natalya's coddling, but his head hurt and he didn't wish to argue. As they finally arrived at their destination, Clare parked his chair in the shade of the plane tree, not far from half a dozen chaise lounges arranged together on the lawn.

"Now, you must meet the soldiers and make friends," Natalya instructed. "I am certain that your being in this place will help you to heal."

Marcus looked up sharply, his pulse quickening. Did she and Clare plan to leave him here as Natalya had suggested at dinner last night?

"Face your demons, Child." A voice emerged, unbidden, from somewhere in his thoughts. It was familiar to him, though one he hadn't heard since he was very young. Was it Father?

He drew a deep breath and surveyed his surroundings. Near the edge of the patio beside the dahlia garden, two patients in night-robes sat at one of the white wrought-iron tables reading newspapers, just as Marcus had seen the other day with Jack. A few feet away, three more patients, hair cropped short and clad in similar garb, sat playing cards. A young kerchiefed nurse had brought a tray and was passing out glasses of lemonade and plates of biscuits.

"See how lovely this is," Natalya said brightly. "You should go and speak with that nice soldier over there in the wheelchair. I think we saw him yesterday during our tour."

He followed her gaze to a table, where a scowling, russet-haired man in nightclothes crossed his arms and pointedly ignored the tall, stocky orderly leaning to speak to him.

The chap looked as miserable being here as Marcus felt. And what sort of intelligent conversation would the two of them have? Talking about the weather or comparing notable features on their wheelchairs?

Marcus couldn't remember much more than that. "I'll stay here, thank you."

Natalya's brow creased as she eyed him. "Very well, milyi," she said. "We must walk before we run, da? I shall go see about refreshments while Mrs. Danner gets you settled."

She nodded to Clare behind him, then touched his hand before following the young nurse who carried the now-empty refreshment tray.

Once she'd gone, Marcus scanned the rest of the faces of the wounded.

"How do you feel, Marcus?"

Clare moved around the wheelchair and again stood in his line of view. She swiftly assessed him, her features still somewhat strained.

"Are you upset with me?" The question spilled from him like water.

"Yes . . . no." She sighed, a rosy hue tinting her pale complexion. "I've just finally come to realize that while we're all equally entitled to our dignity, it doesn't mean our lives are the same."

What was she saying? "I don't understand."

"What I mean is, I'm never going to fit into this world you live in." She looked out toward his Sherwood Forest. "Your family has wealth, title, and lands, while I'm a woman much like Janet, Ellen, or Nellie, polishing silver, stoking fires, and changing bed sheets."

Her eyes turned back to him. "Like my mum, I was a servant for many years. Last night's dinner merely reminded me of my place."

"Preposterous!" Anger surged in him. "I hope I didn't make you feel that way."

"Not intentionally." She smiled. "You are what you are, Marcus, and it's nothing that can be helped."

Disturbed by her words, he leaned back in the chair and studied her. What kind of man was he? He could recall most of the pieces of his childhood, even moments at Harrow School, but what about later as an adult? Had he turned arrogant and selfish, thinking himself above others?

Regardless, he'd managed to hurt Clare, and Marcus sensed that last night's dinner wasn't the first time. But when? How? His frustration nipped at him. If he could have just talked with Jack before the man left for London!

Marcus wanted to know more about the relationship between himself and this woman, and why she refused to speak of it. He felt as though he'd been blindfolded to his own character. Was he a proud man? What were his values? Had he believed in God?

A painful memory flashed in his mind—a boy of thirteen, standing on the crest of a hill overlooking the chestnut grove well beyond the dahlia garden. Shaking with fear as he crushed a telegram in his fist, news of his father's death. Angry at Father for breaking his promise to come home, and raging at God on that hill for betraying a boy's trust by allowing his father to die.

Marcus had avoided church after that—not difficult since Fannie was helpless and grief held their mother captive in her rooms. Only after Grandfather quit his travels to return to them did he force Marcus to attend services again.

Did that young boy's resentment ever fade? Or had it turned him into a monster?

"I never meant to hurt you, Clare," he said, his voice thick. He searched her face, noting once more her smooth complexion, like his mother's finest porcelain. "And if I have *ever* behaved in a way that injured you, then I'm heartily sorry for it."

She looked at him for a long moment, her dark eyes filled with the same pain and longing he'd witnessed yesterday, before she slowly nodded. "I accept your apology."

He smiled his relief, the afternoon's anxiety suddenly releasing him. "Thank you."

She leaned toward him, pressing the back of her hand against his face. "Are you too warm?"

His heart thrummed at her touch. "Yes, it's like Hades out here."

The afternoon's sultry air offered little breeze, and his damp skin itched under the bandage. He could tell Clare also felt the heat, her exposed neck and throat glistening. *Not surprising, after she pushed you the entire way here in this blasted chair.*

She'd said earlier that she baled hay for many months last year and that he wouldn't remember, which meant that he'd been there or at least known of it. When had they first met, and what did it have to do with her little girl? *"You still love Daisy . . ."*

Her plea to him that day in the hospital, and later on the train, when the baby's blond curls rested against Clare's breast as her child stared at him with big dark eyes, pointing her chubby finger. *"Da."*

Shock rolled through him. Was Daisy . . . his?

He tried to recall all that Clare had said to him about her troubles, begging him to save Daisy—

Marcus whipped his eyes to her, his pulse accelerating. She'd said *our* Daisy . . .

"Marcus?" She eyed him with concern. "Would you like to move to one of the tables? You don't have to sit with anyone if you'd rather not, but a chair might be more comfortable than this old thing."

He drew a deep breath. "All right." Though he'd wanted to question her, he resisted, unwilling to tear at the fragile bond they'd mended. And he did want out of this wheeled prison.

"We'll get you seated and remove that blazer, so you can cool down." She wheeled him over to a table near two enlisted men, and after assisting him into one of the patio chairs, she helped as he shrugged his arms out of the jacket.

"Cor, will ye look at 'er, Roberts?"

Marcus glanced up to see a stocky young corporal in a neck bandage leering at Clare. "When did ye arrive, Sister? If I'd 'eard there was such tempting scenery 'ere in 'ampshire, I'd 'ave asked to come sooner."

One arm still in his jacket sleeve, Marcus halted to glare at the insolent man. "Mind your tongue, Soldier."

"Oh, aye?" The other man, Roberts, a sergeant, gave him a smug look. "And who are ye, to be telling my pal Johnson what he can or can't say?" His blond brows slanted. "Ye just got here and already yer thinking ye own the farm, is that it?"

"He does own it. The entire estate."

All three men turned to Clare, her flashing eyes belying the softly spoken words. "Captain Sir Marcus Weatherford is wise to tell you to take care about what you say, gentlemen. I won't have any of that rude talk while you're here at the estate, do you understand?" She raised her head, looking down at them. "And I trust you don't speak of the other nurses in such a way?"

"Aye, Sister! I mean . . . no, Sister!" Johnson was the first to launch from his seat.

His friend quickly followed. "Apologies, Cap'n, I mean . . . yer lordship." Roberts bobbed his head, his youthful face flushed.

"Me too, sir." Johnson, with his neck bandaged, had to wield a salute instead.

"At ease, both of you." The words slipped from him easily, as though he'd said them countless times before. Startled, Marcus turned and caught sight of the russet-haired patient in the wheelchair several feet away eyeing him curiously.

"Such nonsense from those boys."

Clare was tugging again on the sleeve of his coat. Marcus realized the sergeant and corporal had taken his order as their cue to escape.

He glanced at her. He'd been an officer? And knighted?

He loosened his collar. "Which branch?"

She looked at him, bemused, before her features softened, her full mouth curving slightly. "You're a naval captain, Marcus. With the Admiralty at Whitehall in London." She tilted her head. "No one has told you?"

The Admiralty. His heart rate sped. Natalya mentioned Whitehall at tea the other day. "For how long?"

"The past four years of war at least. Maybe longer." She finished folding his jacket. "You were a lieutenant when we first met, but it wasn't long afterward that you moved up the ranks to receive your captain's stripe."

"And the knighthood?"

She shrugged. "That was before I met you, but your grandfather should know."

He eyed her steadily. "And we first met when . . ."

But she merely pursed her lips, giving him a sidelong glance before she set the folded jacket in the empty wheelchair.

Would she not answer him this time? What was she hiding?

Again his memory flashed to the child on the train and Daisy's single word to him connecting them both.

He stared at her, his pulse galloping like a thoroughbred crossing the finish line at Ascot. "Is Daisy . . . is she mine—?"

"Myshka, I am back, and I have found our refreshments!"

Marcus held Clare's shocked gaze another moment before he turned at Natalya's approach. Behind her, the same nurse carried an identical tray of lemonades and biscuits.

"Shall we all enjoy a little afternoon repast?"

Setting the food on the table, the young nurse eyed Natalya nervously—and then knocked the plate of biscuits, sending several rolling across the table onto the ground.

"Oh, pardon me!" she cried and bent to collect them back onto the plate.

"See that we receive a fresh plateful," Natalya instructed, taking her seat. When the girl had gone, she smiled at Clare. "Come, you must sit with us . . . What is wrong, Mrs. Danner? You are so pale." Her gaze narrowed on Marcus. "Myshka, what did you say to her? What did I miss?"

He raised a brow at her sharp tone. "I only asked a few questions."

"What questions?" She looked back to Clare, who slid into the other chair.

"About my life." He frowned at her. "Why didn't you tell me that I'm a captain in His Majesty's Royal Navy and assigned to the Admiralty in London?"

Natalya ignored him, turning her sober gaze on Clare. "In future, Mrs. Danner, you will please consult me first before . . . sharing any details with Marcus about his past."

Her pinched mouth relaxed then, and she smiled. "You see, the doctor at Cottage Hospital explained it might be harmful to give Marcus too much information too soon. It could overwhelm him."

Natalya wasn't wrong; his heart was still racing. *Daisy is my daughter . . .*

"I understand, Mrs. Bryce." Clare turned to him, her eyes still wide. "And I'll take more care in the future."

"Of course you will." Natalya brightened. "After all, Marcus must learn to walk again before he runs."

She reached for a lemonade. "Another reason I did not tell you before, myshka, was because it is not critical to your healing. However, now you should feel more comfortable being here with the patients. Like you, they are all military men who have been fighting to win the war."

"I will visit them, Natalya," he said, nostrils flaring, "but I'm not staying here and that's final."

Clare hid her satisfaction at Natalya's stunned look. It was about time Marcus stopped letting her run him around.

Though Clare, too, was a bit unhinged over his questioning Daisy's parentage. Had she given him the impression her daughter was his when she'd asked for his help? The way he'd looked at her earlier, as if he wanted to know but was afraid . . .

Maybe the London doctor was right, and when she'd gone to plead with Marcus to save Daisy from Randleton, she'd unknowingly caused him to panic. And when the two soldiers needed a good dressing-down minutes ago, had she let her anger at them overrule her good judgment? *Watch yourself, Clare. Natalya may have stolen his heart, but he's still in your care.*

Had the ballerina stolen his heart? Minutes ago, Clare had seen Marcus's distress when he realized he'd hurt her. Not so much last night, but he seemed to understand a rift of some kind had occurred between them in their past. *"And if I have ever behaved in a way that injured you . . ."*

She eased out a trembling breath. With every moment they spent together, her traitorous hopes increased, along with the ache in her heart and the fear that at any moment she would realize she'd gotten it all wrong, and her life would again shatter into a thousand tiny pieces.

Natalya continued prattling on at the table as though nothing had happened. Clare picked up a glass of the lemonade and offered it to Marcus, his hand shaking only slightly as he brought the glass to his lips.

Watching as he drank greedily, her thoughts whirled around his earlier question about Daisy, and a kind of painful bliss filled her—the idea that she and Marcus could have married and had a child of their own together, just like her baby.

221

Be careful, a small voice whispered. She glanced back toward the front of the castle and Montefalco's tree-lined drive stretching to the main road.

Jack had said he would try to return by midweek and bring Grace with him. Tomorrow was Wednesday . . .

Clare prayed for it. She needed her best friend's common sense and support.

23

Clare rose early the following morning, dressing quickly before she slipped through the passageway to check on Marcus.

Relieved that he was still sleeping peacefully, she returned and left her room to ascend the stairs toward the nursery. Already seven days had passed—half of her time until Randleton carried out his threat.

She burst into the nursery, relieved to see Daisy awake and lying in her cot. Ruthie snored softly in the narrow bed across the room.

"Are you my little angel, Daisy Do?" she whispered as she approached, and Daisy rewarded her with a sleepy grin as Clare gently lifted her into her arms.

She cuddled her baby a moment before taking her to the water closet in the adjoining room. Once the task at hand was accomplished and Daisy was praised by her mum, they returned to the nursery, and Clare grabbed the blanket from the cot before settling into the high-backed rocking chair beside it.

"Hosey, Mama." Daisy pointed to the rocking horse at the

room's center. The faded colors of the wooden horse seemed to glow with the sun's early rays through the nursery window.

"You surely love that horse, don't you, baby?" she murmured into Daisy's curls, breathing in the ineffable scent of her child, her heart overflowing. "Maybe one day when you grow up, you can be a woman equestrian."

"Kestyan." Daisy nodded, mimicking the word.

Clare grinned. "That's close enough for now, sweetheart."

Having snuggled her in the blanket, she leaned to kiss her chubby cheek. "And you can ride 'hoseys' all day long."

"Hosey!" Daisy shouted again, and before Clare could shush her, the snoring Ruthie made snuffling noises and squinted her eyes open.

She turned to them, blinking. "Mrs. Danner?"

"Rootie!" Daisy chortled, waving at the young woman in bed.

Ruthie sat up and scrubbed her face with her hands before yawning loudly. "What's the time?"

"It's just seven o'clock now," Clare said. "If you'd like to get a few more winks, I'll take care of Daisy while you sleep."

"D'ye think his lordship is coming back to Hampshire today?"

Clare had awakened this morning with that same hope. "I'm counting on it, especially since he's to bring Lady Walenford with him."

Almost a week had passed since she'd left London to come to Hampshire, and Clare fiercely missed her friend's companionship and advice.

"Ye know, my sister still calls her Grace."

"Becky's a good friend to her ladyship and to all of us." Images arose, and again Clare reminisced over the beautiful Kent countryside where she, Becky, Lucy, and Grace had worked the farms together last year. "Your sister's allowed to be familiar with her when they're not in public. And they see each other at Swan's, of course."

"Aye." Ruthie swung her legs over onto the carpeted floor. "Becky tells me all the time how she's grateful to be workin' at the tearoom for her ladyship's father. It sure helps our family out of a pinch at home."

She smiled shyly at Clare. "I'm grateful, too, being able to work as that sweet one's nanny and help my family as well."

Clare tensed as she smiled at the girl. Last week she'd hoped to give Ruthie a pay rise, but now she prayed the girl's job as Daisy's nanny wouldn't soon come to an end.

So much depended on Marcus . . .

She shook off her morose thoughts. "Ruthie, I've decided this morning to take Daisy out to the garden before breakfast, so you've a couple of hours to do as you like." If she couldn't increase the girl's wages, at least she could offer her some free time.

"Thank ye, Mrs. Danner." Ruthie reached up to finger-comb her hair. "I could do with a nice bath."

"Take your time." Clare set Daisy's feet on the floor and then rose to head for the dresser and get her child fresh clothing.

She turned as Daisy ran to Ruthie and gave her a hug. Ruthie looked down at her, making funny eyes. "And when ye bring little miss back here, I suppose she'll need to ride the *h-o-r-s-e* again today."

"Hosey!" Daisy clapped her hands, and Clare chuckled. "She's becoming a very smart little girl, Ruthie. Take care what you say around her if you don't want it repeated."

"Da!" Daisy proclaimed, turning to point a chubby hand toward the closed nursery door.

Clare sobered. She'd so far been able to postpone giving Marcus answers to yesterday's questions about Daisy, and about when he and Clare had first met. Between Natalya's presence and then Daisy's fussing again in the afternoon—which had kept Clare in the nursery for the evening meal—the two of them hadn't spoken.

And last night, when she'd slipped into his room to sit with him for a while, Clare was relieved that he'd remained sleeping peacefully. *You can't avoid him forever.*

For now, though, she'd enjoy this time with her daughter.

"Come here, Daisy Do. Let's get you dressed. Ruthie wants her bath."

"Bat!" Daisy echoed and ran to Clare, who picked her up and set her in the rocking chair to change her clothes.

Once Clare had dressed and bundled Daisy in the blanket, they left Ruthie to enjoy her leisure and went downstairs to the main floor.

"I'll just get my wrap, little one," she said, making a detour to her room.

She set Daisy on her feet inside and moved to open the armoire, sifting through her meager wardrobe for her shawl. She turned to her daughter. "Now, if your mum only had those dozens of fancy jackets that Mrs. Bryce has in her trunks—"

A loud *thump* penetrated the wall, followed by a groan.

"Marcus!" She rushed from the armoire to the bookcase, and seconds later had the secret door wide open. Peering into the passageway, she turned to glance at Daisy, who stood eyeing her in wonder.

She had to get to Marcus, but what would she find?

"I can't just leave you here. Come with me, sweetheart." She scooped Daisy into her arms and hurried the short distance to the study door.

Entering, her gaze flew to the bed. It was empty. "Marcus?"

She looked past the empty wheelchair to the table before Daisy called out, "Da!"

Marcus lay on the floor behind the wheelchair, still in his nightclothes. He looked dazed, and Clare quickly set Daisy down and went to kneel by his side. "What happened?"

He squeezed his eyes closed, baring his teeth. "I tried . . . walking."

Daisy toddled over beside them. Bending at the waist, she stared at him. "Da?" She placed a pudgy hand against his cheek. "Okay?"

Eyes opened, he stared at the child. Clare held her breath and prayed. *Oh, God, please let him remember her!*

Daisy plopped down on the floor next to him. Marcus's reaction alternated between wonder and fear. Finally, he raised himself to sitting, and she immediately climbed into his lap.

He looked to Clare. "Is she—?"

"No, she's not yours, at least not by blood. Though without a father, you've come to fill that place in her heart." There, she'd told him. Clare studied him a moment before she added, "You often came to visit us in London when you were in town. Daisy still holds much affection for you."

"Fly!" Daisy shouted, stretching her arms wide. "Fly me, Da."

Marcus glanced up at Clare, bemused.

"She remembers how you would pick her up and whirl her around in the air." Clare smiled, gazing at her daughter. "She thrilled at being like a bird in the sky."

"Bird, Da!" Daisy reached for one of his hands, pulling on his fingers with her tiny ones. "Up, up."

"Daisy, stop," Clare said firmly. "Marcus cannot fly with you right now. Mum needs to help him get up off the floor."

She leaned to pluck Daisy from his lap and then moved around behind Marcus, helping to raise him and propel him back onto his feet.

He slipped his arm over her shoulder as she maneuvered him back into the chair. "Why were you trying to walk without help?"

"I'm tired of being a burden." He looked up at her. "Despite what you say."

"You could have lain on that floor for hours," she pointed out. Then she teased him, "And what if Teddy and Lewis had decided to return with the rug? They would have rolled it out right over you."

"A mysterious lump in the carpet?"

"A rather large one, I'd say." She grinned, pleased to see him smiling, too, regardless of the emotional consequences. "Daisy and I were about to venture out for a stroll in the garden before breakfast. Would you care to join us?"

He looked down at his undershirt and pajama bottoms. "I'll need to get dressed first."

"Why should you? After all, you're my patient and this is your home to do in as you please, and that includes strolling about your own grounds. I'll just help you into your robe"—she gave him a quick glance—"unless you'd rather have Hanson come in and get you ready?"

"Help me into my robe," he said. "The fresh air will clear the cobwebs from last night."

She fetched his night-robe from the foot of the bed and once again aided him to standing as he shrugged into the garment and tied it off.

"What about slippers?" Noticing he was barefoot, she turned to her daughter. "Daisy, will you please get Da's shoes?" She pointed toward the slippers beneath the bed.

Daisy tottered over and brought back a single shoe, then tried to put it on his foot, making her and Marcus both grin as it hung skewed from his big toe.

"Now the other one," she said, and while Daisy went after it, Marcus leaned to straighten the slipper and then winked at her, causing Clare's heart to hum with pleasure.

Once he was shod and ready to go, she wrapped Daisy back in her blanket and set her on his lap. "I'll drive while you two navigate."

One of the young maids, Nellie, eyed them in surprise as she crossed their path heading down the hall.

"Have you been to the conservatory since your return?"

When he shook his head, Clare turned the wheelchair in that direction, and after propping open one of the double glass doors, Marcus manned the wheels and pulled the chair across the threshold.

The hothouse was quiet this early in the morning, except for the occasional chirping of birds high above their heads.

"This is a lovely place to be," she said as they rolled along the stone path edged by exotic trees, various shrubs, and colorful blooms. "Do you remember this, Marcus?"

Clare noted her daughter's head thrown back against his chest, her dark eyes staring up at the light streaming through the glass ceiling. She pointed a finger upward. "Sky, Mama!"

"Yes, that's the sky up there, baby."

"I do remember it," Marcus said. "There wasn't so much greenery then, and the trees were not nearly as tall."

"Your sister has been busy working out here and it shows."

"Yes, she's done an incredible job."

"Have you visited with each other yet?"

When he didn't answer her, Clare leaned forward and whispered in his ear, "I think she's been avoiding you as much as you've been avoiding her."

He turned to her, their faces mere inches apart. Clare's pulse leapt as his honey-brown eyes searched hers, the musky scent of his spice cologne surrounding her.

"I don't know what to say to her," he said finally.

"Hmm, yes, she gave me the same story." Clare straightened. "Did you know that she went off to university to become a horticulturist? And that she still remembers your childhood adventures into the cellarium?"

She began moving them forward again. "You really should talk with her, Marcus. She loves you so dearly, and I know if you let her tell you about herself, it might help you both."

He grunted, nodding, and said no more as they continued through the lush maze, finally exiting the conservatory onto the east patio garden.

The spired angel fountain they passed yesterday on their way to the rehabilitation hospital was now spewing water into the pool.

"Flowers!" Daisy cried, spreading her arms toward the red and orange zinnias, pink and white carnations, and yellow lilies on tall green stalks.

"Tell me when we met, Clare."

Abruptly she halted the wheelchair.

"Please," he said, turning his head slightly. "I need to know."

"Last summer." It seemed she couldn't put him off about that any longer. "In Kent when I was working for the Women's Forage Corps on Jack's estate. He introduced you to all of us girls in the work gang."

"And?"

"You and I became friends."

"What about Daisy's father?"

Clare pursed her lips, then said, "He was gone."

"So you were a widow then?"

She stared at his profile. "In a manner of speaking."

"What does that mean?"

She should tell him the truth. He'd said he remembered only parts of what she'd told him in her panicked outburst at Cottage Hospital in London.

Only Daisy's soft babbling broke the stillness, her gaze everywhere, from the fountain with angels spewing water to the flowers and the birds flying overhead.

"I gave birth to Daisy before I met you," Clare said at length. "She's the natural daughter of Sir Elliot Lange, recently killed in the war. When I was . . ." She wet her lips. "When I was removed from the house where I served and whisked off to the Magdalene asylum, Daisy was taken from me by the family after she was born."

"Criminy! What kind of people are they?" His quiet voice held rage, and Daisy paused to turn and stare up at him. He softened his tone. "I remember when you came to see me. You wanted me to save her."

"I did," Clare admitted. "When I met you last year, I was looking for my daughter. You located Daisy in a workhouse orphanage in Kent where she'd been shabbily treated, and you returned her to me."

"And now with the son dead, his family has decided they want her?"

"Yes." Clare gripped the back of the wheelchair. "I'm afraid of what they'll do to her if she displeases them, or if they tire of her, or maybe they're just interested in the inheritance Elliot left her." She swallowed. "Most of all I live in terror of being parted from her again."

Marcus held the small squirming toddler on his lap, her silken curls pressed against his chest. She seemed to view the world around her like a stage play, waiting for the first act to begin. Instinctively, he tightened his hold on her while his mind came to grips with Clare's words.

"You'll need to tell Randleton that you'll testify to what you saw in Kent last year when you found our sweet Daisy . . ."

Her plea to him at the hospital. "That's why you're here," he said. "The reason you wanted to help me to heal. If I can remember what happened, I'll be able to stand up in court for you and Daisy."

Silence. Then, "Jack asked me to come to Hampshire so I'd have the chance to try before it's too late."

"When?"

"Viscount Randleton gave me a fortnight before he intends to petition the courts. Today is the seventh day."

And only seven remained. Marcus closed his eyes, clenching his teeth. How could he help her to help this child when he couldn't manage to keep his balance for two seconds together? And the memories Clare needed from him were still behind a blank wall. *God, why did you let this happen to me again? Not for myself this time, but the child and Clare need me. How can I help them like this, a useless, mindless . . .*

At the sudden warm pressure against his face, he opened his eyes to gaze into twin pools the color of flint. "Okay?" Daisy whispered, touching him with her small pudgy hand.

He forced a smile for her. "Okay."

Seeming convinced, she turned back around on his lap.

"I'll stay in that hospital if you think it will speed things up," he said, twisting toward Clare.

"Oh, Marcus." Suddenly she was around the chair and crouching beside him, her eyes once again soft and wet like rain. She searched his face. "I love you for saying that, but I don't want you to be in a place where you feel uncomfortable."

"I love you . . ." He leaned into the words, holding Daisy tight so that she wouldn't topple out of the chair. "I want to help," he

said gruffly. "Do you think it would be better if I stay with others like me?"

"It might help. But I still think being here with your family is best." She tilted her gaze at him. "Why don't you go and visit the hospital every day, even if it's just for lemonade and biscuits? At least then you can get acquainted with some of the other soldiers, and I'll bring you back here afterward."

Relief coursed through him. He'd much rather stay near her. Near Daisy. "Yes, it's a good plan." He paused. "And you'll start coming to dinner again?"

She nodded. "We'll both make an effort with your family, all right? The more you're able to fill in the gaps here at home, the better chance you can piece your whole life back together."

"I will try." He smiled, his jaw stiff. And not just for this child, but for her mother as well.

He had seven days.

24

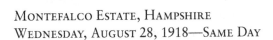

Miss Weatherford? Are ye here?"

At the sound of Deering's voice, Fannie emerged from behind the screen where she'd been rinsing and stacking more pots. She had arrived at the conservatory early this morning and caught sight of her brother out with Clare and Daisy in the garden.

She hoped her friend had brought Marcus inside so he could see for himself the work she'd been doing. At least it would be a place Fannie could start a conversation with him.

Her cheeks warmed to see the orderly had company. Fannie had spied Lieutenant Ainsley reading out on the hospital patio the other day when she, Clare, and Natalya had made their tour.

"Mr. Deering, Lieutenant Ainsley," she said before quickly wiping at the crumbles of soil still clinging to her apron. "You have come to tour the conservatory?"

Now clad in his uniform rather than the robe he'd worn before, the lieutenant colored with the same flush of heat. "I wished to learn more about the sky flowers that need planting."

233

"Oh, the Plumbago auriculata! Of course." She glanced toward the long raised planter still empty from yesterday and then bent to retrieve the crate of sky flower starts. By moving them to the built-in side table beside the planter, it would allow him easy access from the wheelchair.

Her grandfather had built it for Grandmother after she was confined to a wheelchair, and Fannie was glad the table remained. "I'd hoped to get these into the soil today, but I still need to finish planting a crate of Hosta ventricosa."

Silence ensued for several seconds while Fannie stood twisting her fingers together and hardly daring to breathe. Would he accept her task?

"Well?" Deering finally murmured to him in a low voice. "Ye wanted to come to the conservatory, lad, and now yer here."

The lieutenant gazed at Fannie, the soft look in his green eyes heightening her senses. "If you would still like the help, Miss Weatherford, I am at your service."

His husky Scots burr sent a tingle through her. "Oh, yes! Please, come over here by the planter, and I'll bring you a garden spade, a pair of gloves, and a watering can."

Slipping back behind the screen, she pressed herself against the wall, her hand clasped over her racing heart. *Lord, surely you have granted us both a miracle!*

Quickly she recovered and, grabbing the implements, returned to the men and found Deering had positioned the lieutenant's wheelchair on the left side next to the planter. "You're left-handed, Lieutenant?"

"I am," he said. "And you?"

"Right." She raised the full watering can slightly before setting it with the gloves and spade next to the full crate. "Just space the plants evenly apart—"

"Ten to twelve inches and four inches deep, aye?"

She nodded, blinking.

"The lieutenant here is a botanist," Deering explained. "Went to that famous university at Dundee, north of Edinburgh."

Fannie stared. "So you do know quite a lot about plants . . . and all manner of things." It explained why he was so bitter. Botanists usually traveled extensively to discover new species of plants in the wild. Likely the lieutenant felt his career was over. "How long did you practice your science before . . ."

"Before I went to the war?" His mouth twisted. "When conscription came in sixteen and gave me no choice." He gave her a side glance. "I'm no coward either, if that's what you're thinking."

"Oh no, I . . . I am not thinking anything." Her face warmed as she realized what she'd said. *Ninny!* "What I mean is—"

"I ken what you meant, lass."

His smile made her pulse quicken, and her shoulders eased. He had such a nice face. "You were working on a project before that?"

"Aye, experimenting with making chemicals out of several natural substances. Like your grove of *Aesculus hippocastanum*. Deering tells me the harvest is sent to a factory in Dorset, where they convert the fruit into acetone for cordite in munitions?"

She nodded. "Before the war, we sold our horse chestnuts to science institutes for creating topical medicines. Now our harvest is serving a more critical purpose in aiding the soldiers overseas."

"I wasna far enough along in my experiments to get excused from serving my country, and I managed to last a couple of years before this happened." He glared at his feet—or rather right foot, now clad in a serviceable leather boot.

"Well, I'm grateful for your help this afternoon," she said, determined to lighten his mood.

"How long shall I leave ye here, lad?" Deering asked.

The lieutenant considered the starts in the crate, then the soil, and then Fannie. "A couple of hours should do it."

"Righto." Deering gave her a wink as he touched a lock of his hair. "Miss Weatherford."

"So you do all the work in here yourself?" the lieutenant asked when Deering was gone.

"Most everything, unless I need a heavy planter lifted. Then Mr. Bauer, our gardener, comes in to help me." Fannie's gaze traveled the vastness of the conservatory. "After I finished university a year ago, I returned home. Spending time in here and making things grow has become my obsession."

He scanned the plethora of trees and plants. "I have no doubt that you're passionate about your work." He smiled. "I was about mine, too, at one time."

She refrained from probing further on a subject that was clearly still very raw to him. "You did not get a chance to see everything when you were here before," she said slowly. "I could show you around before you get started?"

"Fair enough. I would like to see what you've done with the rest of the greenery."

Fannie smiled. "May I help you?"

"Not necessary. I can move along on my own."

She allowed him to go first, walking behind him as he surveyed her grandmother's life's work and then her own small contribution.

"Your *Hibiscus schizopetalus* are looking exceptional," he said, pausing at the array of frilly red petals, finely divided and each with elongated stamen and pistil draping from the shrub's green-leaved branches.

His approval pleased her greatly. "Thank you, Lieutenant. This split flowered variety is one of my favorites in the hibiscus genus."

"If you like, you may call me Peter," he said, turning to her.

"Why, I would like that very much . . . Peter." Shyly, she added, "My name is Frances, but you may call me Fannie."

"Frances is truly a lovely name. It means 'free woman.'"

Her eyes widened. "Really?"

"Do you feel like a free woman, Fannie?"

"At times." She smiled. "I was able to go to university for a start, and not many women can say the same, though we are trying to change that."

"Women's suffrage, you mean?"

"Yes. Do you support the cause?"

"I smell a trap here." He chuckled. "Actually, I do support the movement, and in my view Scotland's universities are not as restrictive as the staid auld British institutions when it comes to women's learning. Our lassies are braw."

"Oh?" She crossed her arms, giving him a mock pout. "And we British women are not?"

"That's not . . . I mean, I shouldna . . ."

Laughter burst from her, the sound bouncing off the vaulted ceiling. Finally, Peter smiled. "I guess I caught myself in that trap."

"You did," she said, grinning.

"I will make an exception with you, of course."

Her heart fluttered as his green eyes warmed at her, his well-defined mouth tilting upward. "Of course," she said softly. "And you are forgiven."

They continued on, and she was impressed with the vastness of his knowledge. He'd identified nearly every flower and tree species in the entire conservatory.

"You could have taught my horticulture class," she said when they returned to the barren planter and crateful of starts still needing his attention. "You know so much about what took me a few years to learn."

"Well, I did have an early start. My great-uncle Ross was a naturalist, and when he came to live with us on the outskirts of Glasgow, he and I would hike through forests and parks collecting all kinds of plant and spore species. Then we would return to catalogue every kind of organism we'd come across." His expression turned wistful. "I developed my love for nature and exploration during those many trips with him."

"It sounds wonderful," Fannie murmured. "Other than attending university and a few trips into London, I've not been anywhere else. And there is so much plant life I would like to explore for myself in the wild."

His smile waned. "I hope that you'll get the chance someday."

"Yes." She shifted as she realized her daydreaming reminded him of his condition. "Well, these Plumbagos won't dig their own holes, so I shall leave you to it and pop back behind the screen to finish cleaning up."

He reached for the gloves and spade while Fannie returned to her chore of rinsing pots. She prayed he would enjoy the work and re-claim the passion he felt the war had taken from him. She also considered speaking with Grandfather about a prosthetic leg for Peter. If he became proficient enough with using it, he could expand his boundaries once again and return to his vocation.

And you could help him.

Her pulse leapt at the notion. After all, he'd made no mention of her limp and he seemed to want her company, otherwise he would not have returned.

Or maybe he just wanted the company of her plants.

A giggle emitted from her as she finished stacking the clean pottery. It would not be so terribly bad if both of them loved doing the same thing, would it?

Watching him leave with Deering two hours later, she fervently hoped Peter would return and continue sharing with her their mutual love of plants.

25

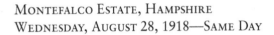

MONTEFALCO ESTATE, HAMPSHIRE
WEDNESDAY, AUGUST 28, 1918—SAME DAY

Two posts for you, madam."

The Weatherfords' butler hovered beside Natalya's chair at morning tea, offering her two cream-colored envelopes.

"Ah, thank you, Yates." She smiled at him, amused when his face retained the sour look he usually wore, and he bowed to her in response.

Yates, the perfect captain for such a vessel as Montefalco! So proper and dignified, and no doubt he was a taskmaster toward the rest of the staff. Much like her old ballet teacher at the Mariinsky in Petrograd.

Her pulse quickened, glancing at the envelopes. Neither carried a return address. She opened the first and gave the message a cursory glance.

Must see you in London. New development.

Noting the sender's initials, she sighed and refolded the missive before opening the second. A smile touched her lips, reading

239

nearly the same message as the first, though the sender's initials were different. Her housekeeper had followed her instructions well.

Anticipation filled her. Both missives had come from Whitehall with news, perhaps the information they had been desperately seeking from Sidney Reilly?

She had so far failed to unlock the critical details from Marcus's mind. And Mrs. Danner insisted that he remain here with his family when he might make faster progress in the west wing!

Tucking the envelopes into the pocket of her skirt, she picked up her teacup and addressed Mrs. Weatherford's curious gaze. "Letters of congratulations on my engagement to your son," she said, smiling.

Natalya turned to Marcus beside her, seated on the settee. At least he was out of that invalid's conveyance. "Milyi, you must hurry and heal so that I can let them know a date for our wedding." She laid her hand protectively over his, her impatience to be away to London battling her reluctance to leave him.

Despite her words to Jack the other day, she had developed a great fondness for Marcus and even now reconsidered her relationship with him. He had been kind to her when she visited their mutual friend at Whitehall, and he was certainly pleasing to the eye.

His family's wealth had also surprised her upon their arrival. Montefalco could easily be compared to the Romanovs' summer home in the Crimea, where she had first been invited to join the Imperial family for a private week.

She squeezed his fingers and smiled when he looked up at her. And she could never forget his willingness to protect her and save her life. Not a chivalry most men in the old country would consider. Mother Russia could be a harsh land, and she bred the kind of men who could survive.

"Myshka, I also received word that my housekeeper is having a domestic problem in London, and I must return for a short time to set things right." She sighed and looked to Mrs. Weatherford. "Finding suitable help becomes more difficult by the day, especially with many leaving to work in the factories. You are fortunate to have a competent staff."

"Indeed, we are." Mrs. Weatherford turned a smile on Yates at the sideboard, and Natalya noted the stiff butler went so far as to crack his lips at his employer.

"I will only be in London two days," she said, returning her attention to Marcus. "Will you be all right here with your family while I am gone?"

"Yes, I'll be fine here," he said. "When will you leave?"

A bit startled, she angled her gaze at him. Marcus seemed more confident, and more like the man she had first met. Was it a sign that he was close to recovery? "I will take the noon train, but I promise I shall not be away long."

"Natalya, when you return, we'll visit the library on the west side of the estate," Frances said from her place on the sofa beside her mother. "I hope you like to read?"

"Very much," Natalya said. Such a sweet *devochka*. "I look forward to it."

"I hope you're able to resolve your household dilemma quickly, dear." Mrs. Weatherford glanced at her son. "I am sure your presence will be missed."

"Thank you." Natalya considered the other vacancies in the Magnolia room. Mrs. Danner had not made an appearance since dinner the other night. Poor little *ryba*. Natalya regretted any embarrassment she might have caused. She, too, had once been in that awkward place—a poor girl from the village of Rostov near Moscow, plunged into the treacherous seas of Petrograd society and the bloodthirsty hierarchy of dancers. Both had threatened to drown her before she learned to use her fins well, gliding through the perilous waters and leaving behind others like her, who either sank or returned to the shore.

Mrs. Danner obviously felt safer on dry land as she took to her room with her meals or with her daughter and nanny in the nursery.

Natalya was somewhat relieved to find Sir Geoffrey absent, no doubt in his "laboratory," as Jack called it. She sensed the old man was not entirely convinced of her engagement to his grandson, and she could not understand why. All of them had seemed shocked to learn about Marcus's intention to marry.

She drew her brows together. What was the depth of the relationship between Mrs. Danner and Marcus? She seemed unknown to his family. Had Jack perhaps overestimated her value to his friend? *"You still love Daisy . . ."*

Mrs. Danner's words to Marcus at the hospital. She had certainly not included herself in the statement. And that scene in the park—then Marcus, silent and brooding on the train to Folkestone and on the ship to Archangel. Had she broken off with him . . . or he with her?

Either way, it must be difficult for her being here now, needing him to remember in order to save her child, with one of them having ended the relationship . . .

Natalya raised new eyes toward the trio of twinkling chandeliers overhead, while a mural of angels and roses spanned the length of the ceiling. Her attention moved to the ornately carved friezes and then along the papered walls, red like rubies and garbed in gilt-framed paintings adding their elegance to the room.

A smile touched her lips. Marcus's eligibility as a husband would indeed require some serious thought while she was away in London.

"Clare? Are you in there?"

Clare turned at the faint knock behind the bookcase, surprised to recognize the voice. "Marcus?"

"Let me through."

"A moment, please." She remained a few seconds longer, kneeling on the gold couch to stare out at the summer drizzle that had started during her lunch with Daisy and Ruthie. Yates held an opened black umbrella over Natalya as she stepped into the Weatherfords' Rolls-Royce.

Only one steamer trunk was strapped to the car's boot.

So she wasn't leaving permanently. How long would she be gone?

Leaving the couch, she went to the bookcase. After removing *Jane Eyre* and releasing the latch, she finally opened the door.

Marcus sat in his wheelchair, face flushed below the bandage and wearing a smile. "Come, I want to show you something."

Curious, she followed him through the dingy passageway back to the study. Glancing at the table, Clare noticed he'd laid out the chessboard, white and black pieces placed on opposing sides.

"Watch this." To her shock, he swung the chair around and sped across the room, his arms pushing at such speed that she feared he'd crash into the wall. Then just as quickly he exerted pressure against one of the wheels, spinning himself around before coming to a halt. "Well?" he said, breathless.

She laughed. "I'm impressed."

"And there's more." He started toward her, this time slowing his speed and giving a jerk to the wheels to raise the smaller front casters off the floor.

"I see you've taken my words to heart." She marveled at his control of the chair. "How long have you been practicing these acrobatics?"

"A few hours yesterday when we returned from the hospital, and then today after our visit to the garden. It wasn't too difficult to learn." He paused. "I've also been practicing getting out of this thing and taking a few steps. A bruise or two, but now I can pick myself up off the floor."

"Your balance is improved from this morning?" Already he was following through on his promise in the garden to help Daisy.

She looked toward the table. "Are you getting ready to play chess?"

"You said you played, so if you have the time and promise not to be a poor loser . . ."

His eyes gleamed, and she chuckled. Why not? When she'd left the nursery, Daisy was down for her nap, and Ruthie was curled up in the rocking chair with a Jane Austen novel. "Very well, but I hold you to the same conditions. Shall we?"

She moved to take her seat, and as he rolled the chair over to the table, pleasure filled her to watch him plant his feet and raise himself to stand and take the other chair. He reached across the board for a black and a white pawn and hid them in his hands beneath the table. "I'll just mix these up a bit to see who starts."

When he held out his fists to her, she chose the left. The white pawn appeared. "White starts the game!" she cried, snatching it from his grasp.

He replaced the black pawn on the board. "You may have been lucky enough to claim the first-move advantage over me, but it doesn't follow that you'll win," he said, amused. "I must simply rise to the challenge of beating you."

She grinned. "We'll see about that."

"Are you willing to play for stakes?"

She paused to eye him. "What kind of stakes?"

"How about a bit of truth or dare? Whoever takes a piece from the other gets to ask a question." He inclined his head, the dark lashes lowered slightly. "And the forfeit for refusing to answer is to follow a command."

Clare's heart thumped. She knew the rules. If she didn't wish to answer his question, then she must do his bidding, whatever that might be. What would he ask of her? Because of his lack of memory, the stakes he suggested put him at a distinct advantage over her.

"All right," she said impulsively. At least she could learn more about his childhood and how much he actually did remember.

As they both focused on moving their chess pieces, all that could be heard was the ticking of the wall clock.

Clare took his first piece—a pawn. "What is your very last memory before the accident?"

He leaned back in his seat, his brow creased. "Examinations. My last term at Harrow."

244

She nodded. He would have been about eighteen then. Only thirteen years to catch up on. "Your move."

Less than a minute later, he'd taken one of her pawns. His gaze narrowed on her. "Have we played chess together before, and if so, how many times have you won?"

Clare released the breath she'd been holding. "Yes, we've played before."

"And?"

She decided to give in to the second question. "We're pretty well matched. I've won twenty-one games . . ."

"Yes?"

"And you've won nineteen."

He gave a bark of laughter, his eyes wide. "I don't believe you."

"But you can't disprove it," she teased. "So you'll have to take my word for it."

"Now I am determined to win."

Once she'd taken his queen's rook, she asked, "How do you feel about Natalya's leaving the estate?" Marcus seemed to her to be in a lively mood and not nearly as anxious as the day of his arrival. "Are you comfortable in her absence or does it upset you?"

He stared at the pieces on the board before looking up at her. "She'll only be away to London for two days. I will miss her, but you're here and I am . . . well."

She smiled, her hopes lifted. "I'm pleased to know you're starting to feel more yourself again. It's a very good sign."

Two moves later, he'd snatched her queen's rook. "Were you and I ever more than friends?"

His gaze pierced hers, and Clare's throat constricted. She swallowed and said, "Give me a command instead."

His jaw hardened. "All right. The forfeit is a kiss."

Her mouth went slack. Why was he doing this to her?

She hesitated, until his brow rose at her in challenge. Slowly, Clare rose from the chair, her knees threatening to buckle as she went to him. Leaning close, she breathed in the scent of his cologne as she cupped his face in her hands, staring at the honeyed flecks in his eyes now blazing gold.

Turning his head slightly, she pressed her lips to his cheek before returning to her seat.

She noted his disgruntled look.

"You didn't specify what kind of kiss," she said, glad her voice didn't wobble along with the rest of her. "And you are an engaged man, Marcus."

Color tinged his face at the reminder, yet any relief she might feel lay buried beneath her agony. How she'd wanted to kiss him properly! But it wouldn't be right.

Marcus had made his decision before the accident. How could she pretend with him now, letting him believe there was still something between them when he couldn't recall his own actions in the park?

The deception would be no better than what they'd done to her.

Their game continued in silence, Clare tensing each time he captured one of her pieces. His mood had changed, however, and his questions turned more toward memories about her growing up. She relayed to him how she started with her mum at the Randleton home and received her education with the Lange cousins. "After the tutor was let go, I attended the local public school until I was of an age to work as a full-time maid for them."

When she'd captured his queen's bishop, she asked, "Do you remember helping your sister when she contracted polio?" Clare still warmed at the memory of his great sacrifice for Fannie, though it also made her ache for what she'd lost.

"I remember," he said, looking past her. "At first, I carried her everywhere. She was only a little more grown than Daisy. I read up on the disease, here in this study." He glanced toward the bookshelves. "And with Mother . . . unavailable, I determined that with time and effort, I would coach Fannie into taking her own steps again."

"You gave up school for a time, didn't you?" she said, the chess game forgotten.

He nodded. "But I worked hard when I was able to finally attend and graduated with my class." His eyes glinted as he focused on her. "It was worth it."

"Indeed, it was. And she is most grateful to you."

He reached across the table for her hand. "Sometimes the sacrifices we must make for those we love are the most painful."

Clare searched his face. What did he mean by that?

He let go of her hand and touched his forehead. "I've a headache coming on. If you don't mind, can we continue our match later?"

"Of course. I'll get you something for the pain." She rose and went to him. "Shall I help you back to the bed?"

When he nodded, she pushed the wheelchair aside. Once he was standing, she fitted her shoulder beneath his arm and guided him toward the bed. Awareness filled her as he pressed the side of his head against hers. What was happening between them? For her part, she'd never stopped loving him, but for him . . . since they'd arrived, he seemed to want to draw closer to her.

What was Marcus feeling, or not feeling, for Natalya?

Once she had him settled, Clare brought aspirin and a glass of water and finished with a cool wet rag across his eyes. "Tomorrow I'll remove the stitches from the back of your head," she said. "You'll wear the bandage a few more days after that, and then we'll let the open air work to heal you."

"Come back later?"

"Yes, before dinner." She touched his cheek. He wasn't overly warm. "Now rest."

Marcus heard the door creak closed as she went through the passageway back to her room. He ground his teeth. Fool! Why had he asked her if they were once intimate before?

And why had he demanded that she kiss him?

Because you're falling in love with her, man. Guilt pierced him at the revelation, and he reached for the cold rag, pressing it against his throbbing brow.

Natalya. She wore his diamond. They had been making arrangements with her family for their wedding before he'd taken the fall. She had more than proven her love to him, saving him before he'd bled to death in the woods, or wherever he'd been when he cracked his head open and done such damage.

And yet she'd barely departed for London, and here he was behaving in such a manner with someone else.

One thing was certain. Clare had accepted the consequences when he asked if they'd ever been more than friends. Had she broken it off with him?

Why was she here? Was it only so that he could help save her daughter from another abduction by that blighter Randleton? Or did she still have feelings for him?

Breathing an oath, he tossed the rag over the bedpost behind him and turned to lie on his side. *You're creating an impossible situation, Marcus. One your heart cannot hope to win.*

Checkmate.

26

MONTEFALCO ESTATE, HAMPSHIRE
THURSDAY, AUGUST 29, 1918—NEXT DAY

did as you asked."

Clare was removing the last of Marcus's stitches the following afternoon when he made the announcement. She paused to glance at him. "What did I ask you?"

"To speak with Fannie."

She stepped back, scissors in hand. "You went to the conservatory?"

"I did. Got there on my own, too." He smiled as he jerked at the wheels of the chair to lift the casters. "Luckily she saw me and let me in."

Clare smiled back. "I'm sure she was happy for the visit."

"I let her give me another tour of the place," he said. "Fannie's green thumb has created a small paradise in the middle of Hampshire."

"I agree." She tipped her head. "So, what did you two talk about?"

"You," he said, his eyes gleaming. "She asked if you were taking good care of me."

"And?"

"I told her that I was suffering through."

"Oh! You're terrible!" She cuffed him playfully on the shoulder. "You'd better behave or I may get clumsy with these." She swished the scissor blades back and forth in front of him. "And I'm not finished yet."

He laughed, and again she delighted in the sound. *Oh, Lord, I can't seem to stop, he just draws me closer to him. Please, give him warts, remove all his hair, and age him another fifty years so I won't love him so much.*

Yet she knew her heart would never change, regardless of what he looked like or how much time passed. She resumed her stitch removal. "Were you able to talk about the past with your sister?"

"Yes, she filled in some missing pieces. Though I remembered we had treasure boxes down in the cellarium."

Why hadn't he mentioned it before? She continued with her task. "What did she say?"

"She told me that once she was walking again, I would sometimes play hide-and-seek with her down there. Apparently, I stumbled onto Father's hidden bottle of eighteen-year-old Buchanan's, opened it, and took a swallow. Fannie said it didn't agree with me because I gagged and spit it out." He looked up and sighed. "A waste of good Scotch."

Clare laughed. "When I was a young maid at the Randleton estate, I did much the same. The family was away, and I got my hands on the key to the liquor cabinet. I'd seen my grumpy employer turn quite happy after drinking a glass or two of the amber liquid, so I tried it myself."

"What happened?"

She shot him a grim smile. "I not only gagged on the rotten stuff, but I also had to clean the room's carpet and then every hall carpet for a week when the housekeeper found out what I'd done. If my mum hadn't been working there at the time, I would have got the sack." She returned to her task. "Needless to say, except for the sherry the other day, I don't touch alcohol anymore."

"I cannot recall whether I drank a lot."

"You didn't."

She felt his eyes on her. "And you know this because . . ."

"I have seen you out in company several times. And whenever you came to visit Daisy and me at the flat, you drank tea. So, I can say to the best of my knowledge you don't imbibe often."

"What else do I do . . . or not do?"

She let her hands drift to her sides. *You're courting more heartache, Clare.* "You have a slight dimple in your left cheek when you smile," she said, despite her misgivings. "You also have a habit of rubbing your right earlobe when you're deep in thought, like those times you're about to lose your queen to me." He grinned, exposing his beloved dimple. "You also prefer your tea with two sugars and go against convention with a dash of cream over milk, and you dislike the opera."

"Have I ever taken you to the opera?"

She hesitated. "No, but you've mentioned a few times being obligated to attend with one of your colleagues at Whitehall." Had he taken Natalya to the opera?

His dark gaze searched hers. "What . . . kind of man was I?"

Clare drew her lips together. *You left me for someone else.* Instead, she replied, "When we first met, Marcus, I admit that I didn't like you." She smiled at his worried look. "At the time, I held a grudge against any titled man with money, though it wasn't long before I changed my mind about you. I thought you the finest of men, hardworking, caring, and funny at times. And . . . you were wonderful with my daughter."

Her eyes began to burn, and his brow creased. "There was more between us than what you're telling me, isn't that right?"

Again she found herself on that same ledge: tell him the truth and he would demand to know the reason why they were no longer together. Marcus had no memory of his hurting her, nor could he change what had happened.

Besides that, whatever remained of their history together had been lost the moment some thug shot him and caused him to fall and crack his head open. "Nothing more," she lied. "But we were friends for a very long time."

"We are still friends, are we not?"

He reached for her hand, his grip firm yet gentle. She raised a smile. *Oh, Marcus, I fear my heart will belong to you until the end of days.* "Always," she said, her voice rough.

She removed the last stitch and rewrapped his head with a lighter measure of the gauze, enough to hide his wounds. Sir Geoffrey wouldn't be fooled by what was clearly the graze of a bullet alongside his grandson's head.

Cleaning up, Clare returned to him. "Now, you've a lot of work to do to get better, and we'll start by visiting the rehabilitation hospital today. I'll take you in the wheelchair, and when you're ready to get out, we'll walk the rest of the way or fall down trying. How does that sound?"

In response, he rose from the chair to stand before her, and again she was reminded of his towering height. "Let's go," he said.

"Since you're so eager, I have an idea—you push the wheelchair. It will help you to keep your balance."

"As long as you take a seat," he said, smiling. "I need the ballast."

Clare settled into the conveyance and allowed him to push her through the passageway into her room. Once they'd reached her outer door, he teetered only slightly as he went to open it and rolled her into the main hall.

"I don't know how to pop up the casters, so I'll trade places with you." Soon she was watching him maneuver the wheelchair like an expert as she opened the door leading outside to the rear garden.

Halfway there, he was ready to try walking on his own. She held out her arm for him in case he happened to fall.

"I used to play in those woods." He pointed to the tree line at the back of the estate. "I remember horse chestnut season when our whole family and many from the village would come to help with the harvest."

"When is that?"

"Next month." He turned to her. "September?"

Clare nodded, remembering last year in late September when he'd left London for a week to come to Hampshire. Likely to pick horse chestnuts. "A family tradition, then?"

"Yes, it was."

They had reached the patio area. A few soldiers sat at tables, playing cards or reading magazines, one pair competing in a game of backgammon.

"Where would you like to sit?"

He chose a table away from the others and sat down. "My legs are shaking."

"That's because you haven't exercised in some time."

Clare spied the young volunteer nurse with her tray of drinks and signaled to her. To Marcus she said, "You sit here and I'll retrieve the wheelchair for the ride back."

When she'd returned with the chair, she was surprised to see the two soldiers from the other day standing beside their table.

"Oh, there ye are, Sister!" Johnson still wore the neck bandage as he doffed his cap. "I saw yerself and the cap'n arrive and wanted to apologize again for my ungentlemanlike behavior."

He'd sounded out *ungentlemanlike* as if it wasn't a word in his usual vocabulary, though it showed he was sincere. Clare smiled. "You're forgiven, Corporal."

"And me, Sister . . . Cap'n?"

Sergeant Roberts wore his sling and glanced at her and then at Marcus.

Marcus looked to her. "Milady's choice?"

She caught the amused glint in his eyes. "I suppose we can forgive you as well, Sergeant, so long as you both continue to behave yourselves."

The young nurse volunteer had brought the refreshment tray. "Would you men like to join us?" Clare offered.

Roberts and Johnson glanced at each other before claiming a couple of the chairs.

"When did you two return to Britain?" Clare asked as the pair took up glasses of lemonade.

"Johnson and me were in the same company over in northern France," Roberts said before taking another sip of his drink. "Took a volley of shots from old Fritzie and shattered my elbow. After weeks in hospital, I came here to learn how to use it again." He removed the sling, bending his elbow a few inches.

"An' a month after Roberts was gone, I took a bullet in the neck," Johnson said, raising his chin to show the heavy bandage. "A miracle it didn't kill me, but it tore muscle." He eyed Marcus. "What are ye 'ere for, sir? Looks like ye got a mighty 'ead wound." He squinted. "Get shot?"

Clare startled at how close to the truth the corporal had come.

Marcus shook his head. "Not so glorious as all that, I'm afraid. I took a bad fall from a high place while in Europe."

"Concussed, aye?" Roberts spoke up. "Nasty. I imagine ye get headaches, too."

"They're becoming more infrequent." He looked around at the other patients. "So how do you two manage to amuse yourselves?"

"There's cards and a bit o' reading, sir. An' table tennis." Johnson indicated the table at the far end of the patio, where two men in wheelchairs held a match.

"There's also a chessboard an' pieces, but neither of us know the game." Johnson glanced at his friend.

"Perhaps the captain might be interested in teaching you?"

The pair of soldiers looked to Clare, then to Marcus.

"Is it 'ard to learn, sir?" Johnson asked.

Clare ignored the sharp look Marcus gave her. "Corporal Johnson, why don't you go and fetch the board and pieces and bring them here? You'll get your first lesson while I sit over there and enjoy my lemonade."

What was she up to? Marcus watched as Clare headed toward one of the chaise lounges. Was she already tired of being with him, or was this her way of pushing him to get better acquainted with the other patients?

Once she'd settled into the chaise, she shielded her eyes and waved.

Johnson had returned with the chess set. Marcus drew a deep breath. He'd made a promise to himself to get better, if not for his own sake, at least for Daisy and Clare.

"'Ere we go, sir." The young corporal placed the board and pieces on the table. Marcus began setting up the game, explaining to the men the placement of each piece, instructing them on the basics. He played a mock match with Johnson first, then with Roberts, and was surprised afterward to realize nearly two hours had passed.

He glanced over at Clare, lying with her eyes closed in the semishade of the plane tree. Her fair skin was likely getting burned from the sun dodging in and out between the few clouds.

"Gentlemen." He held onto the table as he rose to his feet. "I'll leave you to practice."

Waving them off with a smile, he carefully walked to where Clare lay.

Her eyes were still closed, the thick black lashes fanning out across her cheeks. Standing beside her, he caught the slight rise and fall of her steady breathing.

He gripped the chaise, and with much effort he crouched beside her. If only he could freeze this picture of her in his mind, beautiful even in sleep, the dappled rays of sun glinting off her hair and making the thick strands appear almost blue.

So vulnerable without her armor.

He hadn't stopped thinking about what she'd told him yesterday—Elliot Lange and Randleton and how they'd hurt her, using Daisy as their weapon. And earlier, she admitted to him that she hadn't liked him at first because he was titled and had money.

Little wonder with those hidden scars she still carried. Clare Danner had found it necessary to be tough in order to survive, and now the sands of time were running out for her.

255

In just six days, she'd face more hurt, perhaps a wound from which she might never recover. And though he was working hard to try to repair his body, Marcus had yet to do the same with his mind.

Shades of pink had already started to tinge her pale white skin, and his gaze moved lower to her lips, slightly opened, like ripe cherries and no doubt just as sweet, waiting to be tasted.

For an instant he was tempted to lean in and sample what he knew would be paradise.

Yet his guilt quelled the urge, and he drew back.

What kind of wolf are you, Weatherford? You've got to stop this . . .

"Marcus?"

Her lashes had lifted and she was looking at him. Their gazes locked, and as he drowned in the tumultuous gray depths, every decent assurance he'd made to himself yesterday flew out of his head. As if in a dream, he watched himself leaning toward her, pulled by the longing in her expression, his eyes again fixed on her full lips, and when he was just inches away . . . he stopped.

She'd reached up to press a hand against his chest.

Understanding passed between them, and she didn't need to say a word. He already knew.

Pushing himself to his feet, he extended a hand to her, and she rose to stand with him.

Neither spoke as he manned his own wheelchair most of the way back, ignoring the muscles trembling in his arms, angry that he was so weak, not only in body but also in mind. And as they returned to the other side of the estate, he was grateful to her. She'd protected his honor, at least where Natalya was concerned.

He had to quit this foolishness. Get his mind back so he could help Daisy and then get on with his life, whatever that might be. *God, if you're listening to me, then please don't abandon me to what might become a miserable fate.*

27

L eaving Marcus to rest in his room before dinner, Clare returned to her own quarters, her senses rattled. He'd almost
kissed her out on the east patio in front of all those soldiers.
And you nearly let him do it.

She went to the washbasin, cooling her face and neck with a
wet cloth. Perhaps it was her own desire that unnerved her most of
all. She still ached at having refused him, though her pain mingled
with the relief that she'd made him stop and think.

Clare didn't want to imagine his family's reaction at discovering
his dalliance with the nurse. And there was Natalya, who was to
return to Montefalco tomorrow.

What if Marcus confessed to her what had nearly happened?
Would Clare be dismissed from her service, all efforts wasted in
trying to help him recover and to save her daughter?

A soft knock sounded at her door. "Clare?"

Fannie. "One moment."

Drying her face, she went to answer the summons.

Fannie stood just outside, still wearing her soiled apron and a
smudge of dirt alongside her right cheek. "May I come in?"

Clare stepped back and Fannie entered quickly, both settling
on the gold couch. "My brother came to see me this morning."

Clare smiled. "Yes, my ears were burning."

Fannie grinned. "We did talk about you, among other things," she said. "We also discussed the dinners at Montefalco. I stand firm that they've become altogether too fussy for our family, especially living out here in the country." She cast a glance at Clare. "So, I've spoken with Mother, and it's been decided that an evening picnic outdoors is just the thing we need to remember our humble roots and where we've come from. Mother wants me to invite you, Daisy, and Ruthie to dine with us on the front lawn this evening. Even now, Yates is outside directing the footmen concerning the placement of the furniture."

Clare rose to peer out the large-paned windows. Just as she said, the skinny butler was instructing Lewis, Teddy, and Hanson on where to put one of two long wooden tables and several straight-backed chairs.

She turned to Fannie. "I hope all of this isn't because I've missed eating dinners in the dining room?"

"In part, yes," Fannie said. "But honestly, when it's just our family, I do tire of getting all dressed up for a mere couple of hours, and then I have to change again into my nightclothes. Besides, a picnic will allow us to eat with our fingers!" She giggled. "I can hardly wait to see Mother without a basketful of linen serviettes standing at the ready!"

Clare chuckled over the mental image Fannie conjured. She couldn't fathom the regal Mrs. Weatherford ever behaving so undignified. "As long as the dinner is informal and we've all been invited, I accept the invitation for the three of us." She paused. "And Marcus, will he go along with this?"

"It was at his suggestion, and quite innocent actually. He told me that after Father died, there were no more picnics, and we used to have them often. While I was too young to remember, my brother holds those memories very close because it's what he clearly remembers right now."

Clare nodded. Marcus remembered a simpler time, and in an odd way maybe it was a blessing for him. He didn't need to deal with the war or the burdens he once carried daily on those broad shoulders of his. Though she desperately needed him to remember.

"What time shall we meet outdoors?"

"Six o'clock, and dress comfortably, all right?"

"I will." Impulsively she reached for Fannie's hand. "I realize what you and your brother are up to, you know," she said softly. "And I appreciate it."

Coloring slightly, Fannie smiled, her brown eyes searching Clare's. "I . . . think I've met someone," she said softly.

Clare leaned back. "Here? At Montefalco?"

Fannie nodded, and more heat tinged her delicate features. "His name is Lieutenant Peter Ainsley. He's recovering at the rehabilitation hospital. Peter was a botanist before he served in the war, and he knows so much! Why, he named nearly every plant in the conservatory yesterday when he came to help me get a few starts of Plumbago auriculata into the soil."

Clare raised a mischievous brow. "You two are planting together—that sounds a bit serious."

She laughed. "It does sound like an odd way of courting." Her eyes widened. "Not that Peter has mentioned any such thing! We've only met twice, though he was at the rehabilitation center the other day when we were there."

"What does he look like?"

As Fannie described him, Clare recalled seeing the russet-haired young man in the wheelchair. "Well, I think it's wonderful that you've met someone who shares your love of nature and plants," she said. "You both have much in common that way. It's a great start for a friendship, in any case."

Looking pleased, Fannie tilted her head. "What about you, Clare? Marcus mentioned that you became a widow about a year ago. I'm sorry for your loss." Her brown eyes held compassion. "Are you still missing Mr. Danner, or is there . . . someone waiting for you back in London?"

Clare's pulse quickened. She'd told Marcus the truth yesterday about Mr. Danner and Elliot Lange. At least he'd kept her secret.

"Thank you for your condolences," she said, her hopeless heart still longing for the man next door. "And no, I don't have anyone waiting for me in London."

"I cannot imagine why not." Fannie surveyed her. "You are lovely in face and form, and you're kind and compassionate, especially with my brother. In fact, he quite likes you." She smiled impishly. "He spoke of you during most of our conversation, likely because you're with him much of the time. He also told me how you're an expert at chess."

Clare raised a smile. "Did he? And what else did he say?"

"That you're most gentle with him, and you tease him and make him laugh." A sparkle shone in Fannie's eyes. "And you don't put up with any of his nonsense."

Clare nodded, her throat growing tight. "Just so," she managed to say.

Fannie's brows angled then, before a look of dawning lit in her expression.

"What is it?" Clare asked.

Lips pursed, Fannie shook her head. "Nothing important." She rose from the couch. "Well, I'm a mess, even for a picnic. Shall we see you, Daisy, and Ruthie out on the lawn at six, then?"

Clare rose too. "You can count on it."

Fannie took her hands. "It really is wonderful having a friend here I can share my secrets with. I'll let you know how things blossom with Peter."

Clare chuckled. "I can't wait to hear what happens next."

As Fannie left, Clare was touched by the kindness she and her mother were offering to her and Daisy, creating a situation where everyone was an equal and perhaps giving her the chance to get to know them all better.

Marcus was smitten with Clare.

As Fannie drifted upstairs toward her room, her thoughts returned to the conversation she'd had with her brother that morning. While they shared bits of their childhood, the conversation, at least on his part, had been dominated by what he'd experienced in Clare's company.

Of course, she was his nurse and had spent the most time with him so far during his stay, yet there was more going on there.

In fact, he'd mentioned little of Natalya but instead spoke volumes about his chess match with Clare and their joking about her shaving him and having food fights, laughing and talking about their favorite meals. He even admitted to being able to share old memories with her and how she'd managed to help him remember more.

Most importantly, Fannie had watched the energy in his expression as he spoke of Clare and their time together. She'd seen him smile, his eyes warm as he relayed some humorous remark or another Clare had made to him, or his witty rejoinder. He seemed more vibrant than he had for a long time, even before his accident.

So different from when he is with Natalya. With his beautiful and elegant fiancée, Marcus seemed more dependent and reserved, even tense. And though she didn't intend it, Natalya's overly solicitous manner almost encouraged her brother to stay that way.

Clare, on the other hand, challenged him and pushed him forward beyond his fear and back toward his family. Marcus had told her it was Clare's idea that he visit and speak with her, and Fannie was grateful.

In her room, she began to wash up and fix her hair, having already decided the dress she had on would be the one she picnicked in. She smiled into the mirror at her small victory with Mother, then paused. Would Natalya, with all her stylishness and impeccable manners, be the kind of person who would enjoy a picnic?

"Perhaps Mother will need to organize another picnic when Natalya returns," she said to her reflection while adjusting the pins in her hair. "And perhaps we shall invite Peter to join us as well."

Her pulse leapt as the words tumbled out of her mouth. Would her family accept him? Or was she moving too fast with her thoughts? Clare had said that he and Fannie had already made a good start on a friendship, and Fannie did like him very much. Peter was smart and handsome, and those green eyes . . .

She smiled dreamily. Like a lovely forest path, leading her deeper into the recesses of his soul. Perhaps to some future between them?

Fannie straightened the lace against her open collar before taking a seat at her vanity. Turning to one side, she raised her skirt to adjust the tightness on the special short brace Grandfather had made for her right leg.

Her relieved sigh echoed in the room as she eased the tension from the leather straps. Grandfather had customized the fit for her, so that the brace reached only as far as her calf and remained hidden beneath her skirt. She'd been teased so much in school while wearing a full-length brace that he'd sought to alleviate the problem.

Thinking of Peter then, Fannie smiled. *Wouldn't we make a pair?* "A pair of good legs anyway," she murmured, and after re-settling her skirt, she stood to go downstairs.

Her musings continued in that direction, those fern-green eyes and hair the color of copper. And his smile . . .

Hopefully he would return tomorrow to help her graft starts from her dwarf calamondin orange tree. She hadn't asked him specifically, but she'd mentioned the task. Would he come back?

Lord, even if my head is in the clouds about Peter, please let me help him.

"Welcome, Mrs. Danner! And Miss Simmons and dear little Daisy!"

Clare held her daughter against her hip and smiled shyly at Mrs. Weatherford while she and Ruthie descended the portico steps to walk across the lawn toward the gathering. All the family members, including Marcus, were seated in wicker chairs, wearing their summer linen and sipping on lemony drinks.

Not far away were the linen-covered tables Yates had overseen setting up earlier. One of them stood empty and surrounded by chairs, while the other was being loaded by the servants with an array of dishes with shining silver covers. Plates were stacked at one end, thankfully not the good china, and beside them a tall pewter goblet held silverware. At the other end, several crystal glasses surrounded a frothy pitcher of lemonade.

"Please come and join us!" Fannie waved to her, indicating the empty chair between herself and Marcus. Ruthie took the last empty seat on Fannie's other side.

"Is this not grand?" she exclaimed once Clare and Daisy had settled. "A lovely summer's evening, and the fresh air should certainly give us an appetite!"

"Atite!" Daisy blurted with a grin, and everyone chuckled.

"Thank you for inviting us." Clare directed her remark to Mrs. Weatherford. "We're all very fond of picnics, and it's a beautiful day to have one."

"You're most welcome, Mrs. Danner." Mrs. Weatherford looked at Fannie. "I am glad my daughter suggested the idea to me. And I understand it was my son who engineered the scheme." She smiled fondly at Marcus, who lifted his shoulders and then looked away toward the woods on the far west side.

Clare noted the hurt in his mother's eyes as Marcus averted his gaze. Was he angry with her?

She thought back to what he'd told her that first day. He'd felt abandoned when his father died, with his mother grieving and leaving him to fend for himself with his little sister, then crippled from polio. Fannie had been correct; to Marcus, those memories must still be fresh and painful, for he hadn't yet moved beyond them into the years of healing and better memories that followed.

Clare tried to comfort the woman. "I think it's wonderful what you've done in the west wing, Mrs. Weatherford. Sharing half of your home for the wounded coming back from the war. I know the patients appreciate it, and it's been proven that they do thrive in a beautiful and calm environment. After all, it must seem like heaven here to them after being in the trenches. And to be surrounded by your beautiful roses and dahlias. It gives them the chance they need to *truly heal*." Emphasizing her last words, she tipped her head in Marcus's direction.

Her brown eyes looked back at Clare, gratitude in their depths. "Thank you, Mrs. Danner, that is a most kind thing to say. I hope for the patients' healing and as quickly as possible." She glanced at her son.

"The picnic is ready, madam."

At the announcement, Mrs. Weatherford turned toward the food table, where the last servant had placed a handful of serviettes beside the pewter goblet. "Thank you, Yates, that will be all." She turned to Clare and the others. "Well, everyone? All is ready, so take up a plate and fill it, and then you can sit at the other table where there are plenty of chairs."

Clare held Daisy while Ruthie and the others moved to the food table first. Once they were finished and seated, she handed her baby off to Ruthie and filled a plate of her own. Taking the seat next to the pair, they bowed their heads while Sir Geoffrey gave thanks for the meal, and then everyone dove into their cucumber sandwiches and ham and cold chicken, along with tomato aspic salad, assorted cheeses, and more of Mrs. Connelly's blackberry bread pudding. Along with the fare, two bowls of freshly picked blueberries and plums garnished the table.

Clare handed Daisy a slice of the bread from the cucumber sandwich and began cutting up pieces of the ham and chicken into bite-sized chunks. While Ruthie ate with one hand and held Daisy on her lap with her other, Clare offered her daughter the choice morsels, then gave her a sip of the lemonade.

"Your daughter seems to have a good appetite, Mrs. Danner, especially for one so young," Mrs. Weatherford commented. "When Marcus was a baby, he was quite particular at mealtimes, at least until he reached the age of five." She gazed at her son, seated at the end of the table near Clare and tucking into his food. "I remember we had a pair of goats," she said, smiling, "his father's idea for clearing the brush at the back of the estate. My husband had them tethered there, and there was a shed nearby where they were housed.

"When Marcus was about seven, we were having broccoli that evening, and Mrs. Connelly and I were so surprised when his plate was cleared and he received his dessert." She paused, her brown eyes merry. "It was only later that we discovered his stockpile of unwanted vegetables in the shed, before the goats had been brought in for the evening."

Clare grinned and glanced at Marcus. "And all this time, I thought it was your sister who was the picky eater. You were, too, just more sneaky about getting rid of the evidence."

"Not for long." He looked up at her, eyes gleaming with humor. "As I recall, for a whole week Father made me leave the table just before dessert was served so I could go out to the shed and give the goats their feed."

She lifted a brow. "And were your pockets full of broccoli the whole time?"

He laughed, and Clare noted surprise on his mother and sister's faces, while his grandfather's eyes glistened. They all looked to her then, and self-consciously she turned back to feeding Daisy another bite of the ham. "Actually, my daughter isn't always this agreeable when it comes to food, is she, Ruthie?"

"No, she can be downright finicky sometimes," the girl said. "When that happens, I give her milk with a little sugar and she sweetens right up."

"How old is Daisy?" Sir Geoffrey asked, watching Daisy as she waved her slice of bread like a flag before chomping a bite out of it.

"She turned two in July," Clare said. As he nodded, the stiffness in her spine eased. Perhaps she'd been wrong about him. Here she was, seated out on the lawn with the family, with none of the multiple courses or dozens of pieces of tableware to keep track of or even the formal elegance of the dining room. Just four very kind people who had allowed her and her daughter and Ruthie to share their meal with them.

"I'm afraid she made quite a mess of the birthday cake," Clare offered with a smile. "She wore most of the icing in her hair and face. She'd just seen the neighbor's dog at his dish that morning and so—"

Sir Geoffrey gave a bark of laughter. "And so of course she had to try it." His amber eyes shone with merriment. "You've got yourself a future scientist there."

"Oh, I do hope so." She looked to Daisy and handed her a slice of the cheese. "I want my daughter to have every opportunity to follow her dreams, whatever they may be. Madame Curie has done marvelous work for the war, especially with her mobile X-ray machines at the front. Women have much to contribute, and I hope Britain realizes that."

"I believe they are taking the hint even now, Mrs. Danner." His smile broadened beneath the white mustache. "If nothing else, this war has proven women are quite capable and willing to take on the responsibilities of keeping Old Blighty strong while our boys are overseas."

She was relieved to know his views echoed hers.

"Oh, how I wish we could do this every night, Mother!" Fannie cried from her place next to her grandfather. "No dressing up or perfectly boring conversations, and we're eating with our fingers!" She grinned at Clare and then looked at Daisy before popping a piece of chicken into her mouth. She made a googly-eyed face at her daughter while she chewed, and Daisy giggled.

As Fannie reached for another piece of her chicken, Daisy suddenly reached onto Clare's plate for a chunk and threw it at Fannie, laughing, and then tried for another piece before Clare grabbed her daughter's hands. "Daisy, no!" She looked across the table. "Fannie, I'm sor—"

Marcus tossed a blueberry at his sister's head just then, and while Mrs. Weatherford's mouth opened and closed, Fannie retaliated with a plum from the bowl on the table.

"Children, please!" Mrs. Weatherford said, finally managing to get the words out.

Marcus turned, grinning at Clare. "At least it wasn't porridge," he said in a low voice.

She fought back her laughter. Humor right now would not be a good example to her daughter in table manners. But Daisy was clapping, enjoying the game. "More!" she cried.

Clare quickly turned her daughter's attention with a spoonful of the bread pudding. Immediately Daisy's focus changed, and after several bites and more lemonade, she began to squirm against Ruthie's grip. "Down, Rootie!"

Fortunately, Ruthie had finished her meal. "Why don't you take her out onto the lawn for a while so she can run off her energy?" Clare suggested.

Once the pair had left the table, she was finally able to focus on her meal.

Marcus extended a hand to her and held out the plum. "I decided it best to offer this to you rather than toss it at your head." He darted an amused glance toward his sister. "After all, you are taking care of me, Mrs. Danner, and those scissors of yours can be dangerous."

She took the plum he offered. "It's good you remember that, too. Your poor sister is probably bruised."

He arched back against his seat. "From a blueberry?"

"You do have a strong throwing arm, Brother." Fannie laughed.

"Shall I try it again, more gently this time?" He picked up another blueberry while Fannie armed herself with a second plum.

"Your attention, children!" Mrs. Weatherford held in each of her hands a small apple from their orchard. "If either of you throws the first volley, I shall retaliate with these two jewels, and they'll smart a lot more than any blueberry or plum."

Her eyes sparkled as she looked first to her daughter and then to her son. "Well, will peace ensue here or not? I warn you, I was quite good at playing tennis in my youth, and my aim is still true."

What happened next took Clare completely by surprise. Marcus looked to his sister, who grinned at him, and then both the blueberry and plum went flying toward their mother. Mrs. Weatherford easily dodged the small missiles, then threw her apples, one at each of her children. Marcus caught his fruit, but Fannie deflected hers with her linen napkin. Sir Geoffrey began laughing, and it followed that the other three Weatherfords did the same until tears formed in their eyes.

Clare grinned, watching raptly, while a bittersweet ache pulsed through her. It was wonderful to see another side to these people beneath their wealth and affluence, as a real, loving family and the salt of the earth when it came right down to it. Grace Benningham was that kind of person, and so were Fannie Weatherford and Marcus.

She gazed at him, wondering again at his reasons for not telling his family about her and Daisy. Had Marcus been trying to protect Clare and her daughter? *"His work for Britain oftentimes comes with a certain amount of risk."*

Her smile faded. Did he receive his wounds because of his work at the War Office? And why was Natalya involved?

A sudden tap to the side of her head drew her attention, and Clare looked down to see a blueberry rolling around in her plate.

She turned to Marcus.

"You're not keeping up." His lips curved in a knowing smile, and heat rushed through her at the memory of those words during their intimate dinner together almost a week ago.

She reached for the blueberry and popped it into her mouth. "Better?"

Much better. Marcus smiled, loving the way her milky white skin turned rosy, her eyes gleaming with challenge. He'd told her that Grandfather loved fire in a person, and he loved it as well.

He'd sensed it in Clare that first day she came to see him at Cottage Hospital, and then here when he'd tried to intimidate her out of giving him a shave. There was also his obstinacy over visiting the patients in the west wing. She'd stood up for herself after the dinner the other night, too, and he'd apologized. But more than that, he'd seen the unguarded longing in her eyes when she watched him, and he *knew* she must feel something, too . . .

What are you about, man? He straightened and turned toward the lawn, where Daisy and the nanny were running in circles on the grass.

Natalya would return in a matter of hours. Why could he not let go of this woman beside him?

Only Clare knew the answer to that question, and she wasn't telling.

His frustration continued as he stared absently at the pair playing, the inability to remember his past overriding the guilt at his faithlessness toward Natalya, the woman he intended to marry. A beautiful, thoughtful, and kind woman to whom he owed his life.

The woman he was *supposed* to love.

28

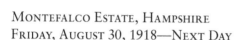

Milyi, I am back, and I have a surprise for you!"

Marcus tensed as he glanced up from the table and the book he was reading to see Natalya sail into the study. He'd discovered her morning arrival from London when Yates reported she'd telephoned a half hour ago, instructing Vickers to fetch her at the station in the Rolls.

"What surprise would that be?" he asked, his voice gravelly from lack of sleep. He'd spent the night tossing and turning, though not from any nightmare. Only his fog-blighted brain trying to decide what to do about the shambles he was making of his engagement to Natalya.

She must have sensed his unease. A few feet away from him she paused, her brow creased. "What is wrong? Are you not happy to see me?"

"Of course I'm pleased." He laid down the book and rose from the chair, walking slowly toward her.

"You are making such progress!" Beaming, she looked up at the thin cover of gauze wrapped around his head. "Did Mrs. Danner remove your stitches, then?"

"The last came out yesterday."

"Wonderful!"

Once he'd reached her, she raised a cheek to him, and he kissed her smooth skin. The strong scent of her candied perfume assaulted his senses.

"This is for you," she said as he stepped back, and she handed him a small box.

Marcus eyed her curiously as he took the offering and began unwrapping the package. "Did you get your housekeeping emergency resolved?"

"Oh yes, and such nonsense." She waved a lace-gloved hand. "A disagreement between my cook and the maid. They refused to reconcile, so I had to make a decision. Since I do enjoy the food served in my home, I let my housekeeper fire the maid and hire another. Hopefully peace will return," she said. "Otherwise I may be in need of another good cook."

Marcus flashed a smile before he opened the box. A polished brass bell the size of a teacup lay wrapped in white tissue. Along with the bell he found a dark beaded rope.

"I found the bell in a shop in London." She reached inside to grasp the metal ring and pluck the bell from the box. She gave it a slight jingle. "See? Does it not sound lovely?"

Again she rang the bell, this time slowly back and forth. "The same sound the bells make in the churches in Russia where I am from. So I had to buy it for you." She smiled. "It will be like the sound of our wedding bells when we marry."

A stab of guilt made his jaw clench as Marcus next withdrew the dark beaded rope. "What's this?"

"A chotki." She eyed him intently. "A knotted prayer rope used by Russian Orthodox Christians, similar to Roman Catholic rosary beads. You do not recognize it?"

He handed her the beads. "Should I?"

Her mouth wrinkled. "I had hoped you would remember. Those

beads belonged to my babushka from the old country near Perm in Russia. You admired them once and so I thought to give them to you." She paused. "Do you remember if you attended church when you were younger?"

"I suppose." Grandfather had insisted he return to church after Father's death, but beyond his leaving Harrow for Oxford, Marcus wasn't certain. Would Clare know?

He checked the tissue in the box and discovered a shred of paper with odd markings. He removed the handwritten note and scanned it—a series of numbers and letters: 2E, 5R, 7L, 3R. Marcus held it out to her. "Any idea what this is?"

"I wonder how that got into the box?" She quickly perused the paper. "What a mysterious message." She looked up, her eyes narrowed. "Any guesses?"

Marcus reread the nonsensical scrawl before crumpling the note in his fist. "I'd say it was rubbish." Pivoting, he tossed the wad of paper into the waste bin next to the bookcase.

She smiled tightly and gave a little shrug, holding the bell up to him. "So, do you like it?"

Marcus nodded, her thoughtful gesture only serving to increase his shame. "The prayer rope is special as well," he said and managed a smile. "Thank you."

Her face brightened. "You could use the bell to ring for your nurse if you like."

He covered his humor with a cough. Clare would take her scissors to him if he tried summoning her in that way. "I'll think about it," he said.

Taking the gifts to the table, he set them beside his book. Natalya followed him. "What are you reading?"

Before he could answer, she picked up the book and glanced at the title. "*Jane Eyre*? I had no idea you enjoyed reading Charlotte Brontë."

"A new author for me." Heat crawled up his neck. Fannie had suggested the novel to him last night after the picnic, bringing him the book from Clare's room this morning. He didn't understand why she chose this particular story, only that it pleased her to recommend it, and he wanted to oblige his sister.

Last evening had been memorable, and he'd come to realize there was much he didn't know about his own family. Mother was no longer the grief-stricken shadow he once remembered, and Fannie had turned out to be an intelligent, splendid young woman.

He hadn't yet talked at length with Grandfather, but his laughter last night at dinner had lifted Marcus's spirits for the first time in weeks. He knew these people, despite all the changes and missing years of his life. And being together with them outside on the front lawn, it was almost as if Father was still with them.

Natalya opened the book to the place he'd marked and skimmed the page. "Ah, I see you are at the part where poor Jane is now employed in the position of governess and has yet to meet the mysterious Mr. Rochester." She closed the book, dropping it onto the table. "Do you find that you like it so far?"

"So far." He was surprised he found it interesting reading. In some ways, the heroine, Jane, reminded him of Clare—the subtle traces of pride and stubbornness, but compassionate as well. Still, he'd only just started the book two hours ago and wasn't yet convinced he would read the entire thing.

"The lord of the manor falling in love with the lowly servant," Natalya continued, and his gaze shot up at her. "Many tragic romances have inked the pages of countless novels." She laid a gloved hand over her heart and sighed. "A young girl's dream, riding off into the dawn with her shining prince."

Marcus shifted, one hand braced against the table while he picked up the book with his other and handed it to her. "See that this gets returned to my sister, will you?"

"Oh, now I have spoiled it for you." She pushed out her lower lip as she took the offering, then eyed him keenly. "Frances gave this to you? I wonder why."

He shrugged before walking carefully across the polished floor to the bookcase. After inspecting several titles among Grandfather's selection of the classics, he chose Homer's *Odyssey*.

At least Natalya wouldn't debase him for reading about one man's journey to find his way home. Marcus had been doing much the same in his search to try to recover who and what he was.

"Once I get settled in my room, would you like me to take you to visit the rehabilitation hospital?"

He turned at her question. "I'd enjoy that, Natalya, thank you." He'd have a chance to see if Johnson and Roberts had sharpened their chess skills.

"Truly?"

She approached him, her dark eyes searching his, her expression so full of hope that his remorse returned tenfold. He owed her more than this cursory politeness. Raising a smile, he took her hand. "We'll even have lemonade and biscuits while we're there."

"Delightful!" She leaned forward to kiss his cheek. "I shall be back for you within the hour."

And like a breeze that suddenly gusted through the room, she was gone.

So much for her grand scheme with Marcus.

Natalya's brows veed into a crease as she sat gazing into the vanity mirror upstairs in her room. Behind her, the maid she had been assigned—Ellen?—began unpacking her steamer trunk and returning her clothing to the armoire.

"'Tis a lovely wedding gown ye've brought back with ye from London, milady."

The young servant girl had lifted the ivory silk crepe and chiffon from its tissue wrapping and held it up, admiring the fabric.

Natalya watched her through the vanity mirror. "Hang that up at once in the armoire. Carefully."

Wide-eyed, the girl blinked before she quickly did her bidding.

Natalya released a huff of air and reached for her face powder. Dabbing with the feathery puff along her chin and cheeks, her frustration kept pace with her anxiety. There was simply too much pressure on her!

Yesterday morning at the MI6 offices in Whitehall, she learned from C that the only "new development" was Reilly's escape from Moscow under the nose of the Cheka police. He was now reported to be somewhere in Finland.

C had questioned her exhaustively about Marcus. What was his current condition? How was he improving? What could he remember?

Despite his longtime friendship with her departed Walter, C had not been pleased with Natalya when she offered only that Marcus recognized his family and remembered his favorite childhood dessert. She was then strongly urged to become more creative in helping her "fiancé" to get his memory back.

Natalya had taken his directive to heart and purchased the bell and Russian rope beads from an import shop in Cheapside, hoping to jar Marcus's memory of his meeting with Reilly in Archangel.

Those clanging church bells had nearly made her deaf while she had tried to eavesdrop on their conversation, and Reilly had mentioned the chotki Marcus would ask for once they arrived in Perm to find the missing Romanovs.

Yet her gifts—even ringing the small bell for him in the same clanging fashion as those in the belfry of Dormition Church weeks ago—had produced no response. Nor had Marcus responded to the chotki beads. And then the note . . .

Natalya tossed the powder puff onto the vanity table. She had made a copy of the mysterious scrap of paper she found in his pocket after he was shot, hoping the number-letter sequence would trigger his memory and give her something to go on!

Marcus had simply thrown the paper away.

Closing her eyes, Natalya drew a deep breath. Not only did C pressure her, but time itself was weighing heavily on her—days passing without any marked improvement in Marcus's condition—and now Reilly's disappearance into Finland. Both reminded her she had yet to complete her task for the sake of

Mother Russia. And every hour lost increased their chances of failure—

"Milady, will there be anything else?"

Natalya jerked her head around. "You may leave now . . . Ellen. I shall call if I need help dressing for dinner later."

"Very good, milady."

Once the servant curtsied and left, Natalya turned back to the mirror. A slight smile began to curl the edges of her mouth, and her skin flushed warm at the memory of her second meeting at Whitehall yesterday. A relief compared to the first, and after a brief exchange and then dinner at his flat, it was several glasses of Bordeaux later that the rest of their evening was spent relaxing and entertaining each other . . .

She had not seen Stephen since Lord and Lady Walenford's party when she had literally fallen into his arms. A chuckle rose in her throat. With both of them shocked to be caught out in the open together, they froze in place for several seconds, like some marbled piece of romantic art, before he had passed her along to Marcus.

Stephen's shyness amused her, especially his insistence they keep their amorous trysts a secret. Natalya imagined he feared his uncle's reprisal. From what she knew of Viscount Randleton, he would not approve of his dear nephew associating intimately with a widow several years his senior and a "common foreigner" at that—despite her once being renowned in the arts.

Her smile twisted in the mirror as she reached to remove her earrings. Even in these modern times, some of the English peerage still clung to their taboos on mixing social class, though Randleton could hardly count himself among them now, not after Mrs. Danner's near hysterical plea to Marcus at Cottage Hospital in London.

Natalya knew of Stephen's cousin Elliot, the former heir to the viscountcy; she also knew he had dabbled in something he was not supposed to. Now Randleton wanted the return of his son's little mistake, and Mrs. Danner counted on Marcus to help her stop him.

Was being his nurse and helping with his recovery the only reason she was here with him? Natalya again wondered at the depth of their relationship. It was clear Frances had become involved. Her motive for putting the Jane Eyre novel into her brother's hands seemed rather transparent, at least to a woman such as herself. Poor Marcus had no clue.

Did something happen while she was away in London?

Natalya eyed the leather-bound book lying on her vanity table. Perhaps she should be more concerned about Mrs. Danner.

She considered her reflection in the mirror. It was time to start deciding her future, once she was able to extract from Marcus the information they all needed and accomplish the mission. And while Stephen's prospects looked promising with the demise of his cousin, the heir, it could change their "arrangement" with each other.

Marcus, however, while not a member of the peerage, still held a position of power in London. Affluence she could easily adapt to and appreciate. Even better, he and his family did not seem concerned about social pedigrees so that they would reject her. In fact . . .

She smiled at the glittering diamond on her finger. What was it Jack had said about his friend? Marcus was besotted with her.

Natalya rose from the vanity seat, her smile turning brittle as she reached for a light shawl and prepared to go downstairs. With C's recent news about Reilly's escape from Russia, Marcus was also their only means of success.

29

Grace was coming!

Clare tried containing her excitement as she and Ruthie each held one of Daisy's hands and strolled with her daughter along the cobblestoned drive toward the gatehouse.

Afternoon sunlight danced amid the leaves of the plane trees while Clare peered beyond the stone gate, her eyes searching for Vickers and the Rolls that would bring her dearest friend to Montefalco. Each second waiting made her anxious heart race. Just two days remained until Randleton made good on his threat, and oh how she needed her friend's level-headed advice!

"Car, Mama!" Daisy pulled her pudgy hand from Clare's grip to point at the shiny black motorcar making the turn onto the drive.

"It's Aunt Grace, sweetheart!" Clare cried, and her slippery daughter would have run ahead if not for Ruthie's iron grip on Daisy's other hand.

"Hold on, little miss, ye don't want to get run over!" Ruthie pulled her to the edge of the grass as the Rolls passed beneath the gatehouse and drove slowly in their direction.

The trio waited along the drive at Vickers's approach. Nearing them, he stopped the motorcar, and the door opened as Grace emerged and tossed her purse back inside before closing the door.

Jack waved and smiled from the back seat while Vickers continued toward the house. Grace threw herself into Clare's arms. "I've been waiting all morning for this moment, dear friend!"

"Me too," Clare whispered back, wrapping her arms around Grace. Tears burned her eyes despite her grin, and she blinked them back before pulling away to look at her. "You've no idea how glad I am to have you here."

"Ant Gay!"

Grace turned as Daisy ran to her, chubby arms outstretched, and she whisked her up and cuddled her close. "How is my Daisy?" she asked softly. "Are you happy here?"

Daisy nodded vigorously. "Hosey!" She pointed back toward the mansion.

"A rocking horse in the nursery," Clare explained. "You can imagine the rest."

Grace grinned at her daughter. "I bet you ride that hosey every chance you get."

"Hosey!"

The three women laughed.

Once Grace set Daisy back on her feet, Ruthie took charge of her while Grace looped an arm in Clare's and they all made their way back toward the mansion.

Thankfully, Ruthie took her daughter on ahead to run in the grass so Clare could enjoy some private time with her friend.

"Goodness! I wonder why Marcus never mentioned you to his family," Grace said once Clare had finished her tale about meeting the Weatherfords of Montefalco.

"Your husband thinks it may have to do with the risks of Marcus's job." Again Clare wondered about the gunshot wound and

Jack's request for her silence. "He said it could be Marcus's way of protecting us, but I still don't understand why."

Grace eyed her pensively. "I have noticed Marcus is quite reticent about his work and private life. Whenever he visited us in Kensington, he and Jack usually holed themselves up in the study. And both would stop talking when I arrived with the tea." She shrugged. "Secrets to do with the war, I suppose."

"Perhaps." She avoided sharing with Grace her fear that Marcus had been ashamed of her. Though Clare had at first been shattered by the realization, after talking with Jack and then being around Marcus and slowly getting to know his family better, she wasn't so sure what to believe anymore.

"It took you long enough to get here," she said, changing the subject. "I've waited for a telephone call daily. What happened to midweek?" Her mock pout was ruined when she grinned. "But your being here now is more than worth the wait."

Grace squeezed her arm. "There was a good reason for our delay." Her green eyes sparkled. "Our men are not the only ones with secrets."

Our men. If only it were true. Clare ignored the twinge in her heart. "Tell me."

"I seem to remember you asking me at our last party if I had an announcement." She smiled and pressed a gloved hand to her abdomen.

Clare's eyes blurred with tears. "Oh, Grace, I'm overjoyed for you!" She reached to hug her again. "Does Jack know?"

"Yes, as if I had a choice!" She swiped at her own watery eyes. "When my husband left for Hampshire last week, I didn't say anything, but I hadn't been feeling my old self for days. And once he returned home, he arranged for my cousin Daniel to accompany us back here on Wednesday to examine Marcus. But when Daniel arrived in Kensington, he took one look at me and ordered me to bed." She sighed. "After a barrage of questions and a medical examination, he informed me there will be a new little Benningham arriving in March of next year."

"This is the best news." Clare was still grinning as they continued walking arm in arm. "And I hope our children will have the chance to play together."

"Absolutely." Grace flashed a determined smile. "Daisy will become an honorary older cousin to our little girl or boy." She hesitated. "And I cannot tell you how relieved I am to know you'll be close by, holding my hand should I need it, Clare."

"Of course I'll be there for you, count on it."

Grace smiled her relief. "Now, enough of my news. How is Marcus getting on with his recovery? Any progress?"

"Not enough." Clare tried to quell her panic. Only two days remained and it wasn't looking hopeful. To make matters worse, since Natalya's return, her time with Marcus had been drastically curtailed. The ballerina saw to his every need, even taking him to visit the west wing hospital. And she now remained in the room whenever Clare came in to check on him.

Clare told Grace about his childhood memories and how they extended only as far as his final exams at Harrow. "As you can see, the situation is bleak," she said, her mouth pinched. "And my time is running out."

Grace frowned. "There is something I need to tell you."

"What?" Clare's pulse leapt. "Has something happened?"

Grace hesitated. "We brought someone else with us on the train," she said finally. "Or rather, he invited himself along, and we could hardly refuse since he works with Jack and Marcus." She angled her head, green eyes dark with concern. "He said he needs to speak with you about a matter of utmost importance."

Fear washed through her. "Not . . . Randleton?"

Grace shook her head. "His nephew, Stephen."

Clare's world teetered, and she clutched at her friend's arm.

"Are you all right?" Grace asked, gripping her.

Clare nodded, regaining her balance while her panicked thoughts whirled. Had he come to deliver a court summons for his uncle? "Do you know why he's here?" she rasped.

"He only told us that he intends you no harm."

Clare choked on a bitter laugh. "Stephen may not wish to hurt me, but his aunt and uncle will destroy my happiness." She fought back a sob. "My . . . reason for living."

Grace stopped walking and held her close. "Before you become too upset, let's hear what he has to say, all right? He may have swayed his uncle into changing his mind about Daisy."

"Really, Grace?" Clare leaned back, staring at her.

Grace lifted her shoulders. "You just never know. But right now you need to stay calm and focused." Her eyes narrowed. "Do not let that temper of yours loose." She smiled then. "I'm here for you, remember? And if you like, I shall stay by your side when you speak with him."

Clare nodded. She would try to be calm, but if Stephen Lange had a court summons with him, Grace could stand on her head and it wouldn't change a thing.

Marcus was still in no condition to offer his help.

She was about to lose her baby again. This time forever.

Once they finally arrived back at the house, Clare was relieved to learn that the unwanted guest had already been escorted up to his room.

Leaving her friend to get settled in, Clare was desperate to see her daughter. She mentioned to Fannie in passing that she wouldn't make the afternoon tea and then bounded up the stairs toward the nursery.

Inside, Clare grabbed up her napping baby from the cot and sat with her in the rocking chair while Ruthie dozed on the bed, her book lying against her chest.

"I cannot lose you," she whispered tearfully, rocking her sleeping child. Had Randleton sped up the court process without her knowledge? Did he discover her whereabouts and decide to execute his demands through his nephew?

"I wish we could run away, little one," she murmured. "Go

back to Wicklow or north into Scotland where we might finally be out of their reach."

Daisy slept on, peacefully unaware that in just days—or perhaps this afternoon?—she would lose her mum. Tears tracked silently down Clare's cheeks, her pulse racing like a wild rabbit as she tried to think.

She hadn't enough money to go anywhere. She couldn't even manage to get out of that slum of a neighborhood she lived in. Even if she did have the funds, Randleton had reminded her at their meeting that in the eyes of the law, unwed mothers had few rights, especially if someone with the viscount's power and influence should go up against her.

Randleton would surely hunt her down wherever she went.

Was Stephen here to take her child?

Why don't you ask him and quit hiding up here like a coward?

She ignored the inner voice. If Randleton's decision had only affected her, she would face it squarely, but for her baby . . .

No! She pressed her wet cheek against Daisy's soft curls.

"Mrs. Danner?"

Ruthie had awakened and set aside the novel. "Are ye not going down to tea?"

Clare dried her eyes and glanced at her watch. It was just past the start of teatime. "I suppose I should."

She rose from the chair and gently placed her child back into the cot. "Guard her with your life, Ruthie," she said, ignoring the girl's wide-eyed look. "I'll check in with you later."

Clare started toward the door, forcing each step. Surely at tea with Grace and Jack and everyone present, Stephen wouldn't deliver any terrible news to her in front of them. Would he?

Perhaps he intended to do just that while Clare had the support of her friends present.

The notion of receiving a public summons from him stole what little courage she had left, and Clare passed up the turn leading to the Magnolia room to head toward the back of the house and the conservatory.

Even if Fannie wasn't there, Clare longed for the peaceful silence of the sanctuary.

Head down, she pushed her way through the double glass doors.

"Mrs. Danner?"

Stephen Lange reached out to steady her as the two nearly collided.

Clare gaped at him. "I . . . you are not having tea with the others?"

"Actually, I came here hoping to find you," he said. "I learned from Miss Weatherford earlier that you would not be at tea, and she told me you might visit the conservatory or at the least she would bring you here afterward." He arched an amused brow. "I hope you were not trying to give me the slip?"

Her face warmed at being caught doing just that. She raised her chin. "I was needed in the nursery to check on my daughter."

His blue gaze behind the glasses turned knowing. "I completely understand," he said with a grin, showing off his straight white teeth. He waved her toward a small bistro table and two chairs. "Shall we sit?"

Reluctantly, she led him over to the table and sat down before her knees gave out. "What do you want to say to me?"

He continued standing, his eyes focused on her while her attention was drawn to his dark blue suit, the silk-print vest and tie the color of gold.

"I wish to start by saying I am on your side." His voice had softened, and she looked up into his gentle expression. "I did not come here to cause you pain or distress. In fact, I hope to offer a solution to your current situation with my uncle Montague."

"Solution?" Clare crossed her arms to hide her shaking hands. "Has he changed his mind about Daisy?"

"I'm afraid not." His eyes held regret. "Uncle is still quite adamant about getting his granddaughter back."

"That is irony, don't you think?" Anger surged in her. "When his wife tossed her away like rubbish in the first place? Of course, now she comes with an inheritance."

He lowered his head, and it was a moment before his gaze returned to her. "What they did to you was—" he paused, then said—"in a word, despicable."

She jerked a nod, arms still crossed.

"I hope it will ease some of your hurt, if nothing else, knowing my aunt and uncle have come to appreciate just how deeply they wounded you." A flicker of sadness crossed his expression. "They are still mourning their son."

Clare relaxed her arms in her lap. Had Randleton and his wife received their just deserts? She wasn't certain. What she did know was that during her own desperate search for Daisy and fearing what had become of her baby, Clare had still kindled the hope she would find her daughter and be reunited with her.

Elliot Lange's military death certificate had denied Randleton and his wife of that hope. Their son was never coming back.

It didn't mean that she was going to surrender her daughter. "Why are you here, Stephen? Do you have some scheme in mind to save my daughter for me?"

He finally sat down in the chair across from her, hands resting against his knees. "I've spoken with my uncle, and he has already petitioned the House of Lords to make me his heir to the viscountcy."

Clare leaned forward. "Is . . . that what you want?"

He grinned, and she remembered he'd always had a nice smile. "How like you, Clare." He straightened, holding his hands outward. "Who would not wish for such good fortune? A title, wealth, lands, power. Most men dream of those things."

"Congratulations then." Stephen was not his cousin after all, and she should wish him well in his newfound success. "Though I don't see how that affects me and my daughter." She lifted a brow. "Unless you think Randleton will keel over in the next two days so you can take his place and countermand his threat?"

Stephen laughed as he reached for her hand. "Clare, I have a proposal."

Too surprised to react, she stared at the hand he held in his larger one.

"I want you to be my wife."

Her head shot up. She hadn't heard him correctly. "What did you say?"

He slid from the chair and dropped to one knee. "Marry me."

No! She reared back, trying to pull her hand away. He held on firmly. "Please hear me out before you reject my offer."

Clare stared at him, slack-jawed. This prominent man, destined to become a viscount . . . was kneeling before her, proposing marriage?

She closed her mouth and swallowed. "Please take your seat first."

His blue eyes held hers a moment before he did as she asked.

"I appreciate what you've said, Stephen, and I confess to being completely surprised, but . . . why would you wish to marry me?"

"While you and I and Elliot were more or less growing up together, I became quite . . . enamored with you." Color tinged his cheeks. "My cousin made for a more dashing catch of course, and even now I'm still somewhat shy around women, but my feelings have never changed. I still think of you with great affection." He stared down at his hands, clasping and unclasping his fingers. "In fact, I was sure even then I was in love."

Love? Stephen had suffered no more than an adolescent crush. "You can have any woman you want, especially now that you stand to inherit," she said. "She could be rich, beautiful, titled. But I was the upstairs maid, remember?"

"You are beautiful, Clare." He looked up, his face inches from hers. "You're also clever and courageous." He hesitated. "I was not told of your . . . circumstances with my cousin, until Elliot confessed to me once he'd rebelled against his parents and arranged for your departure from that hellish place. I lost track of you after that, until you appeared in London. As I mentioned at Lord and Lady Walenford's party, I'd seen you in town a few times, either in her company or with Captain Weatherford. I assumed the two of you were—"

"We are not together." She leaned back against the seat, her voice curt. "The captain is engaged to Mrs. Bryce, who is staying here at Montefalco with the family." She thrust out her chin. "I am here only as the hired nurse."

"You are much more than that," he said softly, reaching to give her fingers a gentle squeeze. "Will you . . . consider my offer? I've already taken the liberty of introducing our match to my uncle, and after pointing out to him the advantages, he has agreed."

A glimmer of hope ignited in her. "What advantages?"

"Uncle Montague needs an heir, and except for his second cousin in Suffolk, who is a bachelor and years older than him, I'm the only relation left." The corners of his mouth lifted. "And as I want you and Daisy, I told him that if we marry, he'll have access to his granddaughter without exposing himself to an ugly court battle."

She eyed him warily. "Why should I trust you?"

Hurt flashed in his eyes, and she instantly regretted her words. Stephen had never been unkind to her. Truly, his only offense was being related by blood to the Langes.

But then so was her daughter. Now he offered her a way to keep Daisy. "Please forgive me, I did not mean to insult you." She raised a smile. "I know you have good intentions."

"Of course I do. And think of it, Clare! Daisy would be my daughter, too. I would love her as she should be loved, and you"— his eyes met hers—"I would cherish and adore always."

She gazed into his earnest expression. With such striking features, he really could have any woman he chose. Did he truly love her? "I thank you for the offer, but I . . . I don't feel the same way about you, Stephen."

"You could learn to love me, too, couldn't you?" He leaned forward. "Many such unions start off with less. And I hope at least that you are fond of me?"

She nodded, her smile coming easily this time while her thoughts raced as fast as her pulse. Could she learn to love Stephen? Even as she ached with longing for Marcus, the man who could have offered her all she'd ever wanted, but now could not give her what she needed most—keeping her and Daisy together?

She remembered him giving the diamond to Natalya in the park, yet despite that, here at Montefalco she'd held on to hope as they laughed together and she'd shared a few of his memories. But in the end, he'd made it clear with Natalya's return whose company he preferred.

And time was whittling away the hours she had left with her daughter. "Yes," she said, before she could give herself more time to think. "I will marry you, Stephen."

He laughed his relief, and before she knew what was happening, he hauled her up out of the chair and into his arms, and her hands slowly went around his waist.

"You have made me a happy man," he said softly in her ear.

She leaned back to look up at him. "Are you certain about this? I am no viscountess. I would embarrass you—"

He touched a finger to her lips, stifling her protest. "I know just as little about being a viscount, so we are even." His smile nearly dazzled her. "And since I doubt my uncle will 'keel over' anytime soon, we both have time to learn. I'm certain we can ask our mutual friends Lord and Lady Walenford to assist us in that regard."

But you are leagues ahead of me, Stephen. Clare tried to smile. At least he was right about Grace; her friend would help her to learn. And surely Randleton wouldn't vacate the title anytime soon. They could wait a few months until both felt suited to their new roles before they married and entered society.

And perhaps before then, Marcus would have his memory back?

"Shall it be a Christmas wedding, then?" she asked.

"How about a summer wedding," he said, his eyes alight. "Next week, in fact."

"No, I can't!" Panic flooded her. "That's too soon, Stephen. I . . . I could never learn so much so fast."

"It was my uncle's condition." His expression sobered. "He wants a special license obtained and he's already creating a new . . . persona for us."

"I see." A chill seeped into her bones despite the warm weather.

"In other words, he's making me acceptable to your London crowd."

"His crowd, not mine." Stephen grimaced. "It pains me to be related to that kind of arrogance, but I meant what I said, Clare. I will love and cherish you always."

He leaned in then, as if intending to kiss her on the mouth. Clare turned her head slightly, offering him her cheek instead. His kiss was warm and light, and when he straightened, a smile creased his lips. "Just so," he said in a low voice. "We'll have a lifetime together to get acquainted."

"About the wedding date." She hesitated. "I will marry you, but first I want time to get to know you again. Instead of a special license, would Randleton agree to the three weeks it takes to read the banns?"

He considered her a moment. "Very well. Can you return to London with me tomorrow?"

"I doubt it. Lord Walenford has hired me to care for the captain and try to help him with his memory. He said it's quite urgent."

"Of course." His brow creased with his obvious disappointment. "What if I hop the train out here on the weekends? Stay as a guest at Montefalco? That should give you enough time to get accustomed to the idea, and for us to become better acquainted than we are now. We'll marry right here in Hampshire."

"I believe that can be arranged." Her mind still reeling, Clare smiled in relief. She wasn't ready to leave yet, and perhaps Grace would stay on for a time and teach her what she needed to know about being a viscountess. Or Marcus would heal . . .

She tipped her face to him. "This isn't some kind of dream, is it? Will I wake up in a moment to find you gone, and myself just staring at the flowers over there?"

"You're not dreaming." He grinned and reached for her once more, embracing her gently. "We will have a wonderful life together, Clare. You, me, and Daisy."

She let Stephen hold her in his arms, his warmth seeping through while she breathed in the scent of his bay rum cologne.

Yet she felt nothing for him but kindness and gratitude. Could she learn to love him?

Surely, Clare, any man who's to inherit title and lands and still wants to marry you to secure your happiness with Daisy is someone you could love.

"I believe you," she whispered into his good ear, knowing it was true.

30

Marcus?" Clare called softly as she opened the passageway door into the study. With her recent attempt to avoid Stephen Lange, which in the end had failed, she was long overdue in checking on her patient.

She planned to inspect his healing progress before cornering Jack to find out if she could leave off with the gauze entirely.

Keeping her mind on the task—any task—was difficult, however. She was an engaged woman! And in three weeks to become a future viscountess.

Clare shook her head. It still seemed fantastical, and likely she would wake up tomorrow and all would be back to the way it was.

Yet Stephen had held her in his arms, his solidness and tender kiss against her cheek real enough. It was no dream, and the sooner she came to terms with that, the better.

She looked toward the table and met Natalya's piercing gaze.

Marcus sat beside her in his wheelchair. Clare straightened as she approached, and he turned to her, a smile lifting a corner of his mouth. His gaze flicked over her and then he turned away, but not before she caught his look of regret.

She had that same feeling as well. "I came to see how the patient is doing?"

"Marcus is doing well, as you can see." Natalya rested her hand on his. "I have been telling him about London and the lovely trousseau I brought back with me. Hampshire would be a beautiful place to marry, do you not agree, Mrs. Danner?"

My future husband thinks so. Clare schooled her expression. "So I've been told."

Then to Marcus she said, "I'd like to inspect your wounds. May I?" She moved in beside him.

He looked up at her. "Of course."

He seemed despondent, almost melancholy, and once more Clare thought about the kiss they'd almost shared out on the west wing patio. Glancing at Natalya, she pursed her lips and began unwinding the gauze. "This will just take a moment—"

"Hey, old boy, are you decent?"

Jack's voice accompanied his rap on the outer study door, and all three turned.

"Come in," Clare called, and the door opened to admit Jack and a familiar silver-haired man carrying a doctor's bag. "Dr. Strom, how wonderful to see you again."

Clare smiled at Grace's cousin, the man who had tended her wounds last year after the air raid over Margate.

"Mrs. Danner, it has been far too long." His mouth curved beneath the salt-and-pepper mustache. "Are your injuries still ailing you?"

"Not at all. I'm perfectly recovered, thanks to you."

Clare ignored the curious looks from Marcus and Natalya as Dr. Strom smiled and then turned to Jack.

"Well, Marcus." Jack came to stand beside his friend. "You likely don't remember Dr. Strom, but he's my wife's cousin and a good doctor. I'd like him to give you a once-over if that's all right?"

Clare stepped back, and Natalya rose from her chair to stand next to her as both women watched while the doctor opened his bag and withdrew a stethoscope.

"I will come back later, *myshka*." Natalya made a show of checking her watch before giving Clare a glance. "An old proverb in my country says that 'too many cooks spoil the broth.'" To Marcus she said, "I must go and write letters to the tailor for your wedding clothes and to the stationer for our invitations."

Marcus raised a hand in farewell, and Dr. Strom cast a surprised glance at Clare, who struggled to hide her anguish. It seemed Natalya was determined to marry Marcus whether he remembered her or not. *And you've agreed to marry someone else.*

She tried to focus on the doctor's examination. After he'd checked Marcus's vital signs, he removed the rest of the gauze and shot a silent look at Jack. At Jack's grimace, Dr. Strom turned his gaze on her.

Clare dipped her head in acknowledgment of the gunshot wound.

"Your injuries have been tended to nicely, Captain," Dr. Strom said, "and they should heal without too much scarring."

He looked at her then. "You've done a fine job, Clare. I could certainly use an assistant at my Kent practice if you ever decide to settle back into country life."

Clare warmed at his praise, and when she looked to Marcus, he was watching her. "Thank you for the kind offer, Doctor. In truth, Marcus did most of the work in healing. He ate all his vegetables and sat still while I doused him with antiseptic." Mischief made her add, "Though at times I did have to show him who was boss."

Marcus chuckled, and Clare's heart leapt.

"I don't doubt it for a moment," Jack said, grinning. "She has a reputation for keeping her patients in line."

"Indeed, she does," Marcus said.

Clare's temperature kicked up another notch as all three men looked at her. "I wondered at the bandages," she said, turning her attention to Dr. Strom. "Should they stay on at this point?"

Once again the doctor raised a silent look at Jack, who gave a firm nod.

"Just a while longer," Dr. Strom replied. "But you can let the air at them for a while each time before reapplying a fresh bandage."

"Very well. I can take care of adding new gauze now."

"No need," he said. "I wish to stay and talk with Marcus awhile, and we'll let nature have a crack at those wounds."

Clare nodded, leaving the room through the hidden door. No doubt Dr. Strom would later want an explanation for her using the passageway, though now it seemed Marcus had few emergencies if any. And that meant from now on she would need to enter his room by the proper means, especially since she'd promised to wed Stephen.

Oh, Lord, what have I done?

31

Are you serious?" Grace's eyes bulged. "Stephen Lange asked *you* to be his wife . . . and you said yes?"

"Well, don't look so shocked." Clare made a face at her friend as the two sat on Grace's bed upstairs. Jack's room adjoined his wife's next door. "It's not like I have snakes writhing in my hair."

"Of course you're not Medusa! And you know that's not what I meant. It's just . . . he's Randleton's nephew!"

"I realize that." Clare clasped her hands in her lap, conflicting emotions still churning inside her. Just minutes ago, she'd left the three men in the study, with Marcus smiling warmly at her when she'd teased him about her being the boss. He'd also smiled at Natalya before she went off to order their wedding invitations.

She raised her chin. "Stephen is a good man, Grace. He says he's always loved me, and he wants to cherish me and Daisy as his own. He did go to some trouble to persuade his uncle to approve the plan."

"And Stephen is to become the next viscount . . ." Grace shook her head, clearly stunned. Then her eyes narrowed. "Are you certain this has nothing to do with Elliot's letter, his last will bequeathing to Daisy his money and lands? Randleton might have agreed to Stephen's request so that he can control her inheritance once you marry . . . or perhaps Stephen himself has that in mind."

Clare had considered the possibility but only briefly. "I don't believe Stephen would abuse any funds my daughter is to inherit. And Randleton may have it in mind, but it doesn't matter to me, so long as my baby and I are together."

Grace reached for her shoulder. "But you don't love Stephen."

"What's love to do with anything?" Clare pulled from her grasp. "I have no other choice." She stood and began pacing. "Downstairs in his room right now is the only man who can help me win against Randleton, and Marcus can't recall what happened last month, let alone recall the events from a year ago." She turned to her friend. "Stephen has thrown me a lifeline. I get to keep Daisy, and Randleton gets to see her occasionally. Even if he wants to control her money, the threat of losing my daughter is gone."

Grace's eyes shimmered with unshed tears. "I just want you to be happy, Clare." She stood too. "And I *know* you still love Marcus."

Clare pushed air through her nostrils, her mouth tight.

"See? You cannot deny it. We've been friends for too long. I let you cry on my shoulder just weeks ago while your world fell apart, remember? And being here with him daily, caring for him, surely your heart hasn't turned to stone."

"I wish it had." The rash words tasted bitter as her memories of their time together returned. The budding new awareness between them, the teasing and bantering back and forth. Marcus's smiles and laughter filling her heart and the way he'd opened up to her about his childhood—both the happy times and the hurts, and the sacrifices he'd made.

The hunger in his eyes when he'd leaned over her as she lay in the sun on the chaise, his lips a mere breath away from touching hers before she stopped him. And the longing in her to feel the press of his mouth against hers . . .

She shook her head. "Not everyone gets a happily-ever-after, Grace, not like you and Jack. I live in the real world, where Marcus has a woman he's going to marry, who is making their wedding preparations as we speak."

"No!" Grace said, blinking.

"*Yes*," Clare bit out. "Regardless of that, I've only hours before Randleton carries out his threat."

"But Marcus *could* still get his memory back." Grace approached her. "Miracles don't always happen precisely when we want them to or in the way we expect." She paused. "You have two days. And if you pray—"

"I've *been* praying," Clare said angrily. "But I'm out of time, and God isn't listening." She drew a shuddering breath. "The letter from Elliot claiming Daisy as his daughter only strengthens Randleton's case in court to take her from me." She swallowed back a sob. "Marrying Stephen is my only guarantee."

Grace's eyes searched hers. "I do understand, Clare, and I am in no position to argue." She pressed a hand to her abdomen. "I cannot imagine what I would do if . . ."

"As a mother, you'll do whatever you must," Clare said in a low voice. "And you're right, miracles don't always happen in the way we expect. What if it is Providence that brought Stephen Lange here today to propose marriage?" She raised a little smile. "And love, well, it may happen in time, but for now this is what I've had to choose for me and my daughter."

Grace nodded, and suddenly Clare's ire fled while anxiety took its place. She reached to grasp her friend's hands. "I do need your help," she whispered. "I don't know the first thing about being a proper lady, let alone a future viscountess. I'm terrified I'll embarrass Stephen—and myself, more than I have already."

"All right." Grace smiled for the first time. "I'll stop haranguing you for your choice, but I'm still going to pray. And I will help you as much as I can. Once you learn and practice the basics of etiquette, it's really quite easy." Her eyes glinted with mischief. "Of course, if we had the dowager countess here with us, I'm certain Lady Bassett would get you into shape in a week's time."

Clare blinked back tears and chuckled. "I don't doubt Lady

Bassett would have me spend hours learning to stir tea just so."
She pretended to row an imaginary spoon in a cup. "And teach me
how to hold my head aloft as I saunter into any room like a queen."

"Or a duchess," Grace said, and they both laughed. "Actually,
you do saunter rather well, so that's a lesson you can forgo." She
hesitated. "And since Lady Bassett is not here, I suggest you speak
with Marcus's mother."

"What?" Clare eyed her sharply, all humor gone. "But . . . you'll
be here for a while, won't you?"

"Only for a couple of days." Grace eyed her with regret. "Jack
needs to get back to his father's business dealings, and he wants
me home where he or Knowles can keep an eye on me." She rolled
her eyes. "My husband learns I'm pregnant and suddenly I must
have a bodyguard at all times." She smiled. "Regardless, Mrs.
Weatherford is kind and quite lovely. I should think she'd be happy
to help you get safely through the gauntlet of social decorum. Why
don't you speak with her?"

Clare bit her lip. "Maybe you should tell her first. You know,
get her used to the idea that I'm going to be . . ."

"Her superior among the peerage?" Grace's eyes sparkled. "You
should see your face, Clare." She laughed. "Of course I'll tell her
if you'd like me to do so. Is Stephen planning to share the news
while he's here?"

Clare's heart pounded. Suddenly her engagement and becoming
Mrs. Stephen Lange in just three weeks had become all too real.
"I'll need to ask him."

"Where do you want these *Codiaeum variegatum* planted?
Along either side of the Plumbago?"

At Peter's question, Fannie lifted her attention from an overgrown *Phalaenopsis intermedia* she'd been repotting, the fourth
orchid of its kind that would yield a pink labellum surrounded by
beautiful white petals, reminding her of little angels.

298

Her heart thumped as she gazed into his inquisitive green eyes. Since that first day working beside her with her beloved plants, Peter had visited the conservatory every day after tea. And each time she'd sensed his growing interest toward her.

She looked out toward the path leading deeper into her forest of plants. "Actually, I think the bright colors in that pair of Crotons would go nicely next to the *Schefflera arboricola*."

Peter had followed her gaze to the dwarf umbrella tree. He turned to her, his rugged features pensive.

Fannie ignored his look and walked to the place where she wanted him to put the plants. She'd purposely chosen the spot because he'd need to leave his wheelchair to complete the task.

"Fannie, I dinna think so . . ."

"Well, I do think so, and it's the perfect spot." She looked at him with affection. "I know you can do this, Peter. All you need to do is try."

His mouth hardened. "I canna leave the chair. Or have you forgotten?"

"Yes, you can, and I have a set of crutches that will aid you in getting up and down."

"What?" He sneered. "You offer them to all your visiting cripples? Are you especially keen to watch invalids try and fail in your company?"

She braced herself against his harsh words. "I am very keen about trying." With her jaw set, she slowly lifted her skirt, enough to let him see her steel brace. "And I was once an invalid myself."

His eyes widened as he looked to the brace and then at her face. "Is it painful?"

"Sometimes, when I've been on my feet too long." She held his gaze. "But compared to a time in my life when I couldn't take a single step on my own, I'm grateful for this." She dropped her skirt to hide the brace.

"How did . . . ?"

"Polio." And Fannie relayed to him her two-year battle and how Marcus had helped her to walk again. "It was a painful struggle, but I succeeded," she said softly. "Though I'm sure you must have noticed my limp."

"No, lass," he said, his voice husky. "I'm afraid I've been too busy ogling your bonny face and fine figure."

A warm blush crept into her cheeks, and she averted her eyes, but not before she caught his smile.

"All right, get me that crutch and I'll give it a try."

Fannie hid her delight as she moved toward the screen. "Would you help me to get the tools?"

He followed her behind the enclosure. "I think I saw your brother the other day out on the west wing patio. A captain, is he?"

"Yes, Marcus is a naval captain with the Admiralty. He works in London."

"He had a woman with him, dark hair. Is that his wife?"

"Oh no, she's not his wife." *Even though I wish it.* Fannie looked at him. "That's his nurse, Mrs. Danner. My brother recently injured his head in an accident, and he has what they call retrograde amnesia." She pursed her lips. "He remembers us and most of his childhood here, but not anything recent over the past several years. He's here recovering, and it's our hope that he'll regain the memories he's lost."

"Och, I'm sorry, lass." His green eyes softened. "Is he seeing our hospital doctor for it?"

Fannie shook her head. "Mrs. Danner—Clare—takes care of his wounds, and the rest is up to God." She paused. "Dr. Strom arrived today from London to examine my brother."

"Aye, I noticed you had company. I saw the Rolls-Royce from the west wing as it was coming back from town."

Fannie nodded. "Yes, Lord and Lady Walenford. Dr. Strom is Lady Walenford's cousin. And they brought with them their friend, Sir Stephen Lange."

"So, the gentry have stormed the castle."

She angled her gaze at him. "Are you against those who have money and title?"

"Not at all, so long as they dinna get full of themselves and think they're better than everyone else."

"Well, Lord Walenford has been my brother's friend for years, and he's a good sort. I met his wife, Lady Walenford, at tea this afternoon, and she seems quite lovely, and so is her cousin the doctor."

"And the other one, Sir Stephen?"

"He wasn't at tea," she said. "He wished to meet with my new friend—"

"What are you thinking, Stephen? A marriage to the nurse, Mrs. Danner?"

Fannie tipped her ear in the direction of Natalya's voice. She glanced at Peter and held a finger to her lips.

"I've asked Clare to be my wife. Is that so hard for you to believe, Mrs. Bryce?"

Fannie blinked. Sir Stephen Lange?

"Oh, now it is Mrs. Bryce?" Anger vibrated through Natalya's tone. "So where does that leave us, Stephen?"

A long moment of silence before he replied, "There is no *us* any longer, Natalya. No more assignations, no more secrets. We both know our relationship was never about love. I have loved Clare for some time, and now that I'm to become a member of the peerage—"

"Peerage! Listen to yourself. You were nothing when I found you, Stephen. I helped you to get that job at Whitehall, and now you abandoned me for what, a common hospital worker? And you intend to make *her* a viscountess?"

Clare . . . a viscountess? Fannie nearly gasped before she clapped a hand over her mouth, her eyes wide as she stared at Peter.

"So, does your *nurse* love you, Stephen?" Natalya laughed, an ugly sound. "And will you still love her when she embarrasses you with her awkward manners and countrified ways? Or perhaps when you *both* become the laughingstock of London?"

A heartbeat of silence, then, "I never imagined this kind of jealousy in you, Natalya."

Sir Stephen spoke quietly, so Fannie barely caught his words. "Clare and I will be happy together, and I shall become involved with my uncle's affairs. I won't have time for—"

"For me or for our arrangement, is that it?" Bitterness edged her voice.

Fannie blinked. Sir Stephen was jilting Natalya for Clare! Why had Natalya been seeing this man at all when she was engaged to Marcus?

"That's right. No time for you or for your games. We're finished."

A deep sigh issued, followed by, "I will not let you go, Stephen. You can say all that you want, but my mind is made up. Play your little game with her if you like, but you belong to me. In every way."

Fannie heard Sir Stephen's curse, then heavy footsteps against the tiled floor as he stormed from the conservatory. She looked to Peter as they both listened and waited for a second set of steps, the click of a woman's boot heels as they, too, faded away.

Another minute passed before Fannie peered around the corner of the screen. She and Peter were alone now.

"What should I do?" She turned to him. "Natalya has been seeing Sir Stephen Lange while she's engaged to my brother!" Fannie started to chew on a fingernail, then realized her hands were still full of dirt. "I cannot possibly tell Marcus. In his compromised state right now, it might devastate him."

"What about the nurse, Clare? Could you tell her?" Peter asked.

"I suppose I should. But oh, the poor dear! It's going to crush her."

"He didna answer when Natalya asked if Clare loved him. He only said that he loved Clare and that they would be happy together."

"True." Fannie shoved her hands into her apron pockets. "It did seem that Stephen at least wants to be honest in his affections for Clare, don't you think?"

"Aye." He grimaced. "Except for the wee fact that Natalya is pressuring him."

"Mmm, yes, I've found her on occasion to be rather . . . daunting." Fannie hadn't forgotten the sparring contest between Natalya and Clare at tea some days ago. While her brother's fiancée had done her best to insult Clare, Clare retaliated quite admirably.

She remembered, too, having observed Clare with her brother and how happy he seemed when he was with her. And then his quiet, almost subdued manner when he was with Natalya.

Admittedly, she'd done a bit of meddling when she brought Marcus the copy of *Jane Eyre* from Clare's room, hoping the novel would enlighten her brother as to what was in his own heart.

But then Ellen had returned the book to Fannie's room along with a note: *"Not interested, but thank you for the thought. Marcus."*

But it wasn't Marcus's handwriting.

She looked at Peter. "I believe I shall wait, at least for a little while until I know more. I want to first talk with Clare and learn her true feelings for Stephen before I decide what to do."

"A very logical way to proceed." He smiled up at her. "A good scientist always collects sufficient data before he or she begins a project." He cocked his head. "And you're not only bonny, lass. You're canny as well."

She warmed at his praise even as her insides churned. The burden of what they had just overheard weighed heavily on her, and she must bear it until she could find the right moment to speak with Clare. If her friend was ambivalent in her feelings for Sir Stephen as Fannie hoped, it might not be so terrible to reveal his . . . amorous proclivities with Natalya. However, if her friend was in love with the man . . .

Fannie's pulse leapt. The news would surely send Clare flying back to London for good, and Marcus might end up making the biggest mistake of his life.

32

Montefalco Estate, Hampshire
Sunday, September 1, 1918—Same Day

I t was time for her to beard the lion.

Clare gazed at her reflection in the cheval glass that evening, the blue silk and chiffon dress accentuating the gray in her troubled eyes.

Having straightened the daisy pendant at her throat and adjusted the pearl comb in her hair, she pressed her lips together while pinching her cheeks, forcing color back into her pale skin. "Now you look ready to do battle," she murmured. "Formal dining."

A smile broke into her somber reflection, recalling the food-fight picnic she and the Weatherfords had enjoyed just days ago. She'd kept her word to Marcus to attend more family dinners and was grateful when Mrs. Weatherford spoke to Yates, requesting a simpler, informal setting when they had no special guests at Montefalco.

Tonight, however, with Lord and Lady Walenford, Sir Stephen Lange, and Dr. Strom in attendance, the meal promised to feature a profusion of tableware, bouquets of flowers, and seating placards all arranged on an elegantly formal table in the dining room.

She was about to leave when a knock sounded at the secret door. "Marcus, is that you?"

"Open the door," he called.

Quickly, she went to the bookcase and noted the copy of *Jane Eyre* had been restored. The novel had gone missing on Friday. Perhaps Fannie had borrowed the book?

Clare removed the novel and pressed the lever. Once the bookcase swung away, she opened the hidden door.

Marcus stood looking tall and fine in his tailored white-tie dinner suit, and except for the gauze around his head, he seemed quite fit. Jack had requested she postpone removing the bandage for another day. Likely he wanted to tell Marcus the truth first.

She observed his right hand resting on a polished black cane. "Where did you come by that?"

"My sister." He smiled. "Fannie has an arsenal of medical appliances she no doubt nicked from my grandfather's laboratory."

Clare had yet to see this mysterious place where Sir Geoffrey spent most of his days.

"You look ravishing, Clare." He spoke in the barest of whispers, his dark gaze traveling leisurely over her length. His deep voice reverberated to her soul. "It was my real reason for coming here," he said. "I wanted to see you."

She blushed, then made a point to do the same to him, her eyes absorbing every detail from his head down to his polished shoes. Stephen had a similar build, but he lacked Marcus's breadth of shoulders and taller stature. "You look rather dashing yourself, Captain."

He grinned, the flash of his white teeth and the mischievous look in his golden eyes making her heart throb. *If only you could save me from my fate!*

"Now that we've complimented each other, will you let me escort you into the dining room?" He extended his elbow to her.

Clare hesitated, the temptation to walk proudly into the dining room on the arm of this handsome, wonderful man almost too much to resist. Yet it would likely invite trouble between her and Stephen, and she couldn't afford to take that risk, not now. "Marcus, you know I would if I could, but . . . it isn't proper."

He relaxed his arm while the gleam in his eyes faded, along with his smile.

Clare's chest ached. "We must stop this . . . this playing with fire," she whispered, her eyes searching his beloved face. "You are to marry Natalya, and she's made it clear that our relationship cannot go beyond that of nurse and patient."

His throat worked as he nodded, sadness in his expression. "You're right, of course," he said, his voice rough. "I should have considered . . ."

He turned to walk back through the darkened hall toward the study. She nearly called out to him before she grasped at the daisy pendant at her throat. *"Needs must when the devil drives, lass."* Another of Mum's sayings when fate compelled one to do what one disliked most.

She held her breath, stifling a sob as she closed the hidden door on him. On their happiness. She must prepare herself now for marriage to a man she didn't love, but one who would safeguard her and Daisy and their being together always.

As Clare took her seat across from Stephen at the dinner table, she glanced first at her fiancé and then at her place setting. A smile touched her lips. Just one spoon—for the soup—lay beside the solitary fork, and on the other side of the decorative serviette were only two knives, one for meat and the other for butter. A small dessert spoon rested parallel above the linen serviette near her water glass.

She looked to Mrs. Weatherford, seated at the far end of the table, her honey-brown eyes gleaming warmly. Clare swiveled her attention to Fannie, who winked at her from her place between Stephen and Grace.

Her heart surged with affection for them both. Though their

gesture wasn't necessary, as she'd made a point to memorize the order of the tableware from her last formal meal with them, mother and daughter had clearly wanted to make her feel comfortable. Clare returned their smiles and then placed the napkin on her lap just as Hanson paused beside her with a tureen of fragrant savory soup.

Marcus sat beside her tonight, with Natalya on his other side—which suited Clare just fine. She didn't want to feel the ballerina's eyes on her in case she did make some unintentional blunder in etiquette.

As the soup course was served, Clare began tucking in along with the others. Every so often she looked across the table at Stephen, who flashed her a knowing smile that set her nerves to jangling. Would he make the announcement tonight? She hadn't yet spoken with him about it, but she hoped they would at least discuss it first.

Once Mrs. Weatherford had welcomed their new guests, she announced the entrée for the evening—baked rainbow trout, a rare treat this late in Hampshire's summer, courtesy of an enterprising angler from the local village of Mattingley.

As Teddy began clearing the empty bowls, Clare hesitated, eyeing the platter of trout and creamed leeks with boiled potatoes that Hanson was offering her. She triumphed in that as well, however, landing the fish and vegetables onto her plate without making a mess.

Marcus glanced at her and winked as he showed her the clean serviette on his lap. Clare couldn't help but grin, though as she locked eyes with Stephen, she caught the concern in his expression and quickly smiled, hoping to reassure him. She must stop this nonsense with Marcus!

Sir Geoffrey and Dr. Strom had begun discussing the latest prosthetics, with Dr. Strom offering a few amusing anecdotes that drew chuckles from around the table. Clare only half listened, doubts having crowded her mind.

Was Stephen going to make the announcement tonight? What

would everyone think? She'd shared the news with Grace alone, who had likely told Jack.

Her thoughts turned to Marcus. She should have told him when she had the chance, but oh what a painful conversation that would have been!

Finally, the last of the plates were being removed, while Hanson supplied the dessert—blackberry trifle.

Clare couldn't resist. "Is it your birthday?" she teased in a whisper to Marcus.

He grinned. "I think Mrs. Connelly is happy to have me home—"

The clinking of crystal sounded from across the table, and Clare's humor fled as Stephen rose from his seat, tapping the dessert spoon against his wine goblet. "May I have your attention, everyone? I'd like to make a toast if I may."

Clare's mouth parched as she met Stephen's determined smile. He cast a brief glance at Natalya before turning to Mrs. Weatherford. "Madam, if your man would refill our glasses?"

"Of course. Yates, if you will, please."

Clare watched as everyone's glasses were refilled, including her own. All held their wineglasses aloft, waiting with anticipation for what Stephen would say.

"Today I have good reason for being the happiest of men," he began. As he spoke, he slowly scanned the family and guests around the table. When his gaze finally came to rest on Clare, love shone in his eyes as he raised his glass. "The woman I love has agreed today to be my wife and my future viscountess."

He hadn't even finished the toast when Marcus—and it seemed everyone else except Grace—turned to stare at Fannie, who seemed clearly shocked as she fell back against her seat.

Clare downed her glass of white wine.

"I give you all my beautiful bride-to-be, Mrs. Clare Danner."

Again the multiple pairs of eyes shifted, this time in her direction.

Marcus stared at her, wide-eyed.

Natalya quietly excused herself and left the table.

KATE BRESLIN

Jack—who apparently hadn't been told—merely gaped at her in astonishment. Mrs. Weatherford looked equally shocked, and Fannie's face now burned a bright red.

Grace offered her a weak smile of encouragement.

Sir Geoffrey scowled.

Pasting on a smile, Clare battled the overpowering urge to follow Natalya's cue and flee the dining room. But then she looked to Stephen, his striking features radiating joy, and she thought of her baby girl sleeping peacefully upstairs.

The vicar's words at the church services this morning suddenly rose in her mind; he'd spoken of making sacrifices for the Lord, the way the Lord had sacrificed for His people.

Her mum's words also came back to her, about doing what was necessary even if it wasn't what she wanted. Clare forced herself to remain seated, not moving so much as a big toe in her shoe. Committing herself to this arrangement. *As a mother, you will do whatever you must . . .* She'd said those words to Grace, and she believed them to the core of her being.

"Congratulations to you both." Mrs. Weatherford broke the silence, having recovered from her surprise. She eyed Clare. "When will this . . . happy event take place?"

"We've agreed to be married this month," Stephen answered for her. "Once the wedding banns are read."

"Oh my! That is quite soon, indeed." Mrs. Weatherford's gaze narrowed. "I trust this plan also meets with your approval, Mrs. Danner?"

"Yes." Clare's voice trembled. "Stephen's uncle wishes for us to marry as soon as possible."

"I see." She pursed her lips, and humiliation burned in Clare. No doubt Fannie's mother thought her in need of a hasty marriage, much as Clare had been years ago after Elliot Lange tossed her away.

She stared hard at her abandoned dessert. *You can do this, Clare. Christ suffered mockery when on the cross. This is nothing in comparison to that.* She raised her chin, smiling at Stephen. "We plan to marry here in Hampshire," she said, then turned to the others at the table. "I hope you will all wish us well."

"Of course. Lady Walenford and I offer you both our happiest felicitations," Jack said, glancing at Stephen and then at Clare, his smile fixed while his eyes hardened on her. "I trust you can remain in your capacity as nurse until the wedding, Mrs. Danner?"

"Yes." She held her shoulders back. "I haven't forgotten the importance of helping my patient complete his healing process."

"I hardly need a nurse anymore," Marcus growled. "I'm doing much better with each day that passes."

"Shall we discuss this later, old boy?" Jack's razor-sharp gaze slid to his friend. He then smiled at Stephen. "This is a joyful occasion for the couple, and we should celebrate."

Sir Geoffrey's frown waned, though sadness filled his amber eyes. Clare recalled the man's jovial laughter the other day at the picnic, and regret pierced her now that somehow her news had caused him pain.

After she and Stephen had been toasted, everyone tucked into their desserts, except for Marcus, who simply stared at his trifle.

Food no longer interested Clare either, yet she forced herself to finish the parfait and was grateful when Mrs. Weatherford rose and suggested the ladies go through.

Once more, Clare considered making her escape, but Grace anticipated her and moved swiftly around the table to hook an arm through hers as she led her toward the Magnolia room. "You're doing admirably," she whispered. "Try to be patient. Let them get accustomed to the idea. They will come around, I promise you."

Knees wobbling, Clare offered a wan smile. If only Grace were right. "Mrs. Weatherford thinks I have to get married," she whispered back.

Grace looked at her, surprised, before a pink hue dusted her cheeks. "Oh, I hadn't thought of that. I could make certain Mrs. Weatherford knows the truth if you'll allow me to share your circumstances with her?" Then abruptly she frowned. "Of course, that would mean telling her the truth about your past with Randleton, and she might still pass judgment."

"I'll speak with Stephen," Clare said. "Once he realizes the implications, he can offer them all a reasonable excuse. It would be true enough to say that it's a condition of his uncle's if he is to be Randleton's heir."

"Brilliant!" Grace brightened. "All will be well, then."

As they reached the Magnolia room, Clare took up her place in the rose-colored Queen Anne chair while Grace occupied the settee.

"Dear me, what has happened to Natalya?" Mrs. Weatherford seemed to have finally noticed the ballerina missing.

"Perhaps she had a headache, Mother," Fannie offered.

"Oh, that is too bad. I hope she starts to feel better."

As Marcus's mother proceeded to take up a conversation with Grace, Fannie leaned close to Clare. "Would you be able to speak with me tomorrow morning in the conservatory?"

Clare looked at her. "Is something wrong?"

Fannie averted her eyes and shrugged. "Not necessarily. I would just like your opinion on a particular romantic matter."

She wanted more advice about Peter? Clare nodded. "I'll meet you there after breakfast."

Fannie's expression seemed strained as she nodded back.

Grace was appeasing Mrs. Weatherford's curiosity about her cousin Dr. Strom when the men finally came through. Yates had already provided chairs for the guests, so while Jack sat beside his wife on the settee, Sir Geoffrey and Dr. Strom each took a chair, leaving Stephen to sit on the sofa next to Mrs. Weatherford.

"Mrs. Danner, please come and sit with your fiancé." Mrs. Weatherford patted the empty cushion between herself and Stephen. "There is plenty of room."

Clare glanced toward the drawing room door. Marcus had not yet entered.

"I'm afraid we are one couple short this evening," Jack said, his eyes darting to her. "Apparently Natalya and Marcus are both calling it an early night."

His words weighed heavily on Clare as she moved to sit beside Stephen. She should have told Marcus earlier about her engagement, having suspected Stephen would make the announcement at tonight's dinner. *In Marcus's mind, you've betrayed his heart as much as he betrayed yours with Natalya weeks ago.*

Yates began serving drinks, offering a sherry to Grace. Jack quickly intervened. "I believe Lady Walenford would much prefer tea, wouldn't you, darling?"

Grace flushed pink. "Yes, of course." Seeing the curious looks, Grace was quick to make the announcement of their coming child.

"Congratulations!" erupted around the room, and Sir Geoffrey called for champagne.

As Clare received her glass, Mrs. Weatherford eyed her sharply. "Are you certain that is wise, Mrs. Danner?" she said in a low voice.

"I assure you, Mrs. Weatherford, there is no cause for alarm, nor for the haste you might imagine."

The woman's stately features colored slightly. "I'm relieved to hear it."

Clare leaned closer. "I'd very much appreciate your help, though," she said on impulse. "This is all very new to me, and once my friend returns home, I must continue to learn how to prepare to be a future viscountess."

Mrs. Weatherford's brows rose. "And you wish my aid in this?"

Clare offered a tremulous smile. "You've been more than kind to me, Mrs. Weatherford, especially in hosting our picnic the other night. And such a refined lady as yourself could surely teach me what I need to know so I don't make a fool of myself."

Mrs. Weatherford held her glass of champagne in one hand and placed her other hand on Clare's shoulder. "It would be my pleasure, Mrs. Danner."

Hope flared. "Thank you, and please call me Clare."

"Very well, Clare. I shall for now." She tipped her head, eyes gleaming. "But at some point in the future, I shall refer to you as either Lady Lange or Viscountess Randleton."

Lady Lange, Viscountess Randleton. Clare shivered. How she despised the very name! Yet once she married Stephen, she must claim it. How would she ever become accustomed to that title or such a life?

"Now, since my grandson has retired early, I'd like to hear what Dr. Strom has to say about Marcus's condition."

All eyes turned to Sir Geoffrey and then to Dr. Strom.

"Certainly, I can offer my opinion." Dr. Strom set down his glass of whiskey. "I would like to say first that Mrs. Danner has done an excellent job tending Sir Marcus's head wounds. And from what Lord Walenford has shared with me, she has also made some progress with the patient with regard to his memory."

Clare found herself the center of attention once again. Stephen gently grasped her hand. "I am proud of you," he said.

She smiled and looked away, feeling guilty that she'd just been thinking about Marcus. "Thank you," she whispered back.

"Yes, we are most grateful to Mrs. Danner for the work she's done," Sir Geoffrey said gruffly, and Clare looked up to see his sour expression had faded, and she nodded her thanks.

Dr. Strom sat forward in his seat. "That said, you must all understand his type of amnesia and the gap of memory he is trying to recover."

Mrs. Weatherford's face paled, and Clare reached for her hand to give it a squeeze. She smiled in response, though her expression held anguish.

"I think his current course is best," Dr. Strom added. "Sir Marcus seems to be thriving here at home, and his daily visits to the hospital in the other wing have been restorative. I understand he's playing chess with a couple of the patients?"

Clare nodded. Corporal Johnson and Sergeant Roberts. Natalya might have commandeered her job of taking Marcus for his daily visits to the hospital, but it was good to know he'd found enjoyment in the company of the two soldiers.

"I would caution all of you that while conversation is fine, you should not push him too hard with questions about the time he can't remember. We don't want him unduly upset, as it could affect the outcome of his complete recovery."

"As Mrs. Danner has told us, we are to be ourselves around him and encourage him if he does recall some particular memory," Fannie said.

"Just so," Dr. Strom agreed.

"I did tell him, quite inadvertently, that he was a captain in the Admiralty," Clare confessed. "Natalya pointed out that I must clear through her whatever Marcus is to know regarding his job."

"That would be best," Jack said. "Too much now, especially with the war on, could pose a security risk." He looked to Dr. Strom. "We will also proceed carefully."

"Have you any idea when Marcus will recover?" Fannie asked the question they all wanted to know.

Dr. Strom rubbed the back of his neck. "It's difficult to say. The mind is still a mystery to science. He could wake up tomorrow and have his full memory back, or it could take months or even years." He eyed Fannie gravely. "Or possibly never."

"Then we must pray that Marcus wakes up tomorrow and returns to his old self."

Jack made the comment, and they all looked at one another somberly. Like Clare, each of them had no doubt been praying, but it seemed God chose to leave Marcus in the dark for now.

She turned to Stephen, his expression sympathetic. "A rotten business," he said.

It was a rotten business, all of it. She could take a leap of faith, trusting that God would heal Marcus in two days' time and free her from this obligation. But if that miracle didn't happen, she must plan her future with Daisy by marrying Stephen . . . like it or not.

33

MONTEFALCO ESTATE, HAMPSHIRE
MONDAY, SEPTEMBER 2, 1918—NEXT DAY

What is this romantic matter you'd like to discuss with me?"
Clare had wandered into the conservatory shortly after
breakfast the following morning to find Fannie already
there in her dirty yellow apron and gloves, mixing a somewhat
smelly fertilizer into the soil around the trunk of the soaring Japanese maple.

Fannie whipped her head around, her usual brightness replaced
by a tense smile.

Clare had worn the same look at breakfast. Stephen, his mood
ebullient after she'd agreed to his proposal, had turned everyone's
mealtime into a discussion about their upcoming wedding while
she'd counted off the minutes until the food was consumed and
her fiancé was off on the early train back to London.

Natalya and Marcus were also conspicuously absent from the
breakfast table, and Clare still regretted having put that look of
hurt in his eyes. Regardless of her own heartache, Marcus's inability to recall the past surely made his wounds all the more painful
now.

"Come, let's sit." Hoisting herself onto her feet using the handle of her shovel, Fannie removed her gloves before leading Clare toward the same table where Stephen had proposed.

"I would like to know how you met your fiancé," she began as they both sat down. "He certainly seems eager to marry. Have you known Sir Stephen long?"

Fannie wanted to discuss her relationship with Stephen? Clare hesitated. "I met him when my mum went to work for Lord and Lady Randleton," she answered. "As a child, I was allowed to be tutored with Stephen and his cousin Elliot for a few years."

"So, you know him quite well?"

"Not exactly," Clare said. "That is, when he and Elliot went off to school, I rarely saw them except during summers. I went to work for the family as a maid, and when the two men attended Cambridge together, I occasionally saw them on the weekends they visited." She looked away. "I . . . left service almost three years ago, and I hadn't seen Stephen until recently in London. And then yesterday here when he arrived."

"He does seem to love you, as he proved last night with his engagement announcement." Fannie's look turned pensive. "And this morning's talk of nuptials at breakfast." She eyed Clare. "I hope you do not think my curiosity impertinent. I have only good intentions, I promise you."

"Not at all." Clare smiled. "I consider us good friends."

"Then would you please tell me how you feel about Sir Stephen?"

Clare startled at the question. "Why would you ask me that?"

"It all just seems rather sudden, this marriage and . . ." She leaned against the table. "Oh, Clare, I have seen how you look at my brother when you think no one is watching!" She inclined her head, gazing up at her. "I've also seen the way he acts when he is with you. Marcus is so . . . so alive!"

Clare's chest tightened. "Fannie, you mustn't say that—"

"But it's true!" Her delicate jaw hardened. "I love my brother, but I don't believe he has made a good choice in Natalya. Marcus becomes so quiet when he's with her, and I worry she is not the right person for him."

Clare gripped the edges of the chair, only half listening. She couldn't deny her love for Marcus or that he was more than just a little attracted to her. And it seemed his sister had noticed as well.

Still, none of it mattered; what she and Marcus had was only her wishful thinking. Because whether he regained his memory and reverted to the past, or he remained the way he was now, he and Natalya were bound together.

And right now she must rely on Stephen to keep her with her daughter.

Clare couldn't explain any of this to Fannie, despite their friendship. Jack and Grace had been right about the Weatherfords; they were good people and had shown her compassion and generosity. To suffer their shock and disappointment at the truth now didn't bear thinking about.

"I appreciate your concern, Fannie, but there's no need to worry about me." She relaxed her hands, though every muscle in her body remained taut. "Stephen is a kind man, and he's willing to provide for my daughter and me. As for your brother . . ." Pain lanced her heart, knowing she must finally give him up. "Only Marcus can decide if Natalya is right for him."

Leaning back, Fannie crossed her arms, her expression dubious. Obviously she wasn't convinced, but it was all Clare was willing to offer her.

Clare rose to her feet. "I should go. I must speak with Dr. Strom before he leaves on the noon train to London." Though anxious to evade Fannie's skepticism, she didn't want to damage their friendship. "You've been more than kind to me, especially that first day I arrived here at Montefalco." She smiled despite her uncertainty about the future. "I hope that . . . when I am married and return to London, we can continue to correspond with each other?"

"Of course." Fannie rose, her eyes misty. "And I didn't mean to probe. I just wanted to make certain that Sir Stephen was deserving of you."

Touched by her loyalty, Clare reached to brush Fannie's cheek, wiping at a streak of dirt she'd missed. The temptation to share her secret with her new friend made her pivot abruptly and head toward the door.

"I'll see you later," she managed to call out, blinking back tears. Maybe the sooner she wed Stephen and left this place, the sooner she and Marcus might both get on with their lives.

Hogwash. Fannie stood at the table, watching Clare retreat into the main house. She took a deep breath, her mood teetering between anger and sadness.

Clare hadn't trusted her with the truth—she honestly didn't love Stephen, though he was *"a kind man willing to provide for her and Daisy."*

Fannie knew Clare loved Marcus, but Natalya had claimed him first. She'd seen for herself last night at dinner how Clare changed. She was grinning with Marcus over some private joke one minute, and in the next she wore a stunned look as Sir Stephen made the announcement of their engagement. Clare had been more defensive than happy as everyone gazed at her.

And poor Marcus! Her brother looked like a walking thundercloud afterward, and he'd refused to come to the Magnolia room with the other guests.

Natalya's disappearance had been telling as well.

Fannie returned to her work, and once she'd donned her gloves, she lugged the pail of fertilizer to the dwarf palm. How would Clare react if she knew the conversation she and Peter had overheard yesterday?

Just to appease your own selfish motives, Fannie? She dipped her gloved hands into the bucket, only vaguely aware of the fertilizer's odor. In truth, she wanted Clare for her brother and possibly one day as her sister-in-law—not Natalya Bryce.

Not only had she been unfaithful to Marcus, but there was also an arrogance about Natalya, that "being full of herself" Peter had meant when they spoke of the gentry.

Unlike most in her position, Fannie had been something of an outcast growing up due to the effects of polio, yet she'd immediately bonded with Clare. Clare made her feel comfortable.

Even if that wasn't the case, Marcus loved Clare, and Clare loved Marcus, and Fannie didn't wish to burden either of them with the truth. It would only hurt them at this point.

"Hello? Fannie?"

Peter hobbled toward her on crutches, his handsome face red as he gasped for breath.

"You . . . walked all the way over here on your own?" She eyed him incredulously.

He glanced back toward the door and then shrugged. "I dinna see Deering trailing behind me anywhere."

His mouth split into a wide grin, and he looked pleased with himself. She removed her gloves and went to him, her spirits instantly lifted at seeing his wonderful progress.

"Are you steady on those?" she asked, reaching him.

"I am." Curiosity flared in his beautiful green eyes. "Why?"

She didn't answer; instead, she wrapped her arms around his waist and hugged him. "I'm so proud of you," she said softly. "I knew you could do it."

His lips touched her brow. "It was you, lass," he said in his soft Scots burr. "You've rekindled the flame in me and given me new purpose. I wanted to become better for you."

Her face warmed as she stepped back, her eyes searching his. "Why is that?"

"So I can keep up with you, for one." He grinned, then sobered again. "And then, lass, it's off to exploring the wilds that nature has to offer." This time he leaned to gently kiss her on the lips. "Together?"

She blinked up at him while her fingers touched her lips, feeling the warm imprint he'd left. Joy spread through her like fire. "I'm certain I should like that very much," she whispered.

Was this love? *"You've rekindled the flame and given me new purpose."* His words made her heart swell . . . and fueled Fannie with new determination.

Marcus needed Clare for the same reason, and Clare needed Fannie's brother.

"I'm meddling, Grandfather."

Sir Geoffrey glanced up from the worktable in his laboratory and gazed fondly at her. "Care to tell me exactly what you're meddling in, Granddaughter?"

Fannie pulled one of the wooden stools closer to the table, and after some maneuvering with her good leg, she hauled herself up onto the raised seat. "Love," she said. "Not mine, of course, but someone else's."

He lifted a white brow, the hint of a smile on his lips. "Why not yours? I hear we have a lieutenant visiting the conservatory quite often lately. Apparently, he's been helping you with your gardening?"

Heat ignited her face while he turned his attention back to the wooden leg he'd been working on. "You know as well as I do, Fannie girl, nothing gets past Yates."

Their butler had been with them for years, and he certainly did have a penchant for ferreting out any and all happenings in the house. Had he also overheard yesterday's exchange between Stephen and Natalya? If so, he'd likely tell only Grandfather. Yates was a bank vault when it came to gossip.

"Peter is very nice," she said, sitting up perfectly straight on the stool. "He's a botanist from Scotland, or he was a botanist until the war broke out."

"A man of letters, then?"

"Yes, he attended university just north of Edinburgh."

"He seems like a nice fellow."

Her eyes widened. "You . . . know him?"

He looked up and smiled. "Lieutenant Ainsley asked through the hospital about getting himself fitted for a leg."

Fannie's heart did a flip-flop. "Truly?"

Grandfather nodded. "I saw him just before lunch today. Took his measurements. I shall have a prosthetic leg ready for him in a few days."

"Oh, Grandfather, I'm so pleased!" Fannie clapped her hands. "I've been praying he would get used to the idea of using a prosthetic. When I first met Peter, he was angry and had lost all hope. He wouldn't even use crutches until I showed him my leg brace."

Grandfather eyed her sharply.

"I raised my skirt only a couple of inches," she said, "just enough to let him know that if I could do it, then so could he. Nothing is impossible for the Lord." She smiled. "And for a very special brother of mine."

"I see." His eyes held a twinkle. "But you like Peter?"

She gave him a shy look. "I do. We both love plants, and he knows so much about everything."

Grandfather grinned. "I can see that he's impressed you."

"Would we . . . be able to invite him to dinner one night?"

Grandfather wedged the wooden joint into his vise. "I don't see why not. Talk to your mother, but I have no qualms about it." He looked up. "So, whose love are you meddling in?"

In her excitement over Peter's new leg, she'd nearly forgotten her purpose. "Clare and Marcus."

At this, Grandfather set down his tools and crossed his arms, leaning back against the stool. "Go on."

"Clare loves Marcus, but she's going to marry Sir Stephen. And Marcus loves Clare, but he's going to marry Natalya. And I have good reason to believe Natalya doesn't love my brother."

"And what good reason is that?"

"Promise that you will not tell a soul?"

Grandfather nodded and crossed his heart.

She summarized for him what she and Peter had overheard between Natalya and Sir Stephen. "Sir Stephen seems to want to make a clean break with her, but Natalya doesn't want to let him go," Fannie finished. "And I don't know what to do." She wrung her hands. "I'm afraid to tell Marcus or Clare what we heard, because it could do my brother more harm than good and make Clare utterly miserable knowing her fiancé had been dallying with Natalya."

"Blasted war business," Grandfather grumbled. Then louder, he said, "Well, what do you propose to do about it?"

"I need your help, Grandfather." Fannie leaned forward. "You could talk to Natalya. Tell her the game is up. Then talk to Clare about all of this. She does seem a little nervous around you, but I think if you offer an olive branch, she'll listen to what you have to say." She shrugged. "After all, the rest of us do."

"You want me to tell her about Lange and Natalya?"

"Only if you have to. Otherwise tell her how much you loved Grandmother, and how much your son loved our mother. Tell her that true love is more important than money and title and lands and . . . physical appearances." She couldn't think of anything else to add.

Relaxing his arms, he leaned over the table and reached out to brush back a lock of her hair, his eyes full of love. "Fannie girl, you are a prize without price. I hope this Lieutenant Peter Ainsley appreciates what a treasure he's found."

She smiled her love back at him. "And the meddling?"

"I want you and Peter to stay out of it, do you understand?" The love lighting his expression moments ago had faded to form new creases in his face. "I'll deal with Natalya. And I'll talk with Clare." He sighed. "I think our conversation is long overdue."

34

MONTEFALCO ESTATE, HAMPSHIRE
TUESDAY, SEPTEMBER 3, 1918—NEXT DAY

W hat in blazes are you about, Natalya? I thought we had an understanding."

Jack confronted her the following morning as they stood along the banks of the small creek running parallel to the east side of the estate. It was early yet, an hour before breakfast, and his stomach rumbled as he again wondered what he could do to change Clare's mind about marrying Stephen Lange and to appease Sir Geoffrey, who had instructed Jack last night in private to handle Natalya and end her phony wedding plans with his grandson.

Natalya arched a brow. "I find it interesting, Jack, that with all your responsibilities, you still have time to worry about my personal life."

"I'll make the time because this involves my friend. You've carried this role of fiancée way too far, Natalya. First with those fake announcement letters to London last week, and then on Sunday telling Marcus, in the company of Strom, Mrs. Danner, and myself, that you were arranging his wedding costume and ordering invitations." He crossed his arms. "I thought it might be some petty vengeance for Mrs. Danner's benefit, but the servants' scuttlebutt is that you've also purchased a wedding gown? What happened to your cover for the assignment and the deal we made last week about easing off my friend and Mrs. Danner?"

Lifting a shoulder, she returned to watching the gurgling water flowing rapidly back toward the woods. "I made no deal with you, Jack. I told you that I would not pose a threat to Mrs. Danner's relationship with Marcus once he regained his memory. However, with her recent decision to marry Sir Stephen, I have decided . . . how do you say? All bets are off."

"And that means . . ."

She faced him then. "It means I have come to admire and hold a deep affection for your friend. In fact, just days ago I realized how much I have become attached to Marcus in the past several weeks, even before we left for Russia. And unlike Mrs. Danner, I am willing to wait until he regains his memory, unless he wants to move up our wedding. In that, too, I am agreeable."

"Unbelievable." Jack stared at her. "You'd marry a man who doesn't even remember you?"

"Arranged marriages start on much less, Jack," she reminded him. "And even if Marcus does remember the past, he would still love me as much, perhaps even more, than he does now. And Clare will be someone else's wife and a future viscountess." Her dark eyes searched his. "It may even be that my love will help him to overcome whatever feelings he might have had for her, but I doubt he is as enamored with her as you think. The Weatherfords obviously know nothing about Mrs. Danner and her relationship with him. Why do you suppose that is?"

Jack's mouth hardened. He wasn't about to relay to her his talk with Sir Geoffrey last night. He'd been right; the old man knew about Clare, and he understood Marcus's reasons for secrecy had been to protect her and Daisy, though Marcus insisted his grandfather keep silent.

Anyway, what good would it do to tell Clare the truth, other than make her more miserable? As of today, her fortnight with Randleton was up. Stephen Lange offered her what his friend could not—the ability to keep her daughter.

Nonetheless, he despised the idea that Natalya was taking advantage of his friend's vulnerability. But there, too, what could he do? Ask her to hold off on her affections for Marcus? Not only was that like trying to stop the tide, but his friend still didn't know his own past, and according to Grace, Clare was convinced that even if he did get his memory back, Marcus would remain with Natalya.

Of course, Jack had known otherwise before his friend's injury, but now he wasn't so sure. Marcus certainly wasn't putting up a fight. Had he fallen in love with her?

Jack had tried speaking with him yesterday, but Marcus remained most of the day in his room with a bad headache. Now he must leave with Grace for London. The newspapers announced last night that Lenin was shot on Friday and presumed dead. Immediately he received a telephone call wherein he was summoned back to the War Office.

At least he could try to borrow some time for his friend. "Three weeks remain until the wedding," he told Natalya. "It is possible Marcus will remember by then and he can tell us himself what his intentions are."

"And if he doesn't remember by that time?"

Jack grimaced. Clare would go through with her unhappy marriage to Lange, while Marcus might wed himself to Natalya Bryce.

He prayed that his friend would never have to awaken one morning to discover he'd lost everything. "Then I suppose you're right, Natalya. All bets would be off."

Papa had taught her to keep her options open.

Natalya sipped on her lemonade later that morning while Marcus played chess at one of the patients' tables. Having taken her seat near the hospital's entryway, she inhaled the fragrance of roses trellising the outer wall.

She had done as Papa instructed—like the wedding gown. Admittedly, the purchase was impulsive, a client having canceled the order with her London dressmaker. Yet as Natalya was being fitted for the costume and gazed into the mirror, she had envisioned another way out even then.

It was true what she had told Jack, that her affection for Marcus had deepened, and now with Lenin hovering near death, the Cheka's bloody retribution, and the Red Terror spreading through her beloved Russia, the decision had been made. Her mission was over. She had failed.

Natalya gripped the glass in her hand, and for the umpteenth time since the news of the shooting, her memories rose to haunt her. Eavesdropping on the steps below the church belfry in Archangel, the voices of the two men. Reilly's words to Marcus about Lenin and the discovery of other disturbing news—before the blasted bells rang painfully in her ears. She must have cried out because she was forced to flee to avoid detection.

If only she had stayed.

Reilly had known what was to come, and he had surely told Marcus. Leaving Natalya's only chance to find out to end in the woods near Vologda, when Marcus took a bullet for her and lay unconscious and bleeding on the forest floor. She had been in such a rage . . .

Her attention now turned to him, and she was filled with new hope. She could still salvage this, make herself a valuable asset once more and at the same time secure her future.

She sighed. Why did Jack insist that she wait? Could he not realize that Marcus and Mrs. Danner no longer had a relationship?

The nurse was smarter than either of them had given her credit for.

Natalya smirked. Mrs. Danner must have thought the sky rained diamonds when Stephen proposed and gave her a way to solve her dilemma with the child. Though what an absurdity on his part, wanting to take such an uncultured woman as his bride and make her into a future viscountess!

The only bright spot was that it had cleared the way for Natalya with Marcus.

Mrs. *Weatherford*. She eased back in her seat. Like she had with her dear Walter, she would support her new husband and embrace his elite and powerful circle of friends. Perhaps they were also card players? Walter had fondly called her his "queen of spades," such a clever and thoughtful wife, he'd said, allowing her to become involved in his important work at the Moscow Consul.

With Marcus, too, she could become the asset she had been before. Make amends to those she now owed . . .

Even if he failed to remember and never returned to Whitehall, she could still cut her losses and enjoy this comfortable haven in Hampshire. Thanks to C, she was already in place. And with a handsome husband doting on her, and his family appreciating her more sophisticated tastes, Natalya would no longer need to degrade herself in clandestine trysts with Stephen Lange.

Still, Papa had taught her well, and she would not close that door on Stephen just yet. If within Jack's requested three weeks, Marcus was to awaken to the past and Natalya had miscalculated his relationship with the nurse, then Stephen Lange would still have his uses.

And future viscount or not, she was not against employing whatever means were necessary to persuade him—including black-mail.

"My dear, you seem to have taught yourself about most of the silverware," Mrs. Weatherford said, "except perhaps for those we haven't had occasion to use, like the oyster fork"—she held up the miniature three-tined utensil—"and the lobster pick."

Clare eyed the odd-looking swizzle style utensil alongside the salad fork before raising a smile of gratitude to her instructor. Mrs.

Weatherford's guidance had worked to ease her lonely heart after saying good-bye to Grace and Jack an hour ago, and it also kept her mind occupied, lessening some of her anxiety about the future.

"Now we shall learn proper tea etiquette, as you will be hostess at many such events, and knowing how to serve and drink a proper cup of tea is critical to your social standing." Mrs. Weatherford turned to the stoic butler, standing attentively in the dining room. "Yates, would you please serve the tea fifteen minutes early in the Magnolia room? I wish to help my friend here before Sir Geoffrey and the others join us for elevenses."

"Very good, madam."

After his swift departure, Clare followed her kind instructor into the drawing room.

"Please, take a seat on the settee so you can watch me by example." Mrs. Weatherford smiled. "While we wait, is there anything you need for the wedding? Lady Walenford is to provide your wedding gown, yes?"

Clare nodded. "Her ladyship will hand-deliver the gown the week before the wedding. And Stephen is making church arrangements with the vicar here in Mattingley." She twisted her fingers in her lap, again jarred by the enormity of her decision.

Mrs. Weatherford noticed and smiled warmly. "You know, Clare, a viscountess must always appear calm, collected, and far above the menial troubles the world presents, even if her knees wobble beneath her skirts."

Clare grinned, forcing her muscles to relax.

The tea service soon arrived, and Mrs. Weatherford reached for the small strainer. "Each cup of tea is poured individually and served before pouring the next," she began, then continued to explain holding the pot with two hands when pouring and the proper way to stir and drink the hot brew—no clanging of the spoon against the cup. "Finally, one leans in to drink their tea, never downing it as one might a pint of beer in a pub. And a raised pinkie finger while drinking, or slurping your tea, is absolutely forbidden."

Once Clare had successfully mimicked her teacher, Mrs. Weatherford beamed. "You are an intelligent woman, and I daresay I was skeptical at first. However, I believe with a bit more training, you shall pull this off."

"I pray that you're right, Mrs. Weatherford," Clare said. "I sincerely appreciate your time in giving me instruction."

"Just my small way to thank you for your wonderful care of my son." She paused. "In fact, he has responded to you like no other."

Did she detect sadness in his mother's gaze? Once more the reality of what she was about to embark upon—and what she was giving up—seized her. "It . . . has been my pleasure to take care of him," she managed softly. "He is like no other patient I have ever cared for."

Mrs. Weatherford reached for Clare's cup, now rattling in her trembling hands. "Continue to work on your comportment, but otherwise I think you've learned enough for one day. The others will join us for tea shortly, and you shall pour and serve."

"Me?" Clare blinked.

"Better to practice on those who hold affection for you rather than strangers in London," Mrs. Weatherford said pointedly.

Those who hold affection for you . . . A lump rose in Clare's throat. At last, when she was about to leave this family and the man she loved, she had found acceptance with them. *Oh, Lord, why this torment? Haven't I paid the price for my foolishness years ago? Why will you not hear me?*

She blinked back the dampness blurring her vision. "I shall not embarrass you."

"Never," Mrs. Weatherford said.

Clare wanted to believe her, that she and Sir Geoffrey would accept her even knowing the truth about her and Daisy and why she must marry Stephen.

Don't forget the real world, Clare. A place where dreams seldom came true.

35

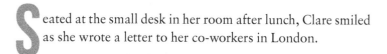

Seated at the small desk in her room after lunch, Clare smiled as she wrote a letter to her co-workers in London.

> *Dearest Beatrice and Sally,*
>   *You won't believe what I am about to tell you . . .*

She imagined Sally's delight in re-creating yet another romantic tale about Guinevere and Lancelot. Only this time it wouldn't be Marcus and Natalya in the park, but instead Clare and Stephen Lange in Hampshire.

She missed her two friends at the hospital and the other staff. Would Stephen allow her to continue her work? When Grace married Jack and took on the responsibilities of viscountess, she'd had to leave her post at Swan's.

Perhaps Clare's own days of independence were nearing an end, too.

Beatrice would want to know all the wedding details—flowers, the lace on her gown, and if she got along with Stephen's family. Clare's smile waned. The bitterest pill of this whole affair was having to suffer Randleton and his wife once she'd married their nephew. And then watch as they cooed and made a fuss over

Daisy, the child they'd dumped off at a workhouse orphanage two years ago. Or maybe they were simply interested in her child's inheritance.

Clare hoped for the latter, for then Randleton and his wife would leave her baby alone.

Though she'd tried, Clare continued to struggle with forgiveness, yet she had made her peace with Elliot. He'd been as young, foolish, and irresponsible as Clare years ago, and he did finally muster enough conscience to pay her way out of that slave house before going off to war. He'd also left a legacy to their daughter.

Clare paused in her writing. In truth, his death saddened her, in more ways than one. If he'd lived, she might not be in this terrible fix now.

Once she'd finished the letter, she sealed the envelope while listening for any sounds coming from the adjoining study. The silence told her Natalya had likely steered Marcus off to the west wing again. She rose and went to take her letter to Yates for the post.

The telephone rang as she placed her missive in the silver tray in the grand hall. As she turned toward the stairs, intending to search out her daughter and Ruthie, Yates appeared.

"The telephone, madam," he said. "Sir Stephen Lange. If you will follow me . . ."

He led her back along the hall to an alcove containing a small telephone desk with a tufted upholstered seat.

Did Stephen miss her already? He'd been rather reluctant to leave her yesterday, as if he thought she might change her mind. Clare had let him kiss her on the cheek again to reassure him, and he'd promised to return to Montefalco on the earliest train Saturday.

Taking up the pedestal telephone and receiver, she thanked Yates before he discreetly disappeared. "Hello, Stephen?"

"Clare! How are you, my darling?"

She stiffened at the endearment. "I'm . . . well enough. And you?"

"I am wishing it was already Saturday," he said, his tinny voice strained. "Though I have news. Are you sitting down?"

Her pulse sped as she took a seat on the padded chair. Had Randleton changed his mind about the marriage? "Tell me."

"Uncle Montague has refused my request of the banns," he said, anxiety in his voice. "I tried every argument with him, but he's impatient and insists our wedding take place as quickly as possible." A pause. "And he doesn't want it made public."

Hot and cold rushed through Clare. It shouldn't surprise her. "When?"

"He wants it done immediately, but I convinced him to allow us until Saturday." The seconds passed in silence before he said, "Clare? Will you please say something?"

Still dazed, she leaned back in the chair and stared unseeing at the doors of the conservatory. "I . . . I suppose then we have no choice," she said faintly.

"Oh, my darling!" Relief filled his voice. "I prayed you would understand, and I told you before we will have a lifetime to get to know and love each other. I shall make all the arrangements from here for a Saturday afternoon ceremony in Mattingley." He paused again. "Would you like me to explain the situation to Lord Walenford so he can release you from your nursing duties?"

"No." She gripped the telephone. "I will tell him myself."

"All right. Expect me early on Saturday. I'll drive out myself."

"Yes," she said, her own voice numb. "Good-bye."

Once she'd rung off, Clare walked toward the green sanctuary. She would tell Fannie first and then the rest of the family before she telephoned Jack and Grace. And Marcus . . .

She dreaded telling him most of all.

"Did you finish your letter, Clare?"

Fannie glanced up from sweeping dirt off the conservatory's path back into the garden when she spied her friend and smiled.

"I thought you did splendidly pouring the tea earlier. Just like a true viscountess . . ."

At Clare's wooden expression, she dropped the broom and rushed to her. "Oh, dear! Something's wrong, I can tell. Come, sit with me at the table." She led Clare to the small bistro table and chairs. "Now, what's happened?" Fannie asked as they both sat. She reached for her friend's damp palm. "Is it Daisy?"

Clare shook her head. "I'm getting married on Saturday," she whispered.

"What?" Fannie blinked. Had Grandfather not spoken to her yet? "I don't understand . . ."

"Stephen just telephoned. His uncle refused the banns." Misery tinged Clare's voice. "Viscount Randleton wants us to wed quickly and quietly, no doubt to minimize the scandal of his nephew's choice of bride."

"Oh, Clare!" Fannie's heart went out to her, and she leaned forward to embrace her. It was on the tip of her tongue to reveal what she and Peter had overheard between Natalya and Stephen the other day, but she held off. *I want you and Peter to stay out of it.*

Grandfather had insisted that he would take care of things. Still, she said, "Are you certain this is what you want, Clare? Married into a family who feels this way about you?"

She looked up. "I have no choice . . ."

Fannie eyed her sharply. "What do you mean, no choice?"

But Clare just stared at her for a long moment, the gray eyes dark with anguish.

"Tell me, Clare," she said softly. "You know you can trust me." *Oh, how I wish I knew why you were going through with this marriage!*

Clare wet her lips. "What I mean is, if I want to become Stephen's wife, then I must abide by Randleton's terms. Stephen must do the same." She averted her eyes. "His uncle holds the viscountcy over his head, and Stephen wants it just as badly as he wants our marriage."

Fannie still wasn't certain she believed Clare's explanation, but for now she must trust Grandfather to get to the bottom of it. "I honestly don't know why you're going through with this wedding, but I understand your being anxious at the sudden change in plans." Fannie rose, grinning. Her friend could do with some cheering up. "How about a little intrigue to take your mind off things?" she asked with a wink.

Clare smiled her relief. "I could use a good diversion right now."

"Good," said Fannie. "I think it's time I showed you the other secret passageway." She held out her hand. "Come with me."

Curiosity overshadowed Clare's anxiety as she let Fannie lead her back through the glass double doors toward the staircase leading up to the bedrooms. She'd hated having to tell her friend only a half-truth about why she and Stephen had to marry so quickly, but Clare had to protect Daisy at all costs.

On the wall beneath the stairs hung a small oak cabinet that housed a variety of glass and porcelain curios. Beside it stood one of the potted palms Clare recognized from the conservatory.

Expecting Fannie to open the cabinet, she was surprised when instead her friend slid the potted palm over three feet and pressed her hand against a corner of a framed, tiled wall mural behind it.

She must have released a latch, as the mural swung wide to reveal an entryway downstairs. "Shall we?"

"The other passageway." Clare now burned to know what lay beneath the house. Once they were inside, Fannie flipped a switch and a string of lamps illuminated the space. "This is the monks' old cellarium," she explained.

Clare peered into the cavernous room below. "Who else knows about this place?"

"Only Yates and Grandfather and probably Mother." Fannie closed the panel door behind them, latching it. "We shall leave by the same method."

Clare followed Fannie down the steps, the air cool against her skin. She could faintly make out a series of vaulted stone arches, and as they paused at the foot of the steps, Fannie flipped another switch, illuminating the farthest corners of the underground grotto.

"The cellarium extends to the west wing below the hospital," Fannie said. "Back on the other side of us are the kitchens, scullery, and laundry." She pointed to the wall near the stairs. The east wing had been closed off entirely from this side of the house. "Yates comes here to select the wines for dinner," she said as they walked through, and Clare marveled at the myriad wine racks filled with bottles, many needing a good dusting. "Back here are the cubbyholes where I hid my secret treasure box."

Clare spied the hive of uniform holes against the wall. A few held wooden kegs, while others lay empty, their interiors dark. They moved around a corner and found the same series of holes, though much smaller, perhaps sized for glass bottles.

Fannie silently numbered off with a finger each consecutive hole at the very top until she halted and began counting downward. Reaching into a cubbyhole to remove a small tin box, she brushed away the surface dust. "My secret treasures," she said and opened it for Clare.

On top lay a photograph of a strapping young man holding a little girl in his arms. Clare noted the metal braces on the child's legs. "You and Marcus?" she said, her voice echoing through the cavern.

"My fourth birthday," Fannie said, nodding. "Grandfather took us to the zoo in London and then to a carnival performing in the area. We stayed overnight with one of his friends—I don't remember where—and returned home the next day." She looked at Clare. "It was just a few months after Father died. I think Grandfather wanted to allow us time to enjoy a child's amusements, especially Marcus."

Clare studied the young man's sober expression and ached for the loss he must have experienced. *"Father never came back . . ."*

The words Marcus had spoken to her during their intimate dinner together suddenly took on new meaning. Had he also felt abandoned? Was it the reason he'd been so intent in his quest to find Daisy last year?

The box contained other trinkets: polished stones, likely from the creek outside, and dried flowers. "I see your love of blooms started early," Clare said.

"Not just any blooms." Fannie gave a wistful smile. "Another birthday, and I was older and attending boarding school, where life can be challenging when you're not . . . like everyone else. After a particularly beastly day and taking the train home for the weekend, I arrived to find my brother waiting with a bouquet of the most beautiful roses. It was—" she cleared her throat—"it was like he knew what had happened at school and he wanted to make me feel special. He even bought me a yo-yo toy and made me laugh as he reeled it in and out, each time pretending to drop it on the floor. I still have it."

She dug inside the box and produced the wooden toy. "I pressed and dried one of those roses, and I've kept it all this time."

Love, bittersweet, surged through Clare as she discovered a side of Marcus she hadn't really known. Though he'd always been wonderful when he spent time with her and Daisy, it was often during his somber moods or when his thoughts were a thousand miles away that he'd missed the signs of what she had needed from him.

"Would you like to see where the monks' honey mead was kept?" Fannie had returned the items to the box and was placing it back inside the cubbyhole.

"Any idea where your brother keeps his treasure box?" Clare asked.

"I haven't a clue now." Fannie stared up at the warren of holes. "My secret cubby is my birthday—September twelfth."

Clare retraced the number of holes Fannie had counted off. Nine across and twelve down. "Did you try Marcus's birthday?" She knew it was May 15, and a moment later looked toward the cubby where it could be.

336

"I certainly did and found it a few weeks ago, though he'd reversed the numbers." She sighed. "But I made the mistake of crowing to him about it when he was here last and so he hid it somewhere else."

"Any other ideas?" Clare's pulse increased. "It would be wonderful if we could find it again. Perhaps he'd remember some of the items in the box."

"Maybe Mother's or Grandfather's birthdays?" Fannie's excited voice echoed through the cellarium. "Perhaps even Father's birthday. We'll try them all."

Clare gathered new energy as they spent the next several minutes trying different combinations of the Weatherford birthdays, including Fannie's deceased grandmother, Charlotte. "Nothing," Fannie said at last. "I suppose we should head back . . ."

"I've an idea," Clare said. "Try going across fifteen spaces and down just one." Her own birthday but backward.

Fannie did as she asked and stood on tiptoes to reach inside the hole. Her face lit up. "Incredible! How did you know where to look?" She removed the tin box from its hiding place.

Clare merely smiled. "Open it."

Fannie did and withdrew a war medal, a pocketknife, a rock, and a photograph. "Marcus and our father, before I was born." She offered the picture to Clare, an image of a handsome dark-haired man and his young son.

"Oh, my goodness."

Clare looked up to see Fannie staring into the box.

"I'd never opened this before," she whispered.

"What is it?"

Tears welled in her friend's eyes as she wordlessly handed the box to Clare.

Beneath the boyhood trinkets was like a shrine, honoring someone Marcus had loved—no, adored and cherished.

Clare's eyes burned as she spied the lock of her own hair tied in a sapphire ribbon, and she recalled when he'd asked to have it before his work had taken him into Europe last winter. He wasn't certain he could return for Christmas and wanted a keepsake to remind him of home.

Beneath the lock of hair lay her missing pearl comb. Had he taken it while she was napping with Daisy on the sofa? Clare had realized it was missing shortly afterward.

There were more photographs—of her, working the hayfields in Kent, and another at the seashore in Margate when a photographer had taken their picture. Marcus's big strong arms holding her baby. The wind had been brisk, and it took her several minutes to pin her hair for the picture. Afterward he'd laughed and leaned with Daisy to pluck out all the pins again, letting her hair blow freely in the wind.

Another picture showed just the two of them in London, dressed in their heavy coats on her birthday in January. He'd taken her to the cinema that afternoon and then to dinner at a pub where they enjoyed a Burns Night supper. Later, he came back to the flat, where they had played chess well into the night while Ruthie put Daisy down for the evening.

The pictures continued: Clare working at the hospital or with Jack and Grace, images she'd given to Marcus when he'd been away for some time. There was also a dried stalk of what had been a flower, the daisy her little girl had picked for him when they strolled through St. James Park after his return in June.

More trinkets, and at the very bottom of the box she caught the glint of glass, and her breath caught as she removed a ring, the small garnet with two tiny yellow stones set in gold.

"Grandmother's ring," Fannie whispered, looking up at her. "And the photographs, the pearl comb, your hair . . ." Her brown eyes narrowed. "I think you've got a lot of explaining to do, Clare Danner."

36

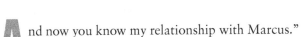

And now you know my relationship with Marcus."

Fannie had listened in shock to Clare's story as the two sat on the gold couch in her friend's room. Outside, the rain was streaking rivulets along the large windowpanes.

"So, you and my brother began courting a year ago." Why on earth had Marcus never brought Clare and her child to Montefalco or even mentioned them?

"He and I spent time together when I worked on the farms in Kent," Clare said. "Though after Daisy and I moved to London, your brother's work for the war kept him quite busy at the Admiralty, and often he was away traveling." She sighed as she reopened the tin box they'd brought upstairs from the cellarium. "The time we did spend together was wonderful, and he was so good with Daisy. Like a father to her."

Clare looked up, and Fannie ached at her sad expression. How could Marcus prefer Natalya over this loving, generous woman?

Disappointment mingled with her confusion at her brother's callous actions. He should have at least broken it off with Clare honorably instead of going behind her back. Fannie remembered the tender, caring older brother who once helped her to take her first steps after the polio, and who had given her so much through the years.

The change in him was almost unbelievable.

Clare reached inside the box and withdrew a chess piece. "We played often when he was in town, and I remember this." She held up a white king. "It was a rainy afternoon like today, and each of us had won a game. He then took the rubber match and kept my king as a trophy." She smiled. "He used to tease me about winning it back."

"It sounds as if you two were very happy together," Fannie whispered.

Clare's eyes shone bright with tears. "I thought so."

"And you came to Montefalco with my brother hoping to help him recover even when you knew of his feelings for Natalya?"

Clare seemed to hesitate, then nodded. "Lord Walenford said Britain needed me, as it was imperative Marcus get his memory back. And I wanted to make sure your brother received the proper care."

"That had to be a huge sacrifice for you."

"It wasn't easy, I'll admit." She returned the piece to the box. "Though I am glad I had the chance to meet you. I meant what I said—I hope we'll continue to correspond once I return to London."

Fannie smiled, only half listening while her thoughts raced. It was obvious Marcus still had feelings for Clare, and Clare for Marcus, even though the two seemed at cross-purposes. Surely they could reconcile with each other?

She pressed a hand against her stiff leather leg brace hidden beneath her skirts. After all, miracles *did* happen, and her own faith was strong. Fannie also knew she didn't want a deceitful, untrustworthy woman like Natalya as a sister-in-law.

Oh, Lord, please help my brother set things right with Clare!

"Ah, there you are, madam."

Yates had hailed her from several feet away, and Clare turned her face from the sun to look in his direction. She and Ruthie sat on the white bench in the garden that afternoon, having decided to get some fresh air once the clouds had departed, leaving the sky clear.

Daisy knelt beside the angel fountain's shallow pool, splashing with her fingers and talking two-year-old gibberish to the statues spouting water.

"I apologize for the intrusion, but Sir Geoffrey wishes to speak with you."

Clare shaded her eyes, gazing up at the stiff butler. Marcus's grandfather was the last person she wanted to face right now. The change in her wedding date, then discovering the mementos in Marcus's treasure box, and finally having to explain them to his sister still had her rattled. She'd hoped to relax out here and sort through her thoughts while spending time with her baby and Ruthie. "Does he want to see me now?"

"If it is convenient, madam."

"Keep an eye on her," she said to Ruthie. Clare darted a glance at her daughter. "Or the next thing you know, she'll be bathing with the angels."

"Don't I know it," Ruthie said, smiling. "I'll take good care of her."

Clare touched Ruthie's hand. She'd been blessed the day young Ruthie Simmons had agreed to live in and care for Daisy. "I shouldn't be long."

Marcus paused in his slow return to the east wing with Natalya, his pulse thumping rapidly at the sight of Clare. She sat beside Ruthie near the fountain, while Daisy crouched at the pool splashing water at the angels.

Tipping her face up toward the sun, she closed her eyes, and he was reminded of the day he'd knelt at the chaise and nearly kissed her.

He'd made his appearance at midmorning tea earlier, the first he'd seen of Clare since Saturday's dinner. Marcus had been avoiding her, taking his meals in his room or visiting the rehab hospital, even allowing Natalya to wrap him in her protective cloak while he licked his wounds and tried to forget.

But Clare's humor and the way she made him laugh, that expressive face revealing her moods, had branded him for life. And at night, he longed to be surrounded in honeysuckle perfume mingled with her soft, musky scent.

He had understood when Lange announced their engagement why she'd agreed to it. Clare was simply doing what was necessary to keep her daughter. Yet Marcus was angry—at her, for not telling him first, and at himself and his broken memory that refused to heal. How well did she know Lange? Did she even *want* to be his wife? *Did you give her a choice, man? You were supposed to get better, you could have saved her from this—*

"Myshka? Are you all right?"

Marcus turned to the woman he'd promised to marry, and a new heaviness settled in his chest. He didn't deserve Natalya, either. "It's the heat. I'll be fine," he said, offering words that he hoped would convince them both.

He turned again to find that Yates had come outside and was approaching Clare, and within moments she'd risen from the bench to follow his butler in their direction.

"Ah, we get to see the future Viscountess Randleton twice in one day," Natalya said as they closed the distance. Marcus ignored her, his heart racing as his desire to be nearer to Clare warred with his pain in knowing he could no longer tease her or touch her . . .

They were still several yards away when Yates opened a side door into the building. Clare stood a moment, looking at him, her eyes pleading, and new despair filled Marcus. If he could have worked harder in his efforts to heal, she wouldn't have to go through with this marriage.

Clare startled to see Marcus and Natalya walking toward them as Yates took her along the path around the conservatory toward the west wing.

Marcus had attended tea this morning, the first time she'd faced him since Saturday evening. Still wearing his thin gauze head bandage, he'd been quiet and tense, Natalya doting on him, and Clare ached, realizing that soon she'd never again be able to laugh with him or share his precious memories from the past. She knew he was angry with her for not confiding in him about her engagement to Stephen. Would he ever forgive her?

She paused as Yates stopped to open a heavy door to her left and indicated Clare should enter first. Yet she turned her eyes on Marcus, hoping he'd look at her and know how very sorry she was for having abandoned their plan, that for her child's sake she'd had no choice. She couldn't wait any longer for him.

His gaze finally found hers, yet as she glimpsed the torment in his golden-brown eyes, Clare wished she could take it all back, and that they would be the way they once were with each other. *Oh, Marcus, if only you had healed . . .*

"Madam?"

She glanced at Yates and nodded, then cast a last look at Marcus before stepping into the shadowy interior of the west wing.

Yates led her toward a flight of stairs, but rather than ascending, he knocked on a door beneath the steps, and Clare was reminded of her recent trip to the cellarium with Fannie.

"Good afternoon, Mrs. Danner. Thank you for joining me here."

Sir Geoffrey smiled as Yates ushered her inside before disappearing, and her eyes widened at the vast array of prosthetics that Marcus's grandfather kept stored on shelves and hanging from the walls.

He sat at a worktable cluttered with metal joints and rods and leather straps, and she recognized an artificial arm and the metal rods he was tightening for the elbow joint.

"Sir Geoffrey," she said, facing him. "You wished to see me?"

"Sit down, sit down." He waved her toward a stool on the other side of the table. "I take it you're familiar with these appendages I've been repairing?"

Clare nodded. "In my work, I see many patients fitted with prosthetics before they leave the hospital." She eyed him curiously. "Did Dr. Strom get to visit this place before he left?"

"Yes indeed, we continued our dinner discussion later that evening. He seems a very learned man."

"I agree. I was injured last year, and he did wonders to patch me up."

"At Margate, isn't that right?"

She startled and then sighed. "Of course, Dr. Strom told you."

"No, my dear, not the doctor." His amber eyes turned warm like brandy, and he set down his tools and reached out to her.

Too stunned to consider her actions, she gave him her hand.

"My grandson told me about you and Daisy," he said gently. "He spoke of you quite often."

Clare blinked. Had she heard him correctly? "Marcus . . . he told you about us?"

He nodded, and tears flooded her eyes. *Oh, Marcus, you were never ashamed.* Having glimpsed him only moments ago, her guilt returned, not only for going behind his back with the engagement to Stephen but also for believing the worst in his hiding her and Daisy from his family.

Sir Geoffrey squeezed her hand, his lined face full of compassion. "He showed me several photographs of you and Daisy, but you're much lovelier in real life."

"I . . . I didn't know." Her voice broke. "I thought he didn't want you to know."

"He was keen on keeping you safe, Clare." He grimaced. "I'm not privy to the details of my grandson's work for the Admiralty, but I do know it can be dangerous." Her head shot up, and he nodded. "As his nurse, you're aware of his most recent bullet wound?"

"Yes, Jack asked me to leave the bandage on after the stitches were out so we wouldn't upset Marcus."

Confusion lit Sir Geoffrey's eyes. "What wound are you referring to?"

"The wound on the side of his head." She narrowed her gaze. "What wound are you talking about?"

He uttered an oath, his features thunderous. "That boy will get himself killed." Then he said, "I was referring to the bullet wound in his thigh that he received in April."

In April? Marcus had been away two months then, and he'd missed Jack and Grace's May wedding. "Hanson has taken care of his . . ." She stopped and cleared her throat. "No, I haven't seen that particular wound."

"Yes, well, there are others as well." He shook his head. "Marcus has also received a few threats from his enemies over the years. He worried they might use you and Daisy as a weapon against him."

"So, he did act to protect us." Just as Jack had said. "Does your—?"

"Elaine and Fannie know nothing of this," he said quickly, reading her thoughts. "And Marcus only decided to confide in me in case something happened to him. He wanted to ensure you and Daisy would be taken care of."

"I don't understand." Her anguish and confusion returned. "He left me for Natalya, so why would he care what happens to us now?"

"Why indeed." Sir Geoffrey hesitated. "I think Marcus may be more enamored with Mrs. Bryce now than he was before the accident." He raised a gnarled hand when she opened her mouth to question him further. "I cannot tell you any more than that."

Clare huffed out a breath. "More secrets with Lord Walenford, no doubt."

"I was told you had spirit." His eyes twinkled. "And you handle yourself quite well with Mrs. Bryce."

"I'm not letting the likes of her trample me into the ground."
Clare inched up her chin. "I may not be elegant or worldly, but
I've come to believe I'm as good as anyone else."

"You are that and more, my dear," he said, then tipped his
head. "Which begs the question . . . why do you plan to marry
Stephen Lange?"

Clare stiffened. Had Marcus told him everything about her and
Daisy? "I've known Stephen for years. He's kind and he loves me
and will provide for me and my daughter once we're married,"
she said briskly.

"You would give up on my grandson without a fight?"

He was scowling again. Clare frowned back at him. How could
Sir Geoffrey possibly know her agony? "He didn't fight for *me*
when he had the chance," she bit out. "And while I may wish it
otherwise, I . . . I need Stephen." She crossed her arms. "And I
cannot tell *you* any more than that."

"Then I am sorry." He leaned back on the stool, sadness in
his eyes. "And I wish you and Lange both well in your upcoming
marriage."

What did Sir Geoffrey expect from her?

After she'd squeezed out her thanks to him, Clare stormed back
toward the fountain. Clearly, like Fannie, he'd been unhappy at
her decision to wed Stephen, and soon she must tell the others of
her new wedding date on Saturday.

Well, let the crumbs fall where they may, because unless something changed with Marcus and his memory, she had no other
choice.

Clare arrived to find the bench seat vacant and Ruthie and Daisy
nowhere in sight. Likely they'd returned to the nursery. She looked
around the garden, her nerves frayed, before deciding to head for
the sanctuary of her room.

Afternoon tea would be ready in three-quarters of an hour,

and Mrs. Weatherford would likely insist she serve everyone once more. Clare loathed having to memorize all the dos and don'ts of polite society, yet she was thankful to Fannie's mother for her help.

Clare ran upstairs first to check on her daughter and Ruthie, and finding both of them napping, she made her way back down the steps, crossing paths with Natalya.

"Mrs. Danner, I hope you enjoyed your little tour with the butler?"

"Yes, it was . . . interesting" was all Clare said.

Natalya smiled. "And shall you be our hostess again at afternoon tea?"

Because Natalya was being amiable, Clare made the effort as well. "I will if Mrs. Weatherford wishes it. Are you going up now to get ready?"

"Yes, and I do weary of changing clothes so many times in one day." She sighed. "I should much prefer to be like you with only one costume to worry about."

Clare bristled at the remark, then pasted on her best smile. "I can imagine how tiring it must be dragging all those steamer trunks everywhere. Thankfully, I need very little to look my best." She dipped her head. "Now, if you'll excuse me."

She continued down the stairs, still fuming over the ballerina's snide remark. She might not have a different costume for every hour of the day like Natalya, but what she did have was clean and presentable. And who needed to look like the Queen of England anyway?

Entering her room, Clare glanced at the bookcase, behind which was the hidden portal. The copy of *Jane Eyre* was missing again. Had Fannie taken it?

She glimpsed the secret lever in the empty space, and the temptation to seek Marcus out again was irresistible. It was also the perfect time, as her highness was upstairs changing into what were likely her tiara and the fourth gown of the day.

Clare glanced at the treasure box, still sitting on the table beside the couch. *Perhaps he'll remember something.*

Impulsively she retrieved it and took it with her once she'd opened the hidden door. She knocked softly at the other end. "Marcus?"

Silence. Clare opened the door and entered. She was surprised to see the copy of *Jane Eyre* lying open on his bed.

She glanced toward the mantel, where he stood staring at his reflection.

The bandage was gone.

Her fingers gripped the box she held behind her back. "Are you all right?"

"Far from it." He glared at her through the mirror while he touched the wound. "Why didn't you tell me about this?"

Marcus had watched her enter his room, anger and misery belying his rapid pulse at seeing her once more. He drank in the sight of her, even now as she walked toward him, her full lips parted slightly, the dark eyes wide with concern.

"I thought Jack had told you," she said, drawing nearer to him.

He stared back at the groove of scarred flesh. Clearly not from a fall. His greatest rub was that she'd known and not told him. Like her engagement to Lange. It seemed Clare liked to keep secrets. "Who shot me?"

Her eyes were the color of smoke as she met his gaze in the mirror. "I was told thugs attacked you in Paris," she said at length. "You protected Natalya and got in the way of the bullet."

"Thugs?"

She nodded. "Your grandfather knows, but no one else except perhaps Natalya. They wanted to protect you from too much trauma—"

"I've had nothing but trauma," he growled as he turned to her, his need to hold her in his arms driving him almost mad. He resisted. "Why didn't you tell me you were going to marry Stephen Lange?"

348

"He'd only asked me just that afternoon before dinner. There wasn't time—"

"There *was* time." He gritted out the words as he leaned toward her, breathing in her scent. "When you told me we were playing with fire, remember?"

And we both still burn, Marcus. Pain seared through Clare as she stared into his eyes, brilliant with gold flecks. "You're right, I should have told you, I just didn't want to hurt you."

"Not telling me hurt even more."

She reached up her free hand and cupped the side of his face, now smooth to the touch. Was he shaving himself or had Natalya taken over that responsibility, too?

Clare swallowed the hurt. "I've brought you something. I hope it will help you to remember." She withdrew the tin box from behind her back.

"Where did you find this?" He took it from her and opened it, scanning the contents before he carried the box to the table. Clare joined him.

"Your sister took me into the cellarium earlier, and with some luck we found it."

Marcus removed some of his boyhood items first, including the photograph of his father. "I remember these," he said, pausing with the pocketknife and the medal in his hand.

Then he withdrew the blue ribbon holding a lock of her hair.

"More than friends, surely," he said and glanced at her, rubbing the black strands between his thumb and forefinger.

He set the keepsake aside and next withdrew the photographs. Clare waited, breathless, as he studied each image carefully, his throat working while emotions flitted across his face.

Would he be able to recollect when the photos were taken?

"We look happy," he said, though when he set the photographs aside, Clare's hopes flagged. He hadn't remembered.

He examined the chess piece next and then her missing comb, along with several other trinkets, and each time his expression was void of any recognition.

Tentacles of despair tightened around Clare, drawing her deeper into the abyss of her misery. Time was running out.

"I remember this." He'd fished the ring from the bottom of the box and eyed the stones from various angles before he looked at her.

Clare's pulse leapt. Did she detect a flicker of awareness in him? "What do you remember about the ring?"

"My grandmother's. And it . . . seems important," he said, his voice rough. "I don't know why, but I feel it is . . ."

"Yes?"

"Somehow connected to you." His golden eyes met hers. "I sense it, in here." He pressed a fist to his chest as he'd done days ago when she was with him. Marcus had been talking about *her* before, not Natalya.

Renewed longing threatened to consume her. "How I wish you could remember," she whispered, unaware of her own tears until he'd set down the ring and reached with both hands to wipe at the dampness along her cheeks.

"Tell me that you loved me once." His eyes searched hers. "Please, I need to know."

"I can't!" She pulled back from his touch. "I've already been forced to choose between you and my child. It would hurt me even more to have to say the words." She stood. "This was a mistake. I have to leave—"

"No, wait!" He rose swiftly from his seat and towered over her, his beloved expression half wild. "I need you to kiss me," he whispered. "Clare, you make me ache down to my soul, and I don't understand why."

Her tears continued as she pressed her hands lightly against his chest. Being with him was wrong, and kissing him would surely damage her even more than his actions had that day in the park.

Yet some great force compelled her, and powerless to resist, she slid her hands upward, his heat warming her palms, and suddenly he pulled her in and bent his head, crushing his mouth against hers.

She surrendered easily to him, her eyes drifting closed while she clasped her hands around his neck. He began stroking her back, gentling his mouth against hers, his lips warm and inviting, and oh so achingly familiar.

Clare imagined them as they once were, without past or future but only this moment. The way he'd always made her feel cherished and safe in his arms. She returned his passion with her own, fingers curling into the thick brown strands at his nape. A soft groan rose in his throat, bringing her pleasure, and he held her tighter as though never intending to let her go.

Yet all too soon their lips finally drew apart, each of them breathless. She laid her cheek against his chest, the racing of his heart echoing her own rushing pulse.

Reality returned as well, crashing into her consciousness. The pain and her sense of loss were excruciating. Never would they be together like this again.

She gazed up at him and saw the same answer written in his agonized look, the golden eyes dark with pain. He knew it, too.

"I . . . I must go. Get ready for tea," she whispered, then moved out of his embrace.

He cleared his throat. "Please make my excuses," he said, his voice thick. "I cannot . . ."

"Yes, all right."

She turned at the door to look at him once more before walking back through the secret hall. *A kiss to remember each other.*

But moments later in her room, as she brushed and repinned her hair at the mirror, Clare knew what she'd done was unfair to more than herself. Stephen had said he loved her, and he was counting on her to be worthy of that love.

Even if it meant she must break her own heart.

37

MONTEFALCO ESTATE, HAMPSHIRE
SATURDAY, SEPTEMBER 7, 1918—FOUR DAYS LATER

Hold still."

Clare eyed Grace and obediently stopped fidgeting as her friend, along with Ellen, slipped the shimmering fabric over her head. The gown was designed to lace down the back, and once Ellen adjusted the dress to fit at her waistline, they gathered the train as the three moved to stand in front of the mirror.

The reflection held Clare's dazed look as she surveyed the gauzy chiffon and ice-blue silk. Grace had outdone herself with such a beautiful wedding gown, and for a moment Clare imagined herself as the storybook Cinderella, a princess garbed in the magic of a fairy godmother.

If only she were truly going to marry her prince.

The past four days at Montefalco had been a flurry of activity after Clare's announcement of the new wedding day. Stephen arrived early this morning before breakfast, followed in a second car by his uncle, Viscount Randleton, and another finely dressed gentleman, Mr. King.

Once introductions were made announcing King as Randleton's

attorney, poor Stephen had turned as red as the roses he'd brought her for the ceremony.

Clare's misgivings over the coming event increased tenfold.

"You look stunning," Grace said, and Clare refocused her attention on her friend's approving smile in the mirror. "I see you also found your missing pearl comb. The pair certainly complements the gown's seed pearls."

Clare's throat bobbed in the mirror as she swallowed. Marcus had returned her comb, along with her photographs and other keepsakes from the tin box. A sign that he'd surrendered to her decision and the fact that whatever they'd had together was lost.

"I know you're nervous." Grace eyed her sympathetically. "I trust Mrs. Weatherford has been helpful this week in teaching you the finer points of what will soon become your duties as Lady Lange?"

"I think so. But a future viscountess? Not yet," Clare said. "Though she's been more than patient with me. And after her swift course in etiquette this past week, I think I can manage hosting a tea on my own and arrange the silverware if necessary. I've also practiced my 'comportment,' as she calls it."

"Ah, yes." Grace's eyes gleamed. "Head held straight, shoulders back, and 'we do not walk, we float.' Is that about right?"

Clare grinned despite her somber mood. "Lady Bassett's instruction?"

"Who else?" Grace turned to the young maid. "Ellen, would you please go to my room and get the veil lying on my bed?"

Once the girl had left, Grace turned to Clare in the mirror. "I do not like the looks of that Mr. King. Did Randleton make you sign anything?"

"No, thank goodness." Clare took deep breaths, trying to settle her nervous stomach after the recent lunch. "Stephen said the attorney is here simply to act as a witness to the marriage." She turned to Grace. "I'm thankful Randleton's wife didn't come with them. I couldn't go through with this if I had to see her again."

"It's not too late, you know." Her friend's eyes searched hers. "You can still refuse."

"Please, Grace. Don't torment me." Blinking back tears, Clare straightened her shoulders. "I've waited as long as I dare for Marcus to recover, and still he remembers nothing. My wedding to Stephen starts in two hours and I can't go back now." She looked to her friend in the glass. "Just stand by me, all right?"

"You know I will."

Clare gave her a tremulous smile. She needed every ounce of strength her friend could lend her for the coming ordeal.

It seemed her meddling had come to nothing.

Fannie knelt beside the low planter, working furiously with her spade to dig a rather large hole. Beside her, the *Ficus elastica* awaited its new home at the start of the path leading through the conservatory's greenery.

Grandfather had said his talk with Clare had come to naught. Her friend was still going through with her marriage to Stephen Lange.

Fannie still resented the arrival of Stephen's irritable uncle and the pompous attorney who had unexpectedly descended on the household early this morning, sending the maids scurrying to ready more rooms. The two men had joined her family at breakfast as well, looking sour, while Stephen bubbled over with the wedding arrangements, and Marcus was again noticeably absent from the table.

Natalya avoided coming to both breakfast and lunch as well. At least Fannie knew her reasons. The woman had no conscience when it came to deceiving Marcus, but she would hardly stand by and watch her former secret lover wooing Clare.

Seething anew, Fannie scooped out another spadeful of the dirt. She'd seen her brother earlier, walking with his cane toward the west wing hospital. Likely he planned to stay away until after the wedding and the newlywed couple's departure.

Fannie shared his view. While she adored Clare, her friend wasn't marrying for love, especially after confessing her past relationship with Marcus—and the evidence of photographs and keepsakes her brother had kept.

Proving to Fannie without a doubt that they still belonged together.

What had happened to Marcus to make him change his mind about Clare? She puzzled over finding their grandmother's ring hidden inside his secret treasure box. If he'd loved Natalya so much, why not give her that ring instead of the oversized diamond she flaunted? Was Grandmother's garnet not sufficient in size?

Fannie had approached her brother two days ago and asked him that very question. He couldn't answer her, but when she'd pressed him about his feelings for Clare, he told her to mind her own affairs. There were "circumstances" she wasn't aware of, and for Clare's sake, Fannie was to cease in her attempts at matchmaking. He'd even returned to her the copy of *Jane Eyre*, telling her brusquely that fiction rarely imitated life.

Undeterred, Fannie had gone to Grandfather next to ask about the ring. Scowling, he'd shaken his head, mumbled something about "war business," and told her to say nothing, reminding her that he would handle Natalya.

Should she ask Mother? Fannie pressed the outline of the ring in her apron pocket. Clare had handed the ring over to her when Marcus returned the keepsakes.

Her heart still ached at the anguish in her friend's eyes. Yet Clare refused to say any more about why she was marrying Stephen, so Fannie could do little except work out her own frustrations by getting her hands dirty.

She missed Peter! It was early yet and he wouldn't arrive until later after tea. By then Clare and Stephen would be man and wife and return to the house to collect Daisy and Ruthie for the trip back to London. Stephen's uncle and his henchman attorney would no doubt depart as well, and good riddance to the both of them!

Finally the hole she'd burrowed was large enough, and Fannie reached for the root ball and settled the glossy leafed rubber plant into its new abode beside the path. After spreading the dirt around it, she was about to reach for the watering can when she heard the sound of voices.

"This is the last time, Natalya," Stephen hissed. "My debt to you is paid. We are finished, do you understand?"

Fannie paused. Stephen and Natalya were back in the conservatory together?

"I suppose we are finished." The crackle of paper accompanied Natalya's agitated voice. "Very well. Go off and live a happy life. I plan to do the same here with Captain Weatherford. Which means our past assignations will remain in the past, da?"

"Yes, of course." Stephen's voice held relief. "That is what I want, too."

"Then we are agreed," Natalya said briskly. "Now, I suggest you go and get dressed for your wedding."

"Just so. Good-bye, Natalya."

Moments later, both had abandoned the conservatory and Fannie was once again faced with a difficult choice. Despite Grandfather's edict, she must tell her brother about Natalya's perfidy with Stephen to ensure Marcus never married the woman. Yet by doing so she'd also be ruining any chance Clare might have to be happy with Stephen. *"There are circumstances you aren't aware of, Fannie . . ."*

Would she be making matters worse than what they already were?

Still kneeling in the dirt, Fannie bent her head and clasped her gloved hands together as she prayed. *Oh, Lord, please give my brother and Clare a miracle!*

Lips dark as cherries smiled at him while he kissed the ebony lock of her hair and tied it with her blue ribbon . . . her laughter, gentle like rain, washing over him as her slender fingers grabbed up his black queen from the board . . . *the feel of her warm, soft curves molding to him like sunlight as they danced together on the beach, listening to the music of the sea . . .*

The sea. Still half asleep, Marcus turned onto his side. *Gazing out at the cold ocean, icy wind stinging his face . . . candlelight blazing around holy icons inside a church, bells all around him, whispered voices with numbers and letters . . . miles of passing forests and tundra. Men grabbing him . . . grabbing Natalya, her scream . . . Ivan!*

Marcus startled awake, sweat beading along his brow. He blinked against the bright noon sun as he tried to get his bearings.

The hospital rehabilitation center in the west wing.

He must have dozed off a couple of hours ago. The chaise was warm beneath him as he rolled onto his back. Lifting his gaze, he stared into the plane tree's leafy branches.

He'd skipped lunch to come here and get away from the bedlam of so many people in the house, including Stephen Lange and his uncle. Nor could Marcus bear to see Clare dressed as another man's bride.

New agony pierced him. He'd failed her.

A loud clatter of dishes interrupted his thoughts.

"Oh, my goodness!"

He rose on an elbow to peer across the patio. The young volunteer nurse had cried out, having dropped her tray of refreshments at someone's feet. She quickly crouched to clean up the broken shards, and Marcus glanced up to see that the victim was Natalya, who had obviously arrived while he slept.

She leapt from her chair, her expensive shoes covered in the sticky lemonade and tea cakes.

"Idiot! *Chto vy nadelali?*" she screeched at the girl.

Idiot! What have you done? Her words crashed over Marcus like a tidal wave, the sudden flood of memories knocking him back against the chaise.

That phrase—Natalya had screamed it that day in the forest after they were taken off the train, the gun pointed at his head . . .

He closed his eyes while more pieces of his dream returned: Archangel and his meeting with Reilly at Dormition Church. The tower bells clanging around them as he learned the location of the tsarina and her son and about the mole at Whitehall. He and Natalya had taken the train to Vologda the next day, their three escorts serving as guards. Traitors all . . .

He opened his eyes and tried to catch his breath, his pulse racing. He'd been shot trying to protect her. So why did she call the Bolshevik an idiot when her own life was in danger?

"Oh, Mrs. Bryce! You're bleeding!" The nurse rose to her feet. "Please, let me take you inside and I'll clean out the shards of glass and bandage you—"

"Do not touch me!"

Marcus saw the nurse reach for her while Natalya backed away toward the hospital door. "I will find someone more competent inside. You leave me alone!" Whirling, she stormed into the west wing where he heard her shriek for a doctor.

The weepy volunteer finished loading her tray and then eyed the table where Natalya had left her belongings. The other patio tables were taken, and there were two patients wheeling in her direction.

Sniffing back tears, she glanced in the direction Natalya had gone, then turned to look at him. "Captain, may I leave Mrs. Bryce's belongings with you?"

He nodded, and she brought him Natalya's purse and the magazine she'd been reading. "It was an accident," he said, trying to ease her misery.

"Thank you, Captain, but I always seem to get clumsy when I'm nervous."

Particularly around Natalya. He recalled the spilled biscuits from the other day as he watched her retrieve the tray of broken glass and hurry inside.

Natalya's sharp words to the Bolshevik continued circling his thoughts. Just before pulling the trigger, the leader in his heavy beard and felt cap had angled dark eyes at her and smiled. Though not in a threatening way . . .

Ivan. Hair rose along his nape. Natalya had called him Ivan, not idiot. She knew him. And her scream—the last sound Marcus heard—was filled with rage, not fear.

More memories rushed him: Russell Square in London . . . giving Natalya the diamond—*on loan*—to complete their ruse.

There had been no promise of marriage . . .

Clare! He sat fully upright, his heart thundering in his chest. Her image that day blazoned across his mind, her eyes filled with angry tears, her beautiful face marred in disbelief and despair . . .

He started to rise from the chaise when he spied the purse in his lap. His instincts were already warning him something about Natalya was off. How did she know the Bolshevik? And why continue this ruse of their engagement?

Keeping his eyes on the hospital door, Marcus opened the handbag and sifted through its meager contents: a powder compact, a lace handkerchief, a coin purse, and a pair of gloves. He opened the coin purse. Only a few folded banknotes, nothing more.

He stared at the powder compact. Lifting the cover, he struck gold when his eyes landed on the note jammed inside. Removing the paper, he unfolded it and scanned the brief message.

VIU shot 8.30. Critical. K wants compensation—T3

VIU. Marcus went still. *Vladimir Ilyich Ulyanov.* Lenin! Reilly had told him of the plot to assassinate the Bolshevik leader on August 30—last week.

Critical. Lenin's condition? Moscow would be on high alert with the Cheka police swarming the city.

K wants compensation. He narrowed his eyes. K . . .

Kaiser? His gaze darted toward the hospital door as he pocketed the note. The Huns would have wanted to know of the assassination plan and would be just as eager to prevent Lenin's demise as the Allies were to see it through. Germany didn't want Russia back in the war fighting against them. *"Ivan! Chto vy nadelali?"*

"Ivan, what have you done?" Marcus whispered, coldness sweeping over him. Natalya had wanted that information from him *before* Ivan shot him. She must have arranged the ambush!

He breathed an oath as he checked his watch—an hour before the wedding. He had to get there and stop Clare before it was too late.

"I need your help, men."

Marcus had entered the hospital after leaving the chaise in search of Johnson and Roberts. He had to stop Natalya first before he went anywhere.

The pair were playing chess in the library.

"Cor, that's some nasty scar ye got, Cap'n." Johnson glanced up first, staring at his bared head. "And it don't look to me like it's from a fall."

"You're right about that, Corporal." Taking a seat beside the two men, he glanced behind him at his father's old leather chair and recognized the russet-haired patient he'd seen outside in the wheelchair. A lieutenant by the look of his uniform, and he was reading one of Fannie's books on plant pharmacopoeia.

Marcus shifted his attention back to Johnson and Roberts. "This particular wound wasn't due to a fall," he said, touching his scalp. "But the one at the back of my head knocked a big gap in my memory"—he eyed them both—"though I'm relieved to say that now I have my faculties back in full."

Marcus had his memory back? Natalya stood poised outside the open library, her pulse thumping at her throat. Leaving the physician only moments ago, her ankle now bandaged, she'd planned to return outside when she heard his voice.

Anxiety mingled with her relief. Would he still wish to marry her?

Stephen and Mrs. Danner would be married within the hour . . .

"I need to find Mrs. Bryce. Have you seen her?"

Marcus. Her hope rekindled. He was looking for her.

She imagined a brief informal wedding, then moving back to London, where Marcus would immediately wish to return to Whitehall. Once he allowed her to help with his work, just as she'd done with Walter, Natalya would learn enough to pacify her German friend after failing to prevent Lenin's shooting last Friday.

She still prayed the people's hope for Russia would survive his injuries. No doubt the Cheka were still on a rampage, seeking out the guilty parties, but they would protect Tunney so he could remain her link to Moscow.

"I think I saw her here in the hospital, Cap'n," Roberts said. He glanced at the purse Marcus had brought in with him. "Ye lose her, sir?"

"In a manner of speaking. I need her located and detained as soon as possible." Marcus then gave them a vague sketch of his job with the Admiralty and his suspicions about Natalya.

Roberts whistled softly. "So ye think she's working with Fritzie?"

"I'm certain of it." Natalya's traitorous charade had nearly gone unchecked, and all the while made Clare's life a living hell. "My grandfather has a key to this library," he said. "Once we find her, you'll keep her locked up here until the authorities arrive."

Natalya froze. Marcus knew? But how did he find out?

The note!

Her gaze flew toward the patio area. Her purse! That clumsy oaf of a nurse had made her forget to take it from the table!

Panicked, she whirled to flee the hospital, her mind sifting through her options. She strode across the patio past the chaise Marcus had occupied and spied the ambulance parked near the admitting office. She needed transportation!

"We'll find her, Cap'n!"

As both soldiers rose from the table, Marcus did the same.

"Excuse me, Captain Weatherford. May I be of service?"

The lieutenant had left the leather chair to hobble over on his crutches. "I'm Peter Ainsley, sir. I know Fannie and I've met Sir Geoffrey as well."

"Yes, Lieutenant, my sister mentioned you." Marcus nodded. "You can find my grandfather and apprise him of the situation. Ask him for the key to this room and have him contact Scotland Yard. Tell him—" he paused, swallowing—"tell him that his grandson is back."

"Aye, sir!"

Natalya breezed past the ambulance and headed toward the garage, glimpsing the Rolls-Royce parked inside. Thankfully, Vickers was nowhere to be seen, and once she'd set the throttle and cranked over the engine, she slipped in behind the wheel.

Her pulse beat wildly as she tried to think. Where could she go that Marcus would not find her? She had no money—it was in her purse, which he had obviously taken. Her pistol though . . .

Natalya's pounding heart slowed as a smile stretched her lips. She needed leverage against Marcus to give her enough time to escape. Or perhaps barter with him for her safe passage back to Russia?

Fannie had finished scrubbing the dirt from her fingernails and rinsed her hands. Reaching for a towel, she continued battling her conscience over when to seek out her brother and tell him about Natalya's deceitful ways.

There was still time—an hour before Clare said her vows to Stephen. But if Fannie waited much longer, it would be too late for Clare and Marcus to be truly happy together—

"Frances, darling?"

Fannie whirled at the familiar voice. "Natalya . . ." Her eyes bulged as she stared at the pistol aimed at her. "What are you doing?" Fear followed on the heels of her shock. "You're p-pointing that weapon at me!"

"I am making certain your brother does exactly what I want." Natalya's smile soured. "Now, let us move outside."

Fannie felt the press of cold steel at her back as Natalya urged her through the outer door, where the Rolls was running. "Where are you taking me?"

"You'll find out soon enough. Get into the back seat."

Fannie opened the door and did as she asked, though when she tried scooting over, Natalya gripped her by the apron. "We did not bring rope." She made a tsking noise. "So you must close your eyes for me, darling."

"No!" *Oh, Lord, don't let me die . . .*

Natalya cocked the gun. "I said close your eyes!"

Swallowing her fear, Fannie obeyed. *Dear Lord, please let me go to heaven . . .*

In the next instant, she felt a sharp pain at the back of her head. And then nothing at all.

38

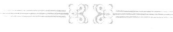

an I really go through with this?

Clare stood on the small dais in the bridal chamber at Mattingley's church while Grace and Ellen repeated their fitting of the gown she would wear down the aisle in an hour.

The vicar had yet to arrive, and at last glance only those who accompanied her to the church were in attendance. Viscount Randleton and Mr. King had taken seats on the groom's side of the church, and for the hundredth time, Clare wondered how often she must endure their company and share Daisy with them after what they did to her and her daughter.

"How are you holding up?" Grace's eyes searched her face as she adjusted the silk and pearl neckline near Clare's throat.

"As well as I can," Clare whispered hoarsely while Ellen fitted the elaborate tulle veil.

Grace removed her own strand of pearls and offered them to Clare. "Would you like to exchange these for the pendant? Pearls would be the perfect addition—"

"I'm wearing my daisy." Clare pushed her hand away. "In fact, I'll never take it off," she said. "A reminder that I am doing this for my baby girl and for no other reason." Tears blurred her eyes then, and she angrily blinked them away.

"I'm sorry, Clare," Grace whispered. "I wish I could change all of this for you."

"And I'm sorry I'm being so cross," Clare said. "Why don't you go and see if the vicar's arrived? I'm praying Randleton's wife doesn't decide to make a last-minute appearance, otherwise I may go off screaming into the night."

Graced chuckled, wiping at her eyes. "I shall investigate and return with my report."

Her friend departed as Ellen pinned the veil to her upswept hair. Would Marcus change his mind and come to the wedding?

Clare hoped not. She couldn't bear to see the pain in his eyes.

"Take a look in the mirror, Mrs. Danner."

Clare turned to see a reflection of that same pain as she gazed at herself, her beautiful gown and veil settled perfectly into place. She was dressed and ready to marry, at least on the outside. But what about her soul?

Dear God, is this to be my sacrifice? Please, Lord, hear me and show me your mercy!

Thirty minutes later, Natalya was nowhere to be found.

Gritting his teeth, Marcus returned to the library, again checking his watch. Half his time gone before the wedding started.

Johnson returned, his face grim. "No luck, sir."

Roberts entered right behind him. "Cap'n, one of the blokes outside told me he saw her a half hour ago headed to the car garage."

Marcus growled as he started to leave the library. "She took the Rolls," he called over his shoulder—and nearly ran into Lieutenant Ainsley blocking the door.

Ainsley's ruddy face was now pale, his breathing heavy. "Captain, I . . . got a telephone call at the admitting office." His lungs wheezed. "I tried running all the way to the conservatory on these blighted crutches to see if it wasna some prank."

365

"What prank?" Marcus's pulse sped. "What are you saying?"

"Mrs. Bryce," he gasped. "She's got Fannie!"

Strains of wedding music suddenly began to permeate the walls of the bridal chamber, and Clare turned to Grace in alarm. Now that the bride was dressed and ready, Ellen had departed, leaving the two of them alone.

"Relax, it's Bach," Grace said. "And you still have half an hour. The organist is merely warming up while the local villagers find their seats."

"So they like a good hanging, do they?" Clare spoke more sharply than she'd intended, twisting the bouquet of roses and baby's breath in her damp hands until a few pink petals drifted to the floor. "Is Jack ready? You know, I never thanked him for his offer to give me away."

Grace smiled. "My husband was honored by your request and he's standing ready outside the door." She touched Clare's shoulder. "Now, let's pray, dear friend," she said gently, "that sooner or later you will get your happy ending."

Clare bent her head, wanting nothing more than that.

"Natalya wants to meet me where?" Marcus asked tersely.

Lieutenant Ainsley shifted on his crutches. "The auld Basing House at three o'clock."

"Criminy, that's in Basingstoke! Fifteen minutes by car and I'm without transportation."

"The ambulance is parked outside," Ainsley said.

Marcus ground his teeth. Even if luck was with him he couldn't make it there and back and still have time to get to the church to stop the wedding. And if he went to the church first, he wouldn't make it to Basing House by 1500. And what would Natalya do to his sister?

"Blast it!" he roared, startling the three soldiers. That she-devil was making him choose! "I need a pistol."

"Your grandfather gave me these, Captain."

Ainsley withdrew a pair of Webley revolvers from inside his tunic.

Marcus took both guns and then turned to Roberts. "Call the church in Mattingley and tell them to stop the wedding. All will be explained shortly."

Roberts looked confused. "Sir?"

"Just do it!"

"Aye, sir!" Roberts took off at a run for the admitting office.

Marcus left his cane behind and started toward the door.

"I'm coming with you, Captain."

He turned to glare at Ainsley, hobbling up behind him. "If Natalya sees you, she'll take out her anger on Fannie."

"I'll hide in the back of the ambulance until you need me, sir. And I'm a good shot."

Marcus eyed him a moment before handing him back a revolver. The two men then headed toward the ambulance, and while Ainsley hoisted himself into the back, Marcus got the engine running.

"Stay alert, Lieutenant," he called back as he released the brake.

"Aye, Captain. I'll be watching you from here."

The fifteen-minute drive passed in tense silence. Had Natalya hurt his sister? She'd proven she was capable of treason, and she claimed to know how to use her pistol . . .

By the time he'd pulled the ambulance up beside the Rolls now parked in front of the dilapidated ruins of the old Basing House, his gut was tied in knots.

Natalya stood a few feet from the car, her pistol in hand. She smiled as he exited the ambulance. "I see that you are still very resourceful, Marcus. And right on time."

"Clare, are you going to be all right?"

Fifteen minutes had passed. She glanced at Jack as they stood together in the alcove at the rear of the church. The soft music still floated through the vaulted interior, but in moments the organist would play in earnest and her walk down the aisle would begin. "I'm fine." Her voice sounded hollow.

"I'm glad to hear it." His smile held sympathy. "Because I promise that I will not let you go."

She looked at her gloved hand tucked into his arm and realized she held his elbow in a stranglehold. "I'm sorry." She tried easing up on her grip, but Jack held her firmly.

"You know that Grace and I support you, whatever may come."

Clare offered a grateful smile, despite her jittery nerves and dampened palms inside the gloves. Her attention shifted to the clusters of people now seated in the church. Nearly all of them were strangers, and some—she eyed Randleton and his lawyer—she would much rather avoid altogether.

She was disheartened at Fannie's absence, even Sir Geoffrey's, though Clare understood his reason for refusing to attend. He'd wanted her to fight for Marcus, yet he didn't know the stakes and that she couldn't afford to wait.

Grace had returned to her place on the bride's side, seated beside Mrs. Weatherford. Clare was touched that the woman had come.

The loud, strident tones of the "Wedding March" began. Startled, Clare looked at Jack. "It's time," he said. "Are you sure this is what you want?"

Clare had to stop herself from shaking her head. "It's what I need to do, Jack."

And then she started to move alongside him, leaving the alcove to begin down the aisle. It wasn't until she spied Stephen at the altar, Mr. King acting as his best man, that she realized her life was truly about to change. An unknown future with a man she knew little about and a family who once nearly destroyed her and her baby.

She gripped Jack's arm, thinking she might faint.

"Where is Fannie?" Marcus demanded.

Leaning against the old estate's crumbling gatehouse wall, Natalya smiled. "Sleeping."

"What have you done with her!"

He'd already started toward her when she took aim with the pistol. "I'll take that weapon from your coat pocket first, Marcus."

He stood defiant, unmoving.

"Please," she asked sweetly, cocking the hammer back.

Snarling, he withdrew the gun and tossed it to the ground.

"Kick it this way."

He did as he was told. "I want to see my sister. If you've harmed her . . ."

"You think I killed her the way I did that stupid oaf who shot you?" She sighed. "The back seat." She waved the pistol toward the Rolls.

Marcus rushed over and jerked open the car door to look inside, his heart in his throat. Fannie lay eerily still, her eyes closed and half of her small body lying at an angle on the seat while her legs lay trapped against the floor. Fury rolled through him like thunder, and he fought for control as he leaned in to check her pulse.

Weak but steady. Relief overwhelmed him. His baby sister was alive.

As he reached in to lift her from the cramped floor, he noticed her leg with the brace had twisted. Still fighting his rage, he gently straightened the brace and settled her back onto the seat.

He turned on Natalya, baring his teeth. "What did you do to her?"

"Only a little tap with this." She showed him the butt of the pistol.

Marcus sucked in air. *Dear God, please don't let Fannie lose her memory.* "What do you want from me?" he gritted out.

"A trip across the Channel," she replied. "Southampton's coast is less than an hour's drive from here. We shall take the Rolls, and once we arrive, you will arrange passage for the three of us on a ship to France."

"And you think you can get away with this?"

"I do." Her eyes blazed like hot coals. "Once we dock, you and Frances can remain on board while I disappear."

"Where will you go? The authorities will find you easily enough in Paris." He tipped his head. "Spain maybe, or Portugal? You'll need to hide once the Allies and the kaiser are both after you."

"I would have succeeded if not for that imbecile, Ivan!" Her elegant features twisted into an ugly rage. "Bolshevism will save our Mother Russia, but those ignorant peasants need to be dealt with or they will ruin what we started."

"We?"

"Lenin," she said. "And my little agent in Moscow." Magically her anger turned into amusement. "There is also my correspondent at Whitehall." Her eyes gleamed malevolently.

The mole. "Who is it?" Marcus demanded.

"You shall find out soon enough." Then she raised her laughter to the gray skies. "Oh, Marcus, how I would love to see your face when you do. Such agony!"

"Witch!" he roared as he barreled toward her, not caring for his safety, the pistol firing off as he knocked her to the ground.

Pain seared him, but he ignored it. "Ainsley!"

The lieutenant soon appeared, hopping along on a single crutch while he aimed his pistol at Natalya.

Marcus tossed her weapon in his direction, along with the borrowed gun. He then freed his necktie and flipped her over, binding her hands while she began screaming at him, "You will not stop us! Russia will never again be controlled by the Imperialists!"

"You're mad," he said. Then to Ainsley, "See to my sister."

Marcus pulled Natalya up from the ground and dragged her toward the back of the ambulance.

"Marcus?"

He glanced back to see Fannie, Ainsley now standing protectively beside her as she leaned out from the Rolls.

His taut muscles eased. "Are you all right, sweetheart?"

She nodded and then winced, reaching for the back of her head. Her eyes widened. "Marcus, you're bleeding!"

He glanced at his arm. A red stain had seeped through his tan jacket below his shoulder. Likely just a flesh wound. "It's not serious."

As he settled his prisoner into the back of the ambulance, Fannie clambered into the front while Ainsley cranked over the engine.

"We'll send Vickers for the Rolls," Marcus called from the back. He checked his watch: 1515.

Already fifteen minutes into the wedding.

Had Roberts got through to the church? Marcus returned to the front of the ambulance, his chest aching as he slid in behind the wheel. He could only pray, because there was no way he would make it in time.

Dear God, please hear me . . .

39

D early beloved, we are gathered together here in the sight of God . . ."

Clare stood numbly beside Stephen as the vicar began intoning the words that would soon bind her to this man for life.

Jack had walked her up the aisle moments ago, and while everyone stood, Clare had anchored her frightened gaze on Grace, who offered an encouraging smile.

Mrs. Weatherford had nodded, compassion in her eyes.

Alone on the groom's side, Randleton had looked grim. Even now Clare's stomach clenched as she imagined him and his wife demanding to take her baby to their estate in the North. What if Clare was forbidden to join her daughter? Would Stephen defend her position?

Again she hoped they were only interested in the inheritance and not her daughter.

". . . which is an honorable estate, instituted of God in the time of man's innocency . . ."

Honorable? Clare tried to pay attention to the vicar's words. How honorable was it to marry a man she didn't love?

". . . and therefore is not by any to be enterprised, nor taken in hand unadvisedly, lightly, or wantonly . . ."

She looked away. Wasn't this *her* enterprise in being able keep her daughter?

". . . but reverently, discreetly, advisedly, soberly, and in the fear of God . . ."

Clare compressed her teeth. *Dear God, forgive me.*

"I now require and charge you both"—the vicar eyed them sharply—"as ye will answer at the dreadful day of judgment, when the secrets of all hearts shall be disclosed, that if either of you know any impediment why ye may not be lawfully joined together in matrimony, ye do now confess it."

Clare looked to Stephen, hoping against hope he would object. Yet his smile destroyed her expectations, his blue eyes warm as he searched her gaze. *Say something to him, Clare! Tell him that you love Marcus, that you cannot do this!*

Instead, she reached for the daisy pendant at her throat.

The vicar next looked to the congregation and made the same charge. Clare darted a gaze around the church at the sea of curious, unfamiliar faces, praying by some miracle one of them would choose to speak out.

Jack now sat beside Grace and cast Clare a worried look despite his weak smile, while Grace and Mrs. Weatherford dabbed their eyes with lace handkerchiefs.

Randleton and his attorney shifted impatiently in their seats.

"Very well." The vicar turned to Stephen. "Stephen Harold Lange, wilt thou have this woman to thy wedded wife, to live together after God's ordinance in the holy estate of Matrimony? Wilt thou love her, comfort her . . ."

When the vicar had finished the vows, Stephen looked at her. Again Clare prayed he would call it off and allow her to go free with her child. "I will," he said softly, beaming.

The room began to spin, and she grabbed for his sleeve to steady herself.

"Clare Irene Danner, wilt thou have this man to thy wedded husband . . ."

She faced the vicar as the words droned on, her dazed senses reeling.

"Well, child?"

She straightened, staring wide-eyed at him.

"Will you?" The vicar's graying brows slanted at her.

Good-bye, Marcus. Eyes welling with tears, Clare said the words that would forever seal her fate. "I will . . ."

Marcus arrived back at Montefalco to find two men in dark suits waiting on the portico steps beside his grandfather, along with a familiar stocky, middle-aged orderly he'd seen over at the hospital.

"Deering is here," Ainsley said.

Sergeant Roberts was there, too.

Marcus stared at the sergeant through the windscreen. Hoping, praying . . .

Roberts looked at him, his eyes sad as he shook his head.

Marcus gripped the wheel. He was too late . . .

He turned to Ainsley. "Tell the authorities what happened and keep Natalya at the house until Lord Walenford returns."

"Where are you going, Marcus?" Fannie said.

He didn't answer her, but instead exited the car and walked toward the back of the estate, past his Sherwood Forest where he'd played as a child, and climbed the small hill overlooking the chestnut grove.

Marcus stared beyond the trees in the direction of the church a few miles away. On this same spot he'd stood as a boy, holding the telegram that changed his life, raging over the broken promises given to him not only by his earthly father but also his Eternal One.

He dropped to his knees, tears tracking down his cheeks. "Lord, forgive me for my anger at you and Father," he whispered. "And forgive my cowardly lack of faith."

Always he'd used the war and the next assignment to avoid

what should have mattered most. "I had to protect them, men like Father fighting overseas, keep them from breaking promises to *their* sons and leaving their widows to grieve like Mother." He closed his eyes, his chest aching. "And in my fear of doing the same to Clare, I waited too long. And now I've lost her."

Lifting his head, he stared dully beyond the forest. His great cause for the war no longer mattered. Only the love he'd let go.

"Marcus!"

Jack. Marcus took a moment before rousing himself back to the present, and he noticed almost the entire sleeve of his jacket had turned sanguine with his blood.

He ignored the flesh wound and rose to his feet, then stood a moment, wobbling a bit before he regained enough of his balance to descend the hill toward his friend.

"Good grief, man, you'll bleed to death if you don't get yourself to a doctor!" Jack took his arm when he finally approached. "Come, I'm taking you to get patched up."

"It's not that bad."

"Well, you might not think so, but your mother's already had one scare with Fannie's tale about Mrs. Bryce taking her hostage and conking her out. Seeing you like this, the poor woman might faint."

Fifteen minutes later, Marcus was bandaged and wearing a clean shirt as he emerged from the hospital. Young Ainsley, Fannie, and Grace were there to greet him.

"Goodness, Marcus, that woman really shot you!" Grace eyed him incredulously. "Are you all right?"

"Darling, I've seen worse on Marcus. Trust me, he'll live."

"I gather from Fannie and the lieutenant you had quite a tussle with Mrs. Bryce?" Jack asked.

"You gathered right," Marcus said. "Where is she?"

"I had Scotland Yard take her to the local constabulary. Once you and I discuss the situation, we'll drive over there and see what she knows."

"She knows more than you can imagine, Jack."

His friend smiled. "It is good to hear you say my name, old boy, and know who you're talking to. The two soldiers, Johnson and Roberts, said you got your memory back this afternoon?"

Marcus nodded and briefly explained the events of the past couple of hours, with Ainsley filling in his part.

"Heavens, and I thought the wedding was exciting," Grace said.

"So it's over." Marcus eyed her bleakly. "The bride and groom are off to London."

"Oh! Oh, dear, no!" Grace blinked at him. "Clare surprised us all when she stood at the altar, and right in the middle of her vows, she said, 'I will . . . not!' and then stopped long enough to tell me and Jack to care for Daisy before running from the church."

"What!" Marcus's heart froze. "She's . . . not married?"

"You should go after her, Marcus. My guess is she's somewhere in the village," Grace said.

Marcus started past them and then stopped. "Blast! The Rolls is still in Basingstoke." He turned to Jack. "How did you two get back from the church?"

"Your mother requested the vicar loan us his car." Jack grinned. "Come on, let's go get Clare. Mrs. Bryce can cool her heels awhile longer."

"Wait!"

Fannie stopped them. "Take this." Digging into her apron pocket, she withdrew Grandmother's garnet. "You might need it, Brother," she said softly. "I hope you do."

He took the ring from her and smiled. "I hope so, too."

But an hour and a half later, Marcus's spirits flagged. He imagined he'd knocked on the door of every single home in the village of Mattingley looking for a runaway bride, and while several of the townsfolk wanted to keep him there and chat more about the scandalous event, he chafed with impatience to find Clare. God had given him this second chance, and his love would wait no longer.

Meeting Jack back at the car, however, his friend was just as weary and out of answers.

"Wherever she's gone, Clare is staying well hidden," Jack said. "No doubt she'll return to Montefalco in the morning once she learns Randleton and his jilted nephew have left for London. And we still have her daughter."

Marcus didn't want to give up the search, but Jack was right. Soon enough Clare must return, for Daisy if nothing else. They'd combed the village clean, questioning nearly every local about Clare's whereabouts without success.

"We should return the vicar's car while we're here so he can give us a lift back," Jack said.

Minutes later, they pulled up in front of the church. As he exited the car, Marcus said, "I'll get him."

He went inside to find the vicar. The church's interior was cool, with only the windows shedding light into the vaulted space.

He found Clare sitting in the last pew at the back.

Moving closer, his heart drummed in his chest. The vicar stood near the altar, his aging features worn with concern. Marcus raised a hand to him, and the old clergyman nodded before disappearing into the sacristy.

Marcus stood behind his beloved and paused, the faint scent of her honeysuckle perfume surrounding him. Even without the memory of her, he'd known her scent.

Removing the ring from his pocket, he gazed at the colored multifaceted stones. Would she reject him now after what he'd put her through in the park, and then here in Hampshire with Natalya? *Lord, did you bring me this far only to teach me a lesson in faith?*

Silently he leaned over her, holding out the ring for her to see. Her sharp intake of breath sounded before she launched from the seat, whirling around to face him. "Marcus!"

She looked like a queen.

He went down on his knee then, gazing up into her beautiful face. He wouldn't wait another moment, whatever the consequences.

"Clare Irene Danner, will you do me the honor of becoming my wife?"

Clare stared at him, tears swimming across her vision. She'd come back to the church, having nowhere else to go, at least until she was certain Stephen, Randleton, and the attorney had left Montefalco. She'd prayed, too, that Jack and Grace would protect her daughter in case the monster decided to take her baby with him.

But now her love was here, kneeling in front of her in this quiet church. Asking her the question she'd waited so long to hear. *God, you answered my prayer!*

"Forgive me for waiting so long, my darling." Emotion roughened his deep voice. "I should have told you before how much I love you. I should have made you my wife." He swallowed, his throat bobbing. "My work, I feared . . ." He looked down. "If I died, I couldn't bear leaving you to suffer the way Mother did, or leaving Daisy to anguish like Fannie and me."

Moved by his words, it took Clare a moment before she realized he'd used her full name when he proposed and he now spoke of the past as though he knew it. "Are you recovered?" she whispered, hardly daring to hope.

"I remember everything, my Chiara." Rising, he towered over her. "The park and the phony diamond I was ordered to give to Natalya for an assignment with the War Office—I couldn't tell you about it then, and I know I hurt you." His golden eyes searched hers. "But I never stopped loving you, Clare, and even if I had no memory, I'd still be here, telling you I want to spend the rest of my life making up for every hurt I've caused you and to be worthy of you—"

"Hush, Marcus." Smiling through her tears, she raised a gloved finger to his lips while her heart threatened to burst with joy. "You told me from the start that if I don't have trust, I'll never find

378

happiness," she said softly. "And though I've tried, I only began to understand when I stood at the altar with Stephen."

Hurt flashed across his face, and she again regretted the old fears.

"I was afraid, much like you. But God knew that you were the man for me, even when I believed we were lost. He was merely waiting on me to decide to surrender myself wholly into His care so that He could help me. And when I walked away from that altar, I trusted that He would 'make my paths straight.'" Her lips trembled. "And here you are, my way to happiness."

He gave a rueful smile. "Too often through the years I've also 'leaned on my own understanding,' but I've since found that I need to put my trust in Him."

She cupped his face with her hand. "And you also have to trust *me*, Marcus. Start by telling your family about me and Daisy, though it seems your grandfather already knows."

"I only wanted to protect you," he whispered, reaching to cover her hand with his.

"I understand, but we still must share our lives together or not at all. I realize you have your secrets with work, but I want the rest of you with me and Daisy." She gazed at him, her love almost painful. "We need to *live* our love. It cannot be boxed up and put on the shelf until it's safe or when it's convenient or just when bad things happen. And they will happen, Marcus. But our love . . . it's alive, right here." She pressed her free hand to her heart. "Whatever comes, we have to trust God to see us through."

"I love you, Clare Danner." His eyes blazed. "More than life itself."

"And I you," she whispered back. *And only you, Marcus, my match made in heaven.* She removed her left glove and held out her bare hand. "Yes, Marcus Geoffrey James Weatherford, I *will* be your wife."

He slid the ring onto her finger, and she noted that it fit perfectly. She looked up at him, surprised.

"I had it sized a long time ago," he said. "It was always you, Clare, and I'm sorry I made you wait—"

Her kiss cut him off as she rose on tiptoes and pressed her mouth against his, silencing him. Instantly his arms went around her, enfolding her in his warm strength, and Clare surrendered when his lips parted on hers, inviting her to taste and feel and revel in his passion. Together they allowed their hearts to speak what words could not describe.

When at last they parted and drew breath, Marcus touched his forehead to hers. "I wish we didn't have to post the banns—we've already waited so long," he said, smiling.

Clare breathed a laugh. "It is too bad the vicar can't issue us a special license, especially since I'm already dressed."

"No, love." He raised his head, his eyes glowing. "You deserve the very best, and so we'll do this properly, in a church with family and friends gathered around us, and most importantly with our Daisy."

"I would be happy to simply marry in a field with just the three of us," she murmured, gazing at him. "You and Daisy *are* my world, Marcus."

And then she slid her arms up around his neck and kissed him once more.

40

Clare Irene Danner, wilt thou have this man, Marcus Geoffrey James Weatherford, to thy wedded husband, to live together after God's ordinance in the holy estate of Matrimony? Wilt thou obey him and serve him, love, honor, and keep him in sickness and in health; and forsaking all others, keep thee only unto him so long as you both shall live?"

Clare almost smiled at the sudden look of uncertainty in Marcus's expression.

He'd granted her wish, obtaining a special license through the archbishop's office so they could marry four days later. And instead of a wedding in a field, he'd agreed to a ceremony surrounded by his mother's beautiful roses in Montefalco's west wing. Clare had been given away by a very pleased Sir Geoffrey and now stood beside her love in her gray silk wedding gown, the heady scent of blooms all around them.

Marcus, too, had been granted his wish. His family and friends were in attendance on the special day, including Jack and Grace and several other gents from the Admiralty and their wives, along with the patients at the rehabilitation hospital. And Daisy wore a white satin frock, which her new grandmother, Mrs. Weatherford, had commissioned in haste for the wedding.

"Will you?" The vicar frowned, making it clear he didn't want a repeat of Saturday's ceremony.

Clare eyed Marcus, who had already given his troth to her. Did he really think that she would run from him now when she finally had her heart's desire? Still, she made both men wait the extra heartbeat before she smiled and said, "I will."

The relief on the vicar's face was almost comical, and Clare couldn't help but grin. When she looked at Marcus, however, he winked at her and flashed a devilish smile. Her pulse raced. Had he anticipated what she might do?

At the vicar's direction, Marcus reached for her hand and slipped the yellow-gold wedding band on her finger, fitted exactly to the contours of his grandmother's ring.

"With this ring I thee wed," he said, his golden-brown eyes full of promise. "With my body I thee worship, and with all my worldly goods I thee endow: In the name of the Father, and of the Son, and of the Holy Ghost. Amen."

A shout of encouragement erupted from one of the soldiers—Corporal Johnson—and chuckles followed from the crowd while Clare and Marcus smiled at each other.

The vicar continued, Clare and Marcus making their vows, holding each other's gazes. The love between them seemed alive and tangible, never to be broken again.

"I pronounce that they be man and wife together," the vicar finally announced. But before he completed the next sentence, "You may now kiss the bri—" Marcus had slung back her veil and lifted her into his arms, capturing her mouth in a breathless kiss, much to the pleasure of the hospital patients if their shouts and whistles were any indication.

"So now you've joined the rest of us, taking on that yoke of wedded bliss," Jack said later, the reception now in full swing. A couple of patients played the fiddle and accordion while Mrs. Connelly and Swan's chief baker, Becky Simmons, had joined with the hospital's cook to prepare and serve several dishes of simple yet tasty fare for everyone to enjoy. "How does it feel, old boy?"

Marcus's eyes were still on his wife, seated with Grace and Lady Bassett and two other young women he recognized from Endell Street Hospital in London. Finally he turned to his friend and smiled. "I couldn't be happier," he said, holding Daisy on his lap, his new daughter leaning comfortably back against him as she dozed in the warm air. "And I feel . . . complete."

"Just so." Jack nodded, eyes glistening. "And I'm happy for you, Marcus. It's about time you thought of yourself for a change and not just the next assignment. Marriage *is* a mission after all, involving adventure and intrigue of the best kind." He smiled. "Trust me, there will be more than a few surprises along the way, but without the bullets."

Marcus laughed, causing Daisy to stir. The little girl turned her face up to his. "Da?" She grinned, and he leaned down to kiss her forehead.

"Have you told Clare about Elliot's letter?" Jack asked.

"I did, and we both thank you and the army chaplain's office in London for the wedding gift." A clean copy of Elliot's letter. Marcus had been disgusted with Randleton's ploy in showing Clare his son's blood- and mud-splattered copy of the will. Clare wouldn't have been able to discern her name amid the stains or that Elliot Lange put Daisy's trust inheritance in both her and her daughter's names. Now Clare would have control over her daughter's money, not Randleton.

"Getting back to the mission," Jack said, glancing toward the aging head of MI6, who had attended the wedding and was conversing with Marcus's grandfather. "How did C react when you told him the results of our interrogation? No doubt he was upset to learn Natalya had set us up with the missing tsarina and tsarevich scheme. Even Sidney Reilly was fooled, and that's no mean feat."

It still infuriated Marcus that their search for the Romanovs had been merely a ruse cooked up by Natalya and her double agent in Moscow, Sir Lionel Tunney III, "T3" of the British Consulate, who had concocted the fiction and fed it to Reilly to get the real information they wanted—the day and place of the planned assassination of Lenin.

"It was fortunate C decided to wait in sharing with His Majesty the details of our mission to Archangel in the event the Romanovs were impostors," he said. "However, he soon had reason to believe Natalya was a suspect, which is why he'd told her to remain here at Montefalco and maintain her cover, so that my grandfather could keep an eye on her."

Jack cocked his head. "Did C give you a clue as to how he knew?"

"Sidney Reilly," Marcus said, his smile tight. "In Archangel, Reilly gave me a playing card, the queen of spades, and told me to pass it along to C. He wouldn't tell me why, just that my boss would understand."

"I saw the playing card," Jack said. "C held it in his hand when I was in his office." He eyed Marcus sharply. "Old boy, it was covered in *your* blood."

"I'd tucked it into my cap before we left for Vologda." He grimaced. "I thought if I didn't survive, odds were my body would be returned to London with the clothes on my back. Anyway, it seems that C, Reilly, and Sir Walter played poker together on occasion, and Walter would affectionately refer to his wife as his 'queen of spades'—the card symbolic for a woman who is intelligent, well-organized, but also malicious."

Jack shook his head. "I daresay Sir Walter hadn't considered that latter quality."

"Probably not. An investigation is underway, yet C believes the treason began on Walter's watch."

"Natalya, obviously."

"Indeed." Marcus sighed. He'd been shot, lost his memory, and put his darling wife through torment, and all of it for nothing. At least Lenin had been neutralized for a time as he struggled to recover, though the future for Russia remained grim. "It's probably a blessing Sir Walter isn't alive to learn that his treacherous wife married him simply to gain access to sensitive information."

"A viper in the truest form."

"More like a zealot," Marcus countered.

Jack nodded. "At least she's in a London jail now awaiting trial. I take it you spoke with Randleton while you were in London?" He smirked. "Doubtless he's already got his hands full without taking anyone to court for custody rights."

"True enough." Marcus instinctively tightened his hold on Daisy. He'd been ready to testify in the courts about having found her last year in the blighted workhouse orphanage, courtesy of Lord and Lady Lange. But now Randleton had bigger problems. With Stephen Lange's confession as the mole in Whitehall, passing sensitive information between Natalya and Tunney—to whom Randleton introduced his nephew last year, requesting he work for Tunney at the War Office—the viscount now faced a scandal of colossal proportions.

"Stephen will likely be tried for treason." Marcus recalled Natalya's taunts in Basingstoke and shuddered to think Clare might have married a traitor. Apparently, Fannie had told Grandfather about overhearing a conversation between Natalya and Lange in the conservatory regarding the pair's amorous trysts. Grandfather then passed the information on to C, who sent men to the church that Saturday intending to question Lange before he tied the knot. But their car was waylaid on the road, and by the time they'd arrived at the church, the wedding was off, with Lange, Randleton, and the attorney en route to London.

Thank God his love had made the decision to walk away.

"I admit I feel sorry for him," Jack said. "The chap seemed sincere in his desire to start a new life, but Natalya knows how to weave her web over men, and Lange wasn't immune to her charms." He eyed Marcus, smiling. "Neither were you."

"I knew my true love." Again, Marcus turned warm eyes toward his bride. "Even while I couldn't remember Clare, I was drawn to her."

"You're a lucky man, Marcus," Jack said. "You got to fall in love with her twice."

"Don't I know it." And he wasn't about to bungle things again.

He'd told his family about Clare and Daisy, and they had all welcomed mother and child with open arms. Fannie, now seated beside her young lieutenant, hadn't been surprised at all, though she still wore her grin at having a new sister and niece as she waved to him from across the patio. And Marcus had made some other changes . . .

"Have you told her the other good news yet?" Jack asked, reading his thoughts.

Marcus shook his head. "I'll tell her at the right moment." While in London, he'd spoken to C about his work for the Admiralty. He was grateful when the head of MI6 informed him that he was to be reassigned to the London office, giving Marcus a chance to completely heal and some precious time to spend with his new wife and daughter. It was more than he'd hoped for, and while he felt a twinge of guilt for leaving behind the young men still fighting the war, he had every reason to believe the conflict would end soon and they all could be reunited with their loved ones.

Clare smiled at him then, love shining in her eyes, and he rose to his feet, lifting his daughter into the crook of his arm. "Let's go see your mother, Daisy." He leaned in and whispered softly, "Because love won't wait."

Author's Note

My dear readers,

I hope you've enjoyed reading *In Love's Time* and the chance to revisit several old friends featured in my first WWI connecting-series novel, *Not by Sight*. Much like that earlier novel, I chose to include more romance in this story since Captain Marcus Weatherford has carried the burdens of war and espionage during my past four books, always putting duty first, and he deserved his own happily-ever-after. Still, it came with a lesson in his understanding that love was more important in his life—especially when he believed he'd lost it—and realizing God's love is ever patient, ever forgiving, and always willing to wait for us to return to Him, however long it takes.

While this novel is a work of fiction, I did glean a few story ideas from history. Marcus's trip to Archangel with Natalya was inspired by the Romanov sightings after the Bolsheviks murdered the former Russian tsar, Nicholas II (cousin to Britain's King George V), his wife, Alexandra, and their five children—Tatiana, Olga, Maria, Anastasia, and the young tsarevich, Alexei, on July 17, 1918, in Yekaterinburg, Russia. The *Pravda* and other Russian newspapers publicized the tsar's execution but withheld the truth about the deaths of Alexandra and her children, instead promulgating the Bolshevik lie that they had been moved to a safe location.

The immediate search for the family led nowhere. Not until the following January 1919 did a thorough investigation begin when Admiral Kolchak, "Supreme Ruler" of the White government in Siberia, selected Nicholas Sokilov, a trained legal investigator, to undertake the task.[1] MI6 did make inquiries in Russia as well, but to no avail. The family deaths would not be officially confirmed until 1926, and even then the Soviets refused to accept responsibility for the executions.[2] During the early years, several impostors came forward, posing as one of the missing Romanovs, in particular as young Alexei or his sister Anastasia. It wasn't until 1991, after the collapse of the Soviet Union, that the official truth of the Romanov family came to light when the first graves with their bodies were revealed.

Another real part of history was Endell Street Military Hospital in London during WWI. The concept of the Women's Hospital Corps was created and instituted in 1914. Previously met with hostility by officials, Dr. Flora Murray and Dr. Louisa Garrett Anderson decided to bypass the British government by going directly to the French Embassy with their offer to run a military hospital in Wimereaux, France. Their idea was accepted, and in less than two weeks, Murray and Anderson had recruited enough medically trained women to staff an entire hospital—doctors, nurses, orderlies, and clerks.[3] When in early 1915 the British Army began sending their wounded home to England to be treated, the two suffragette women doctors, because of their remarkable patient success, were asked by Sir Alfred Keogh, Director General of Army

1. Robert K. Massie, *Nicholas and Alexandra* (New York: Atheneum Press, 1967), 519.

2. Toby Saul, "Death of a Dynasty: How the Romanovs Met Their End," *National Geographic History Magazine*, July 20, 2018, https://www.national geographic.com/history/history-magazine/article/romanov-dynasty-assassination -russia-history.

3. Wikipedia, s.v. "Endell Street Military Hospital," last modified February 18, 2022, https://en.wikipedia.org/wiki/Endell_Street_Military_Hospital.

Medical Services, to relocate their hospital to Endell Street in Covent Garden. As expected, this decision faced much male resistance; however, Keogh was an ardent supporter of Murray's and Anderson's ability to create and operate the Royal Army Medical Corps' newest all-female-run facility in London. Keep in mind that during the early twentieth century, Clare, an unwed mother with a child, would have faced near impossible odds in landing a decent job and certainly would have been forbidden from working in the male-run hospitals. And so I imagined that Endell Street Hospital would be a very plausible solution for her.

Plotting the assassination of Vladimir Lenin could well have been a boardroom discussion in the War Office during WWI, and though I did take some license with the history, the Bolshevik leader was in truth gunned down on August 30, 1918, and left in critical condition. A social revolutionary, a Jewish girl named Dora Kaplan, fired two shots point-blank at Lenin as he was leaving Michelson's factory in Moscow.[4] In retaliation for the attempted murder, Moscow's Cheka secret police went on a killing spree in what was called the Red Terror. Despite Kaplan's socialist affiliation, the Bolsheviks blamed the British for the assassination attempt, and speculation remains on whether real-life MI6 agent Sidney Reilly and British Consul to Moscow Bruce Lockhart were hatching some sort of anti-Bolshevik plot. Reilly and Lockhart *were* misled by a pair of Latvians, who claimed to be Allied supporters but were in fact working with the Bolsheviks. After the Lenin shooting, Reilly managed to flee arrest by the Cheka, while Lockhart landed in a Lubyanka prison cell until he finagled his way back to Britain. Such was the real life of spies!

I'll leave you with one last tidbit. Marcus's boss at Whitehall, Captain Sir Mansfield George Smith-Cumming, was a real-life character and chief of the Secret Intelligence Service, later to become known as MI6. The monocled leader of the SIS carried a

4. R. H. Bruce Lockhart, *British Agent* (New York and London: G. P. Putnam's Sons, 1933), 192, pdf.

sword stick, worked especially long hours, and was reputed to have used a penknife to cut off his half-severed leg—which had him pinned down after a car crash in 1914 in France—in order to crawl to his son, who lay dying several feet away. Smith-Cumming wrote in green ink and signed his correspondence with a C—a habit continued by his successors, including Alex Younger, the sixteenth C, a letter that now stands for chief of MI6.[5] (Incidentally, as of 2022, the current chief of MI6 is Richard Moore.) Smith-Cumming also recruited Sidney Reilly as a British agent working in St. Petersburg.

Enjoy the history!

—K.B.

5. Richard Norton-Taylor, "Sir Mansfield Cumming, First MI6 Chief, Commemorated with Blue Plaque," *The Guardian*, March 30, 2015, https://www.the guardian.com/uk-news/2015/mar/30/sir-mansfield-cumming-first-chief-of-mi6 -commemorated-with-a-blue-plaque.

Questions for Discussion

1. As part of his job with the Admiralty and MI6, Marcus Weatherford must keep many secrets from the civilian population. This becomes a problem when he learns Clare has witnessed his rendezvous with Natalya in the park. Do you think he should have told Clare the truth there and then, or do you believe he acted appropriately in keeping the information from her? Discuss your reasons.

2. From Clare's perspective, Marcus is often away on one trip or another, and when he's with her, he seems distracted with work and reticent about sharing his feelings and concerns. He's also at times oblivious to what she needs from him. With our busy lives today, discuss ways couples might carve out quality time to honestly express themselves to each other, breaking away from shop talk or the daily drama in the news. Do you know of any helpful passages from Scripture that teach us about taking time for those we love and being present for one another?

3. In the past, Clare suffered cruelty at the hands of others, including the trauma of having her newborn child taken away

from her. Consequently, she finds it difficult to trust others despite her efforts to overcome the voices of self-doubt and recrimination. She doesn't realize that she's also been withholding her trust from God, unwilling to surrender wholly to Him, until she faces the most important decision of her life at the altar with Stephen, who is not the man she loves. Why is it we often try to control the outcome of our day-to-day lives and decisions before we catch ourselves and surrender all to God? Do you have a favorite Bible passage that might help with this and serve as a reminder?

4. Clare's employer, Endell Street Military Hospital, was a remarkable place and the first all-female-run military hospital in the UK. Surgeons Flora Murray and Louisa Garrett Anderson were two pioneers in this field of medicine for women and, along with most of their staff, made no secret of the fact that they were suffragists and fought for equality. During WWI, many women stepped into jobs traditionally held by men, who were off fighting the war. These jobs included Land Army women (farming and hay balers), loggers, munitionettes, nurses, scientists, railroad workers, policewomen, firewomen, aircraft technicians, welders, secretaries, and more. If you could have held any job during this time, what would your choice be? Why?

5. Fannie Weatherford made a miraculous recovery from polio as a child due in large part to the help of her older brother. Because of the bullying she experienced from other children, and being conscious of her hidden leg brace, Fannie keeps much to herself. Yet when Clare points out that she has become stronger and more resilient because of her struggles, Fannie begins to think of herself in a new light. Discuss how hardship and suffering can build character and make us stronger for the next challenge. And if you're comfortable, cite a personal experience where this was true for you or someone close to you.

6. When Marcus finally regains his memory, he realizes he's about to lose Clare, but duty intrudes once more, demanding he choose between his sister's safety and his own happiness. Later, when he believes all is lost, he surrenders his anger to God and admits the truth of his folly in waiting to make Clare his own. Yet he gets a second chance when he learns she has left Stephen at the altar. Marcus determines not to waste another moment and goes in search of her. If you're comfortable, share a time when you had doubts or believed things would not work out and yet God gave you that miracle. Or discuss the times when you've seen God's miracles in action.

7. Who was your favorite character in the story and why?

8. If the story were to be continued, which character or characters would you like to know more about?

Acknowledgments

For me as an author, creating a historical novel starts with an idea sprinkled with a dash of imagery, a few rare gold nuggets from the past, and most important, lots of prayer and hard work. So I thank God above all for His gifts of inspiration and strength in seeing me through the process of writing this work. I realize I accomplish nothing on my own, but only by His grace and understanding.

I thank my husband, John, who's always ready to do a quick read or offer me technical help with a difficult scene. Your love and support mean everything to me.

As always, I offer my sincerest appreciation to my network of sister writers and critique partners. I'm so grateful for your continued support, especially during Covid-19. My special thanks to Alisia Camp, Darlene Panzera, Patty Jough-Haan, and Rose Marie Harris for giving generously of your time to read through the first draft of this manuscript and offer me wisdom along with your enthusiasm for the story. You are such a blessing!

To my dear agent, Linda S. Glaz, and my wonderful editors, Rochelle Gloege, Luke Hinrichs, Christine Stevens, and all those at Bethany House who helped to bring this project to fruition, I thank you for your guidance, encouragement, and support.

—K.B.

About the Author

Former bookseller-turned-author, **Kate Breslin** enjoys life in the Pacific Northwest with her husband and family. She is a Carol Award winner and a RITA and Christy Award finalist who loves reading, hiking, and traveling. New destinations make for fresh story ideas. To learn more, visit her website at katebreslin.com.

Sign Up for Kate's Newsletter

Keep up to date with Kate's news on book releases and events by signing up for her email list at katebreslin.com.

More from Kate Breslin

After a deadly explosion at the Chilwell factory, munitions worker Rosalind Graham leaves the painful life she's dreamt of escaping by assuming the identity of her deceased friend. When RAF Captain Alex Baird is ordered to surveil her for suspected sabotage, the danger of her deception intensifies. Will Rose's daring bid for freedom be her greatest undoing?

As Dawn Breaks

You May Also Like . . .

In spring 1918, British Lieutenant Colin Mabry receives an urgent message from a woman he once loved but thought dead. Feeling the need to redeem himself, he travels to France—only to find the woman's half sister, Johanna, who believes her sister is alive and the prisoner of a German spy. As they seek answers across Europe, danger lies at every turn.

Far Side of the Sea by Kate Breslin
katebreslin.com

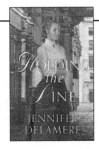

When widow Rose Finlay notices a young woman about to be led astray by a roguish aristocrat who could ruin both her and her family's reputation, bitter memories arise and she feels compelled to intervene. Rose and the young woman's uncle, John Milburn, join forces, putting everything they hold dear—including their growing attraction—in jeopardy.

Holding the Line by Jennifer Delamere
LOVE ALONG THE WIRES #3
jenniferdelamere.com

When their father's death leaves them impoverished, the Summers sisters open their home to guests to provide for their ailing mother. But instead of the elderly invalids they expect, they find themselves hosting eligible gentlemen. Sarah must confront her growing attraction to a mysterious widower, and Viola learns to heal her deep-hidden scars.

The Sisters of Sea View by Julie Klassen
ON DEVONSHIRE SHORES #1
julieklassen.com

More from Bethany House

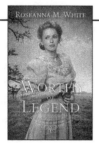

After uncovering a diary that leads to a secret artifact, Lady Emily Scofield and Bram Sinclair must piece together the mystifying legends while dodging a team of archeologists. In a race against time, they must decide what makes a hero. Is it fighting valiantly to claim the treasure or sacrificing everything in the name of selfless love?

Worthy of Legend by Roseanna M. White
THE SECRETS OF THE ISLES #3
roseannamwhite.com

Discovered floating in a basket along the canals of Venice, Sebastien Trovato wrestles with questions of his origins. Decades later, on an assignment to translate a rare book, Daniel Goodman finds himself embroiled in a web of secrets carefully kept within the ancient city and in the mystery of the man whose story the book does not finish: Sebastien.

All the Lost Places by Amanda Dykes
amandadykes.com

After years of being her diva mother's understudy, it's time for Delia Vittoria to take her place on stage. Attempting to make amends for a grave mistake, Kit Quincy is suddenly pulled into Delia's plot to win the great opera war and act as her patron and an enigmatic phantom. But when a second phantom appears, more than Delia's career is threatened.

His Delightful Lady Delia by Grace Hitchcock
AMERICAN ROYALTY #3
gracehitchcock.com

BETHANYHOUSE

CPSIA information can be obtained
at www.ICGtesting.com
Printed in the USA
LVHW110736010223
738383LV00002B/35